The Trophy Wife

The Trophy Wife

Diana Diamond

ROBERT HALE • LONDON

© Diana Diamond 2000
First published in Great Britain 2000

ISBN 0 7090 6748 8

Published by arrangement with
St Martin's Press, 175 Fifth Avenue,
New York, NY 10010, USA

Robert Hale Limited
Clerkenwell House
Clerkenwell Green
London EC1R 0HT

2 4 6 8 10 9 7 5 3 1

Printed in Great Britain by
St Edmundsbury Press Limited,
Bury St Edmunds, Suffolk and bound by
Woolnough Bookbinding Ltd

To Bill,
with gratitude.

Sometime Before

ANGELA LAY BESIDE HIM, a frost of sweat covering her breasts, her flat stomach heaving with her heavy breath.

"Incredible," Walter gasped.

She smiled. "You're the one who's incredible"

"I can't believe . . . I'm still alive." His words were labored. "You're dangerous!"

She rose up on an elbow and tossed her head to swing her long, light hair away from her face. "You seem to like living dangerously."

Walter managed the beginning of a laugh. "You bring out the best in me." He glanced at his watch.

"I hate it when you do that," Angela said. She let herself fall away from him, back onto her pillow.

"What?"

"When you look at your watch. It's like you're saying, 'Time's up, Angela. On to my next conquest.' As if you have something more important to do."

"You know I have to get back for the limo."

"Let the damn limo wait." She turned her back to him. "The drivers get paid the same for waiting as for driving."

Walter lifted her hair and kissed the back of her neck. "When they wait, they talk. I don't want them talking about us."

He rolled out of the bed and walked into the bathroom, pausing for an instant before the full-length mirror. His stomach muscles tightened instantly, in a reflex action that didn't even bother to check with his conscious brain. Walter was proud of his physique even if the onset of fifty-something sag was showing. His pectorals, while still prominent, were no longer sharply etched. There was a pleasant softness around his waist. His buns were flattening and his legs were thinning. But overall, he had survived the onset of middle age quite well. He was in decent shape for

1

any age and in excellent condition for his sedentary lifestyle. True, his sandy hair was thinning and there was puffiness around his deep brown eyes. But he flattered himself that the overall effect was character and maturity, which fitted perfectly on a better-than-decent body.

He closed the glass shower door behind him, turned the faucets absently, and jumped away from the blast of icy water. "Christ," he cursed. But the anger had nothing to do with the shock of cold. Walter was always angry when he had to leave Angela and go back to the lie that his life had become.

He lied to his wife, Emily, at the beginning of the day when he told her he would be working very late. Lied to Joanne, his secretary, when he asked her to arrange for a late limo to his home in New Jersey horse country. Lied to the other officers at the bank when he lingered until they had all left. Lied to the limo driver whom he met in the bank lobby. And then ended his day with still another lie to his wife as he slipped quietly into bed beside her. Walter hated the lies. They put him at the mercy of small and insignificant people who relished his discomfort and were always a threat to expose him. Lying to inferiors made him feel small.

"Christ," he cursed again as he adjusted the temperature and stepped under the stream to wash himself clean.

He knew he had to put an end to it. He had to confront the truth. Angela was perfect for him. She shared all of his interests, was enlivened by the same challenges, breathed deeply in the intoxicating air of his success, and aroused passion that he hadn't felt in years. Perhaps Emily had been just as right for him when they had begun their life together. But the fire of their passion had burned down to warm, comfortable embers. His new life with Angela was just beginning to fuel itself with oxygen. There was no limit to how high the flames might climb.

Emily would have to be made to understand. With Angela at his side, there was nothing beyond his reach; no success that he couldn't achieve. He could face challenges that Emily might once have found exhilarating, but now probably would find frightening, and go to places where she once would have been intrigued, but now would feel hopelessly lost. All she could do was hold him back and that was something that she would never want to do.

His children, too, would have to understand. Their mother was a wonderful woman, intelligent, boundlessly cheerful, physically attractive, generous to a fault. But she could no longer keep pace with him. They would recognize that there were miles on her odometer and while she had all the grace and beauty of a fine sedan, she simply wouldn't be safe traveling in the fast lane where he was now moving. It would be unfair to expect him to slow down so that she could stay by his side.

The shower door clicked open behind him.

"I'm sorry." Angela's hand reached past him for the washcloth. She moved close to him in the shower and began washing his back. "I keep promising you that I won't be a bitch. And then . . . I hear myself say something bitchy. I know this isn't easy for you, either."

"No," Walter protested, "it's my fault." He started to turn to her.

She held his shoulder. "Don't. If you turn around you'll never get out of here."

"I have to tell her. I have to tell her what's happened and explain exactly how I feel. And then I can get my things together, move out, and we can all get on with our lives. I can't keep living a lie. It's not fair to anyone . . . least of all you."

"Will you tell her about me?" She wondered.

"Of course."

"What will you tell her? That I'm a great lay? She'll hate me."

He turned on her abruptly. "Don't say that, dammit. I loved you before . . ."

"Before you got into my pants . . ."

"Stop it!" Walter pushed past her and reached for a towel. "You make me sound like all I'm after is a young piece of ass."

She followed him into the bedroom, dripping water onto the carpet. "What will you tell her?" Angela persisted.

He dried himself furiously, trying to work off his anger. "I'll tell her that you're wonderful. That you've brought me new life and I can't take another breath without you."

She looked at him and then slowly shook her head in despair. "Then she'll really hate me." Angela turned back into the bathroom and stepped into the shower. "It will be easier on her if you just tell her I'm a great lay."

Walter talked over the hiss of the water as he buttoned his shirt. "She'll understand. She'll want the truth."

"She'll want me tarred and feathered."

3

He stepped in front of the bathroom mirror while he adjusted his tie. "Of course she'll be angry at first. But not at you. I started this. I hit on you. You didn't want anything to do with me."

Her hand reached out, feeling for a towel along the empty towel bar. Walter took one out of the linen closet and gave it to her. "It was no one's fault," he went on. "These things happen. We're all sophisticated people."

Suddenly modest, Angela secured the towel around her before she stepped out from behind the shower door.

"When will you tell her? Tonight, when you get home?"

He shook his head angrily.

"Tomorrow, over breakfast?"

"Damm it, Angela, why are you doing this? You know that I can't tell her now. You know what's at stake."

She sagged against the wall. "Hollcroft might not step down for another century," she said mournfully.

"He'll announce it in the next few months," he told her. "Year end at the latest. I know what I'm talking about. I meet with the man every day. And then I'm heir to the throne. Unless I do something stupid to fuck up . . . like bringing a marital scandal into the boardroom."

"It means that much to you?" she asked, sounding as if she already knew the answer.

"To us!" he corrected. "It will affect our whole life together. Isn't that worth waiting a few more months?"

Angela moved into his embrace. "I know, I know," she admitted. "It's just that even an hour seems too long to me."

"How do you think I feel? You are my life, Angela, and I want to begin living it. When we're married, it will seem like such a short time to have waited."

She put on a robe so that she could see him to the door and delayed him for a moment by adjusting the handkerchief in his jacket pocket. "You look terrific," she said and then kissed him good-bye.

"I love you," he said as he slipped out and quietly closed the door behind him.

"You lying prick," Angela laughed to herself as she turned back into her apartment. All he *was* interested in was a young piece of ass, a trophy to flaunt in front of his friends, a woman who would be seen looking over his shoulder in the pages of *Fortune*.

· · ·

4

Walter used his security card to open the lock from the side street door to the bank's lobby. Then he proceeded around the center concourse of elevators so that he stepped up behind the uniformed security guard.

"Good night, Harry."

The guard wheeled around and found him standing in front of one of the cars as if he had just ridden down from his office.

"Long day, Mr. Childs," Harry sympathized as he turned the sign-out book toward Walter.

"You don't know the half of it," Walter responded while he checked his watch and made the appropriate entries.

"Your car is waiting," the guard mentioned.

Walter nodded gratefully and then pushed through the revolving door that opened out onto Park Avenue. Omar, the limousine driver, was instantly standing beside the car, holding the back door open. He offered a sing-song "Good evening, Mr. Childs" in an accent that was either Indian or Pakistani. Then he smiled knowingly, as if he could see semen stains on the front of Walter's trousers. Walter felt his face redden.

The car moved south, crossing town below the crowded theater district, and accelerated into the cut that led into the Lincoln Tunnel. Within minutes, they were on the New Jersey side of the Hudson River, looking back at a panorama of the midtown lights reflected over the water, and of the financial district skyscrapers farther to the south. New York was the most important city in the world, the center of management and finance for all the economies of the global village. Japan might build the automobiles. England might sew the suits. And maybe the Pacific Rim would eventually produce all the electronics. But it was New York that decided what would be produced and raised the money to build the factory. With a one-letter change in a bond rating, New York could turn out the lights of a shoe factory in Italy. A small drop in a stock price on a New York exchange could kill an entire company in Brazil. New York was the most important player in the world and Walter Childs was one of the most important players in New York.

He was senior vice president at InterBank, which was the financial community's shorthand for the Bank of International Trade. There were five men on his level, whose offices shared half of the Park Avenue building's fifty-second floor, the other half devoted to the offices of the chairman, president, and chief executive officer, Jack Hollcroft. Walter's expertise was in international monetary transactions, where he moved enormous pools of currency from bank to bank, country to country in order to keep the mark, the yen, the pound, the franc, and the dollar in some sort of logical hierarchy. Since this was the most critical and the most profitable of the bank's many roles, Walter was the logical successor to the chairman's suite of offices. He would be running the most important bank in the world's most important financial center.

That's what Angela had to understand. He was within a few board meetings of being the acknowledged leader of world finance. He would be sharing head tables with presidents and prime ministers and whispering into the ears of princes and sheiks. As president of InterBank, his life would be a tour of the financial capitals of the world. Certainly, all that was worth waiting for.

Emily, in her prime, might have enjoyed such an environment. But her prime was history. She was, Walter thought with a touch of regret, no longer up to it. Angela, on the other hand, would star on a worldwide stage. Her beauty was genuine and her poise unfailing. She exuded self-confidence, which might have reached into arrogance were it not grounded in such obvious ability. Walter was still in awe of the assurance she had brought to their first meeting.

Angela had blown away her competition at the University of Virginia, emerging as the class valedictorian, and then moving on to the Harvard Business School. Once again, she had outdistanced her class and become the target of all the campus recruiters. She had been invited to visit InterBank as part of the wooing process and had been scheduled for a half-hour interview with Walter, who was then the bank's youngest vice president and a shoo-in for an office on the fifty-second floor.

Walter remembered his annoyance at finding her on his schedule and had reluctantly decided to spare her fifteen minutes. He hadn't even taken the time to study her background folder.

When he had looked up from his work and saw her, the pen fell from his fingers. She was in a chalk-striped business suit that whispered *banker*, with the skirt cut high enough to say *beauty queen*. And when she leaned across the desk with a firm handshake, she showed just enough cleavage to suggest *you might even get lucky*.

She took a chair with her briefcase balanced on a crossed knee, admired the painting that had come with the office and which Walter scarcely noticed, commented on other works by the artist as a way of approving Walter's taste, and then asked him about his work. Walter began to de-

scribe the importance of monetary movements and she nodded her agreement. At the first opportunity she mentioned her research into the flight
of hot money from the English pound that had brought down a conservative government and then asked a very pertinent question about the
excessive gold holdings of several Swiss banks. How was InterBank handling the situation? It was at this point that Walter realized he was the
one being interviewed and that he wasn't making a very good impression.

He had pulled out all the stops, using his working knowledge of the real
market to counter her theoretical preparation, but she clung to his thinking
like a pit bull. Then, when he was just about to pull away, she ended the
interview, thanking him for his time, appreciating the conversation, and
once again complimenting his taste in art. She had left him staring at the
door she closed behind her, hoping that he had made a favorable impression. It took seconds for him to recover, realize that *she* was the one who
should have been trying to make an impression and then get angry at her
impertinence. But his momentary pique hadn't stopped him from calling
personnel and ordering her hired onto the bank's fast-track program with
him as her mentor. He wanted to see a great deal more of Miss Angela
Hilliard.

"Beautiful!" It was Omar's voice from the front seat and for a moment
Walter thought the driver had entered his thoughts and was sharing his
image of Angela.

"What?" he demanded.

"The city," Omar said obviously. "It is very beautiful reflected in the
river."

"Yes, it is." Walter wondered exactly how much the driver had guessed.
How much others had guessed. Did Emily have any suspicion? Could his
affair be a whispered joke in the executive washroom?

He closed his eyes and made a great show of catnapping in order to
discourage further comments from the front seat. His mind lurched abruptly
to the confrontation that he faced with Emily, the dark cloud that invaded
all his dreams of rapture with Angela.

He wasn't terribly worried about the property settlement. Emily didn't
care much about money, nor was she overly impressed with the status that
wealth could convey. She had resisted leaving their first starter house even
when he had become a bank officer. And she was furious when he had
driven her from their second house, a very substantial colonial in a good
suburb, to show her the estate where they now lived. "Why the hell do

we need a paddock?" she had asked. "We have a dog, Walter, a not a horse."

"Emily, I'm a senior vice president, for Christ's sake. The bank expects me to move in wider circles."

"And you need a paddock so you can walk in wider circles," she had taunted.

But her indifference to the trappings of success didn't mean she wouldn't clean out his accounts. Emily was a fighter, and once he put her in an adversary position, she would fight to win. She'd take his BMW 740 for the simple pleasure of parking it at a shopping center where supermarket carts could ding its doors. She'd fight for the house so that she could fill in the swimming pool and knock down the white paddock fences. Probably she wouldn't be angry with Angela. Emily would expect ambitious young women to have a run at their powerful superiors. But she would expect him to be true to his marriage and sensitive to the obvious ploys of children who pretended to find him attractive. In court, she could make his affair look tawdry and ridiculous. In the boardroom, that would very likely make him an unacceptable heir to the presidential office. Jack Hollcroft would never allow a hint of infidelity into his bank. Banks were built on faith!

No, there would be no facing the truth. The truth was overrated. He needed a plan. He had to find a way to move Emily out of his life without encouraging her to battle. He had to find a way to move here out quietly. Better still, a way that would reflect to his credit. There had to be something that he could offer.

The limousine turned off the highway and quickly lost itself in the winding roads that linked the secluded country estates with civilization. Ironic, Walter had often thought that the greater one's success with modern economic realities, the greater the need to imitate the lifestyle of the agricultural barons. His business associates—all men of great accomplishment—housed themselves in the manors of the eighteenth-century landed gentry and relaxed aboard sailing ketches rigged for a seventeenth-century crossing. Tycoons who had mastered the electronic global markets felt the need to prove their skills as vintners, buying into wineries that would never yield a good bottle. Software geniuses, who had raised intangible property to incredible values, somehow felt the need to lapse back into animal husbandry. They not only bred their own horses but even hammered their own horseshoes.

They turned through the gates that announced his driveway and popped over the Belgian blocks that paved the road to his door. Omar lowered the headlights so as not to disturb the sleeping residents and then waited discreetly to make sure Walter had no difficulty fitting his key into the lock.

He went immediately to the alarm panel that was hidden behind a tapestry and pounded the wall when he found that Emily hadn't even turned it on. He had spent ten thousand dollars for a sophisticated system that detected not only forced entry but any sort of movement in any of the rooms. "It's a damn nuisance," Emily had told him, explaining that the system was constantly summoning the police. "I'm the only one it ever detects." So instead of trying to remember to turn it off, she had apparently decided never to turn it on.

Walter stepped into the kitchen, spent a few seconds shuffling through the day's mail, and then walked to the wet bar for a nightcap. He was pouring the scotch over the ice cubes when he heard her behind him. He turned and found her wearing an oversize T-shirt as a nightgown. There was a Grateful Dead tour promotion printed across her chest.

"Want one?"

"No thanks," she answered. "I took a sleeping pill."

"Doesn't seem to have worked," he allowed. He gestured a toast and then sipped at the scotch.

"I guess I don't like to be alone."

He shook his head at the irony. "That's why I put in the alarm, so you'd feel secure when I'm away. You really ought to turn the damn thing on."

"Sure. And then when I get up during the night, I get to make coffee for the cops who are suddenly shining their flashlights through the window. One of them even had his gun drawn. They're more dangerous than a burglar would be. Besides, I don't need security. I need someone to talk with."

Walter sagged into a soft, family-room chair. "We'll talk when I get upstairs. I just need a few minutes to unwind."

She leaned over and kissed his forehead. "A tough day?" she asked.

"A real ballbuster," he sighed.

Emily turned up the gracious staircase that wound up the wall of their circular foyer. Walter downed the rest of the drink and went back to the bar for a refill. The Grateful Dead, he thought. She'll never catch up.

"I'll bet it was a ballbuster," Emily whispered to herself as soon as she was out of his sight. "Why the hell can't men smell the perfume of the women they're sleeping with."

Monday

EMILY RIPPED A FOREHAND crosscourt, aiming for the corner.

"Out!" Mary Anders yelled, pointing at the ball mark she pretended to see just beyond the base line. "We're at deuce."

Emily nodded and took her stance to receive the serve. She waited back for her opponent's looping, topspin serve to bounce up high. Then she pounced on it, drilling a rifle shot that cleared the net by half and inch, bit into the sideline, and ricocheted past Mary.

"Nice shot," her opponent said, trying to sound casual. She was glad the shot had been away from her where she didn't have to try for it. If she had reached it, it would have taken the racket right out of her hand. She set up in the add court, tossed the ball, and hit another spinner at Emily's backhand. Emily slashed at it and sent a whistling return into the alley just outside the singles line. "Out," Mary yelled and walked back to the deuce court.

Again, she spun her serve to Emily's backhand. This time Emily blocked a return to center court. They rallied back and forth with easy top spins until Emily decided to put her away, first with a slashing backhand into the right corner that Mary Anders just managed to return, and then with a forehand to the vacated left corner. But her forehand was too strong, whistling past the base line. "Out," Mary announced. "My advantage."

Mary switched her serve to Emily's forehand and Emily tore into it, hitting a rocket that aimed right back down Mary's throat. For an instant, Mary Anders hesitated like a deer caught in the headlights. But at the last instant she leaped aside, letting the return whiz past her, a foot out of bounds.

"Out!" she screamed triumphantly, raising her racket to the ladies applauding in the gallery. She rushed toward the net with a gushing display of sportsmanship. Emily congratulated her sincerely, smiled at the applause that was her consolation prize, and collapsed onto the bench. She toweled her hands and face and then gulped down her jug of water.

"You threw that one away."

She looked up at Bill Leary, the club pro, who tossed her a fresh towel. "She played well," Emily breathed.

"She played you for an idiot," Leary said. "All she did was feed the ball back to you and let you kill yourself trying to hit winners. Jesus, she even kept complimenting you just so you'd keep trying to hit the lines."

"I hit some lines," Emily said, zipping the cover over her racket.

Leary shook his head. "How many times have I told you? Just keep it in play and let your opponent try for the winners. In the Monday Morning League, no one is good enough to hit the lines consistently."

"No one ever will be if all we do is keep tapping them back."

"Yeah, well, that's why you lost."

She handed the towel back to him and picked up her sweatjacket. "I'd rather lose trying. It's better than standing around waiting for someone else to make a play."

He held her jacket while she backed her arms into the sleeves. His hands lingered on her shoulders an instant longer than necessary. "Well, if you're going for winners, you've got to work harder on your setup," he told her. "Maybe we ought to pencil in some lessons. I could come up to your place so we can get in some real work."

She smiled knowingly. "I'm free right now."

He nodded. "Okay. Give me a minute to freshen up and get my racquet."

Emily broke out of his embrace. "Forget the racquet." She walked across the court, throwing a withering glance back over her shoulder. But he didn't wither. He winked.

Bill Leary had made a quick appearance on the pro tour right after he left college. In two seasons, he had earned $4,500 in prize money and hadn't been offered a single endorsement, even by local car dealers. He was bright enough to get the message that while he could be a consistent winner in the country club set, he would be a consistent joke on tour. He joined the clubs.

For the past ten years he had worked his way up the country club ladder, advancing from equipment manager at a tennis center to assistant professional at a decent club, and now to professional at a very prestigious club. He had enough photos of himself on the same court with John McEnroe and Mats Willander to satisfy the men and the athletic good looks that appealed to the women. He was ten years younger than most of the ladies in the Monday League, which was the right age gap for stirring memories that their successful husbands had no time to rekindle. With a few flattering words about a woman's tennis form, a flash of his outdoor smile, and an accidental erogenous touch as he positioned a student's hip for a better backhand, Bill Leary could pretty much name his game.

Emily had been an obvious target. She was a serious player who welcomed the advice and help of a professional. She had a long, sinewy, athletic body that, if too broad for a runway model, was attractively curved and moved sensually. Her mouth, while severe under stress, looked delicious whenever it spread into her spontaneous smile. Her shoulder-length dark hair seemed never to have been under a dryer, but fell naturally into place. She neither looked nor acted her age. It was a combination that Leary found irresistible and in her dark eyes he saw signals that she was probably available.

They were angry eyes. Clear, narrowed, precisely focused on a point of reality rather than open to vaporous dreams. In his years as a club professional he had seen them often, usually on woman who had been given everything they wanted and then at middle age realized they had wanted the wrong things. There was no defeat in them, as in the eyes of a downtrodden house drudge. These were women of accomplishment. No sadness, as in the eyes that had suffered a great loss. The country club ladies were all winners. Just anger. The anger of pride that has been wounded and which is determined to get even.

Leary could see it in Emily's eyes. She was a woman who had been given a room full of toys to keep her happy by a husband who found his own happiness elsewhere. In his career. With another woman. She knew she was being treated shabbily and was determined to have satisfaction. A tennis pro wasn't an original way to get even, but Leary had long appreciated that his services could be soothing.

At first, Emily showed no interest, pretending to be unaware of his advances even though she was hurting from displacement and neglect. She didn't like the big estate with the paddock. She particularly didn't like being left alone in it under the watchful eye of a security system. She wanted to hurt Walter for tearing her away from her friends just to satisfy his ego. But her need for revenge wasn't developed enough to stomach the thought of a stud like Billy Leary pulling down her panties.

Then she had found out that Walter was sleeping with one of the bank's rising starlets. It wasn't his first infidelity. She had known of a brief fling he had enjoyed with an aspiring model and a liaison in a posh hotel with a lovely representative of a California bank. She had been hurt but not wounded, disappointed but not completely disillusioned. The current affair, however, had been going on for quite some time. More significant, Walter wasn't rushing home to dote on her, make amends, and purge his conscience. He was staying away and leaving her behind. Her pain turned into anger and the anger roared into rage. If she had grown indifferent to Walter, she now felt active hatred. The next time Billy had raised the subject of private lessons, she had signed up for his first available opening.

He had arrived at her tennis court in the early afternoon, dressed in fresh whites with a bucket full of tennis balls. They had volleyed until the balls were scattered, Emily all the while worrying about what was going to come next rather than concentrating on his stream of helpful suggestions. Then he had detected the fatal flaw in her swing that required him to stand close behind her, his arms around her to help her grasp her racquet properly. He had then led her through a series of maneuvers, turning from forehand to backhand, that could have passed for kinky sex, or at least a new Latin American dance step. His arms were caressing her breasts first from the left and then from the right and all the while his groin was grinding against her rump.

This was the point that separated the serious students from the serious lovers. Women who were worried about their tennis games ordered him back to the other side of the net. Women who were worried about their love lives collapsed panting into his arms. Emily had done neither. Instead, she had started to laugh. A smirk, then a giggle, and then gut-wrenching laughter that caused her to drop the racquet, double over, and stagger away from a bewildered Billy. When she had turned back, there were tears in her eyes.

"Is that your idea of foreplay?" Emily had howled.

Then Billy had started to laugh. "Hey, sometimes it works. It's hard to be subtle on a tennis court."

"Well, it's not working now. I don't feel hot. I feel ridiculous." Her words had broken as she choked back laughter.

"How do you think I feel," Billy had answered. He began picking up the scattered tennis balls. "I'm the one making a complete asshole out of myself just to get things moving. If one of us doesn't do *something*, we could be out on this damn tennis court all day."

Emily had helped him deposit the balls back into the basket and then handed him the leather covers that he zipped over his racquets. "You look like you need a shower," she had said. "I'll scrub your back."

Emily had stopped him when he tried to drag her into her bed. They were both naked and dripping wet and she wanted to pull back the bedspread. Then she had delayed him again while she went to her desk and returned with Walter's picture. "You don't mind if I put it here on the night table, do you? I think I'll get more into it if I know he's watching."

It was an hour later when Billy managed to pull out from under her. Involuntarily, his hand went to his heart to keep it from exploding through his chest. He had looked up at Walter's picture. "You give him that kind of a good night kiss every night?"

"He doesn't always come home nights. He has pressing business in the city."

Billy had struggled for breath. "He's crazy. Poor bastard doesn't know what he's missing."

"No, but he seems to like what he's getting."

He had looked at her with a touch of genuine caring. "Hey, I'm sorry. You're a nice lady and you don't deserve that kind of treatment."

Somehow, she had known that this was a departure from his usual line. "No, dammit, I don't. So maybe you can explain why an otherwise considerate human being abandons a loving wife and chases after a younger woman."

Billy had stumbled out of bed and headed toward his crumpled tennis outfit that was piled on the bathroom floor. "I guess it's a guy thing . . . like getting a new car. The old one is running fine, but all of a sudden you can't live without the latest model."

"An old car," Emily had snapped indignantly.

"Well, there are old cars and then there are classic cars. Like you. They just don't build them like you anymore."

Emily stood for a moment in the tennis club parking lot, trying to remember where she had left the car. Then she pressed the button on her keys and a Lexus in the next row barked and blinked like a happy puppy dog. She threw her racquets in the backseat, climbed in, made all the adjustments, and finally fixed her seat belt. She didn't realize she had already started the engine until she turned the key again and heard the starter grinding. "Idiot," she chided herself. It was typical of the mistakes she had been making lately. Stupid little oversights and absences that she attributed to the pressure she was under. Well, the pressure was going to get worse, and in the days ahead, little mistakes could be more than embarrassing. They could be dangerous. She had to get hold of herself.

Emily drove the car directly into the garage, parking it between Walter's BMW and his Italian motorcycle. She used the side door into the kitchen, walking past another deactivated alarm panel. At the bar, she poured herself a glass of wine after glancing at her watch to make sure that it was past noon. If I start drinking in the morning, she had promised herself, it will make more sense to simply cut Walter's throat. She reasoned she would rather live in a jail than disappear into an alcoholic fog.

She carried the wine up the stairs, unbuttoning the warm-up jacket on the way, set the glass on her vanity, and threw the jacket across her bed. She kicked off her tennis shoes, balanced like a stork as she pulled off the sweat socks, and left her tennis skirt in an abstract shape on the floor. She tossed the socks and her sweat-soaked blouse at her laundry hamper as she walked into her bathroom, scoring a near miss. She pulled the athletic bra over her head and dropped it outside the shower tub along with her panties.

In her more reasonable moments, Emily could understand what had happened to her marriage. She and Walter had married young, fresh out of college, filled with romantic notions of family bliss. She had held down a job that kept the refrigerator stocked while Walter had gone through business school and joined InterBank. His starting salary had been more than enough for her to leave her job so they could start a family.

Walter became a captive of the bank, bringing home larger and larger monthly checks with each passing year. Emily didn't care much about the house, so she avoided much of the normal domestic involvement. But she did care about their son and daughter, so she joined Cub Scouts and Clover Buds, church groups and PTAs, and dozens of other organizations that existed to benefit her children. As they got older, she worked in Safe Rides, MADD, Sex Education, and the Alliance for a Drug Free Society, all in an effort to keep Amanda and Alex sober, straight, and free from venereal disease. When they finished high school they weren't particularly interesting people, but at least neither had a prison record. And with Walter's ability to pay full tuition, they were both recruited by prestigious Eastern colleges.

It was at that point that Emily had been able to take a deep breath and look around. What she found made her angry. Walter had used the years to make himself a Very Important Person, surrounded by other over-achievers who also thought of themselves as Very Important. She hadn't used the years to become anything. Aside from her appendage to Walter, she had no identity at all. So, in her reasonable moments, she could understand why he was no longer kneeling at her feet offering a diamond or panting at the prospect of bedding her down.

But Emily wasn't having too many reasonable moments of late. Past all the rationalism was a simple, glaring fact. He was leaving her. She had carried him this far, but now he was stepping onto a faster train. How did Billy put it? He was trading her in for the new model. And if he had the right to put his own interests first, then so did she. At least that's what she had kept telling herself during her tennis lessons.

Bill Leary had proven to be very good for her. Not the solution to all her problems and certainly not a permanent solution to any of her problems. She never forgot that he was a young stud on the make and always paid the bills for tennis lessons she had never taken the day that they arrived in the mail. But he flattered her when she felt tattered, never failed to notice and compliment a new outfit, or hairdo, or even a different shade of lipstick. And when he made love to her, he never failed to convince her that she was the only woman on earth.

Most important, he had praised her ability and her intelligence. He made her feel that losing Walter was incidental and that it was he who was holding her back rather than the other way around. "He lends money, for Christ's sake," Billy had reminded her. "He's just a pawnbroker with an Italian suit. But you can be anything you want to be. You've got all kinds of talent." He even agreed with her about the security alarm. "Damn things go off at the worst possible time," he had said. "Believe me, I know. Turn if off and leave it off. If it makes you apprehensive, I'll buy you a gun."

She didn't mind that it wasn't always true. She suspected that Billy might be as much interested in the size of her divorce settlement as in her less fungible assets. But still, she loved the flattery and needed the support. Particularly now, when she would have to stand up to Walter.

She turned the water up to as hot a temperature as she could stand and then leaned back against the sweating tiles. "Relax, Emily," she told herself. "Keep calm. You're going to need all your nerve . . . all your wits."

She heard the click. Even through the echo of the water, the sound was unmistakable. Someone had opened the door to the bedroom.

She focused her attention toward the sound, but now she heard nothing. She eased her hand toward the pressure faucet and shut the water off. The silence was sudden and complete. No one was there. And yet, the latch had clicked open.

"Billy," she called. "Is that you . . . ?"

Emily stood perfectly still, listening to the tap of the water that dripped from her body. There was no answer. No sound of anyone moving about in her bedroom. Slowly, she convinced herself that she must have been mistaken. It must have been some other mechanical sound. A thermostat relay closing to signal for more heat. The alarm system recycling. She turned the water back on, cooled its temperature a bit, and reached for the bar of soap.

She was shocked by the sudden sound of the shower curtain ripping and the rattle of the plastic rings as they bounced against the bar. She turned just it time to catch a glimpse of the curtain falling on top of her and then felt powerful arms wrapped around her like a rope, tying her into the curtain. She screamed into the darkness that suddenly enveloped her, until a hand pressed the curtain over her face. She snapped her head angrily from side to side, trying to free her mouth, but the hand pressed tighter. In terror, she tried to gulp in air, but the curtain sealed her face like a plastic bag. Jesus, she thought, they're going to suffocate me. She forced her hand up inside the plastic, pushing her attacker's hand upward so that she could gulp a mouthful of air. Then she bit through the curtain.

"Ahh!" a pained voice screamed in the darkness. Emily dug her nails into her bite marks and ripped a hole through the fabric. There was an explosion of light, suddenly darkened by a woolen ski mask. She could see angry eyes blazing and then felt the snap of a fist that drove the curtain against her temple. Her knees buckled. Her feet were sliding and she couldn't free her arms to get a handhold. She collapsed in the arms that were holding her prisoner.

"Get her!" the pained voice screamed.

Another man's voice. "Hold her still, for Christ's sake!"

The arms crushed around her and she felt herself being dragged over the edge of the tub.

"Shoot her. Stick the damn thing through the curtain!"

"Hold her still, dammit!"

Her head and shoulders were being wrestled down to the bathroom floor. The edge of the tub was digging into her belly, her legs dangling uselessly in space. She screamed again and this time heard the echo of her voice rattling off the walls.

"Do it!"

She felt a sharp pin prick plunge into her thigh and then the pressure of a hypodermic injection.

"Oh, Jesus!" It was more a prayer than a curse. "Oh, Jesus!"

She expected to feel her body going limp as darkness closed across her mind. But nothing happened. She was still aware of the sting of the needle and more aware of the pain that the edge of the tub was causing across her hips. She started to scream again, but once more the tattered curtain was pressed against her face. Then she found a foothold against the wall behind the tub and pushed herself furiously at the body that was holding her. She felt the man in the mask topple backward and crash against the vanity cabinet.

"Fuck!" he yelled. "Grab hold of her legs."

She kicked and felt her heel score hard into someone's body. The second voice yelped in pain. "Damn you!" A fist struck through the curtain into her side, driving the air out of her body.

"Just hold her! Don't kill her."

"She kicked me in the face."

"She can't kick you if you hold her."

Emily tried to kick again, but was amazed to find that her legs didn't work. The pain across her midsection had gone away. And she really didn't mind the strong hand that was pressing the shower curtain over her mouth. She could hear the water still running, falling on the curtain like rain on a roof. I hope they remember to turn the water off, she thought. And then she lapsed into blissful sleep.

When they knew the drug had taken its effect, the two men loosened their grip. One turned off the shower while the other twisted his face out of the ski mask.

Carefully they dragged the curtain out into the bedroom where they had more room to work. They straightened the crumpled edges and then re-rolled her into a neat package. One of the men took the top half, locking his arms under Emily's elbows. The other lifted the backs of her knees. Carefully, they carried her out into the hallway and then past the guest suites to the back stairs.

"Set her down for a minute," said the one who was at her head. He took a deep breath. "Some tough broad." He looked at the bleeding bite mark in his hand. "Damn near took off my thumb . . ."

"We should have brained her," said the other, touching the clot of blood that filled one of his nostrils.

"You should have gotten the needle into her faster."

"If you held her still."

They grunted as they lifted her again and moved slowly down the stairs. One freed his hand long enough to pick up the Lexus keys and open the door to the garage. They kept it open with their knees as they carried her out to the car and set her down on the paved floor. One fitted the trunk key and then they lifted the package, still dripping wet, over the bumper and onto the trunk carpet. Seconds later, the big tires were popping over the Belgian bricks out toward the gate. Then the car swung onto the country road and moved slowly away.

Walter left his office promptly at 3:00 P.M. and used the fire stairs to dash down one flight to the senior executive fitness center, a dead-serious health club reserved for the chairman and the senior vice presidents. The center was equipped as a gymnasium, with motorized treadmills, stationary bicycles, land-locked rowing machines, and enough hydraulic stair-climbers to make the elevators to the fifty-second floor unnecessary. Recognizing the irreplaceable skills of the senior line and staff executives, and alarmed at the statistics on heart attacks, the board had voted $4.1 million to turn the fifty-first floor into a fitness center with the best gym equipment, a three-tiered sauna, steam room, Jacuzzi, and a locker room with individual stall showers. Then, realizing that they were an equal-opportunity employer with no glass ceilings, they had spent another million adding a women's locker room, sauna, steam room, and Jacuzzi that, as far as anyone knew, had still never been used.

But despite the cardiovascular machines and the body-building stations, the fitness center functioned more as a conference room. At midafternoon, when the New York markets closed, the senior executives changed into athletic togs and jogged side by side on treadmills while they discussed the morning's impact on the bank's activities. Occasional glances at flickering monitors kept them up to date on the Chicago banks and markets, the West Coast, and the Far East business news, which were updated continuously. And should some piece of information gathered either from a fellow jogger or from the electronic ticker tape require action, there was a telephone mounted on every piece of gym equipment.

Because of his physical appearance, Walter thought of himself as young rather than middle-aged, and when pushed, as middle-aged rather than as well beyond the halfway point. Visually, he was in better shape than most of the other men, which he reasoned was probably an indication of superior mental assets, as well.

He offered a greeting to the whole room rather than any one in particular, started his treadmill, and stepped aboard. Within a few minutes he had finished his warm-ups and was jogging at a steady pace up a five-degree incline.

He glanced to his left and saw that he was running away from two of the top executives. Karl Elder managed foreign subsidiaries in thirty countries and was clearly the officer with the most international experience. But trips abroad to the Michelin-rated restaurants of Paris, Vienna, Brussels, and Milan had given him a portly shape and triple chins. While mentioned out of courtesy, he wasn't really a candidate for the top job and certainly didn't want it if it would interfere with his travel.

Laboring next to Elder was Henry Martin, the bank's expert in investments. Basically, he was a trader with all the gambler's instincts required to turn hefty profits out of most of his bets. "A money machine," he was frequently called, and he was proud of the title. But while gamblers were essential in the back room, no bank wanted them out front where they might run into a big depositor. Henry wasn't really a rival for the top spot.

Walter had to look in the other direction to spot the one man who could beat him to the chair when the music stopped, Mitchell Price. He was standing near the free weights, leveraging another railroad wheel on each end of the bar in preparation for his regimen of bench presses. At thirty-nine, he was the youngest of the senior officers, the leanest, and probably the most fit. Mitchell was the bank's expert in the electronic systems that had replaced currency and paper as the arbiters of global wealth. His work was distinctly different from that of any of the other officers and it just might be that Jack Hollcroft, sensing that the future belonged to the computer literate, would nod toward Mitchell Price.

Walter Childs moved vast sums of money from country to country to protect InterBank's position in foreign currencies. His claim to the brass ring was that his skills most nearly fitted the bank's unique role. He had salvaged hundreds of millions of dollars by taking a quick exit from the peso before Mexico's economic woes had cut the value of the currency in half. Then he had *made* hundreds of millions by mounting a rescue operation at usurious rates. At age fifty, he was a bit too old to be a boy wonder, but old enough so that no one would question his experience. While he ran mile after mile on a fast-moving treadmill, Walter tried to present the calm demeanor that was essential for the top man in times of crisis. So while he kept his eyes fixed on the monitors, he showed little surprise with any of the information and rarely used the telephone.

He returned to his desk just as the evidence of a new dollar-yen crisis was appearing. When the yen fell, every Western bank got nervous realizing that local industries would once again be buried under boatloads of cheap Japanese imports. Walter spent the early evening organizing an orderly buy of yen through all the branches and affiliates. The price rose and the momentary crisis was over even before most European banks were aware of it. It was seven o'clock when he summoned his limousine for the long journey home.

He snapped on the courtesy lamp so that he could continue working in the backseat of the car, setting his briefcase on the seat beside him and spreading the papers across his lap. He found himself wishing that he were meeting with Angela instead of heading home. Angela would appreciate the victory he had just achieved in supporting the Japanese currency. She would understand instantly the crisis that had been avoided and would know that he was one of perhaps only a dozen men in the world who could have pulled it off. Emily wouldn't fully grasp his importance to the situation. She would respond with something unappreciative like, "I'm happy for you, dear."

When they turned into the driveway, the headlights showed the open garage door with Emily's car missing. Walter was momentarily alarmed because the garage light was out.

"Looks as if you've been abandoned," Omar chided from the front seat.

"Probably just the last rubber of bridge running long," Walter answered cheerfully as he gathered his papers. But he was uneasy. It didn't make sense that the garage door would be left open.

He thanked Omar, initialed the limousine log, and then let himself in through the kitchen door. He wasn't surprised to find that the security system was unarmed. He flicked on the kitchen light and started into the living room, then pulled up short when he saw the outline of a person seated on his sofa.

"Emily?"

"No Mr. Childs, it isn't Emily." The voice was harshly masculine.

Walter stared at the dark form while he fumbled for the dimmer switch. The track lights over the fireplace came up like theater lights, slowly illuminating his visitor. He was looking at a rather ordinary man in a conventional business suit. The only thing that was extraordinary was the small, automatic pistol that was aimed directly into his face.

"Please sit down ... there ... right across from me." The man was pointing with his free hand toward the soft chair on the other side of the fireplace, separated from the sofa by a four-foot-square coffee table.

"Who are you? Where the hell is my wife?"

This time the man gestured toward the chair with the muzzle of the pistol. "Please ... sit down. Then I'll answer questions."

He was probably about Walter's age, but a fat neck and sagging shoulders made him look older. His soft appearance, together with his clear voice and precise pronunciation, made the pistol incongruous. The man looked as if he would be more comfortable handling a pencil. Walter sat in the place indicated, keeping his eyes focused on the other eyes.

"Who the fuck are you ... and what are you doing in my houses?" He was on the edge of the cushion, his weight still on his feet.

"I'm a messenger, sent to tell you that your wife is fine."

Walter inched forward. "Where is she?"

"I don't know. And that's the important thing that you have to believe. I don't know where she is, and I don't know who's holding her."

"Holding her?" Walter was halfway to his feet when the gun was raised directly into his eyes. He sat back slowly.

"Your wife has been kidnapped by someone who wants you to do something. But I don't know who he is. I don't know who kidnapped her and I don't know who's holding her. All I know is that you're the only one who can save her."

"You don't know? Then what are you doing here?"

"Mr. Childs, please listen to me carefully. Once you understand that I'm no threat to you ... that I'm completely useless to you ... I'll be able to put away this gun."

Walter stared into the worried eyes. "I'm listening," he said.

The man leaned forward. "I don't know anything about this. I don't know you and I don't know Mrs. Childs. I'm simply bringing you information. I got a phone call a week ago, asking me if I wanted to make ten thousand dollars for simply delivering a message. I asked if what I would be doing was legal and the voice answered that if it were legal, they'd use Western Union."

"What voice?"

"A voice speaking through some sort of computer. High-pitched. Flat. I couldn't tell if it was anyone I knew. I couldn't even tell if it was a man or a woman. But I said I'd like to know more. Things haven't been going well for me. I can use the money."

"I can pay you twice that much," Walter interrupted.

The man shook his head. "It wouldn't do you any good because there's nothing I can do to help you. What I agreed to do was wait for a call telling me that I was hired and deliver a message that I would find here, in your house. I came here, found the instructions on the mail table in the foyer along with this envelope . . ."

"How'd you get in?"

"I was told that the garage would be open and the door into the house unlocked. That's the way I found things."

Walter thought and then nodded for his visitor to continue.

"Thank you," the man said, as if Walter were the one holding the pistol. "Now, if you'd look down between the cushions, that's where I put the envelope."

Walter kept his eyes locked in confrontation across the table while he ran his fingers between the seat cushion and the padded frame of his chair. He retrieved a thin business envelope with no markings on the outside.

"The point that's essential is that I have no idea who sent me to deliver this message. I don't know who did the kidnapping. My instructions said that the kidnappers know nothing about me. And none of us knows who's holding your wife, or where. So you see, memorizing my face, or catching me and holding me for the police, will do you no good. I can't say anything that will help your wife because I know nothing about her. I'm not a kidnapper, Mr. Childs. I've thought a lot about this and I think that I'm just a good citizen reporting a crime. Does that make sense to you?"

Walter glared daggers at the man. He tore open the envelope and pulled out a single sheet of paper, computer-printed on one side.

Mr. Childs.
  The man seated across from you is telling the truth. He knows that

Emily has been kidnapped, but has no idea why, or where she is being held. The kidnappers know nothing more than that they left your wife, under sedation, in a parked van. The van driver knows nothing, other than that he has picked up a valuable person, and is to hold her incommunicado until advised.

I am the only one who knows all the players and all the locations. That means that none of them, nor any combination of them, can lead you or the police to your wife.

My terms are simple. On Friday, at exactly 4:00 p.m., you will wire $100 million to a numbered account at Banco Folonari, the Cayman Island branch. You, of course, know the routing number and authentication code. The money will be converted into Banco Folonari bearer bonds and will be delivered to a courier, who will call for the proceeds using the appropriate authentication code. You must make no attempt to follow or intercept the courier. The courier will use legitimate financial channels to deliver the money to me. I will have it Monday morning and will immediately cause your wife to be released. If the funds fail to reach me for any reason, you will never hear from either your wife nor me again.

If you understand these plans, please inform the courier. His actions will tell me whether or not the message has been delivered.

If you contact the police, the FBI, Interpol, or any other law enforcement agency, you can be certain that I will know about it. There will be no further correspondence from your wife or me.

Her life is entirely in your hands.

If you agree to meet these terms, please make a reservation tomorrow for a single table in the window at Casper's. Walk there and have lunch between noon and 2:00 p.m. I will then order that your wife be kept comfortable until Monday. If you choose not to meet my demands, simply neglect the lunch, or else make contact with the police or other authorities. In that case, I will pay the people holding Emily to kill her and bury the body. You will hear nothing further from any source.

Walter looked up from the note at the man seated opposite him. "Do you know what this says?"

The man looked sympathetic. "I've guessed that it's about a ransom. I don't know for sure. But I've been told that if you understand the terms, I'm to stay with my present rental car. If you don't know what's being asked, I'm to change to another rental car company. So I don't need to know anything about the ... arrangements. All I need to know is whether you understand the ..." He gestured toward the letter that dangled from Walter's fingers "... the document," he concluded.

Walter nodded slowly, indicating that he understood. He folded the letter carefully and slipped it back inside its enveloped.

The visitor raised the automatic pistol. "Then I won't be needing this anymore."

"No," Walter agreed. "You can put it away."

The man released the ammunition magazine and pulled the slide to show an empty chamber. "It wasn't loaded. But I thought you might attack me before you understood that I'm in no way involved. I mean, I would never hurt your wife. I have no idea what they're asking of you. Like I said, all I'm really doing is reporting a crime. That doesn't make me a criminal, does it?"

He stood slowly, slipping the pistol into the side pocket of his suit jacket. "I really hope that everything works out well for you."

Walter glared back, about to spring toward the man's throat.

"Oh, just one more thing. My instructions said that they had left something for you in your mailbox."

Walter rushed past the man and out the front door. He was tearing the package open as he ran back up the driveway from the mailbox. In the dim light of the foyer, he recognized the contents: Emily's wedding and engagement rings rolled together in tissue. He looked up into the living room, wondering if his messenger knew what had been left as proof that his wife had been taken. But the man was gone.

He squeezed the rings in his hands as he pumped up the stairs. Their bedroom was in disarray, with Emily's tennis things scattered on the floor. He turned into the bathroom and saw the broken curtain rings on the carpet before he realized that the shower curtain was missing. Then he noticed the bra and pants next to the laundry hamper. It was obvious that they had caught her while she was changing from her morning tennis game, probably while she was in the shower. With the curtain ripped away, the rings broken, and the carpeting soaked, he guessed that she had put up a struggle. "Oh, Jesus ..." There was a small red stain surrounding the drain, where bloody water had run out.

He went back into the bedroom and walked around in an aimless circle as he tried to imagine the scene. The more he thought about it, the more violent the image became until he bolted out of the room to keep from becoming sick. He took the back stairs down to the kitchen, pausing to notice the water stains at the top step. This was how they took her out, he thought, still soaking wet from her shower. He picked up the kitchen telephone and dialed.

Angela picked up on the third ring.

"I've got to see you in the morning, early," he said in an angry staccato.

"What's wrong?"

"Emily . . . she's been kidnapped . . ."

He could hear the air escaping from Angela's lungs. Then a gasp, which was all she seemed able to manage.

"Did you hear me? She's been kidnapped. I've got a ransom note. Jesus, I was coming home to tell her . . . about us . . . and someone had taken her."

Angela's voice was soft and calm. "Did you call the police?"

"I can't. They'll kill her."

"Oh my God . . . dear God! You've got to get her back. Do whatever they ask . . . anything . . . you've got to get her back."

Emily had just plunged the pruning shears into Walter's chest and was taking great satisfaction in the bewildered expression that had flashed across his face. "Emily, this isn't like you. You're not a violent person. You're supposed to forgive me," Walter was saying as his knees slowly buckled.

"Oh," Emily taunted, "did you expect me to just go quietly? Without a scene?"

Walter's knees hit the floor. "A scene, of course. But this?" He gestured to the round handles that were sticking out of his chest. Slowly he rolled over onto his side. His efforts to talk became a gurgle. Emily smiled as she watched him writhe in agony, sick from the taste of his own blood, his strength ebbing away. But as she began to feel her own consciousness, she realized that she was the one who felt sick to her stomach and whose strength had deserted her. She couldn't move her arms or even raise her head. When she opened her eyes, she was blinded by a white glow. Only by squinting could she make out the pattern of perfect squares coming through the white background.

She was on her back, looking up at a ceiling of sound-deadening tiles. There was a ceiling just like it in the finished basement of the first house she and Walter had owned. She struggled to raise her head and was able to see the tops of the walls, light fake wood panels, framed out with rough furring strips. When she tried to sit up, she found out why her arms felt so heavy. Her wrists were handcuffed around the wooden crossbar of the headboard. She was chained onto a bed. She glanced down and saw that she was on a plain mattress with no bedding and was wearing a heavy, plaid nightgown that she had never seen before.

"Oh, you're awake." It was a woman's voice, neither rude nor pleasant but simply stating a fact. Emily turned her head trying to locate the sound, but she was suddenly engulfed in a wave of nausea.

"I'm going to be sick."

"No, you won't. That's just the drug. It takes a while to wear off." The woman stepped into view, leaning over the bed. She had a long, thin face with narrow eyes and a prominent Roman nose. Her hair was jet black and cut off abruptly just below her ears. The part, which showed traces of gray, was as straight as a laser beam, and the narrow lips were colored to a dark maroon that was nearly black. She was in her forties, fitted out to look twenty and achieving midthirties. She seemed very competent, projecting all the authority of a top executive's private secretary.

She took Emily's face in her hand and turned it slowly from side to side. "They probably used Demerol. That shit can give you a nasty hangover. Sodium pentathol is faster, and there aren't any aftereffects."

"Where am I?" Emily managed.

"That's not important," the woman answered. "What's important is that you're alive and well. And you'll stay that way as long as you do as you're told."

Emily lifted her head a bit higher. "A basement? Am I in a basement?"

"It's a cellar in a house. An old dump in the middle of nowhere. There's no way out except those stairs . . ." she nodded to Emily's left ". . . and there's a gentleman up there you really don't want to meet."

Emily followed the direction of the gesture. There was a flight of steps, covered with a faded carpet, that led to a closed door. "How did I get here?"

The woman laughed. "In a shower curtain. You've been shipped around like a sack of mail."

"You drugged me . . . you kidnapped me."

"Hell, no. Kidnapping is a little out of my line. All I'm getting paid for is keeping you off the streets and that's all I'm doing. This is someone else's scam. Someone told me you were coming and the same person is going to tell me when you're going. In the meantime, you and I have to do our best not to get on each other's nerves."

Emily wiggled on the bed, trying to find a comfortable position. "Please. Can you free my hands. My arms are hurting."

"Sure! If you promise not to try anything silly."

Emily nodded. The woman immediately went around behind the bed and snapped the shackles off one wrist, then the other. Slowly, Emily was able to drag her hands down and begin massaging he wrists. "God," she sighed blissfully.

"There's a toilet over there," the woman said, pointing to the stall formed by a framed-out wall. Emily looked. There was no door, just the most basic kind of enclosure. "And there's a table for your meals." Emily followed her eyes in the other direction. A folding metal chair was positioned next to an aluminum camping table. "I'm not a chef and the guy upstairs can't even boil water, so you won't be getting a menu. But you won't starve."

"Please, can I have some water . . ."

"There's a sink in the bathroom." The woman had already started toward the stairs. Emily saw a floral blouse over designer jeans and flats. "I'll bring down some paper cups."

There was a brief flash of light as she opened the door and then darkness at the top of the stairs when she closed it behind her.

Emily vaguely recognized her. Not the woman who had just left her, but a blonde-headed version who had appeared in the paperwork of the Urban Center. A grifter who had swindled twelve thousand dollars and then claimed that she needed a public defender. The center had provided one and the lawyer had gotten the woman off on a technicality. Her name was Rita. Rita Lipton, followed on the rap sheet with a string of ethnic aliases that announced everyplace from Park Avenue to Calcutta. Emily remembered laughing at her gifted imagination. She wondered what name she was signing to her bad checks now. And the change in her appearance was equally creative, but Emily guessed that hair dye and cosmetics were tools of her trade.

She sat up and was immediately dizzy. Her head felt heavy and the bed began to bob like a small boat. She clutched at the edge of the mattress and then swung her feet one at a time onto the floor. It was icy cold; a plain cement floor that had been painted a light gray. There were scuff marks along the walls where furniture or other heavy objects had been dragged. Electric outlets poked through the paneling, along with switches that controlled the lights buried translucent panels in the ceiling.

She could see what had been done. A basement—maybe even a garage—had been finished off with a drop ceiling and wall panels. The bathroom had been started but never completed. Judging by the scuff marks, the space had probably been used for storage and then emptied out in anticipation of her arrival. "Home, sweet home," she managed wryly.

She pushed herself to her feet, wobbled, and then held onto the headboard to steady herself. It was a heavy wooden bed, probably out of an institution, with vertical rungs connected to a slightly curved crosspiece to form a headboard. It sat in the center of the room, completely out of place, as were the camping table and chair and the single wooden Adirondack lawn chair with a green canvas cushion. A place to eat, a place to sit down, and a place to sleep, she thought. All the essentials.

Emily walked slowly toward the bathroom. A toilet with a cracked seat cover. A roll of paper hanging from a wire coat hanger that had been nailed to one of the exposed studs. A basin bolted between a pair of studs with a single cold water tap. All the essentials.

The nightgown was tight on her and seemed a better fit for the extra slim figure of the woman. The plaid pattern was unflattering. But then Emily realized that she wasn't wearing any underwear. She had been attacked in the shower and wrapped in the shower curtain. That was probably how she had been carried from the house, passed around "like a sack of mail" and transported to the cellar. The ill-fitting nightgown, she saw, was a gesture of kindness. The woman could just as easily have left her in the shower curtain, or even worse, stark naked.

Slowly, Emily circled the walls, looking for a door in the paneling that might lead into another room. Maybe a furnace room or a workshop with a tool bench. But there was none. In fact, the barrenness of the area made it a perfect prison cell. There was nothing that could be used as a weapon. No window or opening that might be used to escape, or even to signal to the outside world. Nothing but blank walls. She looked up at the ceiling and remembered that, in her first house, the tiles had pushed up into the space between the drop ceiling and the wooden rafters that the ceiling was hung from. Maybe there was an escape route above the ceiling tiles. She had to find a way out in case her situation became desperate.

Emily tested the steadiness of the folding chair and then used it to climb up next to the table. Again, the room began to roll, and she pressed her palms against the walls to steady herself. The simple exertion of climbing up one step had brought back the drug-induced dizziness. Slowly, she raised one hand and pushed against the tile that was directly overhead. It lifted easily.

She gripped the edge of the opening and climbed from the chair to the table, raising her head into the darkness above the ceiling. She was looking down a channel between two rafters, dimly lit by leaks in the lighting fixtures. The metal framing that supported the ceiling hung down a foot, so there might be enough space for her to crawl up into the narrow area between rafters. But she didn't know whether the framing would support her weight. And the channel appeared to lead nowhere, dead-ending against the concrete foundation behind the wall.

Suddenly, a hand grabbed her ankle and began pulling her leg off the table.

"Now aren't you a curious little bitch." It was a man's voice, dripping in smart-ass sarcasm. "What I can see of you looks sweet as candy. Let's get you down here where I can get a look at the other end."

Emily spun awkwardly on one foot and lost her already precarious balance. She felt herself falling and clutched onto the ceiling framing. For an instant, she was hanging by her fingertips, being dragged down by the hands, which were now locked around both ankles. Then her fingers broke free and she began to fall.

She crashed into the table, which toppled under her, spinning her sidewise toward the hard, concrete floor. An arm caught her under her shoulders and then another under her legs. She found herself looking into a dark, swarthy face with a leering smile.

"Very nice. Very nice indeed. Top and bottom."

She struggled to get out of his grasp and get her feet on the floor, but he held her tightly. "Now what the fuck were you doing up there? Tryin' to get away? That would make us very angry. Besides, there's nothin' up there for you. Just termites and cockroaches." He carried her toward the bed. "Now down here, there's me. And I can do lots of nice things for you." He dropped her from a height so that she bounced on the mattress. "No reason why you should be lonely while you're stayin' here."

His hair was dark and wavy, held precisely in place by a light dab of hair cream. The shadow of a black beard showed through closely shaved skin. He was dressed in a colorful, open-collar sport shirt, with enough chains around his neck and dangling into curly chest hair to anchor a good-size freighter. His slacks were dark with pin stripes and his shoes buffed to a mirror finish. He was handsome, maybe even exciting to the kind of woman who finds violence exciting.

The menace oozed from his eyes, which were enjoying the fear that must be obvious in her eyes. It radiated from a smile that found it hard to contain its delight in her helpless predicament. This was a man who enjoyed pain, particularly when he was inflicting it. He seemed perfectly at ease in a situation where he was towering over a helpless victim.

He reached down and began undoing the top button of her gown.

Emily shuddered. "Get away from me."

"Just a little feel . . . for starters." He was leaning closer, the smile narrowing into a leer.

"Get away!" She kicked out, driving her bare foot against his leg and sending him toppling away. He regained his balance and started back to her, his hand raised in a massive fist.

"Mike!" the woman's voice came from the floor above. "What's going on down there?"

"Nothin'!" he snapped in a voice that sounded like a shotgun blast. His fist slowly dropped and he looked up toward the door at the head of the stairs. "Just bringin' her the paper cups."

When he turned back to Emily, his mouth was a tight line of anger. But he let it relax into a beatific smile. "You really ought to be nice to me, lady. In a coupla days, after these guys—whoever they are—get their money, we'll get a call tellin' us to get rid of you. That's the way it always is. Smart guys don't send the one they kidnapped back to pick 'em out of a lineup and these guys are smart. Damn smart. So when that call comes, I'm goin' to be the only thing between you and a burned-out hole where your brains used to be. You'll be throwin' yourself at me, begging me to do anything to you except stick a gun in your mouth."

The woman called down again. "Mike, what's keeping you?"

Emily's terrified eyes followed him up the steps and lingered after he had closed the door behind him. "Oh, Christ," she prayed out loud. "Who is he? How does he fit into this?" She pulled herself to her feet, smoothing out the nightgown as if he might still be watching. She saw the stack of paper cups that he had apparently been told by the woman to bring down to her. "God, please. Don't let her send him on her errands." She picked up the cups and carried them into the bathroom. He tongue was like glue from her fright. She was desperate for a sip of water.

Tuesday

WALTER HAD TO SEE Angela. He drove his own car so that he could park near her apartment and used the keys to the front door and elevator that she had given him. She opened the door the instant he tapped and welcomed him into a sympathetic embrace.

"You poor dear, you must be going crazy . . ."

"It's been tough," he admitted. "Damn tough. I've been up all night trying to figure how to handle this." He followed her inside, through the small kitchen where she picked up the coffee pot, to the dining area where the table was already set with cups and saucers and a plate of toast.

"I don't think I can swallow," Walter said. But she was already pouring the orange juice.

Angela slid into the chair across from him. "What happened? How did you find out?"

He told her about his arrival at home, remembering his uneasy feeling when he saw the garage door open with no light turned on. "It was so unusual. I guess I knew right away that something was wrong. But I figured, maybe a friend had had an accident . . . that she had gone to help and lost track of the time. I never figured . . ." Walter closed his eyes, trying to fight back the tears.

She reached across and covered his hand with hers. "Of course not. How could you even imagine such a thing."

He described his instant fear when he found a strange man waiting in his living room. Then he told the story of the bizarre scene in which the man calmly explained that his wife had been kidnapped. "We're sitting across from each other having a civil conversation about Emily being dragged from her bedroom. I was helpless. Not just because of the gun. But the son of a bitch didn't know any more than I did. I mean, he didn't know what had happened . . . or why."

"Did you believe him? That he didn't know anything?"

Walter thought. "Not at first. But I guess I did come to believe him. I mean, you'd have to see him. This guy was definitely not a gangster. He kept wishing me well, and trying to convince me that he wasn't part of any crime. 'Just a citizen reporting a crime,' is what he kept telling me."

"That's bullshit," Emily said. "He knew damn well he was being paid to deliver a ransom note."

"But what difference would it make," Walter snapped in sudden anger. "What was I supposed to do? Knock him down and sit on him while I waited for the police. I couldn't take chances with Emily's life. Christ, they could kill her and bury her in a cellar . . ."

"Of course, of course," Angela was already consoling. "You couldn't take any chances."

Walter drank the coffee from trembling hands. Then he drew a deep breath to steel himself. "The problem is that the bank is involved. What the kidnappers want is a transfer of bank funds."

Angela didn't seem to understand.

"The bank has a policy," he explained. "Like the government. We don't bargain for hostages. We thought that someone . . . probably terrorists . . . could kidnap someone at the bank and demand something as ransom. Not just money. Some kind of monetary action."

Her eyes widened. "Like dump some country's currency. Like an Arab country telling you to wreck Israel's economy."

"Exactly," Walter said. "We knew we were open to blackmail so we adopted a very strong and well-publicized policy: *No dealing with kidnappers or extortionists*. Christ, I spearheaded the policy. What I'm supposed to do is inform the chairman that my wife has been taken. The board will relieve me temporarily of all responsibilities and notify the police."

"But, Emily . . ." Angela was interrupting when Walter slammed his fist down on the table. "The policy regards Emily as already dead," he said. "We don't bargain for her. We put the police onto her killers."

"Walter, these aren't terrorists. These are kidnappers who want money for your wife. You've got to do what they want."

He nodded. "I know. Especially with us. I mean, it would look like I wanted it to happen. Jesus, people might even think that I had something to do with her disappearance. You and I . . . we could never be seen together."

"Dammit, Walter," Angela snapped. "This isn't about you and me."

"I know. I've got to think about the bank. I suppose Hollcroft would

34

see it was one incredible act of loyalty if I put bank policy ahead of my own wife."

Angela was shocked into a speechless moment. Walter looked puzzled at her reaction to his analysis. Finally she managed, "Is that what you were up all night thinking about? How your wife being kidnapped might affect your chances of being chairman?"

"I've been considering every possibility. I've been churning it over and over again."

Angela jumped up, throwing her napkin angrily at her chair. "For God's sake, Walter, there's only one thing you have to consider. Not the bank. Not what anyone might think. The only issue is Emily's life."

"I know! I know!" Walter snapped back. "But it's a consideration. If I don't turn this over to Jack Hollcroft. I could lose everything. Not just Emily. But you. And my whole future."

"Walter, listen to me. I said I'd have you under any terms," Angela said factually. "That includes after the board fires you for violating their damn antiterrorist policy, although I don't think they would have the guts to fire someone for trying to save his wife. But I *couldn't have you* if you just . . . turned your back on her. For the love of God, Walter, it's going to be hard enough to get into another woman's bed even after you've given her everything. But if you . . . let her die . . ." Angela was suddenly crying, her clenched fist pressed against her mouth to stifle her sobs.

Walter stood up. "I'm not going to let her die. I'll work this out," he promised her, laying a comforting hand on her shoulder. "I've got to get to the bank and work this out." He reached back to the table and finished the coffee in his cup. Then he kissed her cheek and headed for the door.

Angela stared after him. She felt very sorry for Mrs. Walter Childs. The present one, and any in the future.

Andrew Hogan, InterBank's security director, returned Walter's call just a few minutes after 7:00 A.M. "Mr. Childs. Andrew Hogan here. I just came in and your message was on my voice mail."

"Andrew, I wonder if you could join me in my office for a few minutes."

"Sure! What time's good for you?"

"Right now," Walter said.

Andrew Hogan's job as director of security paid him vastly more money than he had ever imagined possible. He had been an up-through-the-ranks New York City police officer who had made it to the department's top

35

uniformed rank. When he retired, it was simply to change into civilian clothes and walk across the hall to become police commissioner.

But while good police work had been the key ingredient in advancing through the ranks, Hogan had quickly learned that it was not the most important talent of a good police commissioner. He had learned that pointing his finger at a criminal operation could be a career-limiting move unless he first found out who the patrons of the criminal operation were.

He had come down hard on the practice of lending city garbage trucks to private sanitation firms because many of the private outfits were mob-related. Too late did he find out that the payoff for the trucks went to the ranking officers in the sanitation union. The result was a garbage collectors' strike. He also made the mistake of landing on schoolteachers who falsified their hours. Both the teachers' union and the Board of Education demanded his resignation.

The job, he was told by a well-meaning politician, was really intended as the grease between the city's minority population and the uniformed officers who tried to enforce the law. It had nothing to do with white-collar crime, which was the foundation of the city's economy or, God help us, with the financial interests of public officials. "You're the most popular cop in the history of the city," he was reminded. "Just make speeches. Don't try to clean up anything."

Andrew had resigned, ready for a retirement to the trout streams upstate. But his reputation as a skilled and squeaky-clean policeman was immensely valuable to any institution that existed on public trust. Brokerage firms, banks, consulting partnerships, and even law firms had gotten into a bidding war for his services. InterBank came out on top with an offer of half a million a year.

"Andrew!" Walter was on his feet as soon as the security officer appeared in his still-empty outer office. Hogan was a slight man with silvery gray hair, who looked as fit as he actually was. There were many small-time toughs about the city who had mistaken his small stature for weakness and still had limited movement in their limbs as a result. Walter Childs charged out to greet him, shook his hand affectionately, and then led him into the carpeted quarter acre that was his private office.

Hogan's guard was immediately up. He wasn't used to warm, enthusiastic receptions from the bank's top officers and rarely was he invited to the senior executive floor, much less into one of the private offices. As he had learned, the top bankers with their Ivy League diplomas and graduate degrees didn't think much of City College. Nor did those used to winning in the private sector have much use for men who had made their careers in public service. The former police commissioner of New York made a very impressive entry in the bank's annual report, but he didn't make a very desirable luncheon companion.

"Sit down, please." Walter pulled a comfortable chair up to his desk and then ran around to his own massive swivel chair. Andrew Hogan's radar locked on. Walter Childs, he guessed, had a security problem, and one that he didn't want publicized.

"Andrew, the security scenarios your people come up with are always fascinating. It's hard to believe that there are so many ways to attack a bank." Hogan had built a team of experts who were challenged to break the bank's security systems. It included not only a half dozen computer hackers who spent their days trying to break into bank records, but also second-story men who tried to get around InterBank's surveillance and alarm systems. Whenever one succeeded, Hogan developed an antidote.

"I remember one case you had based on extortion. I think you compromised a branch manager and then got him to deposit into a fictitious account."

Hogan nodded. "That's right. We called him Mr. X because it was a classic case of entrapment. It wouldn't have been right to turn him in."

"That's the one," Walter agreed. "I was trying to remember the steps that were taken to protect against such a thing."

"We guaranty complete confidentiality to anyone who reports the attempt within twenty-four hours. After that, the person is on his own."

"That's all?" Walter wondered.

"We also have key employee surveillance," Hogan said. "It's limited, of course. We don't want our people living in a police state. And, as you know, none of this applies to the senior vice presidents, president, or directors."

"I see . . . I see . . ." Walter mumbled. "Now, after someone does report an attempt . . . at compromising him . . . what action do you take?"

Hogan's eyes remained unsuspecting. It was a trick of his trade that his face should never reveal what he was thinking. "We turn the matter over to the appropriate authorities. Police, federals, bank examiners, anyone who ought to be involved. We give them a John Doe for the bank employee in order to assure he's not identified."

Walter was nodding gravely. "But you never deal directly . . ."

37

"Directly with whom?"

"With the perpetrator. You never try to handle the issue . . . confidentially."

"No," Andrew assured him. "Bank policy doesn't let us. We want to make it completely clear that no one has anything to gain by threatening a bank employee."

Walter was fumbling for his next question. Andrew Hogan decided that they had spent enough time playing games.

"This would be a lot easier, Mr. Childs, if you'd tell me what concerns you."

"Oh, nothing directly. Just curious . . ."

Hogan stood. "It's seven in the morning and you called me into your office to satisfy your curiosity?"

Walter tried to look offended.

"When you decide to tell me who's trying to get to you," Hogan went on, "then we'll see what we can do for you. But I should tell you. These things always get worse with time." He turned and started out.

"Mr. Hogan." Walter's words stopped the security officer, who turned back. "Is this office bugged?"

Andrew had to fight back the smile. Walter Childs was one of the senior executives who had exempted themselves from all security measures. "No, Mr. Childs. We have no bugs on this floor. And we sweep every couple of days just to be certain that no one else does."

Walter gestured Hogan back into the chair. "Please, call me Walter."

Oh, he's in very deep shit, Hogan thought, as he settled back down.

"My wife's been kidnapped," Walter began. "She was taken out of my house sometime yesterday. Probably late morning after her tennis match. When I got home, I found a man sitting in my living room with a gun pointed at me."

Andrew Hogan's expression never changed as he listened to the events of the previous night. He interrupted only once, to confirm that Walter's visitor had claimed not to know who had arranged for him to deliver the message. "A recorded voice?" he asked. Walter explained that the messenger couldn't even be sure whether his contact was a man or a woman.

When Walter finished, he took the envelope out of his suit coat pocket, opened it, and pushed it across the desk. He felt foolish when Andrew used his handkerchief to handle the document.

"A hundred million," Hogan remarked when he reached the instructions concerning the money transfer. He whistled softly. When he finished the second page, he turned the pages over, held them up to the light, and then tipped them to a sharp angle. "Computer printer on office store stationery," he said. "Could have come from anywhere."

He set the pages down and looked up at Childs. "Is all this possible?" he asked. "Could you really transfer that much money to an unnamed account?"

Walter nodded. "At *that* bank I can. Very few of the accounts at Folionari's Cayman branch have names." He could see that the security officer didn't understand. "It's a central bank for the drug trade. It pays no interest and makes a fortune on service charges. All it does is change money and launder accounts."

"InterBank deals regularly with such an institution?" the detective questioned.

"When we have to. We work as agents for central banks. The drug dealers have more monetary assets than the central banks of many countries. So, when we have to buy or sell currencies, they become critical partners."

"So someone could simply set up a numbered account, deposit an InterBank loan into it, and then walk off with the cash?" Andrew concluded, realizing his security precautions hadn't taken into account the peculiar practices of Folonari's Cayman branch.

"In just about any currency they wanted. Francs. Lira. Dollars. Or even corporate securities that the Cayman branch owns or stores. It has a healthy supply of everything."

Hogan pursed his lips as he thought through the scenario that Walter had just posed. "This certainly fits under the bank's antiterrorist policy," he concluded. "The only thing we can do is inform Mr. Hollcroft and have him notify the board."

"We're not talking about terrorists, dammit! We're talking about my wife."

Hogan raised his hands in a gesture of helplessness. "It comes under the same policy guidelines. We won't negotiate with these people." He picked up the ransom document again and glanced through it quickly. "Not that they seem interested in negotiation. This is pretty much take it or leave it."

"We can't simply regard my wife as *already dead*," Walter said, hitting each word with its own cadence. "She's alive, and she'll stay alive at least for another day if I make that lunch date."

"And on Friday?" the security officer asked, "When you don't transfer the funds?"

"Maybe we can learn something by Friday. I've got to try to save my wife."

Hogan leaned forward, resting his elbows on the edge of the desk. "We've already learned quite a bit . . ."

"What?" Andrew was shocked that the detective could know anything beyond what he had been told. "What do you know?"

"First," Hogan began, "we know that we're dealing with someone connected with the bank. Someone who knows what you do and how you do it. These people don't just know about financial operations. They know the extent of your authority. Your relationship with the Cayman bank. Where you're apt to eat lunch. Where you live. It seems that they even know what you're wife's daily schedule is like."

"You think it's someone I know personally?"

"Maybe. But more likely it's someone who knows you personally but who you don't generally think of as a friend. Your secretary, for example . . ."

"Miss Carey! That's ridiculous. Why she's . . ."

"I said 'for example.' My point is that if I asked you to list your close friends, your Miss Carey probably wouldn't make the list. You probably don't even think of her as a business associate. Yet she knows your business activities intimately. Has probably spoken directly with the people at this Cayman bank, as well as the top people at every bank you deal with. And I'll bet she knows your wife's schedule better than you do."

Walter looked chastened. "You're absolutely right," he admitted. "There are probably a lot of people around the bank who understand my job. But . . . a kidnapper?"

Hogan again touched the document. "As I read this, the people behind it aren't doing any kidnapping. They seem to have hired the people who took your wife away and hired the people who are holding her. They even hired the guy who brought you the ransom note. And they've arranged it so that none of them knows either of the others. So this could be someone who has never done a violent deed in his life. Just a skillful manager with a few violent friends. Or with contacts among the underworld types who would do these things."

Walter was nodding. "So where do we start?"

"We don't," Hogan said. "We follow procedure and take this to the chairman as soon as he comes in."

"And Emily gets buried in a cellar!" Walter flared. "For Christ's sake, we can't do that. Not while there's any chance."

Hogan sat quietly for a moment. "You know what this could cost me. I'm paid to enforce security procedures. *Your* security procedures."

"It can't cost you your life," Walter came back. "We've got to at least try. Please, Andrew. I'm asking you as a friend."

Despite his years of training, Hogan couldn't hide his disgust. "A friend . . ." he said slowly, weighing the irony.

Walter had to turn his eyes away. "We're not the most cordial people," he allowed. "I suppose none of us has . . . seemed . . . particularly friendly. We just don't know many police officials . . ."

"I'm a cop," Andrew interrupted, "and proud of it. I've gotten my hands dirty. All of you have made it pretty clear that you don't want me cleaning up in the executive washroom."

"It wasn't that . . ." Walter was about to say, *that you weren't good enough for us*. But he knew it was exactly that. Andrew had no reason to think of him as a friend. He had every right to leave him and his fellow senior executives hanging on their own self-righteous policies. "I'm sorry. Truly sorry," was the best Walter could manage. "I'm begging for your help."

Hogan rose slowly, lifting the ransom pages carefully and folding them into the envelope. "I'll take these. And I'll need the keys to your house. There are some lab people who owe me a favor and chances are that your messenger left prints all over the place."

"You'll help me?" Walter was gushing with gratitude.

"Yeah. Some of the people who dirtied my hands know what's happening around town. We may just get lucky. In the meantime, you go have lunch in Casper's window."

"What about my children?" Walter asked. "I have a son and a daughter. They're close to their mother. I'll have to tell them something."

"This is just until Friday," Hogan reminded him. "On Friday, we go to the chairman with whatever we have. That's when you can talk to your kids."

Walter nodded. "I'll think of some way to stall them. Even if we have to go beyond Friday, I can probably come up with a plausible story . . ."

"Friday!" Hogan cut him off. "There's no way I can let you send that money."

"Of course. Of course," Walter agreed. "Just so long as we *try* to do something."

Andrew Hogan found himself wondering why Walter made saving his wife sound like window dressing rather than a matter of life and death. But still, he was enjoying the moment. It was wonderful to see one of these privileged citizens begging for a cop.

Helen Restivo had once been Andrew Hogan's lover. She had been valedictorian in her class from the John Jay School of Criminal Justice at the same ceremony where then-Captain Hogan had been the guest speaker. Hogan had made police work sound so important that Helen had changed her career plans right on the spot, withdrawing her application for a position in social work and entering the police academy. With more than a little self-interest in mind, she had told Hogan how he had influenced her choice when he came to visit the academy. Later, when Hogan looked her up on her first patrolman's assignment, they had both felt a magnetic attraction.

At first, neither of them worried that she might be bestowing favors on a man who could influence her career and that he might be taking terrible advantage of a woman who couldn't afford to incur his displeasure. They were simply two people in love. But then, their relative positions became an embarrassment. Hogan knew he was jeopardizing everything in his fondness for a woman twenty years younger than he. And Helen knew that she had little future in the department if word got out that she was bedding down with a very senior officer. It was easy for each of them to wonder if the other might be on the make. Maybe they could have overcome the difficulties, but they slipped apart rather than address the problem.

They had avoided each other for nearly two years when Hogan heard that a street punk wielding a linoleum knife had cut up a woman officer named Restivo. He had rushed to the hospital and found her in serious condition with a slash across her face that threatened her eyesight and with three fingers missing from her right hand. His solicitude during her recovery had been much more than the police tradition of "taking care of our own." But it wasn't the same passionate love he had felt for her two years earlier.

Helen had been retired on full disability, the department figuring that she couldn't be a cop without a trigger finger on her shooting hand. At that point, Andrew had asked her to marry him, but she understood that the proposal was born in nostalgia and sympathy and promptly turned it down. He did the next best thing he could by helping her launch her own investigative agency and sending her any problems that shouldn't involve the department. Helen now presided over a very large and successful security service and listed InterBank as one of her major accounts. She was the obvious choice when Andrew knew he couldn't use the police or bank personnel in looking for Emily Childs.

Helen had immediately assigned one of her investigators to keep tabs on each of the senior vice presidents. She had sent her best forensic people out to Short Hills to meet Andrew at the victim's home. Then she had assigned herself to Walter Childs and now stood across the lobby from the executive elevators in InterBank's building.

She had picked Childs for herself because she considered him the most likely suspect. The sad truth about domestic crimes was that someone in the household was generally involved. More often than not, wives who accidentally shot their husbands thinking they were blowing away an intruder had known perfectly well who was in front of the pistol when they pulled the trigger. Disappeared children too often turned up buried in the backyard of the family home. And in the cases of missing wives, husbands often proved to have the best motives.

As soon as Hogan had described the case, Helen Restivo's radar had locked onto Walter Childs. She certainly planned to look into the obvious motives, like the wife having a substantial estate of her own that Walter would inherit, or a major insurance policy that named him as beneficiary. That kind of information, quite frequently tied together with gambling debts, bad investments, or other losses that generated a need for a quick infusion of cash. Or the often present *other woman*. Many a man who wanted to change wives saw little sense in leaving behind all his material goods as part of a divorce settlement. Probably, Helen thought, it would be something as routine as one of those scenarios.

But she was more fascinated by the well-publicized runoff for the leadership of InterBank. One of the senior people would win the gold ring and become the planet's leading financial figure. The others would feel that they had been exposed as failures even though they would still be five-million-a-year executives. She guessed that Walter Childs had reached that elite level where he wouldn't know what to do with more money and could have any woman he wanted without expending more than pocket change. Childs, she was nearly certain, wanted something far more significant.

"How," she asked herself, "could a senior vice president parlay the loss of his wife into the top job?" The answer was obvious as soon as Andrew Hogan explained the bank's policy of no negotiations. If Childs sacrificed his wife to the interests of the bank . . . if he in effect announced that his concern for the bank's depositors went beyond his concern for even his own wife . . . then how could they hope to find a more dedicated man to trust with InterBank's fortunes? Was it possible that he had dragged the bank's security officer into a charade, pretending to try and save his wife? And then, at Andrew Hogan's Friday deadline, would he tearfully do the heroic thing and refuse to transfer the money as the kidnappers had supposedly ordered. Helen was playing a hunch that Walter himself might be the kidnapper and that he wouldn't be overjoyed if they were to turn Emily up alive.

Walter stepped out from behind the doors of an elevator, his eyes darting suspiciously from side to side. For an instant, he seemed genuinely frightened, but then he squared his shoulders and stepped out purposefully, looking involved and important. Helen checked his face against the black-and-white security photo that she had palmed in her good hand. Then she wandered out the door, settling a few hundred feet behind Walter. She wasn't so much interested in Walter's route. She knew where he was headed. What was important was the people in the streets around Walter. If what Childs was claiming were true—if Emily had really been taken away by an unknown person—then that person could well be standing in the street somewhere between here and Casper's restaurant. Or, like Helen herself, the person might begin to follow Walter, seeing him to the door of the restaurant and waiting for him to claim his table as the signal that he would be paying the ransom.

She was looking for anyone else who might be paying attention to her suspect. She planned to follow Walter all the way to the door and then station herself across the street to see if anyone was interested in who took the table in the window. And then she planned to take particular note of anyone who left shortly after Walter. The kidnapper, if there was one, would certainly make himself known by his interest in Childs. Helen's problem was recognizing that interest.

Andrew Hogan was standing in the door of Emily's bedroom, reconnoitering the terrain before stepping into the crime scene. Right now, at this point in time, everything in the room should bear witness to Emily and her husband, and then to the kidnapper. If there was something to be seen he had to see it now, because once he and the forensic team stepped across the threshold the process of obliterating the obvious evidence would begin.

The profession was filled with stories of evidence destroyed in the attempt to gather evidence. There was the tale of the FBI agent-in-charge who stepped out of the rain into the scene of a bank robbery and bent over a clear, powdered fingerprint. Rain from the brim of his hat had run down and washed the print away. A ranking Chicago detective had once hung up the telephone at a murder scene to silence the annoying off-hook signal, and in the process had hidden the fact that the victim had been talking to someone who might have heard the last words. Hogan wanted to take everything in before he threw the room open to the professionals.

The first thing that struck him was the size of the room. It seemed sparsely furnished even though it contained two double beds flanking a circular marble-top night table, a triple dresser, a chest of drawers, an electronics entertainment center with an arrangement of leather furniture, and a vanity that was bigger than the chorus dressing room in some Broadway theaters. Hogan and his two brothers had grown up in an apartment that wasn't as big as the bedroom.

The two beds were his next observation. Apparently Walter and Emily didn't fall asleep in each other's arms. He'd have to check the other bedrooms for evidence that they might not share even the same room. Separate sleeping arrangements usually indicated nothing more than a husband with a jackhammer snoring problem, or a wife who needed to keep the light on. But in his years of police work, Andrew found that men who had done in their wives had usually moved to the couch some time before.

Next, he spotted the wineglass on the vanity. That set his eyes searching until he found the small refrigerator that was built into the base of the entertainment center. He remembered the wet bar in the pantry kitchen, stocked like the top shelf at a country club grill. Drinking was part of their lives. In Emily's case, assuming Walter was correct about the time she had been kidnapped, there was no need to wait for the sun to cross over the yardarm.

His eyes followed the trail of the clothes. The scattered tennis outfit pointed from the bed to the bathroom door. Andrew stepped across the threshold and moved carefully along the marked trail.

The tennis shirt was sweat stained and seemed to have dried stiff. Whoever had worn it had certainly exercised vigorously, so if the trail of clothes had been laid down to mislead an investigator, the garments had been peeled off someone's still-sweating body. The bathroom seemed further collaboration of Walter Childs's story. The shower curtain had been ripped down forcefully. The hollow chromium bar was bent, with a screw pulled out of one of its end fittings. There were rings still attached to it that held torn-out eyelets from the curtain. There were broken rings in the tub and on the floor. Without doubt, the curtain had been involved in a struggle.

Hogan noticed the thin, red stain that surrounded the tub drain. Blood had been shed, but he couldn't tell how much. Someone had bled while the shower was still running and the water flow had carried the blood to the drain. He guessed that any wounds had been superficial. At scenes of carnage, bloodstains were usually splattered all over the room.

The missing shower curtain apparently had been taken away along with Emily. The most logical explanation was that it had been wrapped around her, which, in turn, indicated that when she had left the bedroom, Emily had either been dead or unconscious. The battle in the bathroom didn't suggest someone who would allow herself to be rolled in a curtain if she still had any fight left in her.

There were footprints all over the bedroom carpet, created by wet shoes and sneakers. He figured the sneakers to be Emily's, but then realized that she wouldn't still be wearing her shoes when the water was spilled out of the shower. So, apparently one of her kidnappers was wearing them.

Andrew found the entire scenario troubling. The letter that Walter Childs had given him indicated a very intelligent person running the operation, but the crime scene suggested amateur hour. Emily could have been taken much more easily before she ever entered the house. Kidnappers, who knew she would drive straight into the garage, would attack her as she stepped out of the car. It would be a simple matter to hold a drug-soaked cloth over her face, push her back into the car, and take her away. By waiting until she had gotten into her bedroom, they had given her a greater opportunity to escape and had given themselves the problem of getting her back down into the car. If Andrew were hiring people to lift a wife from her home, these guys wouldn't be his first choice.

He called Helen Restivo's lab men into the room and added specifics to their general procedure. Whose blood was in the tub? Emily's? One of the kidnappers? Was there blood in the drain trap? Enough to suggest a serious wound? Or was it as superficial as it appeared? Was there any blood on the bedroom carpet? Or were the stains water marks only? What about fingerprints? Unless the attackers wore gloves, there should be prints all over the bathroom. Given the apparent violence of the struggle, no one could have been careful about where he'd put his hands.

The forensics team hit the room like chambermaids, gathering linens, glasses, and other debris into plastic bags, dusting and sweeping in every crack and corner. Hogan left them to their work and began a very focused tour of the house. After checking the bedrooms, he went to the telephones, both the residential line and Walter's business line. He noted the phone numbers and made recordings of the recorded messages on the answering machines.

In the family room, he checked the television, stereo, and cassette recorders, noting the capabilities of the systems. Someone in the household was apparently an electronics freak. There was enough video and sound equipment to open a fair-size broadcasting station.

The framed photographs and ornaments told of the family dynamics. There were dozens of photos of Walter with world leaders, some showing him shaking hands in front of portraits of kings, others of him squatting on the carpet in some sheik's tent. He was depicted presenting a football to the Super Bowl's Most Valuable Player and in a golf foursome with Jack Nicklaus. He shared two of the photos with presidents of the United States.

There were plaques honoring his contributions to charitable foundations, crystal bowls expressing gratitude for his service to international financial institutions, and engraved bookends from federal reserve banks. The room was a deferential monument to the life's work of a great man. The trophy honoring Emily as champion singles player of her tennis club, and the framed clipping of her triumph in doubles, were clearly afterthoughts, relegated to the periphery of the display. Walter apparently enjoyed the footlights and Emily obviously felt no need to share in the applause.

Andrew went into Walter's office, made himself comfortable at the computer, checked Walter's files and his computerized address book, and copied the name of his Internet service provider. He slipped into the chair at Walter's desk, worked his way through the desktop papers, and opened the locked file drawer effortlessly, using a paper clip for the key. He was still reading through the Childs's family records when the forensics crew finished with the bedroom and began their assault on the back stairs.

Andrew left them with Walter's key, asked them to lock up and leave the key under the mat, and then drove back into Manhattan. It was after seven when he walked into the small Italian restaurant where Helen was in the process of ordering the lobster ravioli that she and Andrew generally shared.

"Nothing at all," Helen said as soon as the waiter had left the table. "As nearly as I can tell, Walter Childs is the invisible man. Absolutely no one noticed him. I didn't see even one head turn in all the time he was sitting in the window."

"How did *he* seem?"

"Good question," Restivo responded. "I think he was nervous, but doing a damn good job of acting normal. One minute, he'd look like he couldn't breathe. Then he seemed to get hold of himself, and he'd look confident . . . composed . . . like a banker. He was just what you'd expect from a guy who's trying to look calm while he's scared out of his mind."

"So what do you think? He's legit?"

She shrugged her shoulders while the waiter was pouring the deep red wine from a basket-wrapped bottle. Then she resumed thinking out loud. "Is he legit? Yeah, I think so. He looks too flustered to be in charge of a scheme like this."

"So then someone really was waiting to see if he went to the restaurant?"

Helen had been asking herself the same question. "Maybe. But if it is an inside job, then maybe no one had to follow him to lunch. I mean, his secretary would know that he had left for lunch at Casper's. Probably the other swells in the executive suites would know. An insider probably wouldn't have to follow him or see him sitting in the window. Maybe the instructions were just supposed to get him thinking that it was an outsider."

Hogan took over. "The crime scene looked like some sort of circus act. They could have grabbed the lady the second she pulled into the garage. No fuss! They'd have been gone in a half a minute. Instead, they wait for her to get into the shower. Then they have to knock her out, roll her in the shower curtain, and carry her down the back steps. Minimum, ten minutes in the house."

"Which suggests . . . ?" Helen wanted to know.

"Our perps were late getting there. My guess is that they never cased the house. That they played the whole thing pretty much off the cuff. I'm beginning to believe that someone has hired a group of unrelated amateurs . . ."

He paused as the food arrived and waited impatiently while the waiter topped off his still full wineglass. Then he leaned back close to Helen.

"Walter Childs said that the messenger didn't seem like someone who could be involved in a kidnapping. Just some guy moonlighting to pick up some extra money. That's about where I'd put the people who took Mrs. Childs. Average Joes trying to do something that they have no experience with. The lady even bloodied one of them up. The blood around the drain wasn't hers, and it wasn't Walter's."

"You think they killed her?"

Hogan shook his head. "No. Not right away, at any rate. Your forensic guys found a used Demerol ampoule in the shrubs outside the kitchen door. Someone had filled a syringe. Looks like they knocked her cold. Or, at least, that's what they were trying to do."

"That's not completely amateur," Restivo mused.

Hogan shrugged. "No shortage of people who need money and know how to use a hypodermic. Could be any druggie from any street."

"You know," Helen said, "that's one thing that's bothering me. How do you recruit average Joes for a kidnapping? I mean, you can't just pick people out of the telephone book and say, 'Hey, how would you like to make a couple of hundred by kidnapping someone?' It seems to me that you'd have to have a pretty wide inventory of down-and-out lowlifes at your disposal. We think that this is an inside job. But whoever did it must have some connections with crooks and junkies. So who in a bank knows how to deal with street scum?"

"Me, for one," he said. Helen's eyes snapped up. "And I suppose some of the people on my staff. I've hired a couple of guys off the parole rolls. You know, 'to catch a thief.' And there's no doubt that they resent some of the suits who pick up million-dollar bonuses at Christmas."

Helen wanted to drop the delicate subject, but she could see that her friend was still tossing it in his mind. "Some of my guys have learned a lot about the bank's systems and procedures," Andrew said. "It's stuff they need to know when they try to break in."

They started their meal in silence, neither wanting to pursue the idea that Hogan and his staff should become important suspects in the investigation but, at the same time, both unwilling to move on to another topic. Helen found her priorities shifting. She had figured Walter as the most likely perpetrator. But where would the senior vice president of a world-class money center make the acquaintance of subculture types who knew how to administer drugs and who would moonlight as kidnappers? Probably not among the members of his country club. Andrew Hogan, on the other hand, could put together a team in an hour. Hogan was squirming under the continuing insult of his treatment by the InterBank executives. What a delicious way to bring them to heel and pocket the biggest bonus in the banking industry.

But she knew Andrew to be squeaky clean and honorable enough to marry her even though he didn't really love her. Robbing a bank wasn't in his makeup, unless he got bored protecting it. When she glanced over at him, she found him staring vacantly around the room. "Are you bored, Andrew?"

"No, just thinking."

"But not about the case?" She knew him well enough to discern when his investigator's brain was turned on and when he had shut it off.

"No. I was just thinking about these other couples." A tilt of his head indicated the couples at the surrounding tables. "How many of them are talking about bodies wrapped in shower curtains or blood in a bathtub drain?"

Helen laughed. "We do have some disgusting conversations. So what else would you like to talk about?"

"I don't know anything else. This is what I've been doing my whole life. I'm beginning to think that maybe it's time for a change."

She was startled by the thought of Andrew Hogan doing anything but upholding the law. Maybe it would be a good idea, she thought, to take a good look at some of his people.

"Oh," said Andrew, suddenly clicking back into focus. "I've got another new name that you should be following closely."

Helen took out her pad and pencil, ready to write.

"Guess who Walter Childs telephoned the second that his courier was out of sight?"

She decided not to guess.

"One of his associates at InterBank. A lovely young thing named Angela Hilliard."

Helen set down the pencil. "You're kidding. A secretary? You're going to tell me the guy is doing the girl from the mailroom?" And then she bit her tongue. Walter's sheepish grin told her that he, too, was remembering when he was doing the girl from the mailroom. He was an officer and she had been a rookie cop. "Sorry," she said. "Let me try to rephrase that."

His hand reached out and covered hers. "No, that *was* our problem. Neither of us were comfortable with it. But this young lady is hardly from the mailroom. Miss Hilliard is a fast-track executive. She runs a few of the bank's biggest accounts. Odds are that she'll be the first person to use the women's facilities at the senior executives' health spa. And when she does, you're going to find the whole executive row dressed in bath towels, because Angela is a perfect 10, even in a business suit. Put her in running shorts, and she's probably a 12."

Rita Lipton yelped with pain, dropped the small tray of fried chicken onto the table, and jammed her fingertips into her mouth. "Damn platter is hot as hell!" Angrily, she slammed the door of the microwave oven where she had just heated the frozen chicken. "I thought only the food got hot!"

Mike laughed without looking up from the tabloid he was reading. "Good thing you know what to do in bed, because you don't have a clue in the kitchen."

"Good thing I have more than a clue in the courtroom," Rita countered, "or you'd be lining up for your meals with other cons."

"I'd of gotten off," Mike said.

She pushed some of the chicken onto his plate and set the plate next to an open bottle of beer. "Sure you would have. Especially when they found the guy's shoe in your car. How did you figure on explaining that one?"

He put down the paper and picked up a chicken breast. "Christ!" he said, dropping it as if it were a ticking bomb. "It's hotter than hell!"

Rita shook her head. "Isn't that what I just told you?" She wondered whether she should have just let them put Mike away for two to ten. He was beginning to wear on her.

She made her money by her wits, convincing people that she could help them double or triple whatever they gave her. For horseplayers, she always had a sure thing. She was putting up two grand that the player would match. Then they'd place their bet. Only there was no horse and no bet. She'd left with the player's two thousand.

For the greedy, she had a sure-fire insurance scam. The insurance company had agreed to pay her twenty thousand to settle her slip and fall claim. All they needed were the doctor's records. And she needed three thousand to pay the doctor for a set of phony X rays and a matching medical report. She'd pay six thousand for the three thousand loan when the check came in. Of course, there was no insurance company, nor any doctor. Rita would vanish with the three thousand sure-thing investment.

Most of the scams required a third party to play the bookie who would take the bet or the insurance representative who was promising payment. They were never big roles. The starring part was always Rita's. All she needed was someone who would show up and say a few lines. Mike could manage a few lines. He needed a bit of help to grasp that the loud shirt went with the bookie role and the striped necktie was for the insurance representative. But if she dressed him and rehearsed him, he could be quite convincing. He looked and sounded like much more than he actually was. And if things went awry, then Mike's real professional skills as a street thug would come in handy. He had been a leg breaker for one of the New Jersey dons and he could punch his way through anyone who decided to hold them for the police.

Rita put a breast and thigh on a plate with the potato salad she had spooned out of a delicatessen container. "I'll bring this down to our house-guest," she mentioned, turning toward the basement door.

Mike jumped to his feet. "I'll bring it down."

She eyed him suspiciously. "No way! Last thing we need is you getting the hots for her. I'd stab you in your sleep."

"Hey, don't worry." He grabbed for the plate. "If she goes for me I'll call you. We can make it a threesome."

She held the plate away from him. "I'll watch the lady, all you have to do is watch the street."

Emily heard the lock click. She jumped up from the bed and moved quietly toward the table and chair. If it were him, the farther she was from the bed the safer she would be. She nearly sighed with relief when the woman appeared at the bottom of the stairs.

"Time for dinner." Rita put the plate on the folding table and set a spoon beside it. "And there's a surprise." She slowly lifted a bottle of beer from her pocket and displayed it proudly. "It's a good thing he can't count, because he wouldn't like me giving away his stuff."

Emily tried to look thrilled. "That's very kind."

Rita shrugged. "Nobody said this had to be awful for you. Remember, I want to get you out of here as much as you do."

"How long will I be here?" Emily asked, the forced smile still painted on her face.

"Not long. They told me Monday. Tuesday at the latest."

Rita was moving away, back toward the stairs, but Emily didn't want to let her go. "What happens then? On Monday?" she asked.

"I don't know. All they said was 'make her comfortable for a couple of days.' They'll be telling us where to turn you lose."

"Who are 'they'?" Emily tried.

"Who knows? It's one of those computerized voices so you can't tell anything. But they've already sent the first payment, so they're for real. I'm not asking any questions."

Emily took a deep breath. "I could pay you much more. If you let me out of here, you could name your price. My husband is very wealthy."

Rita scowled. "Yeah, I bet you could. I've seen you someplace before. Probably in the society columns. I always look at the society pages. It's like a mailing list of suckers waiting to be taken."

"I suppose I've been in the papers," Emily answered.

"Yeah, well, they said you'd try to up the ante. But they said I could end up in a place where money wouldn't matter. So just try to relax. You'll be out of here soon enough."

Rita turned to the stairs.

"Do you suppose I could have a book," Emily called after her. "It's a lot of time to spend by yourself with nothing to do but worry."

"Sure, I'll bring you the paper as soon as he's done with it. And don't worry. It's only going to be a couple of days."

Emily was still staring toward the stairs long after she had heard the door slam shut.

Mike was hunched over the table, already half-finished with his meal. He had opened another bottle of beer and he was tipping up to his lips while he chewed. His fingers left greasy smudges on the bottle.

"Thanks for waiting for me," Rita said sarcastically. "Where did you learn your manners?"

"I could starve to death waitin' for you. What the fuck were you two talkin' about?

"About her," Rita said as she fixed her plate. "I know her. She's in the society columns. Mrs. 'The Donald' or something like it. She told me her husband would double whatever they're paying me."

"Payin' us," he reminded her. "I'm the one who's sittin' on her."

She bowed profusely. "A thousand pardons." That was the trouble with Mike. He thought like a thug. His ambition was to take more hits than Dillinger did in a bloody shootout with the police. The subtleties of avoiding shootouts with the police seemed beyond his grasp. Rita knew that he was dangerous to keep around. Sooner or later, Mike would get confused by someone they were conning, think he was in trouble, and turn a misdemeanor scam into a capital offense. But, so far, she had been able to control him. He was even showing signs of learning. And she had to admit that the guy was an Adonis. It was hard to face the end of the day without him and she always started each new day with a smile.

That was what had brought them together. She was doing a telephone scam in Trenton, making random calls for a nonexistent charity, collecting credit card numbers and then hitting ATM machines. No more than a hundred on each card so that the mark might not even notice when he got his statement. It promised to be good for a thousand a day, for about two weeks. Then she would have to move on.

Her mistake was in not letting the local wise guy in on the deal and cutting him in for half. So Mike had been dispatched to help Rita see the light of day. His real name was Milo. The "Mike" came from the first syllable of his last name, which was a nightmare of unpronounceable combinations of consonants. When he grabbed Rita, he liked what he grabbed, and she made it clear that there were other things he could do to her besides beating her senseless. He had taken fifteen hundred back to the Don and then begged out to visit his dying mother in California. Mike and Rita had been a thing ever since.

"She wanted to know how long we were going to hold her," Rita said while she cut her chicken into slender strips.

Mike sputtered his beer. "Christ, I hope you didn't tell her."

"Sure I did. It will keep her from getting antsy. I told her we'd be dropping her off someplace."

"Into the harbor. Or into a sewer. It ain't gonna make no difference to her."

"There you go again," she said despairingly. "Thinking like a hood. Nobody is going to hurt her."

Mike shook his head in disbelief. "What do you think . . . this is a practical joke? One of your two-bit scams. This is a real slick operation. She's been kidnapped by some serious players. I'll bet they're askin' for a bundle."

"So," she challenged. "She's got plenty of money. She'll pay."

"It won't make a fuckin' bit of difference whether she pays or not. They won't want her walkin' around. Hell, I don't want her walkin' around. We're the ones she'll pick out of the lineup."

"She won't know where to find us," Rita argued. "She can't hurt us."

"Well, the people who lifted her won't want to take that chance. And neither do I. Long about Saturday, we'll get a call tellin' us to get rid of her. And I'll be ready with a nice six-foot hole behind the garage."

"Listen, Mike. We're not killing anyone. It's a lot tougher to walk away from a murder rap than from small con. I didn't sign up for a lethal injection."

Rita was a changed person when she went back down to pick up the dinner plate. She was all business, reluctant to risk even a moment of eye contact with her prisoner. "Do you want to use the powder room before I lock up?"

"You don't need that shackle," Emily reasoned. "I can't go anywhere."

She held out the handcuffs. "We have better things to do than sit up listening to you climbing through the ceiling. But I'll only shackle one hand, just to be sure you stay in bed. Now, do you want to use the facilities or not?"

"You really think you know her?" he asked when Rita was back upstairs. His question had purpose. Something was stirring under the lacquered hair.

"I know I've met her. Or at least seen her picture. I just can't put a name on the face."

He pointed to the newspaper he had been reading. "If she's so important, how come she didn't make the papers. When somethin' happens to important people, it makes the paper. But there's not a word about anyone gettin' kidnapped."

Rita realized he had a point. But then she argued, "Probably the police don't want to put out her name so that they don't get a lot of crank calls. You know what happens when people find out that someone important is in trouble."

"Well, maybe we ought to find out. We're the ones stuck with her. We ought to know who it is that we're mindin'."

Rita thought for a minute and then decided, "It's not important. We're getting paid."

"Could be damn important," Mike told her. "What *are* we gettin' paid? A couple of lousy grand?"

"Ten grand. And there's nothing lousy about ten grand."

"What do you think they're gettin'?"

"Who?" Rita said as she poured orange juice over a double shot of vodka.

"The guys runnin' this show. If she's some rich bitch, I'll bet they're askin' a coupla *hundred* thousand. But we're the ones takin' all the risks. We should be gettin' a lot more than ten."

"Like what?"

"Like maybe fifty."

She looked at him carefully, uncertain of whether he had gone completely crazy or whether, for the first time, he was making a lot of sense. "Mike, they said ten. I don't think they'd go as high as fifty."

He smiled. "Bet her old man will."

She squinted. "Are you trying to get us killed? Right now, no one gives a damn about us. But you know better than I what could happen if we get the wrong people angry. These guys don't plea-bargain. You take over their play and they take you straight to the river."

Mike smirked at his own cleverness. "We're not goin' to cut anybody out. I know better than that. We're just goin' to set up a little side deal of our own. The people who lifted her won't know anythin' about it."

"They'll know when they ask for the ransom and find out that it's already been paid."

"You think they'll believe the guy? 'Jesus, you already paid? Well, then just disregard this notice.' C'mon, Rita, they won't give a damn. We're peanuts next to what they're askin'."

Rita thought for several seconds. There were always pretenders who tried to cash in on a kidnapping. The real players wouldn't waste a second trying to find out who might have been paid pocket change. It wasn't a bad scam. All they had to do was find out who she was and then send a ransom note to her old man demanding $50,000. Whether he paid or not, they would still hold and release the lady just as they were told. So it was really just a side bet that no one would have to know about. If it didn't work, they lost nothing. And if the guy fell for it and paid their ransom, then they were fifty thousand to the good.

"It sounds too easy," she told him. He was about to argue but she held up a silencing hand. "But maybe that's because it is easy. Maybe it could work."

"What have we got to lose?" Mike laughed.

"Our kneecaps, or maybe even our brains. I'll tell you what. I'll find out who she is. I'm not saying we'll do this and I'm not saying we won't. But I'll try to get her to tell me her name and then we'll talk about it tomorrow. Okay?"

"Yeah, okay," he agreed reluctantly. But I won't wait for Rita to coax a name out of the bitch, he thought. It'll take me no more than ten seconds to get her name and anything else we want to know about her.

"Mitchell Price was at the restaurant," Walter said, as soon as Angela had opened her front door. "The son of a bitch was sitting at a table along the back wall, hiding behind one of those computer nerds he has lunch with. But I caught him peeking over the guy's shoulder. He had a clear view, right up the aisle, to my table in the window."

He had left the bank at six o'clock and walked the fourteen blocks to her apartment, his legs pumping like the drive rods of a steam engine. Now he was ranting, venting his explosive anger.

"Calm down, Walter. Relax," Angela said, trying to be comforting.

But Walter would have none of it. He fired his dark blue suit jacket at the sofa and charged to the bar in the kitchen where he splashed scotch on top of a tumbler of ice cubes. Angela retrieved the coat, brushed it with her hand and hung it in the closet. When she reached the kitchen, Walter waved the scotch bottle in her direction. She shook her head and whispered, "No thanks," trying not to interrupt his diatribe.

"The little prick was laughing at me, knowing he had me by the short hairs. I felt like going back to his table and driving my fist right through that bonded smile."

"It couldn't be. He's too smart to do something that obvious," Angela reasoned. "If he set the restaurant up as a signal, why would he ever let you catch him there?"

"Because he wants me to know that it's him. He wants me to know that he's the one who's ruining me at the bank. Hell, he may even plan to pick up the money and put it in his pocket so I can watch him spending it. And there's not one damn thing I can do about it." He took a long swallow from his glass.

Angela moved next to him and put a comforting hand on his shoulder. "Walter, I think you're overwrought. Please, sit down and try to relax."

He gave her a grateful but tense smile and carried the drink to the sofa. Angela settled directly across from him. "Now tell me slowly. Why would you think it could be Mitchell?"

"Because if I wire that money, I'm in gross violation of bank rules. I'd be finished."

Angela nodded that she understood his reasoning. "But, still, to go there himself and risk having you see him . . ."

"Dammit, he wasn't risking anything. He could sit there and smirk at me and what could I do about it? I can't have him arrested for having lunch at Casper's."

"Still," she wondered aloud, "it could be just a coincidence. Maybe there's some way we could find out when he made the date. Or maybe the other person picked the place."

Walter sat thoughtfully for a moment and then agreed with her. Andrew Hogan could check it out. He told her about his meeting with the bank's security officer and explained that Hogan was bending the bank's rules to help him.

She was surprised and asked why Hogan would do a favor for any of the officers. Hogan didn't polish anyone's apple and he had no true friends on the executive floor.

"Why not?" Walter sneered. "It's only until Friday. So if he catches someone by Friday, he's a hero, and if he doesn't, he goes to the board and follows policy. He's not going to let any money leave the bank."

He went to the bedroom phone and dialed Andrew's office. When he came back, Angela was in the kitchen, starting a potluck dinner.

"He wasn't in. And I didn't want to leave a message on his voice mail. Christ, Mitch Price wouldn't have any problem breaking into Hogan's voice mail. He's the one who designed the whole goddamned voice mail system." He began fixing himself another drink while he regurgitated the tangled string of clues that he had thought up since the instant when he recognized his associate at the restaurant. "There are lots of things I should have caught onto," he rambled angrily. "Wire the funds! No one knows more about our leased line situation than he does. It's another one of his electronic wonders. He could easily tap into it and he'd know instantly if I were to try to trick him. It's like the messenger said. If I went to the police, he'd know instantly."

He poured a glass of wine for her and set it next to the cutting board where she was beginning a salad.

"Another thing," Walter went on. "The guy who came to my house said he got his instructions from a computerized voice. Price knows how to do those things. Every time you call the bank, you talk to one of his computerized clerks. It would be a cinch for him to pull it off."

She dumped the salad into a colander and rinsed it under the faucet, glancing at Walter to show her interest.

"Hogan says it's someone inside who truly understands my job. Mitch knows it. I have to describe exactly what I'm doing so that he can design the *perfect* computer and communications system for the job."

Angela didn't seem to agree with him, but she didn't want to add to his obvious frustration. It was easier for her to just nod to show she was listening and shake her head to share his anger. She listened patiently to all the evidence that pointed toward Mitchell Price. There was no doubt that the man had all the computer and communications skills needed to monitor all the details of Walter's business life. And he had sat through many long meetings with Andrew Hogan's underworld characters as part of the effort to build secure walls around all the bank's electronic records and files. He knew all the leaks. But when Walter finally lapsed into silence, Angela suggested that he was stretching the evidence too far. "It just doesn't make sense for him to risk everything in a criminal act so that he can beat you to the presidency," she said. And then, when Walter seemed annoyed that she disagreed with him, Angela added, "Bottom line, Walter, is that Mitchell Price doesn't have the balls."

Walter nodded thoughtfully and, for the first time since he had come through the door, cracked a half smile. "I suppose he doesn't," he allowed. And then he seemed suddenly to realize exactly what Angela had been doing. She was fixing their dinner.

"I really shouldn't stay," he mumbled. "I should be at home, waiting by the telephone. If anyone knew that I was here . . . when . . . Emily . . ."

She paused with the pasta in her hand, hovering over the boiling water. "Well, if you really think it's best . . ."

But instead of backing away, he pressed even closer to her. "God, but I need to be with you. I'll go crazy if I'm alone with nothing to do but think."

She put her arms around his neck and kissed him more affectionately than passionately. "I wish I could help you," she whispered soundlessly. "I want so much to help you."

His kiss was more passionate. "Maybe I could stay for a little while," he suggested.

Angela pulled back. "I'd like you to stay. But I guess you're right, it's not a very good idea. You might have to account for your time and if you're asked where you were the first day after your wife was kidnapped, you wouldn't want to say that . . ." Her voice trailed off, leaving the obvious unspoken. How would it look if his first reaction were to rush into the arms of his mistress? He might think of it as a needed moment of consolation. But to people who didn't know him, it might seem a tawdry moment of adultery and evidence of his total disregard for Emily's life.

"Who would ask me?" Walter suddenly demanded. "Who would I have to account to?"

"Well, Andrew Hogan now. And later, maybe the police. I'm not saying it would ever come to that, but . . ."

He cut her off. "My God, you're not suggesting that someone might think that I . . ."

"There's no way of telling," she said.

He turned away from her, his arms suddenly flailing in bewilderment. "How could anyone think that I would . . . hurt Emily?" Then he wheeled back toward her, his eyes wide. "Sweet Jesus, *you* don't think that I have anything to do with this?"

"Of course not! I love you." She stepped forward to embrace him, but he backed away.

"What if you didn't love me? Would you think that I could do something like this?"

"Don't be silly. All I meant was that you're in the middle of an investigation, and if someone were trying to discredit you . . ."

"No! That's not what you meant. You meant that I was probably a suspect. 'Man kills his wife so he can marry his girlfriend.' That's what you were thinking, wasn't it?"

"Of course not," Angela snapped back. But then she added, "Well, yes . . . in a way. What I meant was that if you stay here, that's how it might look to others. But I didn't mean that I was thinking that way. I know you too well to even imagine you doing anything so dreadful."

He leaned against the refrigerator. "You're right. What a damn idiot I've been. I'm a married man, in love with another woman. She won't give me a divorce, at least not without a messy scandal. So I . . . oh, Jesus, people could think that, couldn't they? The police could think I'd want to get rid of her." He seemed about to sink in despair. But he suddenly shouted, "Andrew Hogan! I'll bet that's what he's thinking right now."

She moved squarely in front of him, her hands hard on his shoulders. "Don't do this to yourself. No one is accusing you. No one suspects you. I was just trying to protect you. To keep the wags from talking."

Walter took her hands in his and held onto them as if they were a lifeline. "I can't be alone tonight," he said. "I'll go crazy, Angela."

She led him into her bedroom, expecting to comfort and console him. But in her arms, he came alive, his passion becoming almost frantic. They rolled over each other for nearly an hour, knotting themselves in the bed-clothes, so that when they finished their lovemaking, they couldn't work themselves apart. Walter seemed to forget his problems and laughed at the situation they had gotten themselves into.

"If you can lift your shoulder, I think I can pull the blanket free," she said.

"It's tied up in the sheet. You have to roll toward me so I can get the sheet free."

But once they were lying separately, his morose mood returned. "I must be a real bastard," he berated himself. "How could I do this? I'm laughing with joy at being with you. And Emily might be locked in some goddamned closet. She might be starving. Jesus, she could already be dead."

Angela sat bolt upright. "Don't put us together with what happened to Emily. We both betrayed her the first time we got into bed together. We knew what we were doing. We knew it was wrong. What's happened to her doesn't make us any worse than we already are."

He was nodding. "I know, I know. But it feels worse. I should be experiencing some terrible pain. But I don't feel any pain when I'm with you. I guess I feel guilty that I'm not torn apart by her disappearance. I'm not sure that I want her to come back and that's god-awful. That's really despicable!"

"You want her to come back," Angela said, "and you'll do everything in your power to get her back. I don't care what it costs you and I partic-ularly don't care what it costs the bank. We both have to know that she's home and safe. Then we'll both go to her and tell her about us. That's the only way we can get on with our lives. Otherwise, every time we're together, you'll be feeling guilty. Whenever you look at me, you'll be wondering what happened to her."

"You're right," Walter decided. "I've got to keep the two things separate. Our love has nothing to do with her being kidnapped."

Angela went on. "There's got to be closure on your marriage to Emily before there can be any marriage with me. You see that, don't you?"

"Of course. I didn't mean that I didn't want her back. I was only saying that I must be some sort of unfeeling bastard to be able to laugh when she could be . . ." He choked, unable to finish the thought.

Angela leaned down and kissed him gently on the cheek. "Don't torture yourself thinking about what might be happening. Just do whatever it takes to bring her back safely."

It was nearly nine o'clock when Walter thought about leaving. His car was in the parking garage across the street where he had left it early that morning and he could be home in Short Hills by eleven. But why? There was nothing for him there. It would make much more sense for him to call a local hotel, get some sleep, and be in his office early in case anything developed.

"A hotel?" Angela shook her head in despair. "Why don't you just stay here. I'll get up early so that I can fix you some breakfast."

"Like you said," Walter answered. "Staying might not be the best idea. Someone might ask . . ."

"You've already stayed. It's not going to look any better if you leave at ten than if you leave at five in the morning. Either way, you're going to be telling someone about us."

He wavered, wanting desperately to hold on to her through the long night, but afraid to appear so completely unconcerned at his wife's disappearance.

When he left her building, Walter went straight across the street to the garage. It would raise fewer questions, he thought, if the car were parked closer to the bank. He had decided to sleep on the couch in his office, close to his business phone. It would look better if it were obvious that he had kept an all-night vigil. And he had a change of clothes in his locker at the fitness center.

When he pulled out of the garage, he nearly hit the rental car that was parked across from Angela's. He glanced apologetically at Helen Restivo, who was sitting behind the wheel.

Wednesday

WALTER PACED IN HIS office for nearly an hour before Andrew Hogan appeared in the doorway. The security officer looked composed and well rested in contrast to the nearly frantic anxiety that Walter exhibited.

"Where have you been?" Walter demanded. He realized that he sounded as if he were dressing down an underling, so he softened his question. "Have you heard anything? I've been going crazy wondering what was going on."

Hogan answered as he eased into a side chair. "Well, let's see. We've covered your house. Looks like it happened pretty much the way you guessed. But we know that Emily wasn't injured. She was drugged and taken out in the shower curtain. There's every reason to believe that who-ever set this up wanted to make damn sure that Emily remained alive."

"Thank God . . ." Childs collapsed into his chair as if a heavy burden he had been struggling with had finally been lifted. But after a fraction of a second at peace, the anxiety reappeared in his eyes. "But will she be safe?"

"I think so. Unless somebody screws up. From what you said about the messenger and what we saw in your house, we think that these are rank amateurs. They probably don't want to hurt anyone. But, on the other hand, they'll probably spook easily. Quite honestly, there's no telling what they'll do."

Walter told him about seeing Mitchell Price in the restaurant and launched into the litany of his suspicions. "You think he'd be capable of planning a kidnapping?" Hogan wondered out loud. "He seems pretty much of a straight shooter."

"He'd have help," Walter suggested. "Mitchell Price would never get his hands dirty. But is he capable of setting the whole thing up? Would he have the stomach for it? You're damn right he would. He'd kill his mother if he thought it was going to get him moved into the big office." Hogan

63

listened to Walter's analysis, shaking his head at the details. It wasn't just the mindless ambition being attributed to Price. Hogan realized that Walter clearly understood his rival's ambition because it perfectly matched his own. The key to the big office had become the center of both men's lives. He listened, nodded, and made a few notes. Then he leaned forward confidentially and told Walter that Price, like all the other senior executives, had been put under surveillance the previous day. "We didn't start following him until he got back from lunch," Andrew monotoned as he read the information from his notes. "We had a tail on him last night, but all he did was stay home. We're also bugging his private line, but there have been no significant phone calls, either in or out."

Walter's face fall into the palm of his hand. "Then you really have nothing?"

"Oh, I wouldn't say that. We've picked up a few significant items."

Walter's face reappeared.

"We've identified the messenger. His fingerprints were on everything. He's a down-and-out lawyer doing public defense work in Newark. He lives near you, but he won't be there much longer. The bank is foreclosing on him."

"What did he tell you?"

"Nothing, yet. But we have his phone tapped and we have a guy following him. Maybe he'll try to contact someone or someone might try to contact him. We'll wait until later in the day to sit him down and ask him some questions. But we tend to believe your evaluation of him and there probably won't be a great deal he can tell us.

"We also found several sets of prints around the shower," Hogan continued. "Emily's and yours, of course, but also several others that, judging by their size, appear to be men's fingerprints. You haven't had a plumber in lately, have you?"

"No . . . not that I know of. No, I'm sure. I would have seen the bill."

"We're running the prints now. We'll let you know the moment we come up with something."

Walter started to rise. "I can't tell you how grateful I am . . ."

"I'm not finished," Hogan said. He waited while Walter sat back down. "If you're really grateful, then do me a favor and tell me everything you know that might bear on Emily's kidnapping. Like, for example, how long you have been seeing Angela Hilliard?"

64

"Angela?" Walter's eyes went out of focus. He stuttered a few defensive sounds.

"She was the first one you called after you learned that Emily was missing. And then you went to her apartment last night, as soon as you left the office. So you're seeing her, aren't you?"

The best Walter could manage was a slight dip of his chin.

"Why didn't you tell me?"

"Because Angela . . . my, eh . . . relationship with her has nothing to do . . ." He raised his hands hopelessly. "I wanted to keep her out of it, I suppose."

"Not a smart decision," Hogan told him. "A married man having an affair. His wife with a claim to everything he owns. And then the wife gets kidnapped by someone who knows your job as well as you do."

Walter remembered what he had suddenly announced to Angela. "You think I did this!"

Hogan waved at him. "Take it easy. I don't think anything. But I should tell you that as far as my investigators are concerned, you've become the number one suspect." He waited while Childs turned away in embarrassment and shuffled to the window. Then he asked, "You want to guess who their second favorite suspect is?"

Walter's face was showing his fear. "You can't mean . . ."

"I'll know better once I've been through her place." He held out his hand. "I assume you have a key."

"Dammit, no! Leave her out of this. She couldn't do such a thing." Walter was nearly screaming, his voice cracking with emotion.

Hogan remained calm. "The fact is, she *could* do it. She knows your job very well. There's every chance you've told her more about Emily's habits than you ought to. And she certainly has a motive."

Walter was sputtering. "But, she wouldn't know how . . . where would she find the people . . . how could she . . . ?"

"That is why I'd like to see her apartment," Hogan answered.

Walter stared helplessly for a moment. Then he went to his desk, took out a ring of office keys, and snapped Angela's key off the ring. He couldn't bare to hand it over to Hogan, so he simply tossed it on the desk.

"I think she has a security alarm," Hogan said

Walter went to his wallet and produced a business card with a security PIN number written on the back. He copied it on a phone memo pad and pushed it in Andrew's direction.

"What about a safe?" the security officer asked.

"No. I told her to get one, but she doesn't think she needs one. She has a hiding place for her jewelry and a few very personal things."

"And where might that be?"

Walter was showing his irritation. "In her closet. The floor molding pulls away and there's a space behind it between the wall and the floor. But, I'm telling you, you're wasting your time. You won't find anything."

Hogan took the key and glanced at the security code. "I'd have thought you'd be hoping that I'd find a lead to Emily," he answered.

Helen Restivo used the key to open Angela's apartment door. She went immediately to the alarm, and tapped in the PIN. Then she took a deep breath and let her eyes roam freely.

The apartment was spacious and tastefully furnished, the decor relaxed rather than impressive. It seemed to be the way the woman wanted to live, rather than the way she wanted her lifestyle to appear. The living room had a small sitting area of the typical sofa and soft chairs surrounding a coffee table. There was a small television on a TV stand, with a remote resting on one of the sofa arms. The longest wall was covered with standing bookshelves, interrupted by a built-in desk that held a personal computer. Most of the books seemed to be business reference volumes and the shelves to the immediate right of the PC were stacked with CDs and floppy disks. The telephone, at the back of the desk, accessed multiple lines and the facsimile and scanner were office quality.

The artwork was striking. The paintings were postimpressionist, with two good prints of works by Bonnard. There was an original oil by a Mexican painter, done in a primitive style. The statuary, resting on the tables and on the floor, were quality pre-Columbian copies and Indian pottery.

Helen entered the kitchen from the living room. Small and suitably cluttered, she thought, very much like her own. Women who generally cooked for only themselves didn't seem to make a big thing out of it. There was a loaf of bread hanging out of the breadbox. The dishwasher door was open and breakfast dishes were set into the baskets. There were several liquor bottles on the countertop near the dining el, all top-shelf brands. Helen noticed the notes tacked to the refrigerator with magnets and reminded herself to copy them before she left. She opened the refrigerator and found a career woman's store of stovetop meals and fast foods, along with a dieter's ration of fruits and raw vegetables. Again, she could have been looking in her own refrigerator.

Nice girl, she decided. The evidence said "hard working and nonpretentious."

She went into the bathroom and searched the hamper, where he found designer underwear and a nearly transparent nighty, and the medicine cabinet where she found contraceptive cream. Helen no longer worried about her underwear and she was pretty sure she had thrown out her old, flattened tube of spermicide along with her diaphragm.

The closets and dresser drawers described the same woman. A mix of the provocative and comfortable that said she knew how to dress for the sport in which she was involved. But everything was understated. The lady knew her own value. She apparently had no need to be anything but herself. Restivo was relieved that the popular battery-powered sex toys or gaming costumes were nowhere to be found A decent girl, she decided with a shrug.

Inside the closet, she pulled the baseboard molding away from the wall and found the secret hiding place that Andrew Hogan had mentioned. She slid out a small jewelry case and found two diamond rings, a sapphire pendant, a pair of diamond earrings, a string of real pearls, and an antique cameo broach. It was a small cache for a very successful young woman, but it all seemed to be fine quality. She found heself liking Angela better and better.

She set to work in the living room office, starting with the computer and opening the file manager so that she could look into Angela's written files and downloaded records. It was like paging through a personal diary. There were letters to her mother, her sister, and to a favorite aunt, all in the "I'm fine, how are you" genre. She shared enough of her success so that they would be proud of her, but not so much that they would feel she was leaving their orbit A thoughtful girl, Helen told herself. Then there were long files of business correspondence, some granting loans and establishing lines of credit, others calling notes and implying legal actions. She was staggered by the amounts of money involved—tens of millions on individual transactions. Helen's security agency was a very successful company, but numbers seldom reached over six figures. Angela's business manners came through clearly. She was bright, authoritative, and to the point. Always there was the assumption that she knew more than her client and that the hoard of money she was dispensing put her in the position of power. A real ballbuster! Helen tried to reconcile the InterBank executive with the Angela Hilliard who swapped recipes with her sister. It wasn't difficult. She had managed to retain her own feminine instincts despite moving in a world of ambitious men. She was glad that Angela seemed able to handle both well.

Helen found other files that seemed almost a tutorial on international monetary transactions. "Steps to create a transferable fund" was a detailed primer of Walter Childs's job. "Routing procedures" explained in great detail how routing numbers could aim funds not just to another bank, but to a branch of the bank and a specific account within the branch. "Passwords and IDs" broke down the identity codes that were used to authenticate transactions. There was also a downloaded file on InterBank procedures for monetary transfers, authored by Walter Childs himself. She chuckled at the imprimatur that Andrew Hogan had added to this document in his role as vice president for security.

But she found Angela's interest in areas of the bank other than her own very disturbing. It was pretty obvious that she had made a very close study of Walter's operations, which were exactly the operations needed to deliver the $100 million ransom.

Helen copied the dozens of e-mail addresses in her electronic telephone directory. Then she connected to Angela's Internet service and opened up the listing of her favorite sites. Surprise! The lady was a bit of a voyeur, judging by her fondness for photos of the Chippendales. She was also an opera buff who had ordered computerized courses in spoken Italian. And she was apparently planning a trip. She had been in and out of travel services on an almost nightly basis.

Helen cross-referenced Angela's discount broker and, within a few seconds, had her trading record up on the screen. Each quarter, for the past year, Angela had put $25,000 into her account, probably a hefty slice of quarterly bonuses. She had traded furiously in a futile effort to latch onto one of the soaring rockets in computers or pharmaceuticals. Most of her investments had floated up with the rising market, almost covering her few big losers and her mounting commission fees. She was down about $30,000 in a year when she could have been up ten or fifteen in even the most conservative funds. Clearly, Angela Hilliard could afford the loss. But if, as the trading record testified, she was in a hurry to make a fortune, she had fallen well behind her schedule.

Restivo shut down the computer and leaned back in the swivel chair.

68

Angela Hilliard seemed like a nice enough young lady, normal in every respect except for the enormous resources she commanded. More of a gambler than she would have expected, particularly for someone who worked in a bank. Maybe a bit more cold-blooded than her mother and sister would ever acknowledge.

Could she be part of a scheme to kidnap her lover's wife? Yes, Helen concluded, and probably for the money as much as for the freedom to marry Walter Childs. There was no question that she knew enough about transferring funds to have set up the ransom scheme.

But there was no smoking gun. In fact, there was no gun at all. Nowhere in her files was there any reference to Emily Childs's typical schedule, nor even a hint of any special relationship with Walter Childs. She *could* be part of the kidnapping, but, by the same token, so could most other women who had risen to management positions in the field of finance. There was nothing glaringly unusual about Angela.

There was, of course, the possibility that something would turn up in the telephone records Helen's operatives were examining. And when she set them to calling the e-mail addresses she had copied, they might find themselves talking to people who could handle a kidnapping for a price. But judging by what she had in front of her that didn't seem likely. She locked the apartment door behind her, hailed a taxi, and rode back to her office on the West Side.

The messenger who had visited Walter was the center of attention, sitting at the head of the conference room table. He had a delicatessen lunch in front of him, a chicken salad sandwich resting on a nearly soaked-through wrapper, and a paper cup of black coffee. Three of Restivo's investigators were sitting along the sides of the table, politely asking questions while agreeing with the man that he had done nothing wrong. Helen slipped in quietly and took a chair at the far end, offering an apologetic smile for interrupting the man's story.

Thomas Beaty was a night-school lawyer who had kept a modest local practice in wills and mortgages, with a little slip-and-fall whenever the opportunity arose. He had thrown everything into property in the Newark slums, betting on a tip that the buildings were going to be bought by the housing authorities. They were still standing, vacated by a court order, but tied up in a political skirmish that had gone on for three years. Beaty owed money for taxes and mandated repairs, was being sued by a family whose child had blown himself up in one of the buildings, and he had lost his office to a foreclosure. The promise of $10,000 for simply delivering a message had been irresistible.

Helen's lieutenants had already established that Thomas Beaty was telling the truth. He knew nothing other than the instructions he had received over the telephone, the down payment that had appeared in his mailbox, and the final payment that had come to him through the mail earlier that morning. His concern had originally been that he was being arrested for a crime and would be sent to prison. Now his only worry was that the private investigators might try to force him to give the money back.

The questioning had taken a new turn. Now they were trying to learn all that they could about Beaty's background, hoping to find a point where his path might have crossed with one of the players in the kidnapping. Could he possibly have had a past connection with Walter or Emily Childs? Did he have any dealings with anyone at the bank? Could he have ever communicated with Angela Hilliard? Someone had selected him as the messenger. Who could have known him? How could they have learned that he had fallen on hard times?

"No, never," he had answered to a question on whether he had ever dealt with InterBank. "Who?" he asked, genuinely bewildered, in response to a question of whether he knew Mitchell Price.

"What country clubs do you belong to?" one of the investigators asked. Beaty began to laugh. "Or did you belong to?" the investigator corrected. Beaty didn't play golf or tennis and he did his drinking at a local bar. "What professional associations do you belong to?" Just the Bar Association and once they knew that he had served as courier in a kidnapping, it was doubtful that he would remain a member. Social memberships? Church memberships? Helen's mind was wandering in the pointless repetition of the trivia of a failed life. Where could winners like the people surrounding Emily Childs have ever crossed paths with a loser like Thomas Beaty?

"The Urban Shelter," she heard Beaty say. "I was on the board for a year. I resigned when things began to mount up on me. Embarrassed, I suppose. I was sitting with a bunch of rich people allocating money to the homeless and I was about to become one of the homeless myself."

Helen snapped to attention. The organization had been prominent in Walter Childs's files. "Mr. Beaty, isn't Walter Childs on the board of the Urban Shelter?"

Beaty smiled at his own surprise. "Yes. You're right. I mean, he was on the letterhead. And I guess I must have seen him at some of the meetings. But we never spoke or sat together or anything like that. I didn't make the connection until just this minute."

"Could he have known about your financial misfortune?"

The man thought. "I suppose so. If he remembered my name, he might have found it in the legal notices in connection with the foreclosures. But he probably wouldn't have paid any attention."

The phone on the conference room table buzzed and Helen picked it up. "Restivo, here."

It was Andrew Hogan's voice. "How's our ransom note doing?"

"Just beautifully," she said. "We're chatting right now."

"Well, stop chatting," Andrew said, "and meet me out at the Childs house. I got your lab report and I think we may have found the one in the sneakers."

"One of the kidnappers?"

"I would assume so, because I don't figure that Emily could have been taking a tennis lesson while she was wrapped in a shower curtain."

Billy Leary was giving a tennis clinic, stealing nervous glances at the man and woman who had just taken seats in the small grandstand. They looked like cops, which could only mean they knew about his activities in the Childs house. For a second, he considered chasing a ball toward one of the exits and just disappearing from the building. Instead, he decided to talk his way out of it. He did his best to focus on his students, but found himself repeating his last instruction. It was easier to arrange the women into two step-in groups and let them practice with each other.

As soon as he picked up his towel the two visitors stood up and started toward him. He pretended not to notice and made his way to the men's locker room. He wasn't completely surprised when the door opened behind him and the man followed him in. But he couldn't help the double take at the woman who followed right at the man's heels.

"Hey, lady. You can't come in here."

Hogan flashed his badge, which had absolutely no police authority but generally fooled people who were expecting the police. "Would you rather talk outside in front of all your students?"

Billy didn't answer, so Helen turned the lock in the door.

"Anything you want to tell us about Emily Childs?" Andrew began.

"She's a member. She plays tennis."

"We're thinking specifically about Monday, when you went slopping through her bedroom leaving fingerprints all over the door jambs and wet sneaker prints on the rug."

Billy turned away and opened his locker. "I don't know what you're talking about."

"We're talking about a capital crime. Kidnapping, and maybe murder."

He dropped the racquet. "What . . . ?" He looked stunned.

"You're saying you don't know about it?"

"Jesus, no! Kidnapping? Murd—" He couldn't get the word out. "I thought . . ." he tried again. Then he decided, "I think maybe I ought to get a lawyer . . . before I say anything."

"Right now," Helen said, "you have a free shot." She held up her hands. "No notebooks. No tape recorders. No one is going to read you your rights. It's Mrs. Childs that we're interested in."

Billy seemed to be trying to make up his mind.

"We know you were in her bedroom," Andrew Hogan announced. "And we know you were there while the bathroom floor was still wet. What we need to know is why you were there, what you did, and what you saw."

"Am I under arrest?" Billy said, his eyes widening with fear.

"That depends on what you tell us," Hogan lied, keeping up the pretence of being with the police department. "Like the lady says, this one time you get to talk off the record."

Billy slumped onto the bench. "I figured it was her husband. I figured he found out."

"Found out what?"

Billy actually blushed. "You know . . ."

"Not unless you tell us," Helen jumped in, trying to sound totally sympathetic.

"Mrs. Childs and I were . . . more than . . . it wasn't just tennis."

Hogan tried to be patient. "How much more than tennis was it?"

"We were very close friends," Leary tried.

"You were banging her," Hogan corrected.

Billy looked shocked at the thought. Then he nodded.

"So what happened? Things get a little out of hand?"

He realized that Hogan thought he had been in bed with Emily on Monday. "Oh, no. I just went over there to give her a few pointers. She had been in a match and wanted some extra help."

"That would explain why your footprints would be on her tennis court, which they weren't. But it doesn't explain why they would be in her bedroom, which they were. Unless you give your tennis lessons back and forth over the bed."

Leary writhed at the confusion. "When I got there, her car wasn't in the garage. The kitchen door was open."

"So you walked in and went up to her bedroom. Pretty pushy for a tennis lesson."

He dropped the pretence. "There was no lesson. I went there to . . . be with her. She was expecting me and I couldn't figure out why no one was home. I called her name, went outside to look for her around the grounds. Then I figured something might have happened to her. I went back inside and up to her bedroom . . ." He ran out of steam and silently shook his head.

"She wasn't there?" Helen provided.

"The room looked like a war zone," Bill Leary went on. "Her clothes were scattered like they had been pulled off. There was water all over the bedroom floor and water leaking out of the bathroom door. The bathroom was torn apart. The shower curtain had been ripped off. One of the towel bars was broken. And there was a puddle of bloody water leaking slowly down the drain."

"What did you think had happened?" Andrew asked as soon as the narrative paused.

"I figured her husband found out about us. Like maybe she told him that I was coming over. Or maybe she told someone else and he overheard. I figured he had knocked her around a bit and that probably she had run away."

"Did she ever tell you that her husband was in the habit of knocking her around?"

"No. She sort of made it sound like he did his thing and she did hers."

Helen tried a question. "Did she ever mention that she was going to divorce her husband?"

He smirked. "No. Rich ladies never leave home unless they get to take the house with them."

"I'll bet that pissed you off," Hogan said. "You were hoping to get together with a rich divorcee, and all she wanted was a quickie every now and then. Makes you real mad to have all the ladies paying you stud fees, doesn't it?"

"She was a nice lady. Her husband was cheating on her."

"*Was*. Is there something you're not telling us, Mr. Leary?"

"That's not what I meant," Billy shouted. "But if anything happened to her, he's the guy you should be talking to. Her death would save him a lot of money and a lot of headaches."

They left Leary in the locker room, advising him to keep himself available.

"What do you think?" Hogan asked Helen as they walked toward their cars.

"I think he knew Emily a lot better than he's letting on. And I think he pretty much had free run of the house."

"You think Walter Childs knows about Billy Leary?"

"No," Helen said quite positively. "If he did, he wouldn't be blaming Mitchell Price. He'd get the lover."

Hogan nodded. "Why don't you follow me over to the Childs house. There's something I want to show you." The two cars left the tennis club in a procession.

"It's for making voice recordings," Andrew said, handing Helen a software package that contained a CD and an instruction book. "You set it up, type in a message, and then load it into a PC that has a sound card and speakers. Here, let me play one for you."

He keyed the mouse. Almost instantly, a computerized voice began to speak, announcing the opportunity to earn $10,000. It told the listener which telephone keys to press on a telephone to proceed with the deal and indicate agreement. A smile spread across Helen's face as she listened. "It's pretty incriminating," she said as soon as the message had played itself out. "Whose is it?"

"Mine," Andrew said. "I made it when I was here yesterday. At the time, I thought it put a noose around Walter Childs's neck. But then I found out you can buy the software in any computer store for fifty bucks."

"So anyone could have done it."

Andrew nodded. Then he added, "Do you think you can find out whether our tennis coach has a copy? Because if he does, given the fact that he was at the crime scene . . ."

"Who in hell are you?"

They both wheeled toward the voice, with Helen's hand reaching instinctively under her jacket. They were confronting a young woman, perhaps twenty, who was looking at them as if they were bugs she had found in her breakfast.

"And what are you doing here?" She stepped angrily into the room, totally unconcerned that she might be calling out a pair of serial killers.

Hogan did his badge trick. "We're police officers. And just who the hell are you and what are *you* doing here?

"I live here," the young woman said, playing her ace card. "Now, would you mind telling me why I need the police?"

She was of medium height and slightly built, wearing the tank top and jeans that were college campus uniform. Her features were attractive and her figure was noticeable but certainly not outstanding. What set her apart was her hair, which was shaved close to her scalp on the back and sides, but which stood up in a long crewcut at the top. The crewcut was pure white in contrast to the brunette shade of the fuzz. As she came closer, Helen noticed the rhinestone stud that was fixed to one side of her nose.

"You're . . . Amanda?" Hogan tried.

"Good guess, Detective," she mocked. "If I live here and I'm not Emily, then I'm probably Amanda. Obviously, there's no fooling you. But that still doesn't tell me why I need police protection."

"Your father called us in," Walter said.

"Why? Are you supposed to arrest me and brainwash me?"

Helen eased closer to her. "You might want to sit down."

"I'll stand," she fired back, "so I can show you two to the door."

Helen nodded and then told her the news. "Your mother has been kidnapped. We're trying to find her."

The sophistication drained instantly and Amanda's eyes widened with fear. "Kidnapped . . . how . . . when?" She settled into the chair that Helen had been offering.

"She was taken out of the house Monday morning by two or three people. She was drugged. It looks as if they were very careful not to hurt her."

"Then she's all right and we're going to get her back."

"We certainly think so," Hogan answered.

"Why? What do they want?"

Andrew and Helen exchanged glances. Helen answered, "I think you ought to talk to your father. He can explain."

"He's going to give them whatever they want, isn't he?"

Another exchanged glance and then Andrew said, "Why don't you talk to your father."

Amanda's expression turned angry. "Talk to my father? That's a laugh. Nobody talks to my father. All you do is listen."

"He's going through hell right now," Andrew said. "This might be a good time to cut him some slack."

"Sure, like all the slack he cuts for me."

"He doesn't approve of . . ." He gestured to her face.

Amanda jumped to her feet. "That, and my friends, and my course selection, and my apartment . . . and Wayne . . ." She kept up the litany as she walked out of the room. "I'll call him. He'll be thrilled to hear from me."

They both stared through the doorway as if an exotic animal had passed through the room.

"Daddy's little girl," Andrew finally offered.

"The nuclear family," Helen added. "Daddy gets it in the office, Mother gets it at the tennis club, and little Amanda gets it at college." She turned to Andrew. "Am I the only one who isn't getting any?"

He smiled. "We could go back to my place."

She stood quickly and picked up the software package she was supposed to investigate. "Been there, done that," she said as she left the house.

Emily prayed it wouldn't be him when she heard the door latch. But then came the footsteps on the stairs, with a sharp knock of heavy leather heels. She pulled the blanket up to her chin and buried her face against the arm that was shackled to the headboard. The footsteps came toward her and then stopped dead at the foot of the bed. Then she felt the blanket being pulled slowly off her.

She sat up abruptly, catching the top of the blanket and dragging it back over her.

"Pretendin' to be asleep," his mocking voice said. "Next thing you'll be tellin' me you've got a headache. What's the matter, baby? Don't you want to get it on with me?" He looked down at her with his openmouth smile. She couldn't stand the obscene leer that danced in his eyes, but when she looked down she saw something even more frightening. He was holding a pair of scissors in one hand and carrying a boom box in the other.

"What are you going to do?" There was no disguising the fear in her voice.

"Not me, baby. Us! You and me together. It takes two to tango."

He set down the portable stereo. "We're going to make a record that we can send to your old man. But first, I need to know his address. We wouldn't want to deliver it to the wrong house."

He took a folded paper out of his shirt pocket. "Here! You better rehearse the words." Emily read the note that was thrust in front of her face.

Dear_____,
Do what this man tells you. He's treating me very nice.
If you pay him, he will let me go. If you don't, his friends
will kill me. Don't talk to anyone, and don't call the cops
or you will never see me again. I love you.

She tried to sound defiant. "You can't do this. He'll never believe you."

He laughed. "Well, now, that would be a real bummer. Because if he doesn't, then you'll never get outta here alive, will you?"

Emily tried to fight back the panic. "But you're just supposed to keep me. Someone else is asking for ransom."

Another big, self-satisfied smile. "Someone else will have to make his own deal. I'm gettin' mine now and I'm countin' on you to make it work. So don't let me down."

"I won't do it," Emily snapped. She tried to sound determined.

"Okay," he said, sounding overly pleasant. "Whatever you say."

His hand moved like lightning, snatching the edge of the cover and tearing it out of her grip. She though she might scream, but the voice caught in her throat. He sat on the edge of the bed. Then he began fingering the hem of the nightgown, which lay just below her knees. He lifted the scissors and snapped the blades open and closed. Then he put the scissors to the hem and slowly began to cut the cloth. "I'm going to just keep cuttin', all the way to the top. Whenever you want me to stop, you just tell me the address where we should send our recordin'."

"Please, don't!" The defiance was gone. She was begging.

He snipped again, this time cutting farther up, above her knees. "What did you say?" he demanded.

"Stop, I'll give you the address." She recited it slowly, while he wrote it on the back of the paper.

"Now, you ready to record?"

Emily nodded and took back the paper. She scanned the words. Mike adjusted the dials on the boom box and set it on the bed with the microphone port in front of her face. "Anytime you're ready," he told her, and he pushed the record button. Emily could see the tape begin to turn through the small, smoke glass window on the front of the machine.

"Dear Walter," she began, filling in the blank. She tried not to mind his big hand, which was resting on her knee, or the scissors that still held her gown locked in their grip.

When she finished recording the message, he punched at he controls until Emily's voice played through the speaker. She sounded breathless with fright, an emotion that came through clearly and made Mike smile broadly. Her husband would be able to picture the groping hands sliding over her body. He would certainly imagine a garrote cutting into her throat, or maybe a silencer pressing into the hollow under her chin. The poor son of a bitch would pay up in a hurry. He shut the machine off.

"You were terrific. Ever think of becomin' an actress?"

"No," she said angrily.

"No problem," he snickered, as he picked up his things. "With me, you're never goin' to have to act. You won't have to fake anything!"

He ran up the stairs and slammed the door behind him. Emily heard the dead bolt slide back into place. She squeezed her eyes shut, trying to blot out the images of the past few minutes.

She had to get out. No matter what the risks, she had to abandon any thought of remaining a prisoner, waiting to be rescued. That had seemed a safe course, but now everything had changed. Rita was obviously sympathetic and was apparently following the rules of the game. But this leering jerk, whoever he was, had invented a role for himself in the affair, and that changed everything. He could screw up the ransom exchange, which would certainly ruin her chances of rescue. Even more dangerous, the pervert was excited by the presence of a captive woman. He could rape her, or even kill her as a punishment when his brainless scheme backfired on him. He certainly wouldn't hesitate to eliminate her and the risk that might be involved in setting her free.

First, she had to break the shackle that held her in the bed. She couldn't free her wrist. She had tried several times to slip her hand through the loop, even soaping her wrist when the woman unlocked her and let her use the bathroom. But the bracelet was squeezed too tight.

The headboard held more promise. It was a gently curved crossbar supported by a series of vertical rungs that disappeared behind the mattress and were supported by the bed frame. The overall impression was that of a bridge truss connecting the two corner posts that rose up from the floor. The chain from her wrist connected to another cuff that was locked around the crossbar in the middle of the vertical posts. It wouldn't be enough for her to force the crossbar out of one of the corner posts, because she still wouldn't be able to slide the locked cuff to the end. What she needed to do was figure out a way of detaching the crossbar completely, not just from the corner posts, but from all the vertical bars, as well. It would take hours of work. Rita, and probably her houseboy, would be coming down at least a few times while she was working. So she had to take the headboard apart without letting a single cut or break show. If they caught on to what she was doing, they could simply tie her to the bed frame.

But even if she succeeded in freeing herself from the bed, there was still the problem of escape from the room. She would have to get back up into the ceiling and hope that she could find another room over the tops of the framed-out walls. And then, she could only pray that if there were a room, it would have a door to the outside.

Walter used the rear door of the InterBank complex and took a taxi to the side street entrance of Angela's apartment. He climbed the fire stairs rather than risk being observed in the lobby and studied the hallway through the small glass window in the fire door before he stepped out into the corridor and hurried to her apartment. He let himself in, surprising her as she came out of her bedroom.

"Walter, what are you doing—"

"Hogan knows about us," Walter said, cutting her off. "He had one of his people go through your apartment this afternoon."

"He . . . what?" Angela was genuinely shocked.

Walter drew her into his arms. "I'm sorry. He confronted me this morning. He said we were both suspects."

"Me?" She seemed horrified as she pulled back out of his embrace.

"Not just you. Everyone I know," he hastened to tell her. "Particularly anyone who understands bank operations."

Rage appeared in her eyes. "The dirty bastard!"

"It's what I need him to be doing," Walter said. "I need him to be looking at every possibility. Jesus, I know you're not involved. But Hogan has to figure that out for himself. I'm sorry, but I couldn't tell him that you were out of bounds. He would have gone straight to the chairman."

Angela calmed as the information sank in. "I suppose so," she conceded. "But couldn't you have called to warn me?"

"I think my phone may be bugged. He said that they had put a bug on Mitchell's phone. It figures that they would bug my office, as well."

Angela's eyes snapped toward her home telephone.

"No, I don't think so," Walter said. "Hogan can do anything he wants on bank property. But I don't think he could cut into our home lines without a court order. Just be careful what you say in the office."

Her anger flared again. "Why should I be careful?"

"Angela, he knows we're lovers, for God's sake! Emily was standing between us and now she's been kidnapped. It's not unthinkable that you and I could have planned this together. At least it's a possibility that an investigator would have to look into."

Her nod was almost imperceptible. "I suppose it's logical," she conceded. "But I don't enjoy being suspected of a capital crime."

"I know, and I'm sorry," Walter comforted. "How do you think I feel when I'm suspected of doing in my own wife."

Angela slipped back into his arms and they stood in an embrace, consoling each other. "God, I need you," he whispered. "But, right now . . . the way things are . . ."

She froze and then slowly backed out of his embrace. "What are you saying. That we can't see each other?"

"It's probably not wise," he answered. She backed away another step. He saw the suspicion in her eyes just before she turned her face away from him. "It's just for a few days. Friday . . . Monday at the latest. Then it will all be over."

"If she comes home," Angela said. "Or if they catch somebody. But if something goes wrong . . . if Emily doesn't come home . . . then it will be a police investigation. With publicity. They'll be watching us forever."

Walter was shaking his head before she could finish her thought. "We'll get her back. I'm going to do exactly what they told me. I'm going to wire the money no matter what the bank does to me."

Her fingertips touched his lips. "Get her back, Walter. Please, get her back." She turned away from him, her shoulders sagging, and disappeared back into her bedroom. Walter hesitated for a moment and then retreated back through the front door.

He returned to his office and shuffled papers aimlessly. The incredibly important work of the bank seemed meaningless. All his attention was focused on the Friday deadline.

His task was complex. There was no $100 million pool of funds just waiting to be transferred. The wealth of the bank was in its investments; the vast array of bonds, securities, properties, and the enormous deposits in foreign banks. Much of its ready cash was in its liabilities, principally in the accounts of its depositors. To transfer funds, Walter first had to raise cash from internal sources. He could sell investments and withdraw cash from the bank's accounts. Or, he could sweep up the idle cash in depositors' accounts. It would take hours to assemble the funds through a series of transactions that were small enough so as not attract attention. Then he would have to set up an account at a different bank, perhaps one of the Swiss affiliates, and fill it with a number of small deposits that he could transfer to the Folonari Cayman Island branch. Eventually, Mitchell Price's computers would retrace the flow of funds through the circuitous routing and Andrew Hogan's lookouts would detect the total amount going into the Caymans. But that would probably be hours—maybe even days—later. By then, the money would have vanished.

During his ride home in the limousine he reviewed his complex scheme, calculating the number of transfers, too small to raise any flags, that would be needed to accumulate the entire amount. His head was spinning with figures.

"You seem terribly occupied," Omar's voice sounded from the front seat. The East Indian cadence to the precisely pronounced English seemed almost condescending. "I hope my money is safe."

It was standard banter. Omar had a small account in one of InterBank's few remaining retail banking locations and often joked about the effect of his deposits and withdrawals on the global financial economy. But at this moment, the harmless remark seemed sinister, as if the driver were amused by Walter's predicament.

"It's safe!" Walter snapped, his eyes still fixed on his worksheets.

"Oh, that's very comforting," Omar chanted. "I would hate to lose my money."

Walter looked up and caught the driver's thin smile in the rearview mirror. The man looked self-satisfied, as if his ethereal Eastern values were superior to those of his money-grubbing Western employers. He had often seen the same look on the faces of clergymen, preaching the true wealth of poverty while adding a few words about the importance of next week's collection. Well, Walter thought, look who's riding and look who's driving.

He turned back to his cash transfer figures, but the melodic voice kept on talking. "It must be very disconcerting for you, Mr. Childs, having to keep track of such fantastic sums of money. To be so burdened with matters that are, at their root, unimportant."

Would the man never shut up! Walter raised his eyes again. "As a matter of fact, Omar, this is extremely important. Much as I'd like to chat, I really have to get through this."

"Of course, of course. I'm very sorry for having disturbed you. I only meant that it leaves so little time for pleasurable things. Human things . . . like the people we love. But I will let you get back to your very important work."

The thin smile came back to Omar's lips. Walter felt his hand move over the work sheets so that the driver couldn't see them in the mirror. Does he know, Walter thought. Could he possibly know what these figures are? *The people we love* . . . Does he mean Emily? Does he know about Emily? He was suddenly very frightened. Maybe Hogan should put one of his people on Omar. Maybe he should call the car pool manager and get another driver.

The headlights dimmed as the car turned into a residential area. Walter folded his papers and slid them into his briefcase. It would be more comfortable working at home. He keyed his code into the alarm and started toward his office. He was startled when he saw his daughter waiting in the living room.

"Amanda. This is a surprise. I wasn't expecting you."

"Mother was," she answered. "I talked to her Sunday and told her I was coming down."

"Your mother is . . ." Walter was fumbling for the right word.

"Kidnapped," Amanda filled in. "The police were here when I got home. I tried to call you at your office but you had stepped out."

He set down the case and gave her a perfunctory hug. "I'm glad to see you," he said.

"Then why didn't you call me? I would have come home right away." She walked back to the coffee table where she had left her cigarettes, shook one out of the pack, and flicked her lighter, knowing that he would disapprove. She was surprised when he let the moment pass. "You *were* going to tell me, weren't you?"

"I thought about it," he lied. "But there's nothing that you or your brother can do. There was no need to worry you."

"Did you think maybe I had a right to worry about my mother? Maybe a chance to give my input on how we might get her back."

Walter went to the bar. He didn't particularly want a drink, but he needed a moment to get his thoughts together. He had given some thought to calling Alex, if only for appearance sake. But the last person he wanted under foot was Amanda. He set a glass on the bar and then remembered that she was standing there. "Can I get you something?"

"Just the truth. The police said you knew what the kidnappers wanted for Mom's return. What is it? All your money?"

He poured his scotch. "Not my money. That would be easy. They want the bank's money. A great deal of it. It's a very complicated situation that I have to work out. I don't think you can help and there's no reason why you should worry. That's why I decided not to call you." Walter endured the cigarette smoke as he passed by her on his way to retrieve his briefcase.

"What are you doing?" she snapped when she saw him lift the case. "You can't just close yourself up with your damn bank while Mother is in trouble."

He took a deep a breath. "Amanda, for once give me the benefit of the doubt. I told you they wanted the bank's money. The bank has procedures that keep me from giving away its money. I'm trying to figure out how to get around them."

She looked suddenly apologetic, but she couldn't bring herself to say she was sorry. Instead, she crushed out her cigarette and followed Walter into his office, where she waited silently as he spread out his papers. "There must be something I can do," she finally tried.

"Just your being here is important," he said.

Amanda watched in silence while he used his pocket calculator to work the figures on his spreadsheets. "Dad," she eventually interrupted, "I know the bank is everything to you. I'm glad Mom is more important."

He nodded. But he was afraid to say that her mother was the most important thing in his life. He might not be able to sound completely sincere.

She jumped up. "I better call Wayne and tell him I won't be back tonight."

Walter's jaw tightened at the mention of the name. "Could you do that from an outside phone. I should keep these lines open . . . in case . . ." He was trying to imply a call from Emily's captors, even though he was sure that no call would be coming. The truth was that he suspected the line might be bugged and he didn't want strangers enjoying the details of Amanda's sordid life. *Away at college* was all the police needed to know.

He heard her go out and then heard her car start in the garage. In a few seconds her headlights panned through the front windows. Walter turned back to his papers.

The telephone rang. His instinct was to ignore it, particularly since it was Emily's line. But on the second ring, he thought better of it. He touched the line switch and lifted the receiver. "Walter Childs," he announced.

"Okay, Childs, listen good, because I'm only goin' to say this once. I have your lovely wife with me here and it will cost you fifty thousand dollars to get her back." His drink slipped through his fingers and splattered on the carpet.

"I want the money in twenties. Random serial numbers. And none of them better be marked because I'm goin' to look them over very carefully."

The voice was completely business like. He couldn't believe what he was hearing.

"Get the money tomorrow and you put it in a black leather briefcase. Then drive the case up to Randy's on Southshore Drive in Greenwood Lake. Be sittin' at the bar at eleven p.m. That's where you'll hear from me. If you're not there, or you bring the police, then I'll sell your dear Emily to one of my Colombian friends. They pay pretty well for women to work in their jungle whorehouses. Now listen very carefully. There's somethin' she wants to tell you."

There were mechanical clicks followed by the electronic hiss of blank tape running through a player. Walter jumped at the sound of Emily's voice.

"Dear Walter, Do what this man tells you. He's treating me very nice. If you pay him, he will let me go. If you don't, his friends will kill me. Don't talk to anyone, and don't call the cops or you will never see me again. I love you."

His hands began to shake and a flood of nausea pushed up into his throat until he thought he was going to be sick. He was still listening to the terror in Emily's voice even though her words had gone silent. "Jesus, this can't be happening," he whispered to himself. Then he shouted, "This can't be happening . . ."

Thursday

ANDREW HOGAN HEARD HIS telephone ringing while he was still asleep. He was a kid in Brooklyn, hitching rides on the back of the old DeKalb Avenue trolley. For an instant, the telephone became the trolley car's bell. He sat upright in his bed and blinked at the phone as if it didn't belong on his night table. Then he lifted the receiver and managed a growl.

"Well, I'm certainly happy that I didn't take you up on your offer if this is the way you wake up," Helen Restivo told him.

"And I'm thrilled you refused my marriage proposal. I'd hate to be living with someone who begins each day with a smile." Hogan looked at his clock and saw that it was only a few minutes after five. "Jesus, it's *five o'clock!* I hope you've found Mrs. Childs, because otherwise there would be no reason for calling so early."

"No, but we have the kidnappers," Helen answered. "The two guys who lifted the lady from her bathtub. I think we should talk."

"Now? At five o'clock."

"I managed an appointment with the young Miss Childs. Her house, at nine. So I can't hang around for your bath and breakfast."

Andrew was already padding across to his bathroom. "How about Rosie's in half an hour?"

"Okay! Last one there pays for the bagels."

He stepped out of his doorway into the deserted West Side street. The pink light of the rising sun reflected in the top windows of the high-rise apartment buildings. But down in the caverns, it was still dark. He liked this time of day when the city was empty except for the occasional limo that carried the very important to their aircraft-carrier desks and the morning television personalities to their still lifeless sets. In his years as a policeman, the early morning hours were the only moments of peace. Crime, which was a nuisance during the day, seemed to flourish in the late night hours. It reached its crescendo around two in the morning, when the drunks staggered into their apartments and confronted their families, when the partygoers stepped out into streets mined with muggers, when the addicts awoke from euphoria and found themselves twisted in agony. From midnight to 3:00 A.M., the air wailed with sirens and crackled with gunfire. There weren't enough ambulances to answer all the cries or enough gurneys to carry the bodies.

But then the frantic pace of violence suddenly exhausted itself. A blissful quiet settled over the city. Crime seemed to fall into a deep sleep, resting up for the next night's celebration. It was in this sunrise interval that a policeman could close his eyes and steal a moment of rest.

Rosie's was an all-night delicatessen in the theater district that Ed Sullivan had once credited with the best bagel in New York. Its owner didn't have time to shut everything down and then start everything up again in the few fleeting hours between the departure of the stage hands and the arrival of the financial types, so he just kept open around the clock. Helen was already at a table when Andrew arrived and she held up her bagel to remind him to pay for it.

While Andrew used both hands to align his first cup of coffee with his mouth, Helen briefed him on the night's activities. The fingerprints in the shower had identified two minor hoods with thick rap sheets filled with misdemeanors and small felonies. One had been picked up losing his fee for the kidnapping at an all-night poker game. "He should thank us," Helen commented. "We got him out before he lost everything." He had told them where to find his partner, who was picked up as he got off a bus from Atlantic City.

Hogan shook his head. A defrocked lawyer. A couple of gutter gamblers. How in hell could these guys be involved in a hundred-million bank fraud? It didn't make any sense.

Like the lawyer, the kidnappers had been hired by a computer voice over the telephone that had offered them a chance to make ten thousand each. All they had been told was where the lady could be found and what they were supposed to do with her.

"They took her exactly the way we figured it," Helen went on. "They cased the place and decided to get her in the garage as soon as she stepped out of the car. But they were late getting there."

"Unbelievable," Hogan interrupted.

"It gets worse," Restivo said. "The lady was in the bathtub when they broke in and apparently she kicked the stuffing out of our boys before one

86

of them finally managed to stick her with the needle. Then they rolled her in the shower curtain and carried her out to the car.

"They were supposed to leave her in a blue van that was going to be parked in one of the far-off sections of the Paramus Mall. But when they got there, they found two blue vans in the section and they didn't know which one she was supposed to go to. They drove around for a while, waiting for someone to move one of the vans, and then they loaded her into the one that was left. Last they saw of her, she was stuffed down on the floor between the seats, still wrapped in the curtain."

"I don't suppose they noted the license plate."

"No, and they're not even sure whether it was black or blue. One thinks it was a Ford. The other is sure it was a Dodge Caravan."

Andrew scratched his head. "Do you think the people behind this are intentionally hiring idiots? Maybe making sure that they're jerks who would never get any ideas of their own? Either that, or they're amateurs themselves. It could be that whoever is running the show is picking his people off the post office wall. But what infuriates me is that it's working so well. We've nailed half of the people involved and still we're no closer to finding Mrs. Childs or the people who wanted her lifted."

"Not so," Helen said, smiling at the delicious secret she had been holding back. "Guess what the last entry on both of their rap sheets was?"

He looked suitably bewildered.

"Breaking and entering," Helen told him. "At a home less than a quarter of a mile from the Childs residence."

"What?" It was too much of a coincidence. There had to be a connection.

"And guess who rushed in to provide the two lads with defense counsel?"

Hogan smiled. "The Urban Shelter. Walter Childs' favorite charity."

"Bingo!" Helen told him. "That damn charity is the link between the messenger, the kidnappers, and the victim. And the person it ties in to all three is the cheating husband."

They sat for a moment staring at each other. Then Hogan said, "Why? He doesn't need to do this. He can have his trophy wife for the price of a divorce settlement. Expensive, but he can afford it. Why would he risk everything? Why would he associate himself with small-time crooks?"

"Maybe so he can show the directors just how much he loves the bank," Helen said, reminding Hogan of a motive that he had dabbled with himself. "Maybe he's found the sure path to the top."

Hogan allowed the possibility, but he didn't think any sane man would put everything in jeopardy just to get the edge in a race for the chairman's chair. "Unless," he allowed, "the lovely Angela was getting tired of waiting. Could she be having second thoughts?"

"No way! Remember, I read all her computer mail. This lady wants the gold ring."

"So then why does Walter Childs play games with his wife's safety?"

They fell into a morose silence. Then they began a meticulous, step-by-step review of the other possible suspects.

Angela came first. It was certainly possible that she had heard Walter talk about the disgraced lawyer who was involved in his charitable work and about a burglar who had been caught on his street. Small talk, to be sure. But if someone was thinking about accomplices in a kidnapping, it could be information that she would have noted carefully. And there was no doubt about her motive. She wanted to become Mrs. President of the Bank and wife of the world's most brilliant financial light. Suppose Walter was dragging his feet about throwing over the mother of his children. Might she have not decided that he needed a little assistance? The fact was that Angela had the most to gain if Emily should turn up dead.

"We're forgetting the most obvious motive," Andrew warned his friend. "There's a hell of a lot of money involved here. Let's, just for the minute, forget sexual favors and boardroom politics. Let's look at this as an uncomplicated kidnapping where someone is hoping to collect a record ransom."

"Our tennis star," Helen filled in. "He certainly has cased all the rich ladies in the neighborhood. So maybe he got tired of balling for dollars. He's counting on Emily Childs getting a big divorce settlement so that they can live happily ever after. And then Emily tells him that she'd rather spend the money herself, thank you!"

"Yeah," Hogan said. "For a while, he was the obvious choice. But I can still see his face when we told him that she had been kidnapped. His jaw damn near fell off. He certainly looked surprised to me." But then he added, "On the other hand, he probably gets a lot of acting practice pretending that he's madly in love."

Helen got up to refill their coffee cups. She was thinking out loud when she returned to the table. "What about the other banker, Childs's rival for the presidency?"

"Mitchell Price," he filled in.

"He was at the restaurant where Childs signaled that he'd pay the ransom," Helen reminded him. "And Walter seems to think that Mitchell would do anything for the top job."

That was true, Hogan admitted. Price, according to insiders, was slipping behind in the race. It might be that he would have absolutely no intention of harming Emily and no thought of ever collecting the ransom. He would simply count on his rival violating bank policy to save his wife, which would knock Walter out of the running. "What makes Price a reasonable suspect is the ransom note," Walter told her. "The kidnapper was positive that he would know instantly if Andrew called in the police. Price is one of the few people who would have that kind of access to top-level information."

"What he doesn't know is that Walter might prefer the top job to his wife," Helen interjected.

Andrew shook his head. "Who could figure a guy acting that way?"

He noticed that Helen quickly broke off eye contact, busying herself with her purse and briefcase. And then he realized what he had just said. Once, many years ago, he had put his career ahead of the woman he loved. She was sitting right next to him. He had broken off their affair because of the risk to his professional reputation. He could have told the department to go to hell. He could have found another line of work. But he had picked his career in preference to her. Wasn't that the root of Walter Childs's dilemma?

They parted company in the street, Andrew hailing a taxi that would take him crosstown to the bank and Helen headed toward the New Jersey hills and her meeting with Amanda Childs.

As she walked to her car, Helen thought about the one suspect that they hadn't discussed. Andrew Hogan was sick of his demeaning position at the bank, where he was clearly an employee who would never be admitted to the inner circle. He couldn't stomach being treated as an inferior. Nothing would give him greater satisfaction than to take one of these movers and shakers to the cleaners and fatten his pension at the directors' expense. Andrew would be the only one close to the affair who would have access to people like the two lowlifes she had just interviewed. And he spent his days studying all the loopholes in the banks security systems. Helen could imagine the joy that Andrew would have in orchestrating the perfect crime and then putting himself in a position to enjoy its intricacies.

She hoped to God she was wrong but, to her mind, Andrew had fallen quite a way from the dedicated public servant who had addressed her graduating class.

Hogan knew that something was wrong as soon as he reached his office. There was a security guard standing beside the open outer doorway. Inside, his secretary was sitting perfectly upright at her desk, her head twitching toward the open door to the inner office. "Mr. Childs," she whispered, identifying the subject of her pantomimed warning. "He had security let him in. He was here when I came and then he made me open your office."

Hogan smirked, and slowly shook his head. "Who can understand people who love power?" he said to the woman, causing her stunned expression to relax into a smile.

But Andrew stopped chuckling when he saw Walter Childs. The man was pacing in aimless circles, his eyes black against the white pallor of his face. He stopped moving when he realized that Hogan had entered the office, but stood dumbly as if Hogan were the last person he expected to find.

"Are you all right, Walter? What happened?"

Walter's response was to hold out a tape cassette that he had been carrying in his hand. Hogan reached out and took it.

"What is it?" he asked, turning toward his cassette player.

"It's a phone call I received last night. Emily's machine copied it while I was listening to it on her extension."

Hogan snapped on the player and listened impatiently to the hiss. Then the smug, self-assured voice resonated through the office. He felt weak as he listened to the ransom demands and the threats. When Emily Childs's voice came on, Andrew Hogan collapsed into his chair. "Jesus," was the only comment he could think of.

"What do we do now?" Walter said, his voice cracking from fear and fatigue.

"Sweet Jesus!"

Childs fell like a discarded rag into one the chairs beside the desk. He sat silently, staring at the detective as he waited for him to come up with an answer.

"This doesn't make any sense. Not one bit of sense. We're dealing with a pro for a hundred million and all of a sudden some jerk is willing to settle for fifty thousand. It just doesn't fit . . ."

"That was Emily's voice," Walter whispered. And then he nearly screamed, "He has Emily."

"I know. I know. The man is genuine." Hogan lowered his face into his palms. "Give me a minute. Let me think," he mumbled.

He had thought he knew the answer the instant he heard the voice. The caller was another one of the absurd thugs. The disgraced lawyer. The two racetrack regulars. One had delivered the note. The other two had done the kidnapping. This had to be the person hired to mind Mrs. Childs; the owner of the van where she had been deposited, unconscious and wrapped in a shower curtain. But it couldn't be. The others had been harmless punks, obviously determined *not* to hurt their victim. This guy was making dangerous threats.

It had to be an outsider. Someone the mastermind behind the scheme had never figured on. Someone who had found out about the kidnapping and was trying to pick up some pocket money for himself, unaware that he was about to screw up a $100 million payoff.

"My first instinct is to ignore the man. His threats to harm Emily are probably empty."

"Harm her?" Walter interrupted. He pointed at the cassette player. "He's talking about selling her into white slavery."

Hogan nodded impatiently. "I heard him. It's a ridiculous threat. And just dealing with him could prove dangerous. If the fool got himself killed, Emily might be left tied up in a closet or someplace where we would never find her."

"Jesus," Walter interjected with complete despair.

Then Hogan reversed himself. "But there are also good reasons for treating him seriously. He may be the best link we're going to get to Emily's whereabouts. If he were caught, he might not know the other people involved. He probably wouldn't be able to identify the computer-generated voice. But he most certainly would know where your wife could be found. Hell, he got her to record the message to you."

Walter was pleading. "Andrew, I don't know what to do . . ."

"I think we have to follow up with this guy," Hogan concluded.

"What about the other ransom?" Walter still seemed bewildered.

"We follow up on both of them. Treat each one of them as if it were the only deal you've been offered."

"We pay both of them?"

Andrew smiled. "No, we don't pay either of them. What we do is make each one of them *think* he's getting paid. Then we follow the money. If I'm right, both trails should lead to the same place."

Walter came out of his trance. "*If* you're right. That's not good enough. It could get her killed. We have to pay the money they're demanding."

Andrew stepped around Walter and put a hand on his shoulder. "We can't do that, Walter. Remember what we agreed right at the start. If you're thinking of transferring a hundred million dollars, then I'll have to take everything I know to Hollcroft. I'm trying to catch these people. I'm trying to save your wife. But I'm not cutting a deal with kidnappers. And neither are you."

Emily stood behind the bed, holding the headboard crossbar in both hands, rocking it quietly back and forth. She had started late at night, when the squeaking of floorboards and the banging of doors over head had subsided and the only sound was the nighttime settling of the house. At first she had used all her strength, trying to break the joint between the headboard and the corner post. But when she pushed hard, the bed had moved, its legs scratching across the cement floor like fingernails digging into a blackboard. To prevent the noise, she had to hold the bed steady with one hand while she forced the bar with the other. The process had quickly become exhausting.

Instead, she had settled for a rocking motion that wiggled the tapered ends of the bar and rungs in their sockets. It had been early morning when she saw the first signs that she might be getting somewhere. The varnish at the joints had cracked and chipped away.

Now, there was brown sawdust forming at the joints. The motion was causing the finials and sockets to grind away. Eventually, the structure would become wobbly, giving her the opportunity to push out on the corner posts and pull the bar free. But she couldn't go on. Once she freed the bar, she doubted whether she would be able to force it back to its original position. She didn't want any sign of her work to be visible when Rita brought down her breakfast or, God help her, when Mike came down.

She was suddenly aware of movement over her head. One of them had gotten up and was shuffling about. The next thing she heard was the sound of water moving in the pipes that rose somewhere inside the surrounding wall. A refrigerator door slammed. She moved around the corner post, stretching her arm over the top until she was able to slide back onto her bed. She sighed with relief that she would be able to take a few moments of rest. But when she looked behind her, she was shocked to see the evidence of her work. There were traces of sawdust running down each of the verticals, with tiny yellow flakes dotting the pillow. She pulled herself up to her knees and looked down at the floor under the headboard. There was a thin covering of sawdust, like a ghosting of snow over a highway. They'd *have* to see it. There was no way that they could miss it.

She slid across the bed, raising her arm over the corner post until the handcuff chain was behind the bed. Then she slipped out and rushed behind the headboard. But only one hand could reach the floor. She could brush at the dust, but she couldn't clamp it between her palms. There was no way that she could pick it up.

Pots banged together in the kitchen over her head. The woman's voice called through the house, "I'm taking her breakfast down to her." The man answered from farther off in the distance, "I'll bring it down." And then the woman's voice. "I'm already here. I'll take care of it."

Emily was trying to scatter the dust with her free hand. But that only made things worse. She was etching designs where the bare floor showed through the dust. The stain of the yellow powder was even more obvious. She licked her fingers and the palm of her hand and began patting the residue. It stuck to her skin and she was able to pick it up and brush it off against the fabric inside the neck of her nightgown. When she licked her hands again, the sawdust coated her tongue, nearly choking her as she tried to summon up more saliva. She kept patting, picking up bits of the stain and lifting them inside her gown. It was working. The dust was less and less noticeable.

The bolt snapped back and the door swung open. Emily stood for an instant, frozen in fright. Then she moved quickly, pulling the chain to its limit and stretching her arm over the top of the post. She had only one knee on the bed when she heard the footsteps on the stairs. There wasn't enough time for her to get back under the blanket. She swung her legs around so that she was sitting on the edge of the bed, her feet dangling down to the floor. She tried to be natural and relaxed, like someone waiting patiently for a meal to be delivered. But when she dropped her arm, the shackle fell outside the corner post. Her hand was pointing around toward the back of the bed, obviously not in the position where she had been left. She looked toward the stairs and saw Rita's face appearing just under the ceiling line. It was too late. She couldn't get her arm back to where it had been shackled.

"Your breakfast," the woman said cheerily, "and a newspaper." She walked past the bed and over to the table, never looking directly at Emily. "It's yesterday's paper, but I don't suppose a hell of lot has happened since yesterday." She set a plate of dry scrambled eggs on the table and put a cup of coffee beside it.

Emily stood up quickly. "Can you take this damn thing off? I have to get into the bathroom." She held her arm straight out, so that her hand didn't seem to be caught up in the chain. The woman fumbled in her pocket as she crossed to the bed. "Sure. I'm sorry. This must be a bitch for ya." She unlocked the cuff and let it fall idly. It jangled down behind the bed, just as if it had fallen between the vertical rungs of the headboard. The woman never spared it a glance.

"Remember." It was Rita's voice following her into the bathroom. "We're both at the top of the stairs."

"I know," Emily answered. "I appreciate your leaving the handcuffs off."

She ran the water in the sink while she listened carefully for the footsteps on the stairs. The door swung shut, followed instantly by the crack of the bolt. Footsteps moved away from the door and into the room overhead. Emily climbed up on top of the toilet and was able to press one of the ceiling tiles out of its frame. But the opening was too far overhead for her to see into. She looked at the sink, bolted through the wallboard. It seemed sturdy, but would it hold her weight when she stepped on its edge? Directly in front of her was the water tank for the toilet, like the sink, bolted through the masonry. It was built to hold the weight of a couple of gallons of water, so it was probably her best bet. She stood on the toilet seat. When she climbed onto the top of the tank, her head and shoulders reached through the opening into the space above the drop ceiling.

Once again, she was looking down the channel between the rafters. But now she could see daylight at the far end. The channel opened into the ceiling of another room. And the fact that she saw daylight meant that the other room had a window or a door.

There were footsteps in the room above. The boards directly over her head squeaked as they flexed. She was right beneath them and she could hear them so clearly that she knew they would hear any sound that she made when she she tried her escape. And, if they became suspicious, they would have plenty of time to find her. This would be no quick dash to freedom. What Emily was looking at was a slow, exhausting process of wiggling through a narrow channel, making sure to keep her weight on the metal framework and off the fragile tiles. Even though the light seemed to be only thirty feet away, she had to figure at least fifteen minutes to make the passage. She would have to wait until they had locked her up for the night and gone up to their bedroom. She eased the tile back into position and stepped down carefully.

The eggs were dry and the coffee muddy, but Emily gobbled it down quickly. She wanted to be sitting in the bed in a nonthreatening pose when the woman came down for the dishes so that there would be no reason for her to refasten the handcuffs. She took the newspaper and pulled the blanket up to her waist.

Angela Hilliard sat in the first-class lounge, her laptop computer open on the desk and her morning coffee raised in her hands. She was connected over a telephone line to the bank's local area network and was going through her mailbox. In a moment, she would download the files she needed for her business trip down to Miami.

Generally, at least one day a week began like this. The limo would pull up at her front door and wait patiently while she packed a few things into an overnight bag. Then she would be whisked over the bridge to La Guardia Airport, sometimes to the marine terminal if she were riding on one of InterBank's three executive jets, sometimes to an airline's first-class lounge if she were flying commercial. Always, she would connect her laptop to a telephone line and then log into the bank's internal information network. She would check her mail for anything that needed an immediate answer and respond in her terse, pull-no-punches style. Then she would download the complete data file on the bank client she was visiting, so she could review all the information that might affect her meeting.

She valued the trips on the company planes because she often found herself riding with important senior executives whom she never failed to impress. But she preferred the commercial flights where she could work without being interrupted by polite chitchat. She could simply ignore the person seated next to her, or if her fellow traveler kept trying to be friendly, call the attendant and asked to be moved. Usually there was no seat available, but even the most persistent talker would take the hint and leave her alone with her computer.

This time, she would have preferred the company plane. The mousy little guy with the wire-framed glasses had followed her right into the lounge. Apparently, he was going to stay with her all the way to Miami.

He couldn't have come aboard the executive jet and she certainly would have been able to spot anyone who tried to tag on to her when she left the private hangar in Miami. Since she was flying commercial, it was up to her to lose him.

He had appeared almost miraculously the instant that Walter had warned her that she was being watched. Probably he had been following her earlier and she hadn't noticed him until she was alerted to look for him. But now he was easy to spot in the reflection of store windows whenever she stopped and racing to the taxi that had pulled in behind the one she had taken.

This morning, he had been sitting in an illegally parked car, a few hundred feet from the door. The car had pulled out behind the limousine and managed to remain behind her on the Triborough Bridge and all the way to the airport. At times it had been so close that she could recognize that her man was riding in the passenger seat with another man driving. He jumped out of the car at the terminal and followed her all the way to her airline's departure area. Angela thought she had lost him when she ducked into the first-class lounge. But within a few minutes he entered the lounge, conspicuously without luggage, and brandishing a first-class boarding envelope.

So it had worked. By ordering her ticket through a different Internet service provider, she had disguised her destination. Andrew Hogan hadn't found her travel plan in the InterBank computer and whoever had searched her apartment hadn't found anything in her usual Internet files. They hadn't anticipated her trip. The man had obviously called his office when he found himself entering the airport and had been instructed to stay with her no matter where she went.

Well, let him try to keep up with her. Angela wouldn't be taking him where she was going.

Amanda had been waiting for Helen to arrive, anxious to do anything she could to help her mother, but it didn't seem as if she could do much. She had learned less about her parents during her lifetime than Helen's investigators had been able to piece together in just a few days.

She described her parents' relationship as happy—at least as happy as any relationship involving her father could be. Her mother was totally loyal to her husband and children. Amanda had no inkling of Emily's involvement with her tennis coach. Her father was a slave to his own straight-laced ambition. She couldn't even imagine that he might be leading a double life with another woman. Helen listened to all this information and made notes as if Amanda were providing priceless gems. She never hinted that she had contradictory information from more reliable sources.

They were all aware that, because of her father's position, she could become a target for kidnappers or terrorists. Walter had sat her and Alex down when they were still in high school. He had scared the daylights out of her, telling her that kidnapping the families of important business executives was a common occurrence overseas and there was nothing to keep it from happening here in the United States. He had gone into great detail on the global importance of his work, intimating that he ranked only slightly behind the president of the United States as a target for radical terrorists. His message was that they had to be on their guard at every minute.

"Then you have no doubt that your mother's kidnapping is an attack on your father's bank?" Helen asked.

"What else could it be?" Amanda answered. "Why else would anyone hurt my mother?

Helen probed carefully into the young woman's opinion of her father. Her anger was obvious. Was there something wrong in his background?

"The bastards may have made a mistake in picking on my father," Amanda said. "He may be the one man on earth who would sacrifice his own wife to his crazy devotion to duty. I always figured that if anyone kidnapped me, I was as good as dead. I didn't have a prayer if he had to choose between me and his fucking bank."

Helen tried to defend Walter Childs, pointing out that he was in a position of trust. His responsibilities at the bank had implications for entire nations, even regions of the globe. "Yeah?" Amanda challenged. "Well, he has no weighty responsibilities when it comes to how I choose to live my life. It's just that he thinks everyone should live by his standards."

Helen managed to keep a straight face.

"Times have changed since he was starting out," Amanda continued. "And he won't let anyone move with the times. Wayne and I have a . . . a relationship. But it doesn't meet his moral standards, so I'm in the dog-house and Wayne is a nonperson. My father won't even use his name. Like it was a curse or something."

"But Wayne isn't his family," Helen began.

Amanda cut her off. "But I am. And he's thrown me over rather than compromise. That's why I think he could let my mother die. I can hear the pompous bastard now. 'Regrettable, but I have no choice. My duties at the bank . . .' "

"You can't believe that," Helen argued.

The daughter shook her head. "I suppose not. Last night he was trying to figure out how he could save her. I guess she's more important to him than I am."

Helen suggested a way that Amanda might help. She told her how everyone involved in the kidnapping seemed to have links with the Urban Shelter. Amanda was surprised, indicating that her father was involved only to the extent of lending his name. "I'll bet he couldn't find the office," she said. "Mom is the one who really put time into it."

Helen thought that Emily might have kept records of her work in the household files or in the family computer. She asked Amanda to sift through the information, hoping to get names of people who might also be involved in her mother's work. She didn't mention that what she was really after would be references to Bill Leary, or to her father, or even to Andrew Hogan.

Walter Childs was shocked when Andrew Hogan outlined his plan.

"You know you're gambling with Emily's life," he charged. "Even if this works—even if you catch them—there's no reason to think that Emily will be released."

"It's a gamble no matter how we play it," Hogan countered. "Even after we meet all their demands, there's no guarantee that they'll let her go."

"But if we give them what they want . . ."

"Walter, there's just no way that I can let you send a hundred million dollars to a private account in the Caymans. If you want, we can go to Mr. Hollcroft and explain the bind that you're in. But we both know that the only thing the directors can do is follow policy to the letter. I think trapping these people is the only chance that Emily has. That's what you asked me for—a chance."

Walter nodded silently. Andrew had already gone way out on a limb by trying to investigate without involving the police. He couldn't be expected to make himself a partner in a $100 million loss.

Hogan had explained that there were two ways of approaching the kidnappers and he was suggesting that they try both. Neither one looked terribly promising, but taken together, the odds were a bit more favorable.

The first was following up on the latest demand that had included Emily's recorded plea. Hogan was convinced that caller had to be connected with the people holding Emily prisoner. Like the other members of the conspiracy, this guy was a rank amateur, Hogan felt, acting without the knowledge of the masterminds who had engineered the whole plan. It was pretty obvious that he was someone local because he used a local place for the payoff. Greenwood Lake wasn't known anywhere, except in the small communities on the New York–New Jersey boarder. Southshore Drive was even more obscure and Randy's wasn't one of its more popular spots. The caller had to be familiar with the area.

"This guy will probably come for the money himself," Hogan had explained. "And if he's like the kidnappers, he won't be very sophisticated about his methods. I think if we get him, we'll have Emily back within an hour."

Walter had swallowed hard. He could raise the $50,000 from his own brokerage accounts, and it seemed safer to pay the man and hope he would keep his part of the bargain. But Andrew had argued that the voice on the recorder probably didn't have the authority to set Emily free. They would end up paying for nothing. "Look, Walter," he had finally said in exasperation, "if it makes you feel better, put fifty thousand in the briefcase. But an empty briefcase will do you just as much good, because either way, we'll only find Emily if we capture this guy and make him take us to her."

Hogan's second proposal was even more frightening. He wanted to transfer a minimum amount to the Folonari branch in the Caymans, probably $10,000, just enough to create an account that could be called for. "We'll have a team of people down there. One inside the bank to watch for anyone who accesses the account and others outside to follow whoever it is. Either the pickup guy is in on the kidnapping or he'll have to make contact with whoever sent him."

"They'll transfer the money electronically," Walter had predicted.

"I don't think so," Hogan had fired back. "I've had my best people try this. No matter how they transfer it, they leave a trail." He had explained several of the war games his people had played to test the InterBank safeguards. "At some point, all the tests concluded, they had to convert the funds into something nontraceable. Cash, usually in a foreign currency, or bearer bonds."

The risks, Walter continued to argue, were enormous. But the list of alternatives was painfully short. He could simply refuse to transfer the funds, which was what would happen if Hogan took his information to Jack Hollcroft. In that case, if he believed the ransom note, Emily would vanish. Or, he could go ahead with his complex transfers of small amounts to a third account and then make the $100 million payoff as the kidnapper had ordered. But Hogan would spot it the moment it was moved to Folonari. He would have it tagged immediately as a fraud, probably even before the Cayman courier could pick it up. So, once again, the ransom would go unpaid. Gradually, he began to see that Hogan's plan wasn't much riskier than any of the alternatives open to him. Use the account to draw in someone connected with the kidnapping and pounce on that person before he could send up a warning. It was probably as safe for Emily, and it was clearly less destructive to his career at InterBank than giving away $100 million of their money.

"I don't want anything to happen to her," he told Andrew, once he had finally given in to the security director's plan. He noticed Hogan's eyebrows lift in surprise. "I'm glad to hear that," he said getting up from his chair and walking to the office door.

Walter was stunned by the remark. The bastard thinks I don't care, he realized, and he was about to call Hogan back. But there was no point to it. Hogan had already told him that he was a prime suspect. And why should anyone believe that Walter would care about Emily when he was in bed with another woman the day after his wife was taken away. One more day, he thought. One more day and then all this will be over.

He got up and closed the inside office door, an unspoken message to his secretary that he didn't want to be disturbed. Then he took his worksheets out of his briefcase and spread them across his desk, next to his computer terminal. He began sweeping up $100 million from small balances and investments that InterBank had all over the world.

Andrew Hogan stepped through the front door of Randy's, a dilapidated, wood-frame roadhouse pinched between Southshore Drive and Greenwood Lake. In the height of summer, it would be filled with high school and college students, some from family cottages along the shoreline, others groupies who were sharing a rental shack, and still other transient weekenders who would be sleeping in the backs of cars or out on the beach. But now, in the early spring, it was nearly deserted. In the restaurant area, the chairs were stacked on top of the tables. The outdoor tables were piled on the dance floor. At the huge island bar only one side was lighted, showing the bartender and two of the locals, a big guy in a baseball hat and hockey jersey and a small, slight character who seemed half-asleep.

Hogan ordered a draft beer, which caused the locals to raise their heads and the bartender to move away from his newspaper. He tossed down a five-dollar bill and walked back toward the men's room, his eyes searching into every corner as he moved. There was the front entrance to the parking lot, a door into the kitchen and office, and several double doors along the back wall that led out to the porch. The only other doors were those into the rest rooms.

In the cavernous men's room, there was a single window high on the back wall. Andrew made a mental note to check the outside. Presumably, there would be a matching window from the ladies' room. He wandered past the double doors and glanced out at the deserted wooden porch. Below the porch was a dock with slips for a dozen small boats. That was something he hadn't figured on. Whoever was planning on picking up the money might be arriving and leaving by boat.

"Nice view," he announced when he returned to his waiting draft. The bartender, who had had gone back to his newspaper, managed a nod.

Andrew wiped the froth from his lip. "You get much boat traffic?"

"Some. In the summer. Not much now," the bartender answered.

"Not much of anything now," the smaller of the two regulars cackled. The bigger one nodded in agreement.

Outside, Hogan circled past the men's room window and confirmed that the women's rest room was laid out in the same way. He went to the porch, pretending to be admiring the view, and noted that the double doors were locked. Even if they were open, one of Helen's people stationed on the porch could cover both the exits and the dock. Another, in the parking lot, would be able to cover the front door. So, he wondered, why had the kidnapper picked this spot for the ransom drop? It was as unlikely a place as he could imagine. At this time of year, there probably wouldn't be more than half a dozen cars in the lot. The car Walter Childs was supposed to leave with the briefcase visible would be easy to keep under surveillance. There was only one exit out onto Southshore Drive, which meant that there would be no problem in picking up a departing car and following it. There was certainly no way that someone could disappear inside the building.

The one problem that Andrew could see was the dock on the lake. If someone left by boat, the only way he could be followed was by another boat or a helicopter. Both would be immediately obvious. So if the man who made the pickup came in a boat, they would have to take him as soon as he stepped out onto the porch. Then he would have to be persuaded to lead them to Emily Childs, which probably wouldn't take more than a few minutes. The lake was still icy cold, and a few minutes was about as long as someone could stay in it submerged up to the chin. If they got him, they'd have Emily.

It was all too easy. One man in the woods on the lake side of the building. Another in the woods across from the parking lot exit. And then two cars on Southshore Drive, one headed in each direction. Maybe one more man in the bar, just for good measure. Someone dressed like one of the regulars.

Andrew took one last look around. The guy, he thought, was going to step into his own trap. He had to be dumber than the courier who had brought the ransom note, or the two clowns who had handled the kidnapping. "Amateurs," he whispered as he started his car and pulled out of the lot.

Back at the bar, the bigger of the two regulars stood slowly and pushed a ten-dollar tip to the bartender. "See ya, Gerry!"

"Yeah, sure, Mike," Gerry answered without looking up from the sports page.

A cop, Mike thought. He could smell a cop as soon as one entered the room. So, Walter Childs had decided to play games. Well, he had a few games of his own.

Andrew drove back down to the city and went straight to Helen's office where they put their heads together over a pencil sketch of the roadhouse layout. Helen agreed immediately that the place would be simple to cover and she nodded while Hogan indicated where her men should be posted. "The guy is crazy," Helen said, agreeing with Andrew's conclusion that there was no way the kidnapper could escape after he had taken the briefcase from the car. "He's just one more amateur."

She folded the sketch and got two bottles of mineral water from the refrigerator while she explained the arrangements that had been made in the Cayman Islands. "You can buy a lot for a little down there. Folonari's cashier only cost us five hundred bucks."

"What's he going to do for us?" Andrew asked.

"He'll tip us off when someone comes to pick up that account. We told him to handle it just as he always does. All he has to do is nod to our guy in the lobby. He'll follow the courier outside. That will give us two men in the street and one in a parked car."

"Suppose the courier tries to phone someone from inside the bank?"

"If he tries to use a cell phone, the cashier will stop him with some bull about fouling up the bank wireless system and offer him the desk phone. If he uses it, or any other internal phone, we'll have the number that he calls before he leaves the building."

Andrew leaned back in his chair, his hands joined behind his head.

"Sounds like you've covered all the angles."

"All the ones that we know about," Helen said. "But there's always the angle that we haven't though of. Like maybe we have this thing totally wrong. Maybe the most obvious suspect is one of the people in your department who spends all his time trying to figure out how to rob the bank. Maybe one of your spooks is the kidnapper."

"Or maybe it's me," Andrew offered. He waited a second enjoying the poor job she was doing of feigning shock.

"Andrew, for God's sake," she protested.

He laughed. "What pisses me off is that you didn't assign your best man to me. What is it? Do you think I'm slipping? That beauty school queen you have following me couldn't be more obvious."

Helen tried to control her expression, but her face cracked and she exploded into laughter. "What am I supposed to do? You know all my best people. Half of them came with your recommendation."

Hogan agreed. Then he asked, "So what do you think? Am I guilty?"

"I think you wish to hell this was your play. I think nothing would give you greater joy than to take down all those stuffed shirts at InterBank."

"And if I was behind it, would you turn me in?"

"Absolutely," Helen answered. "Unless you let me in on the action. I wouldn't mind taking them down a peg or two myself."

"What's wrong with us?" Andrew asked.

"I think maybe we both feel that we've missed out on a lot of the fun."

"Why? We both wanted to be cops. We're both doing exactly what we wanted to do."

Helen agreed. "When I was younger, I wanted to fix the world. Now, I just want to live in it. Does that make any sense?"

"I don't remember that I ever wanted to fix the world."

She laughed and took a long drink from the bottled water.

"What's so funny?" Hogan demanded. "You think I was idealistic?"

She nodded. "Oh, yeah. Somewhere, I still have the draft of the speech you gave at my graduation. Public service was the highest calling and there was no greater service than assuring the public safety."

"Did I really say that?

"You certainly did. But lots of people *say* it. You *believed* it."

He paused, remembering his own words. "What an ass I must have been."

"No, I thought it was the most noble ambition. Until you put it ahead of me."

He patted the back of her damaged hand. "I was an ass."

The phone rang with a call for Helen. She had it patched into the conference room and was about to speak when she was overwhelmed by a torrent of words from the caller. As she listened, she mouthed "Amanda Childs" to Andrew.

"Amanda, are you sure?" Helen asked at her first opportunity. She listened patiently, rolling her eyes in Andrew's direction. "I don't think you should jump to conclusions. You can't be sure what any of this means." More talk came from the other end of the line. "Amanda, why don't you leave this up to me. I'm sure I can get answers much more quickly than you can. And you can keep going through your mother's records. That way, we won't be duplicating our efforts." She nodded several times at the voice on the other end and then concluded with, "Okay, I'll get back to you tonight."

"What's happening?" Hogan asked as soon as Helen was able to disconnect from the telephone.

"Amanda found some of her mother's correspondence. She says that Bill Leary, her mother's tennis coach, was blackmailing her mother. She claims her mother told Leary she was done paying only a month ago."

"Now that's a new wrinkle. But it's possible. No one knew better than Leary that Emily was cheating on her husband. He would have assumed that she would have paid quite a bit to keep her husband from finding out."

Helen agreed, adding, "What he wouldn't have realized is that Emily already had the goods on her husband. She didn't have to worry about blackmail."

"She did if she had plans of taking all of the adulterous husband's money." Andrew reminded her. "Innocent wives get more than the ones who are cheating themselves. What do you think? Do you believe her?"

Helen shrugged. "I haven't seen the correspondence. But Amanda certainly believes it. She was on her way to confront the great sportsman. I think I convinced her that wasn't a very good idea."

Angela Hilliard was in Boca Raton, sitting in a circle of men that surrounded the huge desk of one of her more important clients. He was a Cuban who had fled Castro more than forty years ago, taking $30 million out of the country. InterBank had helped him turn the loot into a company that manufactured communications equipment.

Most of the discussion had been between Angela and the gray-haired patriarch. The other men, all younger and a generation removed from their homeland, had sat in respectful silence, speaking only when spoken to.

Angela tapped the results of the meeting into her computer, which was connected to a high-speed data port at the back of her host's telephone. Instantly, a new and larger line of credit was established in InterBank's central files, along with authorization for her client to issue offshore letters of credit against the line. Then she scheduled a visit by the bank's economists to provide a briefing on economic changes occurring in Central America. Finally, she booked Broadway theater tickets for her client's upcoming visit to New York. By the time she disconnected, there were smiles all around the room.

She took her time packing her things, allowing each of the younger men to find a reason to withdraw from the meeting. When she was alone with the president, Angela got down to the most important part of her agenda.

"Roberto, could I possibly enlist your help on a personal matter?" He spread his hands in a gesture of openness. She had only to ask. "One of my associates," she went on, "has a rather substantial loan opportunity with a company in the Caymans. I'm afraid that he may be getting himself into an embarrassing position."

The suntanned face broke into a wide smile. "And you want me to investigate?"

"No, actually I'd like to look into it myself. But I don't want it to appear that anyone at the bank is concerned about this deal. I've allowed myself a few days and I was hoping that you might know an inconspicuous way for me to get into Grand Cayman."

Roberto's eyes narrowed suspiciously, but they danced with the laughter that was already showing in his smile. "Bank business?" he asked, and then with a lecturing wave of his finger, "Or monkey business?"

She joined his laughter. "Strictly bank business, I'm sorry to say."

He was immediately serious. "There's a charter flight company that we use . . ."

"Oh, no! That would be expensive."

He waved away the suggestion that anything could be too expensive. "My car will take you over to the executive airport. The plane will be waiting for you." Then he added cautiously, "Do you need documents . . . a passport . . . ?"

"No, nothing like that. It's just that if I'm correct, someone could be watching the airport."

"Where will you stay?" he asked as he picked up his phone to make the arrangements. Her embarrassed look told him that she was hoping for help in that area, as well. "So," he announced decisively, "you will be staying at the West Beach town houses. We keep an apartment there."

Angela pretended to be overwhelmed. But she had been counting on the private plane and the anonymous rooms at the town houses. She knew they existed. Long before the meeting, she had found the expenses for both of them in her client's books.

When she pulled out of the office complex in the dark-windowed limousine, she caught a glimpse of the man in the wire-rimmed glasses who had followed her to the airport and into the first-class compartment. He was sitting in a sweltering taxi, fanning himself with a newspaper as he waited for a cab to carry her out through the gate. Angela smiled at his inevitable confusion when the building shut down for the night with her apparently still inside.

As Roberto had promised, the twin-engine turboprop was starting its engines when the limo pulled alongside. Five minutes later, she was climbing out over the coastline.

Mike hovered over Emily, his ivory smile only inches from her face. "Your husband must figure he can do a lot better than you," he tormented. "Because he went to the police. I set a little trap for him at a place where I couldn't miss him. And guess what? He had the place crawlin' with cops."

She tried not to look into his eyes, nor to notice the scissors that he held close to her face. She settled for his unshaven chin, and for the lips that he curled into a snarl at the end of every sentence. The guy was madly in love with himself. She knew that the only thing saving her was that he felt he had played her husband for a fool and was milking his moment of triumph.

She had spent the day working to free the handcuffs from the headboard, frustrated that it was taking her so long. She knew that she could shatter the wooden framework if she could just slide the bed close to the stairs and then bang it against the wall. Be she had to work secretly, so she had been limited to rocking the crossbar back and forth, waiting for the joints to wear out. It was exhausting work. As the day went on, her work periods became shorter as her need for rest grew greater.

She had just cleaned up the film of yellow sawdust and had been stretching her shoulders in the bed when she had heard the bolt snap open. Rita, she had thought, until she heard the footsteps. It was Mike and he was coming down quickly. Emily had been thankful that he hadn't caught her working behind the bed. But when she had seen the sick smile, and recognized the scissors in his hand, she knew that there was little reason for thanks.

"I told him what was going to happen if he tried anything funny. I told him I was going to sell you into a drug dealer's whorehouse. And you know what? He didn't care. Am I right, Emily? Would he rather have you turnin' tricks for an army of wetbacks than part with a little of his money?"

She had been lulled by his calm, pleasant voice, so she was shocked when he was suddenly screaming into her face. "Am I right? Answer me, bitch? Does he care more for his money than he does for your ass?"

"No," she said weakly. She couldn't hide her fright with the scissors now pressed to her throat.

His temper seemed to settle. "Then you figure he'll pay me?" he asked.

"Yes, yes," she promised him. "He'll pay you. He'll do whatever you say."

Mike seemed satisfied with the answer. He nodded thoughtfully, then stood and walked away from the bed. But after a few steps, he turned back toward her. "You know what? I don't think he's takin' me serious. I'll bet the bastard figures that he's dealin' with some low-life punk who's just blowin' air."

Emily was confused. She didn't know where he was leading.

"So I have to figure out some way to get it across to him. I have to convince him that I can get pretty nasty when people cross me. What I need you to do is help me send him somethin' that will prove I really mean business. Will you help me do that, Emily?"

She could only stare at him. She was too frightened to speak, her tongue too dry to make a sound.

Mike snipped the scissors in midair. "How about lendin' me one of your ears? Or maybe your nose. When it falls out of the envelope and lands in his lap, I'll bet he starts takin' me seriously."

Emily shook her head violently. Her eyes were nearly insane.

He snipped the scissors a few more times. "No? Well, what else? Maybe a finger. Or a coupla toes?"

"Please," Emily managed in a cracking voice. "Don't hurt me?"

"I know," he said. "Somethin' he'll certainly recognize." He stepped quickly back to the bed, lifted one of the buttons from the nightgown, and cut it off. He reached for the second button. Her scream was piercing.

Mike's smile spread wide on one side of his face. "Hey, wouldn't it be great if he could hear you screamin' while I'm cuttin' you up. Then he'd really have to pay attention, wouldn't he."

"Oh, God, please don't hurt me."

Mike stood up and made a show out of closing the scissors. "Tell you what. We'll let your bastard of a husband play his little game tonight. Then, tomorrow, we'll make a new tape for him. Somethin' he can listen to while he's examinin' pieces of you."

He sauntered happily toward the stairs. "I'll be back," he promised her.

"Oh, Jesus," Emily said out loud. She struggled to fight back her terror and get control of her own breathing. She could no longer calculate her level of risk. There was no hope that Walter would save her. He would be struggling to meet the original ransom demand. Mike was right. How could Walter take the obscene man and his sick threats seriously? Unless he found part of her in an envelope? Somehow, she had to get out of there tonight, before he returned.

Emily worked herself up to a kneeling position and then lifted her arms over her head so that the two shackles cleared the bedpost. She was facing the headboard, with both hands on the crossbar that secured the other end of her chains. She began rocking it back and forth, adding the weight of her body to the rhythm. The joints creaked but still held together, keeping her chained. But she had to keep trying. Her life was going to depend on it.

Mike was leaning against the compact sedan he had borrowed from the long-term parking lot at Newark International Airport, when Rita came down the front steps. He whistled softly. If she had come out of any other doorway, he probably wouldn't have recognized her. Instead of her severe black hair, she had a red pageboy brushing her shoulders. She was wearing a black dress with a low top and a high hem, dark seamed stockings, and spiked heels that nearly punched holes in the concrete. Her only jewelry was a string of pearls that showed through the embroidered sweater she had hung from her shoulders. She was either an executive wife on her way to a company affair, or a high-priced hooker out trolling for a john. To Mike, she was an irresistible turn-on.

"You know exactly what you have to do," Mike reminded her while she fussed with her seat belt.

"Mike, I was doing this sort of thing before you broke your first leg."

"Don't be such a smart-ass. There's a lot riding on how we play this."

"So you've told me, but I don't like it," she complained. "It's just too damn risky."

"You'll like having an extra fifty grand to spend, won't you?"

Rita shook her head. "You can't spend it in prison, Mike. And if we both get caught, who's going to con the judge into keeping you out of jail?"

Walter drove his car into the parking lot, passed slowly by Randy's front door, and turned into a space at the far end. He set the leather briefcase on the passenger seat, got out, and closed the door gently behind him. When he looked back, he realized that the briefcase couldn't be seen below the window line. So he opened the passenger door and stood the case on its end, resting against the seat back. He checked again to make sure that the door was unlocked and walked across the lot and into the dimly lighted bar.

There were two men seated uncomfortably on bar stools, shoulder to shoulder but seemingly ignoring each other. A few feet away, a woman with dead eyes leaned over a dark mixed drink, in whispered conversation with a red-eyed man who had his hand on her knee. No one paid the slightest attention to him.

"Anyone working?" Walter asked, referring to the lack of a bartender. The two men swiveled their heads toward him and looked curiously at his tie and jacket. "Gerry went to the head. He'll be right back," one of them informed him.

As he waited, the headlights of a pickup truck swung into the parking lot. Seconds later, two young men in T-shirts walked in and sat at the darkened side of the bar. Walter tried for eye contact, but they seemed completely uninterested in him. Then Gerry returned, fixed a scotch for Walter, and drafts for the two newcomers.

The woman downed her drink and pushed the empty glass toward the taps. Gerry reached for a lower shelf blended whiskey and fired ginger ale into the glass with it. Not a word or even a glance was exchanged.

"Slow night?" Walter asked.

Gerry shrugged. "It'll pick up."

Walter wondered if any of his fellow patrons was one of the investigators that Hogan had promised would be on the scene.

More headlights swung past the front windows and Walter caught a glimpse of a small sedan parking across from the pickup truck. A minute later, an attractive woman with red hair came through the door, posed long enough to get everyone's attention, and then took a stool on the dark side next to the recently arrived pair. Gerry drifted over, mumbled a greeting, and took her order for a gin martini.

As she waited, the woman's glance drifted to Walter. Her eyes smiled, telling him that he was her kind of man. She seemed to be laughing to herself as she sipped her drink.

Could she be the one? Walter wondered. Why not a woman? It would be logical as hell if they went back to his car and drove away. She wouldn't have to take the briefcase until she was certain that they weren't being followed. But it was up to her to make the move. If she were the contact, she would have no trouble identifying him. His shoes were shined and his trousers were creased. He was the only one in the place wearing a business suit.

Walter looked around. He recalled the sound of the voice on the tape and tried to remember the face that his imagination had put with it. That face was nowhere in the room. In the stained mirror behind the bar, he could see his car parked outside. It stood alone. No one had parked near it. He looked at his watch. Hogan had warned him that the pickup man would probably let him sit for quite a while, making sure that he was alone. He glanced back at the redhead in the black dress. She had already struck up a conversation with the two young men in the T-shirts. Walter sipped at his drink. It was promising to be a long night.

People came and went. The first woman picked up her purse and left with her boyfriend right at her heels. A slutty-looking woman entered, ordered a drink, and within a few minutes was joined by a male arrival. They left together almost immediately. An older man with a terrible limp pulled himself up onto a stool with great effort. Walter studied him until the man looked back. Then Walter was embarrassed because he seemed to be focusing on the man's handicap.

Two hours went by uneventfully. The man with the limp belted back two shots and left. Walter finished his second scotch. Finally, the redhead pulled her cigarettes and lighter back into her purse, gave Walter a glance that said "last chance," and sauntered out the door. When she pulled away, Walter saw that there were only two cars in the lot, his and the pickup truck that belonged to the two T-shirted characters, who were still working their way through whatever was on tap. He surmised that the woman had probably been Hogan's agent who had cased the place, checked out her two drinking companions, and then left. He decided that he had missed his rendezvous. When he went outside, the top of the briefcase was still visible through the front window of his car.

As he drove away from the roadhouse, he dialed Andrew Hogan's office on his car phone. Hogan picked up instantly and told Walter he was already aware that the kidnapper had never shown up. "As far as we can tell, he never even tried. No cars were casing the place. No one moving through the woods on foot."

"What about the two kids at the bar?" Walter asked.

"They were working for us," Hogan said.

Walter was shocked. "Then who was the woman?"

"A hooker who offered to do both our guys for the price of one."

"Well, if our man wasn't there, where was he?" Walter wondered.

"Probably at home," Andrew speculated. "Maybe he's just a nut who gets his kicks out of playing games."

"We shouldn't be playing games," Walter snapped bitterly. "We should just pay the guy."

"It wouldn't have made any difference if the case was chock full of money. He never even took a look."

"If it's someone real close to me, he wouldn't have to look. He might have known what we were up to without even bothering to show up."

Andrew's tone became consoling. "I know this is tough on you, Walter. But you and I were the only ones who knew the case was empty. No one else. Not even the people who had the place staked out."

"And what about tomorrow? When we wire those funds, anyone who's really looking will know that it's only ten thousand. We're going to get Emily killed."

"Try to sleep on it, Walter. Maybe the best thing we can do is take this to the chairman and let him make the call."

"It won't take Hollcroft five seconds before he'll be on the phone to the police. We've been through all this, for Christ's sake."

"Let's both sleep on it. I don't mind telling you that I'm getting uneasy about setting a trap for a courier."

"Dammit! It's your idea. I was the one who said it wouldn't work."

"Like I said. We'll sleep on it!"

Walter knew that there was no chance of his sleeping on anything. His whole life was coming to an instant of crisis. His entire future would be decided in the next twenty-four hours. He felt desperately alone. If only Angela were with him. If he could just talk to her.

Angela carried her wine out onto the balcony of the town house and looked at the moonlight sparkling on the water. A wonderful night for a swim, she thought. A romantic night. Exactly the kind of evening six months ago when Walter Childs had first hit on her.

She had known it was coming ever since she had joined the bank and learned that Walter was her mentor. She had probably overdone it at her interview. But people looking for a high-paying job *had to* impress the hell out of the people who were doing the hiring. Women had the added burden of making sure which of their many attributes was making the impression.

Walter's interest was obvious. He had monitored her work as if it were the most important activity at InterBank. Weekly, she was summoned to his office for a professional conference on her progress. But always the conversation was more about Walter and the loneliness of command than about any achievement of hers. She had recognized all the opportunities to be sympathetic, to display her concern for his burdens, and to offer an opportunity for a more relaxed meeting.

At one of their sessions, after official business hours, he had gestured to the stack of documents on his desk awaiting his attention. "An all-nighter," he had sighed. "Probably just grab a fast bite and then get back to the desk." And then, as if the idea had just occurred to him, he had suggested, "Say, if you're not terribly busy, maybe you could join me. We could talk over dinner." Angela had agreed with a show of enthusiasm. You didn't get ahead by offending the people in power. Skillfully, she had kept the conversation on her work and the demanding chores waiting back in his office. At the end of the meal, he had no entry to anything except to say good night and call her a taxi. But she knew that wouldn't be the end. Walter regarded her as his personal property. She had to find some way to outlast his interest, or she probably had to find another bank.

The moment had come during a three-day business conference at a Caribbean resort. Walter had found her in the cocktail lounge with two of her colleagues at the end of the first day and had moved in. He had out-waited the colleagues, then suggest a moonlight swim. It was while he was toweling her off that he had pulled her close and kissed her. "I hope you understand the way I feel about you," he had whispered.

She understood, but knew a truthful answer would be a career-limiting move. "What took you so long," she answered, and she had kissed him in return.

The second night of the conference, he had joined her on her patio with the requisite bottle of champagne, and alluded to a family that simply didn't understand the pressure he was under. The wife who no longer loved him was the last act of his play.

On the third night, he had joined her in her bed. A very tender and considerate lover, Angela had thought while pretending to unheard-of heights of ecstasy. Better than the hotshots she had grown up with, more energetic than her fellow MBA students, and certainly more durable than the business ethics professor who began apologizing for his inadequacies the instant their bodies touched. But still, there was no doubt that he was simply taking advantage of their relative positions. It was up to her whether this was the beginning of her career or the end. Right at that moment, she had decided that it would be neither.

She sipped the fine white Bordeaux that Roberto had apparently ordered and that had been waiting in a bucket of fresh ice when she entered the room. Roberto's plane had touched down on Grand Cayman just as the sun was touching the horizon. She stayed aboard while the small turboprop was towed into a private hangar and found only one person waiting when she stepped out onto the plane's swing-down steps. Roberto's agent had been well briefed. His car, with darkened windows, was parked immediately outside the access door of the hangar building. There was no one in the area who could possibly identify her.

She had leaned forward in her seat and asked the driver to take her past the Banca Folonari and then spent the next half hour studying the narrow streets of George Town, capital of the islands, and Grand Cayman's only attempt at even an insignificant city. She was driven by the front door of the bank branch, a two-story structure with an imitation warehouse facade that could just as easily have been a souvenir shop. Then she had the driver take her down the side streets and around the brick structure. She noted the row of windows on the second floor and the small parking area for the executives behind the building. Angela shook her head in dismay. The entire Folonari branch wasn't much more impressive than a typical American late-night convenience store. It seemed anything but the most profitable branch of a major European money center.

But, of course, banks no longer needed impressive facades. Nor was there any reason for barred teller cages and mammoth vault doors. The Cayman branch was simply a computer center, housing small, inexpensive terminals that were connected to the rest of the world by telephone lines and satellite uplinks. Generally, there wasn't anything in the building worth stealing. Grand Cayman had become a world money center not because of the security of its vaults, but simply because of the generosity of its banking laws. The island government didn't require that depositors report their balances to the tax authorities. Nor did it ever ask depositors about the sources of their wealth. Funds transferred through a Cayman branch simply vanished from the radar screens of police departments and tax collectors all over the world. The tiny island nation, once it freed itself from British rule, had become a rival to Switzerland as the safe haven for thieves of every kind.

Angela created a mental picture of the area as the driver spun back and forth over the streets surrounding the building. There was a jewelry store on the corner diagonally opposite the bank. Directly across from the Folonari entrance was a huge imported goods outlet, with open arches looking out over the street. There was a liquor store with dozens of wine racks fronting the street, a drugstore, and a sidewalk cafe. In the daytime, she guessed, the whole area would be swarming with tourists. It was a good area in which to become invisible.

Now, as Angela relaxed on the patio with the white Bordeaux that had been provided by her Cuban customer, she finalized the elements of her plan. She would connect to Walter's computer server and watch for his connection to the Folonari branch. Once she knew that the money had been moved, she would head for the shops she had noticed. She could kill at least an hour looking at gold chains while she watched the bank entrance through the jewelry store window. Then, if no one showed up, she would move down a few doors to the import center and spend another hour selecting a camera. If she needed still more time, she could look at lenses and other camera accessories, all the while keeping watch on Folonari's entrance. She felt certain she would be able to spot a courier, who would be wearing a business suit in an island of sport shirts and tank tops. And she would see anyone who tried to follow him.

Angela finished her wine and stepped back into the suite to unpack. From the side pocket of her valise, she took out a floppy sun hat. Then she spread out a striped, long-sleeved poncho, oat-colored slacks, and leather sandals. She would blend in easily with tomorrow's columns of shoppers.

Emily's voice seemed to come from hell, shrill with pain and nearly breathless with fear.

"Jesus, he's got a razor. He's going to cut off my ear. Help me, Walter! Help me!"

Then, the calm man's voice that was colored with laughter. It was obvious that Mike was enjoying the moment.

"Not an ear? Then maybe one a your tits! You think he remembers what they look like . . ."

Emily's scream. "God, no! He'll pay. He'll get you the money."

Walter screamed, "No! Stop it!" into the phone, but all he heard was a click and then the sound of obscene laughter. "Please, don't hurt her," he begged.

"Why not?" the man's voice demanded. "You brought the cops!"

"No, I didn't. I just . . ."

"Don't lie to me! Who do you think you're dealing with? One of your flunkies at the bank? You had cops casing the place all afternoon."

Walter stammered, "I . . . I didn't mean . . ."

"And then those two kids at the bar. Where did you get them? Out of Mod Squad? They might as well have been wearing badges."

"Please, it wasn't my idea. It won't happen again. I'll . . ."

"I'll give you one more chance. Your old lady still has her ears and her tits. But if anything happens this time, I'll be sending you her heart!"

"I'll do exactly what you tell me."

"Stay by the phone. I'll be calling you back in a few minutes."

A click, and then the sound of an open line.

Walter used both hands to hang up the phone. When he raised his drink to his lips, he could hear the ice cubes trembling.

"Jesus," he said in a whisper. His first thought was to call Andrew Hogan and tell him about the call. He wanted to scream at him for the danger that Emily was in, and to berate him for underestimating the kidnapper. But he couldn't get past the terror that he had heard in Emily's voice. It was as if the madman's razor had been hovering over his own face. He didn't want Andrew or anyone else involved. He just wanted to pay the money and put an end to all this.

He snapped down the drink and rushed to the wet bar to pour himself another. Then he began pacing his living room, glancing at the telephone each time he passed it. "Ring, goddammit! Ring!"

It was only half an hour since he had shuffled from his garage into the kitchen, disarmed the security system, and gone to the telephone answering machine. There was no message waiting. Maybe Andrew had been right. The man was of no account and had probably lost his nerve and abandoned the ransom. Walter had taken off his jacket, loosened his tie knot, turned up his sleeves, and gone to the wet bar to fix himself another drink.

The tension was suffocating. Pilfering accounts. Moving small amounts of money. Assembling the $100 million ransom. At any point in the process, he could have been spotted by any one of hundreds of people who sat bleary-eyed at their computer terminals, watching the flow of funds in and out of banks on three continents. It had taken all his nerve just to keep his fingers on the keyboard.

And then there were the hours spent at Randy's, pretending to drink when his stomach was in knots, eyeing the lowlife regulars hoping for a sign, and all the while stealing glances at his car.

Even though nothing was resolved, it had been a relief just to lock himself in the familiar and safe surroundings of his own home. But then the new worries began. Would he be able to transfer the entire $100 million as he had planned? Would Hogan recognize the transfer in progress and be able to stop it? Would the transfers go through or would they be blocked by some well-meaning clerk, awaiting a confirmation? Would he be summoned to the boardroom instantly or would the money be gone and Emily be free before his theft became known? Walter had none of the answers. But there was no turning back. He would have to plunge ahead and live with the consequences, whatever they were. He had gone to the bar for another drink, hoping that the alcohol might bring a few moments of peace. And then the telephone had rung. Walter had hesitated, sure that it was probably something routine, but fearful nevertheless. He had been greeted by a moment of silence and then the sound of a tape player. An instant later, his head had nearly exploded with the sound of Emily's screams. It wasn't supposed to be this way. He had never intended to hurt her.

Now, the telephone rang again and he sprang to it instantly.

"Hello."

The voice: "You gotta car phone?"

"Yes, of course."

"What's the number?"

He rattled off the number of his cellular telephone.

"Wrap the money up in a brown paper parcel. Keep it outta sight, on the floor of your car, in back of the passenger seat. And bring the leather briefcase with you. Keep it in the front seat, in plain sight. You got that?"

"Yes, I understand."

"Noon on Saturday you go for a drive on the Garden State, by the Paramus Mall. Make sure the car phone is turned on. I'll call you."

"Saturday?" Walter couldn't contain his fear. "What about tonight? Or tomorrow?"

"Saturday! At noon. And don't screw it up. You know what will happen."

Emily lay motionless, her hands chained above her head, the blanket tossed in a heap at her feet. She had hardly breathed since her grotesque jailer had sauntered up the stairs, playing back the screams he had recorded. And now he was on his way back down to the basement.

It had been the most terrifying moment of her life when he had brandished the razor-sharp linoleum knife and fantasized about where he would begin the process of slicing her to pieces. Her plans of escape were forgotten. Her dreams of freedom had become a nightmare. Even though she had come to despise her husband, there had been no pretense in the screams that begged Walter to save her. If he had arrived at that moment and paid her ransom, she would have clung to him in gratitude for every living moment that was left to her.

The leering psychopath had held out strands of her hair and sliced them in front of her eyes so that she could see the capabilities of the blade. He had drawn a drop of blood simply by touching the curved point under her ear. He had cupped her breast and used the back of the knife to trace the ease with which he planned to mutilate her. And all the while, his machine had been running, recording her pleading and begging and, when he seemed about to strike, her screams. Then he had played it all back for her, enjoying the sound of her degradation as much as he would enjoy the feel of the ransom money.

He was chuckling to himself when he came down the steps and obviously enjoyed her fear as he slithered toward her bed. "Your loving husband is scared shitless. He's beggin' me to take his money." Mike leaned over her. "Guess he's finally realized that he's met his match." He touched his fingers to her face. "Or maybe he's not so sure how much he'll be able to love you if I send you home with some of his favorite parts missing."

His hand drifted slowly down her neck and then under to the top edge of the gown. "But maybe if you're very nice to me . . . very nice . . . I'll send ya back to him in one piece. He won't mind havin' seconds." The sick smile curled into a corner of his mouth.

"Hey, Mike! You down there again?" It was Rita, shouting from the floor above.

"Yeah. Just checkin' to make sure she's not goin' nowhere."

He stood up straight, towering over Emily. "I'll be back when she's not around. In the meantime, you better be thinkin' of how you're goin' to make me happy."

Friday

WALTER PAUSED AT THE door of his inner office and set down his briefcase so that he could fit the key into the lock. Then he stumbled over the case as he pushed the door open. He was exhausted, his eyes still red and puffy from his sleepless night, a tiny speck of tissue stuck to the blood clot on his cheek, evidence of his effort at shaving. He picked up the briefcase and dropped it heavily into one of the chairs that flanked his desk. Then he went into his private washroom and tried to make to himself look presentable before his staff began arriving.

He was shocked at what he saw in the mirror. Not just the fatigue, which he had expected, but more the total emptiness in his eyes and expression. The week had taken its toll. In some higher court of justice, he was being fined heavily for his plan to put Emily aside.

Walter had never wanted her hurt. He could have stood before God and sworn that he wished her absolutely no ill. Oh, there would certainly be some embarrassment. Even though he expected her to tell their friends that he was a liar and a philanderer, and blame the breakup on his weakness, she would still feel humiliated that he had preferred another woman. Some resentment was inevitable. But Walter knew Emily to be a strong and practical woman. Deep down, she would be able to admit to herself that he had simply gone off into another orbit. She would know that she had no interest in traveling with him and that her happiness was located exactly where he was leaving her, in a gracious home, with her tennis and travel, in the love and occasional company of her children. His settlement would guarantee that she would never want for anything. It was not even unthinkable that she would find another man to take his place.

Instead, he had left her in the hands of a madman whose ambitions reached only to $50,000 and whose lust would be sated by cutting her to pieces. No matter what, regardless of what it might omen for his relationship with Angela or his future with the bank, he had to save her from the monstrous voice on the telephone. His own needs, important as they were, paled in comparison with her danger.

He held a wet washcloth over his eyes, letting the cold invigorate his dead face. He removed the tissue paper and carefully wiped away the spot of blood. He took his electric razor and completed the job that he had botched with a blade. He gargled with mouthwash to cleanse the paste from his tongue and ran a comb through his hair to cover the thin spots. Then he went to his desk and turned on his computer.

The first step was to check into the accounts in which he had stored the $100 million ransom. Once he had moved the few thousand that Andrew needed to set up his trap in Grand Cayman, he fully intended to follow with the full amount.

Next, he checked his own accounts in the bank's executive compensation files. He had over $100,000 in treasury bills, accumulated from his incentive percentages and available to purchase approved securities. He could draw the $50,000 with a simple coded order that automatically posted the required tax and payroll deductions. His problem would be getting the funds in cash, specifically nonsequenced twenties. Cash was fast becoming a curiosity among money center banks and his request for compensation funds in twenty-dollar bills would certainly raise some eyebrows. The last thing he wanted to do now was call attention to himself. He was going to have to take a bank check for the funds and then go to another bank to cash the check. In fact, he would be better off taking several bank checks and cashing each at a different bank. This was the kind of thing that Andrew Hogan could arrange easily. But Emily's safety depended on his keeping Hogan's people away from the ransom.

He was startled when he heard Andrew's voice. "What did you decide?" The security officer was speaking as he came through the door, acting as if they were still engaged in last night's conversation.

Walter looked up, his expression registering his confusion.

"We agreed to sleep on it," Andrew reminded him, as if there had been any chance of his finding restful sleep. Walter wanted to scream.

"I'll tell you my thoughts," Hogan said, settling into a chair, "but you're not going to like them." He took Walter's silence as interest in his decision. "I think we ought to go together up to Hollcroft's office and lay everything out for him. That's probably what we should have done right off the bat. But there's still time to get this off our backs."

"Jack Hollcroft will call in the police and the FBI," Walter said in despair.

"That's the best move. We were wrong to try to handle this with our own resources."

"And Emily. We just act as if she's of no importance. As if her life isn't worth anything?"

"That's the bank's policy, Walter."

Childs's lips curled in anger. He bit off his words. "Bank . . . policy . . . is that she's . . . already dead." They stared unblinking at each other. "You know she's alive," Walter went on. "You heard her voice. In fact, she might be free right now if you had let me pay the lousy fifty-thousand-dollar ransom."

Hogan broke off their eye contact and glanced down at his hands. "That's not fair. You know as well as I do that the fifty thousand was a side bet."

"Well, the hundred million is for real, dammit," Walter snapped back. "And that's what I've decided. I don't want to take any chances with Emily's life. I want to pay the hundred million just as I've been ordered."

"Maybe Hollcroft will see it that way . . ." Andrew tried.

"No, he won't. He'll see it exactly the way a bank president has to see it, because it's not his wife. He'll follow policy." Walter sagged slowly as if the air were being let out of him. "If we go to Jack, he'll summon the board. And that will be Emily's death sentence." He looked pleadingly across the desk. "Let me send the money. I take full responsibility."

Hogan's head shook so slowly that his gesture was nearly imperceptible. "Security is my responsibility. I can't let anyone give away a hundred million of the bank's money. No matter what the reason."

"Then you're the one who's going to kill her," Walter said. Even though they were only the width of the desk apart, they each disappeared into separate worlds of gloom.

They were called back by Walter's secretary, who brought in the usual morning coffee, setting cups before the two men. When she finished, Hogan took up the discussion. "We've gone in a complete circle and we're back to where we were yesterday. There are a hundred things wrong with the trap we've got set up in the Caymans. But it's the only play we have."

Angela stood before the full-length mirror. Her hair was up, tucked under the soft canvas hat so that its color hardly showed. The floppy brim circled the sides of her face and the sunglasses provided the perfect mask. The poncho disguised her figure and the baggy pants even raised doubts about her sex. Even Walter, she thought, could pass her by without recognizing her.

The outfit itself was her biggest problem. Anyone looking for suspicious characters would be attracted to a costume that made someone impossible to recognize. But in George Town, broad-brimmed hats and opaque sunglasses were de rigueur. And loose, cool cottons were the standard cover for the thongs and bikinis that were ubiquitous on the beaches and at the pools. In the streets and shops surrounding the bank, there would probably be a hundred costumes similar to what she was wearing. She would be as inconspicuous as Angela Hilliard was ever going to get.

Her laptop computer was open on the counter that separated the kitchen from the living room, its power cord plugged in above the toaster, and a phone cord stretching from its base to a telephone jack on the kitchen wall. Angela had simply dialed into the PC in her New York office and then connected that computer to the bank's internal network.

Walter's password, which he had often encouraged her to use, had put her computer online with his server. Anytime he downloaded a file, or connected to the network in order to move funds from one account to another, the information would write out on her screen just as it was appearing on his. As far as his computer dealings were concerned, she might just as well have been standing behind him, looking over his shoulder.

She glanced at the screen as she stepped into the kitchen for still another cup of coffee. Keep sharp, she had warned herself, and alert. She couldn't allow herself to settle into the relaxed mood of her surroundings.

There was nothing yet, which was hardly surprising. It was only 9:00 A.M. Angela guessed that he would probably wait until his colleagues were buried in the day's work before he would key in the ransom transfer. His activities would go unnoticed until late in the day.

She could easily imagine the tension that was seizing Walter's hands and the pressure that was building up inside his head. Walter, she knew, was highly driven and completely obsessive. The danger he was confronting would take possession of all his senses. He had collapsed into her arms only a few nights earlier when his moment of truth was still many hours off. Now that he was down to his final minutes, he was probably becoming a basket case. She could only hope that he wouldn't crack. She was counting on his being able to face up to the dangers and make the only choice that was really left to him.

She took her coffee to the patio and looked up the length of the Seven Mile beach. Pure white sand was pasted on flat blue water to form a piece of impressionistic art. The first sun worshipers of the day were just beginning to migrate down to the water's edge.

This was the kind of place where she would like to live; a paradise with none of the uncertainties of the seasons, reserved for the rich and powerful, and next door to discreet banks that would let her manage her money. When people thought of her as power hungry, they imagined that she enjoyed flexing her financial muscle over subordinates at the bank and clients around the country. But that certainly wasn't high on her list of priorities. The power she needed was the power to command any service and to gratify any need. Money bestowed that kind of power and she planned to have a great deal of it.

But for all its practical attributes, Grand Cayman struck her as a bit too sterile. Its history, a brief tale of European powers that had tried to foist the islands on one another, could be written on the back of a clam shell. It's only geopolitical importance was as a landing strip for resident seagulls and for the longer-range migrant birds. In truth, its real beauty was underwater, visible only to the divers who left its shores every morning.

Europe, she thought, would be more fitting. Perhaps a villa on the Riviera, or a white cement house above the harbor of one of the Greek isles. Or perhaps the Italian coast, south of Naples, where cities with centuries of history rose vertically from the sea.

She looked over her shoulder at the computer, its screen still blank. She could imagine Walter ringing his hands as he circled the machine next to his desk in New York. Come on, Walter, she thought. Let's get on with it.

Walter was, indeed, circling his desk like a caged animal. But he had yet to give thought to the small transfer that he and Andrew Hogan had agreed upon. Instead, he was waiting anxiously for the five $10,000 checks that were coming up from the cashier's office. He had called the appropriate officers at several of the other major banks that filled the blocks of eastside midtown. Each would be delighted to arrange for five hundred used twenties to be available for pickup. No problem whatsoever. "You going down to Atlantic City?" one of his business acquaintances had jibed. A closer friend had ventured that he would like to see the lady who was worth that much money.

He had already lied to his secretary, telling her about an opportunity to pick up a great-looking sailboat that he could put into charter service. "I hate to do this, but the guy is in the middle of a divorce and doesn't want the money to show up in his checking account. Could you . . . ?"

Joanne had agreed to leave early on her lunch hour, bring his checks to neighboring banks, and have the cash back to him before 2:00 P.M.

The messenger arrived and Walter hurriedly endorsed the bank checks. Then he sent the secretary on her way and turned his attention to the small account he was about to deliver to the Caymans. It was a wasted exercise, he thought. No one was going to come calling for the small amount he was wiring. But he had to go through the motions just to satisfy Andrew Hogan. Once Andrew saw the $10,000 transfer and thought he was completely on top of the situation, Walter planned to move the $100 million from his storage accounts.

Angela heard the electronic ping from her laptop and strolled around the kitchen counter to see what Walter was up to. First came an InterBank account number, followed almost instantly by the international routing number that identified the Folonari Cayman branch. Next was the Folonari account number, the one where the ransom instructions had directed that the funds be deposited. She found herself smiling at how easy it was. No masks, no guns, no getaway cars. Just "hello" and "thank you very much." Probably even a "pleasure doing business with you. I hope we can be of service again." It would all be completely polite and civil. Why would anyone stoop to armed robbery?

Next came Walter's authorization code. Somewhere in Milan, at Folonari's headquarters, an old mainframe was checking the code against its file of authorized wire transaction depositors. The cursor on Angela's screen blinked impatiently. It wasn't used to being kept waiting. Then Folonari's confirmation number printed across the screen. The branch could accept the funds with the same assurance, as if they were counting their way through a truckload of U.S. dollars. The sender had the money and had InterBank's authorization to transfer any amount.

Angela looked eagerly for the $100 million figure. She was stunned when the computer wrote out the number $10,000. "What the hell . . . ?" she heard herself mumble dumbly. She hunched down close to the screen as if she suspected her eyes were deceiving her. There was no mistake. Walter was depositing only $10,000. She pulled away. Something was wrong. Someone was playing a game and it was a game in which she hadn't anticipated the rules. What was Walter up to?

She ran through a list of possibilities. He was transferring the funds in small amounts. Smart, because it would be more likely to go undetected than one large transfer. But $10,000? At that rate, it would take all day and a good part of the weekend to complete the deposit.

He was trying to bluff the kidnapper. "Take it or leave it," he might be saying. "I'll let you walk with a few thousand and we'll forget any of this ever happened. Just release my wife and get out of my life." That was a possible ploy, Angela decided, but not for Walter. He simply didn't have the guts for games of chicken, played at high speed.

Most probably this was simply a trial run. He had established the account and funded it out of the bank's coffers. He was waiting to be sure that the transaction went unchallenged before he sent the bulk of the money.

She poured herself still another cup of coffee, set it next to the computer, and climbed up onto one of the stools that served the counter. There had to be more coming. She sat patiently, waiting for the other shoe to drop.

An hour dragged past and Walter's server reported no action. Whatever he was doing, it didn't involve accessing the bank's internal accounts and records. Nor did it seem to involve any correspondence with outside banks. Something was terribly wrong.

She perked up when Walter's machine went back online. Maybe this was what she had been waiting for. But he keyed in a routine transaction and then went immediately back into darkness. Angela jumped down from the stool and switched off the machine. There was nothing happening in New York. She had to find out if anything was happening at the Folonari Cayman branch.

She took her huge canvas bag, which served not only as a purse but also as a shopping bag, and locked the apartment door behind her. The sun was already high in the sky and its heat was radiating from the sidewalk and the black surface of the road. The beach, to her right, was dotted with cabanas and umbrellas and the oiled bodies of physically endowed vacationers. In the streets to her left, the day's commerce was in full bloom.

It was a quaint little town, ugly in the dilapidation of its structures, but pretty in the colorful commerce it housed. The wide, double doors of shops were thrown open, with merchandise migrating out into the streets. Coffeehouses had no front facades, their business reaching out until the tables were threatening to topple over the curb. Automobiles, mostly European and Japanese compacts, were parked with two wheels on the sidewalk and a steady flow of cars through the narrow space left in the roads amounted almost to a traffic jam.

She strolled passed the front entrance of the bank and noticed a tall man, probably in his thirties, leaning casually against the wall, his hands thrust deep into his pockets. His white complexion stood out among the native tans, his sports shirt was brand new, and his shoes weren't typical island ware. Was he watching the entrance, she wondered as she drew close? Or was he waiting for a wife who was spending her day on a shopping spree? His eyes were hidden behind sunglasses, but Angela thought she noticed his head turn to follow her as she passed. Had he spotted her? Or was he just bored enough to look at anyone?

Get hold of yourself, she chided. Anyone could look suspicious. If she were confident she could watch the bank without being recognized, then professionals would be even more difficult to recognize. She and Walter were both certain that a bonded courier would be the likely choice to pick up the money. She was looking for a courier who was prepared to walk down the street with $100 million in Folonari bearer bonds. She could expect a briefcase, probably chained to his wrist, a businesslike sedan that would wait at the curb, and jacketed driver, probably armed, who would be actively scanning the crowd.

Angela turned at the corner, crossed over, and headed back past the bank on the opposite side of the street, toward the import outlet where she would spend an hour examining cameras. She would select a display case just inside the open warehouse doors, giving her a vantage point that looked directly across at Folonari, with enough height to see over the heads of the shoppers.

Then, she saw him. It was the weasel of a man who had followed her into the first-class lounge and had waited outside the Boca Raton industrial park. He had replaced his wire frames with sunglasses and his business suit with a more casual costume. But, like the one in front of the bank, he was in a freshly unfolded sports shirt and heavy dark shoes. He was looking away from her, but his head was slowly panning in her direction. Angela turned away and moved into a souvenir shop to get off the street.

There were two of them, probably with their car parked at the edge of the shopping district. If the pickup man came on foot, they would have no trouble following him. If he came by car, the car would move at a snail's pace until it reached the main beachfront road. One of them could walk beside the courier's car. The other could run ahead to have their car ready. Or maybe they had no intention of allowing anyone to get back to a waiting car. They could just as easily take their man in the bank doorway.

Angela smiled. So that was why Walter had transferred only $10,000. He was going along with Hogan's scheme to catch the kidnapper. He had simply used the ten thousand to create an account. His real intention was to see who came to claim the money. He wasn't planning to ransom Emily at all!

She looked back into the street and found that neither of the lookouts seemed to be interested in her direction. Casually, she sauntered out into the middle of a throng of shoppers and moved away from the man she had recognized. Then she ducked into the sidewalk cafe and took a table just inside the building. She could sit unobserved, but still watch the bank and the man stationed in front of it.

Half an hour dragged by, spent sipping bottled water so that she could hold her place at the table. She was beginning to wonder what had gone wrong that the courier hadn't shown up. Could the courier service be connected into the bank? Had they learned that only a small amount had been transferred and decided to wait for new instructions?

Angela had waited long enough. Nothing was going to happen and she didn't want to linger any longer around people who could identify her. She counted out the change for her bill, stacked it on the table, and was just about to abandon the watch when the car she was waiting for appeared. It came down the side street next to the bank and turned into the dense parade of shoppers. Carefully, it edged up to the curb. She could see two men behind the darkened windshield and watched the reaction of the man keeping watch at the front door as he made a point of wandering away from the his post without glancing back at the car.

One man got out. He looked in both directions, then moved to the door of the bank, turning his shoulders as he pressed through the crowd. There was no mistaking him. The gray, summer-weight suit stood out like a lighthouse, even though it was worn over an open-collar white shirt. The briefcase was a thick, case-file size. All she could see of the man who remained behind the wheel was his silhouette. He was leaning back, away from the windshield, disguised by the black tint of the side window.

The little man who had been posted on her side of the street suddenly appeared, moving into her view as he crossed the street behind the car. He then sauntered past the parked car and went into the bank's front door. Angela allowed herself a smile of satisfaction. She had called it right. One had gone to the end of the street where the car would have to pass. The other had moved into the bank and was ready to follow the courier. Andrew Hogan; she thought, needed to be more original. His operatives were being a bit too obvious.

The minutes dragged by slowly. She had expected the courier to return within a few moments. All he had to do was count the bonds and sign a receipt. Unless he knew the amount that he was supposed to pick up; then, he probably would have called his office for instructions when the account contained only a fraction of the amount.

But he was seemingly at ease when he emerged from the building, moving straight to the car without examining his surroundings and disappearing inside. Instantly, the car eased from the curb, forcing itself into the human traffic. In another instant, the man who had followed her to Florida came out of the bank and began moving along the far sidewalk, keeping in the sedan's blind spot. Angela stepped out and began following on her side of the street.

At first, she moved very quickly, darting in and out of the shoppers. But she realized that, even at a slow pace, she would move ahead of the sedan. She had to hang back in order to keep the car in front of her. She glanced across the street at the man making his way down the other side. He now had one hand raised to his head and was talking into a small radio or telephone, perhaps alerting another member of the team that the car was on its way. Ahead, she could see the line of taxis waiting to take shoppers back to their hotels and beach houses. It would be easy for her to jump into a cab and have him follow the car that the man across the street would undoubtedly get into.

The courier's sedan was near the end of the street, about to break free from the crowds. Angela picked up her pace, knowing that she had to be at the cabstand before the car was able to accelerate away. But when she glanced back to her right, the man across the street had vanished. She suffered a split second of panic as she realized that Hogan's agents weren't following the script she had assumed. But what did it matter? She still had to get to a taxi before the courier's car left the area.

The door of a taxi at the rear end of the line opened in front of her. She started to step around it, hurrying toward the head of the line. Suddenly, hands reached from behind and locked on her arms. Before she could turn her head, she felt herself being pushed forward and into the arms of a man who was already inside the taxi. She had hardly hit the seat, when the man who had pushed her slid in next to her and closed the door behind him.

"Who the hell . . . ?" Angela started. But then she recognized that she was being held immobile between the two men who had been watching the bank. "What do you assholes think you're doing?"

"Following the courier. Same as you," said her friend from the first-class lounge.

"Figured you'd appreciate a lift," said the second man. "So just shut up and watch."

"You can't do this," she protested. "This is kidnapping."

"No, it's bank robbery," said the first man, "and it could get a little dangerous. So keep down and keep quiet."

The taxi had already pulled out of line and was no more than fifty feet behind the courier's sedan, separated by a thinning group of shoppers. As Angela watched, the sedan found its opening and moved onto the shore road. Then it took a left turn toward the airport where her private plane had landed. Seconds later, the taxi maneuvered around the stragglers and turned after the courier car. The driver stayed a good way back in order to avoid being spotted.

"Looks like they're heading for the airport," the guard to her right announced. The driver nodded. Then the guard turned to Angela. "Is that where you were going to meet them? At the airport?"

"Meet who?" she countered, staring straight ahead.

"We figured someone would come down to pick up the money."

"What money?"

She noticed that the guard to her left was examining a photograph and, when she stole a glance, saw that it was the photo of her from personnel file. He glanced at the picture and then over at Angela. Then he chuckled. "Where did you get that outfit? You look like an idiot."

She kept staring straight ahead. "You're the ones who are going to look like idiots when I pick you out of a lineup for assault. If you have half a brain between you, you'll stop this car and let me out. You're holding me against me will."

"They made us!" the driver suddenly announced and the taxi lurched forward, almost as if it had been hit from behind. The sedan had suddenly pulled out to pass a car ahead and was now rapidly accelerating away. The taxi shot up close to the car ahead and then leaned out across the center line. Angela saw a car coming directly at them and closing fast. She squeezed her eyes shut and turned her head into the seat back like a turtle squeezing into its shell. The engine downshifted and roared. Horns blared and tires squealed as the car lurched back across the dividing line. She expected the sound of tearing metal, but instead the horn blasted past, its pitch dropping as it vanished behind.

"You bastards are crazy," Angela shouted.

"We don't want you to miss your pickup," the man to her right said.

The taxi was moving so fast that it seemed to be hopping in a short series of flights and then leaning heavily when the road turned. The traffic sign for the airport exit rocketed past and seconds later they shot by the exit itself. Angela focused on the speedometer and saw the needle hovering around the 100 mark. Far ahead, she could make out the sedan, which still seemed to be pulling away from them.

"Where's he heading?" the guard on her left asked the driver.

His shoulder hunched. "Search me. There are just a few roads ahead. He won't be able to shake us."

"Just keep him in sight, then. Sooner or later he's gonna run out of island."

The road, which had been well paved and protected with guardrails where it circled George Town, had deteriorated to a gravel path that was barely the width of two cars. The sedan ahead was forced to slow down and the taxi was catching up. Then, without warning, the sedan's taillights flashed and the car turned sharply onto a nearly invisible road that ran south toward the sea. It was headed to a small colony of buildings that were at the water's edge.

The cab skidded into the same turn. When the sedan screeched to a stop, the taxi was only a hundred yards behind. The courier and his driver jumped out and raced into one of the buildings.

"Stay here!" The man to her left ordered Angela. Her two captors sprung out the sides of the taxi.

"Fuck you," she shouted as she rolled out through the open door.

She was running after her captors, glancing back at the taxi driver, who was trying to catch her from behind. The building was a dive shed, with displays of scuba equipment guarded by a wide-eyed clerk, who was powerless to interfere with the chase through the center of his store. The couriers were quickly through to the seaside entrance and out onto a wooden pier. They were trying for a dive boat, tied to the end of the dock, but Hogan's two agents were right at their heels.

"You ain't going to make it," one of pursuers called out. A second later, he had a pistol in his hand and fired two shots out into the water. While the shots were still echoing, the courier and his chauffeur skidded to a dead stop and fired their hands into the air. Hogan's two men pulled up next to them. Seconds later, Angela and the taxi driver joined the conference. It was Angela's first-class companion who took charge and steered the group off the pier, back into the dive shop. There, he flashed some credentials, which the owner barely acknowledged, and threw down a pile of twenties, which got the owner's attention. Seconds later, they were all in the dive shop office, the door shut to assure their privacy.

The couriers were fiercely professional, unwilling to say anything about their assignment other than to refer Hogan's people to their superiors at a downtown office. They were unimpressed when they were told that they were involved in a kidnapping. Many of the courier company's clients were using the firm precisely to maintain their anonymity while they retrieved illegally gotten gain, so the threat that they might be involved in a crime came as no shock. But the courier who had gone into the bank was completely flabbergasted when Hogan's man told him what was in the briefcase that was still locked to his wrist and exactly what had transpired inside the bank.

"You guys have been had," Angela's traveling companion told them, "and the kidnapper who hung you out is here on the island. Where were you supposed to take the money?"

"The airport . . ." the courier started to explain, but he was silenced by the threatening glance of the driver. The two men went silent, leaving Hogan's people no alternative but to telephone the courier office and to take the entire party back to George Town to talk with their boss.

"I'm not going with you," Angela protested. "I have nothing to do with these two or whatever they're involved in."

The grip of the man who had been following her was anything but gentle. "Why don't you just tag along and see if anyone recognizes you?"

The cash was impressive. There were 2,500 twenty-dollar bills neatly stacked in twenty five paper wrappers. Walter's secretary had gathered it in a shopping bag from four different banks, dragging cash in and out of a waiting taxi, and praying that the bottom wouldn't fall out of the bag in the middle of Park Avenue. Then she had brought it up in the elevator, realizing that no one cared what she had in the bag and musing how easy it would be to carry the same amount down in the elevator and out the front door. All day, she worked with amounts that ran into the millions or the tens of millions, counting up small fortunes with a few keystrokes on her computer terminal. The vast sums she worked with were vague and meaningless, like the numbers in the InterBank annual report or the frequently quoted total of the national debt. But $50,000 in twenties had a real presence. Joanne had swallowed hard as she stacked the currency neatly on the coffee table in Walter's office. He had thanked her profusely, again forcing her to endure his lame excuse about a friend's boat. As soon as she was out the door, he began to wrap it.

It was a hefty package, a twelve-inch cube of plain brown paper secured with unbreakable tape and tied with a heavy cord. Walter lifted it. Twenty pounds, he guessed. He carried it to his closet and pushed it to the back corner of the shelf. No one would question him at the end of the day when he carried it down in the elevator. He would probably rest it on the guard's desk while he initialed the sign-out sheet.

He used his private line to dial Andrew Hogan's office. "Any news?"

"Nothing yet," Hogan answered.

"It's been over an hour. They wouldn't just leave it sitting there."

Hogan's voice sighed with impatience. "We've got the cashier working for us and the street covered. If anyone shows up, we'll know about it. They're just taking their time. Wouldn't surprise me if they had people watching the street themselves."

"You'll call me?" Walter asked.

"Soon as I hear something, you'll be the first to know."

He sat at his desk, trying to shift his attention to the mountain of work that needed his input. But he couldn't concentrate on anything except the ransom account in George Town. Andrew would have it under surveillance until someone came calling for it. Then, when he thought he had his man and was no longer interested in the paper account, Walter would send down the full $100 million.

But would that buy Emily's freedom? He had never even considered that she could fall into the hands of a psychopath like the man on the telephone. Just recalling the relish with which the smug voice had described her mutilation sent a chill up his back and into his hairline. Even if the man were paid in full for holding Emily captive, he might not obey an order to release her. No matter what happened in Grand Cayman, Walter was determined that nothing should interfere with his turning over the cash he had pushed into his closet.

He went to the locker room, changed into his gym shorts and sneakers, and then slumped into the exercise room where Mitchell Price was already sliding weights onto the bar. "Jesus, you look like hell," Price said by way of a greeting. "Something wrong with the deutsche mark?"

"Sound as a dollar," Walter answered, completing the tired old joke. He climbed up onto the treadmill and set it for a warm-up jog.

Son of a bitch, Walter thought, as he watched Price begin a series of shoulder shrug exercises. It would be Mitchell's computers that would find the $100 million he had siphoned from dozens of accounts and trace it through to the Folonari Cayman branch. It would be Mitchell who would bring him up to the boardroom, confront him, and then listen to his lame explanations. And it would be Mitchell who would be knighted, while he was being led away in disgrace.

He fought against the wretched hope that something might happen to Emily before he transferred the money. Something totally beyond his control that would leave him blameless. But the most logical *something* was that the madman who was holding her would kill her horribly. Nothing he could ever gain would be worth that. Walter wanted to be free of Emily. He didn't want to live with her screams echoing in his brain. Nor was there any way he could refuse to pay. Angela had made it pretty clear that she could never marry him if he left Emily to die.

He really had no choice but to play the affair through to the end. Transfer the money and then run away with Angela. That was certainly a future he could live with, if only he wouldn't constantly hear Mitchell Price laughing from the chairman's office.

The headboard was yielding under Emily's grip. As she leaned her weight on the crossbar, she could see its ends breaking free from the corner posts.

The joints had only a fraction of their grip. If she had a hammer, she could probably knock them free with a single swing.

Not that she wanted to be free right now. Her two guards were still in the house. She could hear them moving around on the floor above. Rita was due to bring down her lunch sometime during the next hour. Mike might come down at any time to record another horror message or just simply to enjoy her terror. She couldn't let them find her in a broken bed. As soon as she was free, she had to begin her escape through the drop ceiling and that would take time. She had to bide her time until they were both asleep or both out of the house. Otherwise one of them might walk in while her legs were hanging down through the roof.

She stopped forcing the bar and bent to blot up the small traces of wood dust that were on the floor. Then she swung the chain over the corner post and got herself back onto the bed. Within seconds, she heard footsteps padding toward the top of the stairs, and then the bolt snapping open. Rita came down with a small tray.

"Just a sandwich," she said as she put the tray on the table. "It's cheese. I hope you like it with mustard." The woman was almost pleasant. She found the key in her jeans pocket and unfastened the hands that Emily offered. Then she watched sympathetically while Emily tried to massage the blood back into her wrist.

"You've been exercising, haven't you?"

Emily felt a jolt of fear. "What do you mean?"

Rita's hand brushed up the side of Emily's face. "You worked up a sweat. What were you doing? Leg lifts?"

"Yes," Emily lied. She stood up from the bed and went into the bathroom.

"I used to do aerobics," Rita called after her. "But it was a waste of time. You can't fight age, can you. Neither of us is getting any younger."

Flattery can't hurt, Emily thought. "I wish I were in as good a shape as you. You probably don't need a lot of exercise." She washed her hands and splashed water on her face and neck. Then she went to the table where she began to quaff down the sandwich.

"Take your time," Rita said. "No need to put the bracelets back on you until I have to go out."

Emily's face snapped up from her plate. "You're going out?"

"Just to get a few things. But I can leave you with only one handcuff. Mike will be here, so you're not going anywhere."

Emily stood slowly, drawing the gown around her. "Please, don't go. Don't leave me alone with him. I'm afraid."

"Don't be. That's to scare your husband. It's not you he's after. It's the money."

"He's been all over me. And he told me that he'd be back when you were gone."

Rita's quickness caught Emily offguard. She crossed the space between them in two lightning steps, her open hand flying through the air as she came. The blow cracked across Emily's cheek, sending her reeling back against the wall.

"Mike doesn't need anything from you," she said in an angry whisper. "I give him everything he needs . . . or wants."

"I'm not lying."

"Just don't try to come on to him. It won't do you any good because he isn't interested in you. And you don't want to do anything that makes me mad, because then you'd really be in trouble."

Andrew Hogan decided not to use the telephone. He wanted to be face-to-face with Walter Childs when he told him. In all his years as a detective, he had never met anyone who could completely hide his reaction to bad news. Walter's expression would tell him exactly how much he knew about his lover's activities in Grand Cayman.

He held up a hand to stop Joanne from announcing him, opened the door, and walked directly to the desk. Walter's eyes showed his amazement when he looked up.

"What?" he stammered. "What happened?"

"Two couriers showed up for the money." Andrew said. "We caught them and ended up talking to their boss."

"What did he say?"

Hogan kept focused directly on his eyes. "They'd been told to make a pickup and deliver it directly to a private jet hangar at the airport. The caller was a woman who said she would identify herself by showing them the account number. She paid with a check for five thousand dollars drawn on the account."

Walter seemed to be digesting the information. Nothing in his expression hinted that he might have known about the arrangements in advance. "The courier service was willing to do that?" he asked in what appeared to be genuine surprise.

"In the Caymans, that isn't unusual. Or at least that's what the couriers say. There's a lot of money laundering by people who don't want to leave their name and who don't wait around for the paperwork."

"Who did you find at the hangar?" Again, Walter seemed honestly eager for information.

"No one," Andrew admitted with an expression of despair. He fell into a side chair.

"No one!" Walter's expression turned to anger rather than to relief. If he already knew all the details of the ransom payment, he was doing a wonderful job of playing innocent. "Then you blew it!" He was up on his feet. "You played Russian roulette with Emily's life and you lost!"

Hogan smiled cynically. "Not quite. My guys found the pickup person before they ever got to the airport. Turns out someone else was following the courier, too."

Walter backed up a step. "Who in hell was it?"

"Your lady friend. Angela Hilliard."

The shock that registered in Walter's eyes looked real. "Angela! That's ridiculous. She's with a client."

"She *was* with a client," Andrew corrected. "We followed her down to Boca Raton where she spent most of Thursday with one of the bank's customers. But she gave our people the slip."

"You followed her?" Walter interrupted.

"Of course. Her. The other officers. Even you. We're keeping an eye on everyone. But when we lost her in Florida, we had no idea she was heading for the Caymans. It was just luck that we identified her. The guy who had followed her to Boca Raton was sent down to Grand Cayman after he lost her. He was the only one down there who could have recognized her and even he wasn't too sure. She was in disguise . . . dressed very differently."

"A disguise?" Walter's mind seemed to be reeling. "What in hell would Angela know about a disguise? This whole thing is crazy."

"She's on a plane right now, headed back up here with our investigators. They're due to land at La Guardia around seven. I think we all ought to gather right here at, let's say, eight o'clock."

Walter bristled. "And in the meantime, what do we do about Emily? Just . . . let her die?"

"No. I think your girlfriend is going to be able to tell us where Emily is. Or, at least, be able to tell us who has her."

"Damn you! Can't you get it through your thick skull that Angela isn't in on this." Walter's eyes were flooding with tears of frustration. "She's been insisting that I do everything possible to get Emily back."

"Insisting that you pay over the hundred million dollars," Andrew reminded.

"She's not involved!" Walter exploded.

"If she's not involved, then we'll just have to wait for another message from the people who are involved."

"There won't be another message. You remember my orders. Either the money is there or I'll never hear from anyone again."

Hogan rose slowly. "Walter, we have our kidnapper. And I think when she understands what she's up against she'll lead us to Emily. Now don't get me wrong. We're not relaxing for an instant. We'll still be watching every one who could possibly be involved and we have people running down every shred of information. But I think Miss Hilliard will have all the answers."

Angela concentrated on the laptop computer on the tray table in front of her, making a point of ignoring the investigator in the seat next to her. She knew he was alternating between obvious interest in the information scrolling across her screen and sneaked glances down at the generous length of thigh that showed below her pulled-up skirt. The pitiful jerk, she thought for a moment. He'd spend his life looking instead of taking.

They had expected her to crumble the moment she had confronted the couriers, and heard them say that they had been on their way to meet the *woman* who had hired them. Instead, she had stuck to her story, repeating that she knew nothing about the money that the couriers were collecting, nor any of the details about a kidnapping. Her only crime, Angela had conceded, was playing hooky from her office long enough to allow herself a long weekend in the Caymans and that was a matter between herself and InterBank. It was none of their business.

They had posted a guard outside the window of her apartment while she changed back into her business outfit, warning her that they would be watching her every minute. Angela hadn't even bothered to pull the shade, enjoying the obvious embarrassment of one of her guards when she began undressing. When she was packed, she had handed one of them her suitcase to carry.

On the way to the airport, she had given them a very clear and formal warning. They were not policemen, nor officers of any court, and had absolutely no right to take her into custody. If this was a citizen's arrest, then she demanded that she be handed over immediately to the island police. "You'll look pretty stupid charging me with . . . what is it? Following you up the street while you were following someone else?" If they insisted on bringing her back to New York, then she fully intended to charge them with assault and kidnapping as soon as she touched down.

Angela offered no resistance when their flight was called, nor did she even glance at the policeman who patrolled the boarding gate. On the plane, she had ordered a martini, while Helen Restivo's detective had accepted a complimentary soft drink. Then she had set up her computer and begun typing her trip report, detailing all the adjustments to Roberto's accounts that had been agreed to at the business meeting.

"You're making this hard on yourself," the investigator had advised her. "We're working for the security people at your bank. They're the ones who want some answers."

"The New York police will want their names," Angela had countered. "If they're really in on this, then they're guilty of conspiracy."

As she worked, she noticed the man squirming in his seat and was amused by his uneasiness. She knew exactly what he was thinking. He was no different than her superiors at the bank or most of her businessman clients. Once they knew that they were outgunned by her intelligence, and intimidated by her daring, they harbored secret thoughts of how they would dominate her in bed.

Sassy bitch, she watched them say to themselves, I'd show her who's boss if I had her between the sheets. I'd knock that smart-ass smirk off her face in one hell of a hurry.

It was the last resort of a man's ego. She'd kicked their asses all through college and then through b-school. But it just wasn't in their makeup to admit defeat at the hands of a woman. Instead, they reached back to a primitive past of sexual superiority and comforted themselves with the thought that they could easily dominate her in the only contest that really mattered. On the few occasions when she had taken up the challenge, she had usually left them exhausted and trembling in fear of a heart attack, without so much as raising a sweat.

That's what the cop next to her was doing right now, Angela assured herself. She could almost hear the rusty, cast-iron gears turning in his brain. Snotty broad thinks she can frighten me with this bullshit about me getting arrested. She thinks she can just wiggle her ass and walk away from a capital offense. Boy, would I like to show her a thing or two.

Then he'd peek down at the inside of her thigh, imagine her breathless under his weight, and reassure himself that he was still in charge. What a complete, absolute nerd! Running roughshod over guys like him was almost too easy to be called a contest. She turned suddenly in his direction, catching him momentarily with his eyes in her lap.

"Be a good boy and order me another drink," Angela said. Then she tugged her hem down a bit, just to let him know that she knew exactly what he was thinking.

Walter closed his door and turned his chair to face the computer. He keyed in his password and the machine answered with his clearance. He could look into any file on the InterBank network and execute any transaction that wasn't in violation of banking laws. Only five people at InterBank had total access and Walter was one of them.

He clicked onto the menu and then onto the first entry, account access. A matrix appeared asking him the number of the account and then for a repeat of his password. He spent the next few minutes checking into each of the accounts he had created and found no surprises in the amounts. They were all exactly as he left them. None of them had any indicated activity—they had not been called up by anyone for any reason. That meant that Mitchell Price's auditors hadn't located them yet.

Walter typed in the number of the account that had been set up in the Caymans. As he expected, the words *access denied* flashed in the center of the screen. It was a private account, one of a list of accounts belonging to drug dealers, dictators, and politicians who didn't want anyone browsing through their affairs. But the fact that it was still listed meant that no one had yet closed it. It could still accept Emily's ransom and then make the money disappear.

His fingers hovered over the keyboard. Andrew Hogan's spooks probably wouldn't be watching. They already knew the identity of the kidnapper. Or at least, they assumed that the woman they held in custody would provide the link to the kidnapper. As far as they were concerned, the case was closed.

He designated the target account at Folonari's Cayman Island branch and was about to list the accounts to be transferred, when a new warning flashed across his monitor: *Access limited. Account under surveillance.* His fingers jumped off the keyboard as if he had touched a hot griddle.

"Son of a bitch!" he snapped softly. Then his fist exploded against the edge of his desk. "Son of a bitch!" Hogan was using his authority to keep a security watch on the account. In theory, Walter could get into it, but couldn't do anything with it. And with Folonari's guarantee of secrecy, he couldn't even look into it. He was dead in the water. "Son of a bitch!"

Angela Hilliard was relaxed to the point of boredom when she was escorted into Walter Childs's office. Andrew Hogan led the procession, walking directly in front of her, and the two agents who had escorted her back from the Caymans flanked her. Helen Restivo was holding up the rear.

"Angela," Walter whispered, coming around his desk to greet her. But none of the men moved aside and Angela, who stood in their midst, seemed completely indifferent to Walter's affections. Hogan pointed her to one of the chairs in Walter's lounge area and then sat on the sofa, directly across from her, so that their legs were almost touching. The others arranged themselves around her, leaving Walter to drag one of his side chairs over and take a seat near Angela's shoulder.

"Walter, do you know these idiots?"

He looked around and realized that he didn't. "No, I'm afraid I don't."

Hogan started his introductions, beginning with Helen, but Angela rode right over him. "I'm glad you don't, because they're all going to be spending the next few years in court, if not in prison."

"You know why we're here," Hogan told her.

Angela ignored him, keeping her attention focused on Walter. "There are two things you can do for me. First, go to your desk and call the police. Tell them that I'm being held against my will. Then call the most expensive tort lawyer you know. You can tell him these bumbling fools are going to be paying me a lot of money and there will be plenty to cover his fees."

Walter looked uncertainly from Angela to Andrew. "You can't just . . . hold her," he tried.

Andrew kept after Angela. "Miss Hilliard, what were you doing in the Cayman Islands, across the street from the bank where Mrs. Childs's ransom was being paid?"

"Walter, will you please make those telephone calls for me?" She wasn't budging at all from her role as the outraged woman.

"They're trying to help us find Emily." He was begging her to understand his predicament.

"And you think I know anything about what happened to her?"

"Oh, Jesus, no. But you may be able to help us. Something you saw, or something you might have heard."

She turned to Hogan. "I saw nothing, nor did I hear anything relevant to Mrs. Childs's situation. I hope that concludes this meeting." She tried to stand, but Hogan leaned forward and blocked her escape.

"You know she's been kidnapped," the security officer said.

"Yes. Walter told me. And he knows he has my complete sympathy."

"And you knew how he was supposed to pay the ransom?"

"He told me. And I urged him, for Emily's sake, not to let you and your Boy Scouts fuck everything up. Which, apparently, you have already done."

"You went there to pick up the money," Hogan pressed on.

She shook her head in exasperation. "I'm going to get up now and I'm going to walk out the door. The only way you're going to going to stop me is by knocking me down. I think that's called a felony." She stood up, but Hogan stood with her so that they were face-to-face. "You better tell him, Walter, what the headlines are going to do to your tenuous grip on the presidency. 'Banker's Mistress Assaulted in InterBank Executive Suite.' "

"Please, Angela. Answer his question. What were you doing in the Caymans?"

She froze him with a glance. "I feel very sorry for you, Walter. You just made the worst decision of your life."

She pushed past Hogan and stepped out of the circle toward the office door. Walter jumped to his feet and took command. "Will you all step outside, please. I'd like to have a word alone with Miss Hilliard."

Angela stopped with her hand on the knob. Helen and her agents looked up at Andrew Hogan for their instructions. "Let's wait outside," Hogan decided. They rose reluctantly and filed past Angela. But Hogan closed the door behind them, turned, and leaned his back against it.

"Please, Andrew," Walter Childs asked.

Hogan shook his head. "I can't do that, Walter. You two have a . . . relationship. And the fact is that you're both suspects. I can't give you an opportunity to coordinate your stories."

"Jesus," Angela said in despair. She reached around Hogan for the door-knob and then looked back to Walter when the security officer wouldn't budge.

"We're trying to save Emily's life," Walter pleaded, "if she's not dead already."

Angela considered for a moment. "You're right, of course," she said to Walter. Then she stepped quickly to the sofa and sat in the chair she had just left. This time, Hogan sat a decent distance away from her and Walter perched on the very edge of his chair.

"We're all in agreement that Emily's kidnapping involved insiders," she began, "people well placed in the bank and familiar with its operating procedures."

"Yes, of course," Walter acknowledged. He looked at Hogan for confirmation, but the detective's expression was professionally noncommittal.

"You do agree with that, don't you, Mr. Hogan?" Angela persisted. Hogan reluctantly allowed that it was a strong possibility. "Then which one of your operatives was going to identify the person from InterBank? Did any of them even know anyone from InterBank? Any of the senior officers or the key people on their staffs?"

Hogan kept staring. She was right. Helen's hired hands wouldn't have been able to identify anyone from the bank who showed up to claim the ransom.

"That's why I went to Grand Cayman," Angela told him. Then she looked over at Walter. "You told me when you were supposed to send the ransom and how it was going to be handled. I knew you'd pay it. You'd never take a chance with Emily's life. And I knew that the only way you would survive here would be if you could show Mr. Hollcroft who the real thief was." She turned back to Hogan. "Someone from InterBank was down there. Probably waiting at the airport for the couriers to make their delivery. And I would have spotted him, if you're people hadn't screwed everything up."

Hogan shook his head slowly. "I've got to hand it to you, Miss Hilliard. You've got balls. We catch you red-handed at the scene and you blame the people who caught you."

"Those idiots couldn't catch the runs in Mexico," she fired back. "First, they couldn't have been more obvious if they were dressed like Batman. I spotted them and I'm not exactly Scotland Yard. Then, they blew whatever cover they might have had by barging through pedestrian traffic to arrest me. Next, they let themselves be suckered into driving right past the airport where the person they were supposed to find was probably waiting."

Andrew was turning red from the description of the operation. "They found the person they were supposed to find," she interjected.

Walter came to Angela's defense. "She does have a point, Andrew. You said yourself that the couriers were supposed to deliver the money to the airport."

"For the love of God, Walter, don't side with her. She knows where Emily is."

"I don't," Angela said, "but I think that maybe your investigators do. It's hard to believe that they could have screwed up that badly if they weren't trying."

"Where is Mrs. Childs?" Andrew kept pressing.

Angela looked back and forth. Then she stood quickly. "I'm very tired. It's been a bitch of a day." She fixed on Hogan. "I'm going home now." And then she said to Walter, "I'm truly sorry about all this. You know I want to help you in any way I can. You have my address and phone number. Your friend Hercule Poirot, here, ought to be able to find me."

They all sat speechless and watched her walk out of the office.

"She couldn't be involved in this," Childs finally assured Hogan. "I know her. She couldn't do anything like this."

"Walter, think with your head instead of your pecker. You don't really believe that she went down there to catch the kidnapper, do you?"

"I know she'd do anything to help me."

"She's not helping you. She's helping herself. Dammit it, Walter, I've been a cop all my life. I know when someone is lying. Your lady friend went down there to collect the hundred million. She knows where your wife is."

Helen didn't agree with Andrew Hogan. She had listened patiently as Hogan repeated the conversation that had been held in Childs's office after Helen and her men had departed. Then she announced, "Of course she's lying. Her story about going down there to identify the kidnapper is pure horseshit. Something that she made up on the plane. But I don't think it follows that she's involved."

"What other explanation is there?" Hogan demanded.

"I don't know. But she doesn't have a motive. Why would she be part of a scheme to kidnap Emily Childs?"

"How about a hundred million bucks. Isn't that motive enough?"

"Not for this young lady," Helen instantly answered. "She has the next president of InterBank wrapped around her finger. Prestige. Power. Money. Even after Emily Childs leaves with half the property and a life's worth of alimony, there's still going to be more money than Angela Hilliard can ever spend. It would be stupid of her to risk all that for money that will come to her eventually. And one thing this young lady isn't is stupid."

"Well, if it isn't her, then who in hell is it?" Hogan's question was more an explosion of frustration than a serious inquiry, but Helen answered thoughtfully.

"That's what doesn't make sense. There are no motives. No one has anything to gain."

Hogan returned a blank stare.

"Well, think about it," she went on. "Why would Walter Childs have his wife kidnapped? He's got his fortune. He has his trophy wife. He's got a big-time job. So he's going to have to give up his house—he'll buy another. And he's going to have to pay serious alimony—he can afford it. To him, it's a simple financial transaction. He pays top dollar for a brand-new wife who's worth top dollar. It's just like trading in his BMW for this year's model. No big deal."

"You said he was ambitious," Hogan corrected, reminding his friend that she had once thought that Walter might use the kidnapping to assure his rise to the presidency.

"Yeah, but that only works if he goes to the board and makes a big show of sacrificing his wife rather than robbing the bank. Childs is trying to pay the ransom, which isn't going to raise his stock with the directors."

Andrew nodded in despair. Then he asked, "What about the tennis jock?"

Helen shrugged. "He's hard to figure. Amanda is right about her mother paying him regularly and Emily did send a note with her last check saying that she wasn't going to need any more lessons. But is that a motive? It's not like she was going to turn him in. He had nothing to fear from her and he still was collecting overtime from all those would-be Steffi Grafs."

"Her note could have come as a disappointment if he was counting on half her divorce settlement," Andrew mused. "But he doesn't know a thing about InterBank activities. And if he were in on it, why would he have come in after the kidnappers and walked all over the crime scene?"

"So who does that leave?" Helen asked.

"The other banker, I suppose. He knows the bank procedures inside out and he has a real interest in derailing Childs's career."

"Yeah, but he already has a seven-figure salary and all the perks. Why would he risk exchanging all that for a jail cell?"

Hogan supplied the answer. "To make himself the world's top financier. For people like Mitchell, finishing second is a complete disgrace."

Helen nodded. "So I guess the only one left is you."

Hogan laughed. "You still think I might be the kidnapper?"

"You're the only one with the underworld contacts," She answered.

"Well, I'm not paying for the chorus girl you have following me," Hogan said.

"No charge. It's the least I can do for an old friend."

They fell into another period of moody silence, both focused on the same set of suspects and motives to see if there might be something that they had missed. Then Hogan put his thinking into words. "Suppose Emily decided that she didn't want to be pushed aside . . ." Helen looked up into Andrew's face, signaling her interest, so Hogan continued with his train of thought. "Walter lays everything out for her one night, tells her he's fallen in love with another woman and explains what a wonderful settlement she's going to get. But instead of demanding more, like any sensible wife would, Emily says flat out no. She threatens to drag Walter and his mistress into the garish light of public disclosure. Walter pleads. Promises her twice as much, but she isn't interested in the money. She's so pissed at the guy that she wants his head on a pole. She's already cutting out a scarlet letter to sew onto Angela's lapel. Wouldn't that be enough motive? Wouldn't Walter want to put her out of the way?"

"Maybe so," Helen allowed.

"Or, suppose Walter accepts the bad news," Andrew continued. "So he goes back to Angela and tells her that he won't be able to marry her because he'll be disgraced and thrown out of the banking world. All of a sudden, a very ambitious young lady who figured she was going to get it all is now going to get nothing except the occasional sexual favors of a middle-aged man. Quite a disappointment, don't you think?"

"It's a motive," Helen conceded. She stood up wearily. "Guess I better find out whether Emily Childs knew she was going to get thrown out of bed."

"How are you going to find that out?"

"Amanda. She's searching through her mother's records. Maybe she found a check retaining a divorce lawyer."

Walter Childs took a devious route from his office. He signed out in the usual fashion, crossed the lobby, and as he climbed into the waiting limo, stole a glance at the man who had been watching his office. The man, presumably one of Hogan's hirelings, waited until the car pulled away from the curb and then turned abruptly to head off in the other direction. That was exactly what Childs expected. Just as on the previous nights, the one watching his office had passed him off to another investigator whose car was just now falling into line behind the limo. The car would tail them all the way out to Short Hills, up to the moment when they turned into the driveway. Then it would roll past, leaving him to the man who was watching his house.

Walter made sure the car was still following when the limo turned south on Park Avenue. Then he leaned forward to his driver. "Omar, I need to head uptown. Take a U-turn here."

Omar looked bewildered. "Where would you like to go?"

"Just uptown. Now!"

Omar braked and turned abruptly into the cross-street cutout in the center island. He found a minute space in the northbound traffic and accelerated rapidly into his turn. The following car was hung up at the intersection. With the light turning yellow at the next corner, Walter yelled, "Take this right!"

"Dammit," Omar cursed quietly as he squealed into an abrupt right turn. As soon as they were safely on the cross street headed east, he added, "You should give me more warning, Mr. Childs—"

Walter cut him off. "We were being followed. I think we lost him on the first turn. But you better make a few more just to be damn sure."

Omar registered a different kind of fright. "Followed?" He reached for the telephone that was cradled in the dashboard.

"Don't call anyone," Walter ordered. "Go north, then east over to Second. Use Second south and get me back to the rear door of the bank." He glanced over his shoulder. There were a couple of taxis hanging on the back bumper, but no sign of the following car. One of the cabs blasted its horn as Omar took a quick left without signaling. There were more angry horn blasts as they angled across traffic and turned into the next eastbound street. Omar backed off to a normal speed, and coasted to a stop at the Second Avenue traffic light.

"I am supposed to call immediately if anything suspicious happens," he said indignantly. "I really have to call."

"Just get me back to the office and then don't hang around. Keep driving. I'll phone you when I'm ready."

"But the procedure is . . ."

"For Christ's sake, Omar, I'll tell you what procedure is. Just do it!"

The driver looked as if his feelings were hurt.

Walter jumped out quickly and went directly to the security lock on the rear doors. He bent over the keypad as if entering his identity code, but kept an eye on the car until it had turned at the next corner. Then he stepped back out into the street and hailed a taxi.

He used the back door and the fire stairs to reach Angela's floor, searched through the wired-glass window to make sure the corridor was empty, and then dashed to her apartment door. He used his key to let himself in so that he wouldn't have to wait outside for the bell to be answered.

He crossed the living room to the bedroom door and tapped softly. "It's me. Please! I have to see you."

The door pulled open. Angela was slipping into her robe. She looked more angry than startled. "What are you doing here?" she demanded.

"I have to talk to you." He led her out to the living room sofa.

"Now?" She questioned. "I thought we agreed that this wasn't a very good idea."

"I know." He left her sitting on the sofa while he went to the kitchen liquor cabinet.

"You shouldn't have come here," she said when he returned with their drinks. "It's bad enough that moron suspects me. Now he'll think that we're working together."

"I'm so sorry," he began. "I never would have allowed them to subject you to that kind of treatment. But it never dawned on me that you would . . . involve yourself . . . in the investigation." He sat carefully on the edge of the sofa next to her, but made certain to keep a bit of distance between them. It was as if he were asking if he were still welcome.

She shook her head slowly. "They had no right. No right at all."

"Of course not. They're a bunch of damn fools." Walter's hand wandered over to touch her shoulder. He was relieved when she didn't pull away. "I should have thrown the whole bunch of them out. But I'm not thinking straight. Jesus, I keep thinking that we've blown it and wondering what they might be doing to Emily to get even. I've read things . . . like people being buried in a box and just left there. Or even worse, like . . ." He squeezed his eyes shut to lock out the ghastly images.

Angela took his face between her hands and brought it close to hers. She kissed his cheek softly and then rested against his shoulder. "I'm the one who should be apologizing, Walter. I was angry because my dignity was being abused. I should have been thinking about what you were suffering. It was selfish of me."

He hugged her reassuringly. "No. We're both upset. It's just too damn much to cope with." He jumped up and began to pace frantically. "I handled this wrong right from the beginning. I never should have tried to play it smart. I never should have gone to Andrew Hogan. I should have just collected the money and deposited it in the account, exactly the way they told me. If I had, Emily might be home now, safe . . ."

"You did what was right," Angela corrected. "You went to an expert. Someone who should have known how to handle it."

"He's a cop," Walter wailed. "I should have known that he'd act like a cop. That he'd try to catch the bastards instead of trying to save her."

"You can't blame yourself. You've tried twice to buy her freedom. It's Hogan and his goons who keep screwing things up. If anyone is responsible, it's he. Jesus, he couldn't have done any worse if he were trying to get her killed. The way Andrew Hogan has worked things out, you're going to get hurt no matter what happens."

His eyes flashed. What in hell was she saying?

"Well, just think about it," Angela said, putting aside her untouched drink. "He didn't go to the board the way he was supposed to. That would have lifted the entire burden off your neck. And yet he won't let you pay the ransom."

"He can't," Walter interjected. "He can't let me give away the bank's money."

"No, I understand that. He's just using the money to bait the trap for the kidnappers. Only he never catches anyone in his trap. The guy on the telephone never took the bait. And down in the Caymans, he arrested me instead of the person who was waiting at the airport."

Walter squinted, suspicious of her logic.

"Don't you see? If you don't pay the money, you lose your wife. And if you do, you lose your career. Andrew Hogan gets to drag you before the board and say, 'Look who I caught with his hand in the till.' "

His expression hardened. She was certainly right. Hogan had screwed things up right from the beginning.

"Walter, is it possible that Andrew has it in for you? Is there any reason why he'd want to destroy you?"

"Hogan? Of course not. We hardly even spoke to each other before all this happened." Then he shook his head. "He'd never be involved in a kidnapping."

"No! But is there any reason why he would use the kidnapping as a way to get back at you? Because everything he does seems to bury you deeper in your problems. He seems to be grinding you into the ground. Christ, he made you sit and watch while he and his bullies were working me over."

The idea was absurd. And yet, Hogan's plans kept backfiring. The kidnappers were never caught. Emily had not been freed. And no money had left the bank. He seemed to be running in circles, chasing after thugs who would probably fit comfortably into Andrew's circle of underworld associates. Certainly, Andrew wouldn't be a kidnapper. But would he enjoy watching Walter, or one of his senior executive associates, swing slowly in the wind? And would he be likely to throw one of them to the wolves just to raise his own stock with the bank's management? The thought wasn't beyond consideration. Andrew was a proud man who had enjoyed sterling success on the public payroll. Yet the senior executives had treated him like a night watchman. Walter couldn't help think that if he were in Andrew's place, he would relish a few moments of sweet revenge.

"I haven't told him anything about tomorrow."

Angela looked up quickly. "Tomorrow?"

"I was contacted again by the bastard who's holding Emily. He threatened to do horrible things to her and then told me I had one more chance to save her. I'm delivering the money tomorrow."

"Alone? Where?"

"It has to be alone. I'm not going to jeopardize Emily again. And I don't know where. He has my cell phone number. He told me to bring the money and just keep driving around the Paramus Mall. He'll contact me. Probably send me on a couple of wild-goose chases. Then he'll tell me where to leave the money."

Her eyes darkened with fear. "Walter, that could be dangerous. You have no experience dealing with this kind of person."

He tossed down the drink. "I've got to do it this way. It's what I was told. And Hogan doesn't know about it so he can't mess it up. I have no choice."

Walter took her into his arms and held her tight. "Please don't worry. I'll be all right. I shouldn't have told you anything about it." He kissed her forehead and then bolted out the front door and down the fire stairs. Twenty minutes later he was in his limousine, with Omar behind the wheel, driving downtown toward the tunnel. I shouldn't have told her about tomorrow, he berated himself as he stared blankly out into the traffic. It was then he realized that he hadn't told her about the previous scheme to pay Emily's ransom. Angela knew how the $100 million was going to be transferred and which bank it was going to. But how did she know when the transfer was going to take place? How did she know to be in Grand Cayman on the right day and to be across from the Folonari branch at precisely the right time?

Suddenly, Walter felt totally alone and completely exhausted. There was no one he could trust.

Amanda and Alex were waiting in the living room, she in jeans and a sweatshirt and he in his shirtsleeves, a print necktie tight up against a buttoned collar. He was taller than his father and more athletic, with a muscular neck and more of his weight in his shoulders. But there was no mistaking his lineage. He had his father's chiseled features and his hair was the same color, thinning in the same pattern. Walter went straight to his son and embraced him. "I didn't want to drag you into his," he said. "But I'm glad you're here with me."

"What have you heard? Is there any news about Mom?" he asked.

Walter nodded. "We're very hopeful. We're following some very good leads."

Alex pulled away. "You should have told me right away. You must have been going through hell."

"Especially with a detective following you," Amanda chimed in.

Walter looked at her and saw anger blazing in her eyes. When he glanced back at Alex he found less than the young man's usual admiration. "Oh, for Christ's sake. What the hell has she been telling you?" he asked in Alex's direction.

"Just the truth," Amanda said from her position on the sofa. "And I think it's time that we had a lot more of the truth. Like how long have you been cheating on Mother?"

"Amanda," Alex said, reprimanding his younger sister. "Take it easy." But when he looked at his father it was obvious that he was expecting an answer.

"I haven't been . . . cheating," Walter answered hesitantly. He was quibbling about her choice of words rather than the fact. "Your mother and I . . . have our differences . . ."

"Stop the bullshit!" Amanda shouted, jumping to her feet. She brandished a stack of papers that she had been holding behind her back. "She hired a detective. She knew all about you. You and your . . ." Amanda consulted the pages for the name that she made sound loathsome ". . . your Miss Angela Hilliard."

He wanted to throttle her. How dare she accuse her father! How dare she make Angela sound like some common streetwalker! He didn't owe her any explanations, her and that doped-up drifter she was living with. Who did she think she was, spouting moral indignation? But Alex seemed wounded. Amanda's accusations, which he had undoubtedly heard earlier, had taken on new impact in the presence of his father. He slumped into a soft chair as if he had been punched in the stomach. His hand was covering his eyes.

"Alex, I'm sorry she had you fly all the way across the country just to listen to this," Walter said.

Alex's eyes appeared above his hand. "Is it true?"

"No, no, it's not the way it sounds." He stepped around the coffee table and put his hand on his son's shoulder. "You have to understand. As you get older, your interests . . . change, mature. Mother and I were finding . . . other interests.

"You hypocrite!" Amanda snapped. "You called me a slut because I was living with Wayne. And then you're bedding down some bimbo!"

The veins in his temple began to pound. How could she equate her humping with that second-rate photographer to his relationship with Angela? But he didn't really care about her opinion. They had agreed years before not to like each other. It was Alex's admiration that he couldn't bear to lose. He dropped down to one knee so that he would be face-to-face with his son, who was still slumped in the chair.

"You have to understand. Things change. Your mother and I have been moving in different directions. I didn't have time to be involved in her sports . . . her activities. And she really has no interest in mine. You know how she hated it whenever I talked about the bank. And how she wouldn't even buy a new dress for a business affair."

"She loves her home . . . her family," Alex interrupted.

"That's not enough!" Walter's voice turned up in volume. "My responsibilities go far beyond my home and family. Your mother doesn't want any part of those responsibilities."

"So you need someone to polish your global image," Amanda said sarcastically.

"No," he answered to Alex. "This isn't about vanity. This is about partnership. I need someone who can share my interests . . . stand beside me in my new ventures. I'm not some clerk who comes home, demands his supper, and then squats in front of a television. I manage critical, global affairs. Your mother doesn't care about them."

"But to cheat on her . . ." Alex whispered in despair.

"That's not true. I simply met someone who was moving in my direction. Someone who could keep pace with me . . ."

"Someone younger?" Amanda asked.

"Yes, younger," he admitted, finally sparing his daughter a glance.

"Closer to my age than to yours?"

"Oh, I don't know. I suppose so."

"Attractive?"

His anger was beginning to boil again. "Yes, very attractive."

"Perfect?" Amanda persisted. "Flawless skin? A model's figure?"

"I said she's very attractive. But that's not important. What's important is our shared interests . . . her grasp of my problems . . . her ease and comfort with the important people I have to mingle with."

"Oh," Amanda said, pretending to understand. "So if she weighed three hundred pounds and had to shave her upper lip, you'd still be tossing Mom over for her."

His jaw locked in rage. Through clenched teeth he bit off every word of his response. "I . . . am risking . . . everything . . . even my life . . . to get your mother . . . back."

"Why? So you can walk out on her?" Amanda demanded. "So that her ghost won't be hovering over you while you and your little bimbo share . . . interests?"

He jumped to his feet. "I don't have to listen to this," he shouted. He started toward his daughter, both fists clenched in fury. It was only Alex's moving in between them that prevented physical violence. "Don't, Dad!" And then turning quickly to his sister, "That's enough, Amanda."

Walter backed away and Amanda settled back onto the sofa. Alex looked cautiously at both of them. "None of this is going to help Mother. Right now, she needs us all."

Walter gained control of himself. "I'm going to get her back," he promised them both.

Saturday

ANDREW HOGAN WOKE UP with a start at the sound of his telephone. He looked around, trying to orient himself, and realized that he was at home, in his den, still wearing his shirt and tie. He had dozed off in his recliner chair while staring at some witless late-night movie.

Andrew hadn't intended to sleep. The Emily Childs kidnapping was coming to a crisis. It was time for that final call offering one last chance to pay a ransom. Nobody walks away from $100 million just because the ransom payment was originally botched, he had assured Walter Childs. And the thug who had been dealing with Walter probably thought his $50,000 was nearly as much as $100 million. He would be even more apt to offer Walter "one more chance" to save his wife. Something should be happening and happening soon.

He keyed the remote to shut off the television and pushed himself out of the chair in the direction of the den telephone. He wasn't at all surprised when he heard Helen Restivo's voice. "It's me! I didn't wake you, did I?"

"Do you care if you woke me?"

"Not particularly."

"Then you probably have something important to tell me." Andrew carried the cordless phone with him into the kitchen. He could smell the fresh-brewed coffee that had been turned on by the timer. He thought he might implode if he didn't get to it quickly.

"Nothing much, except that we may have found our motive," Helen teased.

"Was I right? Emily knew she was about to get dumped?"

"As much as it pains me to say it, yes, you were right."

Andrew chuckled. "And she hired herself a lawyer?"

"Not that I can tell. But she did hire herself a detective. And he delivered a large number of telephotos."

"No shit?" Hogan couldn't hide his interest. "The usual of the sinful couple acting out the illustrations in a sex manual."

"Nothing that titillating. I guess Walter and Angela are too discreet to be seen together near the bedroom. But the private investigator did get establishing photos of Walter going in and out of Angela's building and then shots of Angela arriving and departing. There's a strong suggestion that Walter was paying frequent visits to his young protégée."

Andrew nearly scalded himself gulping down a mouthful of jet black Colombian. "Proves nothing. They might have been consulting on interest rates."

"The PI also showed Mrs. Childs close-ups of Angela on the street, jogging along the FDR, and a few shot through the window of her health club. Believe me, they aren't discussing interest rates. One look at Miss Hilliard was all the proof that Mrs. Childs needed."

Andrew sipped thoughtfully. "You saw the photos? The guy made extra sets?"

"Yes, I saw the photos. The one in the health club makes her look very healthy. But no, it wasn't an extra set. These were the original prints that he showed to Emily Childs."

"And she didn't take them home with her?"

"Curious, isn't it?" Helen responded, answering a question with a question. "The guy said she just set them back down on his desk, took out her checkbook, and paid in full."

"She didn't say anything. She didn't mention a lawyer?"

"What she said, and this is a direct quote from the investigator who claims to be quoting Mrs. Childs, was, 'That prick! He'll pay for this.' According to our man, she didn't get mad, but she sure looked like she was planning to get even."

"Nothing more?" Andrew asked.

"Just that the check cleared."

"Okay," Hogan concluded. "We have a motive. Emily wasn't going to go away quietly. Which meant that a settlement was going to cost Walter plenty and the nasty publicity was probably going to keep him out of the bank's biggest private office. So, he does what . . . ?" Hogan knew the answer but he wanted to hear it independently from her.

"So, he figures out how to get rid of her. He pays a few thugs to kidnap her and a few other losers to hold her. He runs this charade, winning himself all sorts of sympathy, not to mention the brownie points he's going to score with the directors. In the end, he calls the people keeping her, tells them the deal has collapsed, and orders them to kill her." The line went silent as Restivo waited for Hogan's critique.

"Sounds reasonable," Andrew finally allowed. "Now here's one for you. Emily leaves the private investigator's office, goes straight home, and waits for Walter. She confronts him the minute he walks in the door and Walter reacts the way any red-blooded American husband would act."

"He kills her," Helen suggested.

"No, of course not. He drops down to his knees and he grovels. He begs her forgiveness and then he goes back to Miss Hilliard and tells her that they can't see each other anymore. Isn't that the way it usually plays out with a mistress?"

"I wouldn't know," Helen teased.

"Only this isn't just your ordinary mistress. Miss Hilliard sees a fortune slipping through her fingers. Even worse, she knows there won't be much of a future for her at the bank once Mrs. Childs becomes Mrs. Chairman of the Board. So she arranges the kidnapping. And she wins either way. If Walter pays the ransom, she loses a husband but gains more money than the husband has. And if Walter doesn't pay the ransom, then Emily is killed, Walter becomes a bank hero and is immediately elected president, and they live happily ever after." He paused to let Helen think it over. "So how does it play?"

"I like it," she responded. "But I'll give you another one that is really off the wall. Suppose Mrs. Childs has herself kidnapped."

Hogan interrupted. "You're getting desperate, Officer Restivo."

"Look. The kidnappers dropped her off in a van where someone else was supposed to pick her up and stash her until the ransom is paid. But maybe there was no one else. Mrs. Childs unties herself, starts the van, and drives away. The ransom note is delivered and Walter hesitates. But there are more calls—from Mrs. Childs—threatening terrible things unless Walter pays. He may be willing to leave the woman, but he doesn't want her gang-raped and then cut to pieces. So he forwards the ransom. His career is ruined and she walks away with a hundred million dollars. Isn't that the kind of ending she might have had in mind when she said 'the prick is going to pay for this'?"

"That certainly is a unique interpretation," Andrew Hogan allowed. "Except for one fatal flaw."

"Which is?"

"Why in hell would Walter pay the ransom? He's trying to shed a wife at a cost of maybe ten million dollars in property settlements and alimony. And, quite unexpectedly, someone does him the favor of kidnapping her and threatening to kill her if a hundred million dollars in ransom isn't paid promptly. If I were Walter Childs, it would seem that the ransom note must have come from Santa Claus. She's gone; there is no property settlement or alimony. In fact, there may even be an insurance bonus. And his refusal to compromise the bank's interests, even for the life of his beloved wife, would just about assure him of the presidency. It's all too good to be true. The very last thing he would do would be to pay, which would leave the lady with absolutely nothing."

"Still," Helen argued, "she might know that he would never let her die. At least in the terrible way that's been threatened, probably by her."

Andrew thought. "I suppose, if she were absolutely certain . . ."

Restivo took the comment as Hogan's agreement. "Look, if it's true, then Mrs. Childs is the one who was waiting at the airport. She's sitting on the beach in Grand Cayman right now, composing a ransom note that gives Walter one more chance."

"You've been smoking the drapes," Andrew said.

"Authorize a few more dollars so that I can hire some people to look around in Grand Cayman. She won't be hard to find."

Andrew laughed. "Helen, your fee is already higher than the ransom would have been."

"Okay, okay, I'll handle this out of my own pocket. But if I find her down there, you pick up the expenses. Agreed?"

"Agreed. Only don't spend too much of your money. I'll bet anything that Mrs. Childs is nowhere near the Cayman Islands."

Emily listened to the footsteps over her head. Her keepers were up early, moving quickly with an obvious sense of purpose. Something was happening that was changing their routine.

The man had gone out the front door several times, each of his departures immediately followed by the sound of an overhead garage door rumbling open and minutes later, slamming shut. He seemed to be preparing the car for a trip.

Overhead, there was a steady flow of conversation, very different from the moping silence of other mornings. She tried to eavesdrop, but was able to catch only random, meaningless words. "It will work," she had heard

Mike say once in an angry tone that suggested Rita had doubted something he planned. "It's too risky," Rita had shouted a few moments later. At another point, her voice had risen above the murmur to demand, "Why are you taking a gun? Stop thinking like a hood and start using your brains. You don't need that." And most recently, "No way I'm going with you. If they get the both of us, who's going to spring you?"

She could feel her heart racing, keeping pace with her rising anxiety. Just the fact that the routine had changed was frightening. Her captivity was probably coming to an end and at this moment the only end she could envision was at the hands of the madman upstairs. In her imagination, the cargo that he was loading into his car consisted of a saw, ax, and shovel.

Get hold of yourself, she thought, trying to rally her courage. There were reasons to be hopeful. By now, Walter should have paid her ransom. If everything were going according to reason, then Rita and her husband should have been ordered to release her. Emily couldn't remember hearing the telephone ring, but it was possible that all the preparations she was hearing had to do with her release.

Then there was the money that Mike had demanded as part of the threats he made her record. Maybe Walter had paid him off. And maybe Rita and Mike, with their newly found fortune, were planning their own escape. It that case, they might decide to just leave her locked in the basement, planning to phone from some place on the road and tell Walter where she could be found.

Another consoling thought was that the rumble of the garage door had come from the other side of the wall, in the direction where she had seen the daylight between the ceiling rafters. That most likely meant that she would be escaping into a garage where she could easily open a door to the outside.

"Goddammit!" It was his voice, shouting his displeasure at something that had happened above. And then, "Where the fuck is it?" Just the sound of his voice blotted out all reasons for hope. Emily could clearly visualize the egotistical sneer and the depraved eyes that enjoyed the thought of her rape and mutilation. Setting her free would be a disappointment for him. He would much prefer to commit his ghastly crimes and then bury the evidence behind the garage.

Her worst fears returned when she heard footsteps shuffling toward the top of the stairs. The dead bolt flew open and then the footsteps started down.

"Your breakfast!"

Emily sighed with relief at the sight of the tray. "Thank you, I'm hungry."

Rita set a bowl of dry cereal, already awash with milk, on the folding table. Next to it, she put down a gas station mug of coffee. Wordlessly, she crossed to the bed and unlocked the shackles, not even glancing at the sprung fittings of the headboard.

"I'll come back in a few minutes," she said and went toward the stairs. Emily went into the bathroom.

But Rita was still there when she came out, standing at the foot of the steps, a pained expression on her face.

"Is something wrong?" Emily's antennae immediately picked up danger signals.

"No! Have your breakfast."

Emily crossed cautiously to the table and sat down at the bowl of cereal. But her eyes kept track of Rita, who wandered back into the room and sat on the edge of the bed. The frame creaked and the bed wobbled. It seemed impossible that she wouldn't notice the weakened headboard. But her mind was elsewhere.

"Did he really come on to you?"

Emily's eyes widened at the suddenness of the question.

"You know what I mean. Was he really under your nightgown?"

Her lips moved, but she couldn't make a sound. If she repeated what he had done, then Rita could explode into rage just as she had the first time that Emily accused Mike of fondling her. But if she denied it, then the woman would think she had made it all up. That would be another reason for her anger to flash.

"Mike sometimes acts like a punk," Rita went on. "He can be pretty physical with people that give him a hard time. Or even with people that try something with me. At a bar once, some jerk grabbed my ass as I was coming out of the ladies room. Mike threw the guy right through the plate glass window and out into the street." She smiled at the happy thought of how much he cared for her. "But he'd never attack a woman." Rita stiffened to show her indignation at even the thought of him being less than chivalrous. "Well, he did slap me around once when I pushed him too hard about being a punk. But a hour later he was crying on my knee, telling me how sorry he was. So I wouldn't expect him to give you a hard time. Especially when you're tied up and helpless."

"Maybe he was just trying to frighten me," Emily offered. "Just to get my voice on the ransom tape."

"I'll bet that's what it was," Rita said with feigned enthusiasm, as if she were trying to save face with Emily. "He's not sure how he should handle all this. Kidnapping isn't what we bargained for. We were just supposed to mind you. It was easy money and we weren't going to be hurting anyone."

"Then let me go," Emily said. "You could have twice as much money. And I'd be grateful to you. I'd never describe you to the police, or point you out, or testify. You'd have nothing to worry about."

Rita nodded. "That's the way I'd play it. Take the money and run. But Mike wants to see this through. I think he feels that this is the kind of thing that he can do better than me. So far we've made our way playing my game. Sophisticated scams where people pay for being greedy. This is his kind of game. He likes to feel that he's in charge."

"Please," Emily begged. "Help me."

Rita jumped up and started for the stairs. "You'll be all right,' she promised. "I won't let anything happen to you. And you don't have to worry about Mike. He's a real pussycat."

She was interrupted by the sound of a car engine grinding and then catching Emily's face snapped in the direction of the garage. "He's going out. He's going to meet your husband and collect the money. Then you'll have nothing to worry about," Rita explained. She ran up the steps and bolted the door behind her.

Emily stood slowly. She was alone and she was unchained. How far could she get before Rita came back down. Probably not even into the ceiling. And if she waited until after she came down for the breakfast tray, could she move quickly and silently enough to make her escape before the woman's next visit? She had to do something more than wait for the sick thug to return. And, yet, if she angered Rita, she would forfeit the only protection she had.

Should she make her move now? Or should she wait until night as she had been planning? Both choices were dangerous. The wrong choice would get her killed.

Alex watched silently as his father lifted the leather briefcase and laid it conspicuously across the backseat of his car. Then he pushed the tightly wrapped package of cash into the space on the floor behind the driver's seat.

"I'd like to make sure of the car phone," he mumbled as he slid in behind the wheel.

"I don't think you should be doing this," Alex repeated for the third time since they had sat together, toying with their breakfast.

Walter turned the phone on. "Would you dial it for me?" he asked as if he had never heard his son speak.

Alex went back into the kitchen where he lifted the telephone and keyed in the car phone's number. He listened to the ringing and then heard the beeping sound coming from the garage. His father's voice came on the phone. "Thanks. Thanks very much."

He looked at Amanda, who was still sitting at the breakfast table. "Don't leave it like this. He's putting his life on the line for her. He might get himself killed." Amanda turned her face away. Alex marched back into the garage.

"Dad, please don't do this. It could be very dangerous. You ought to turn the whole thing over to the police."

"They want the money," Walter answered. "They certainly don't want me." He started the engine and then pushed the button for the garage door.

Amanda came out from the kitchen. "Please, don't go. You've never done anything like this before."

He showed a wry smile. "I guess I never had to. But don't worry. Everything will be all right."

She put her hands on top of the open window as if she could keep the car from moving. "Dad . . . last night . . . I said some terrible things."

Walter patted his daughter's hands. "Let me do this now. We'll have plenty of time to talk everything out once your mother gets home."

They backed away from the car and watched it ease out of the garage and into the turning circle.

Walter drove slowly, taking meticulous care to observe every traffic regulation he could think of. He had worried all night about the things that might go wrong, and one of them was that he would be pulled over for passing a stop sign and that the policeman would find the money. In his grim scenario, he was sitting at the police station arguing with a desk sergeant while a madman was slitting Emily's throat.

He pulled onto the interstate that ran west to east, toward Manhattan, and fitted into the light, weekend traffic. Cars eased up on either side of his and he found himself shrinking into his seat as if to escape identification. It was absurd, of course. He had been much more conspicuous driving this route every morning as the lone passenger in the back of a gleaming limousine. But now it seemed that his mission was obvious. It seemed that everyone who passed him would know instantly that he was a man on his way to pay off a ransom.

Walter wasn't really afraid. Apprehensive, certainly, because he was dealing with a terrible unknown, and careful because the money on the floor behind him seemed like a bomb that could go off at the slightest jar. But it wasn't concern for his own safety that made him shrink low in the window. It was more that he felt like a criminal about to engage in a despicable act.

He had lived his whole life within the womb of the establishment. Always, it had been us and them. The "us" were the people that the country was truly intended for. Hard-working, dedicated, and fiscally responsible, they created wealth to the benefit of the entire community. They dressed properly, visited the dentist regularly, tried to understand the political issues, and voted in even the off-year elections. You met them at Sunday church services and Ivy League parents' weekends, at charity functions to benefit the downtrodden and at Republican Party luncheons. The "them" were the takers rather than the givers. Shiftless and unambitious, they counted on tenure, civil service rights, and labor unions to keep them in salaries far higher than their worth. They filled welfare rolls and jammed the lobbies of public clinics. When they gathered, it was generally to protest reductions in their civil rights and they inevitably littered the area. They were often darker in complexion, probably unshaven, and most likely Democrats. The best of them were pain-in-the-ass do-gooders. The worst were cutthroats and purse snatchers.

Walter rarely dealt with "them." He had, early in his career, developed a distaste for the consumer side of the business that provided home mortgages, auto loans, and other needs of the common people. He had embraced the investment side of the business, which was inevitably run and staffed by "us." Then he had moved up a class when he entered international monetary movements and found himself dealing with the deities of the business world. They were even more "us" because they had noble titles that proved they had always been "us."

Now he was moving downward to the level of the criminal class. He was acting like a common burglar, avoiding the police, averting his eyes as though he were standing in a lineup, driving stealthily to a clandestine rendezvous with an unsavory psychopath. He was handling the crudest form of money—cash. The televised murder and mayhem that always seemed so far off would be close enough to touch. During the next few hours, he would clearly be one of "them." Walter wasn't so much afraid as degraded. His self-esteem was in greater danger than his physical person.

He swung off the interstate onto the toll parkway and headed north. After a few miles, the road dissected a giant complex of stores that rambled through a mind-boggling panorama of color-coded parking lots. Every day, people got lost in the endless avenues of shops and found themselves searching for the YOU ARE HERE arrows on the backlighted maps. There were dozens of phone calls to security each night from people who couldn't find their cars and felt certain they had been stolen. At its heart, the mall was a labyrinth, the confusion intended to slow down the progress of shoppers and force them to pass more display windows. For the kidnapper's purpose, it was the perfect place to pick up a ransom. There were endless avenues of escape.

The car phone chirped and Walter switched it on instantly.

"Yes?"

The smooth voice demanded. "Where are you?"

"Heading north on the parkway."

"Okay. Get off at the first mall exit. Take a left under the parkway and then drive in from the first entrance off the access road."

"All right. Then what?"

"Then park as close to the side doors as you can get and stay in your car. I'll call you when I'm ready."

"I want to talk to my wife . . ." Walter started, but the phone went quiet. Then the connection was broken. "Christ!" He moved to the exit lane. He could see the skyline of the mall ahead and he wanted to be ready for the exit.

The parking lot wasn't crowded. The marked rows closest to the building were full and there was a steady rush of shoppers around the entrance doors. But there were acres of empty blacktop around the periphery, marked into neatly stenciled parking places. Walter slowed well short of the densely crowded cars and pulled to a stop between two marker lines. He felt conspicuously alone in the center of so much empty space. Hopefully, the exchange would take place in an alley or in the shadow of a building where his crime wouldn't be so apparent.

Time passed slowly; ten minutes that seemed like an hour. Then the phone rang again.

"Where are you?"

"In the parking lot."

"What space? Look at the signs. Everythin' is numbered."

He looked around in panic. "I don't see any signs."

"Look up. You're right under one."

Walter was shocked to realize that he was already under observation. He pressed his nose against the glass and saw the sign fastened near the top of one of the lighting poles. "Red lot, row CC," he said.

"What slot?"

For the first time, Walter saw that all the spaces were numbered. "One twenty-one."

There was a chuckle and then the slick voice saying, "Real good. You've got the system down. Now I want you to drive around the north side of the buildin', and pull into blue, JJ, one hundred."

"Fuck the games," Walter cursed. But he knew the reason. He would be driving out in the open, aimlessly. Anyone who was following him would be immediately visible. He went back to the periphery road, offering an unobstructed view from every angle. Then he circled the mall and navigated himself into the assigned parking area. He could see large glass doors looking out from the building, directly down his aisle. Then he noticed another set of doors, directly behind, that looked out into the red parking area he had just left. His man had to be in that building, where he could keep an eye on both sides. He had watched Walter pull in and then had been able to follow him when he traveled to the new location.

The phone beeped almost immediately. "Very good. Now I want you to keep driving around the building, like a roulette ball rolling around the numbers."

Walter snapped. "No! No more games. I have the money, I want to see . . ."

The phone died in his hand. He looked from the receiver toward the glass doors. There was no sign of his caller. He had an instant of panic wondering if his outburst had driven the bastard away. His heart seemed to stop with the realization that he might have blown the deal. But then he figured that the man must have still been watching him. He turned on the engine and began a counterclockwise circle around the enormous central mall.

His anxiety mounted as he completed the first cycle. He had passed all the close-in parking spaces and had received no word. There were signs pointing to auxiliary lots on the other side of the parkway, but he didn't think he should include them in his search. Emily's captor was somewhere within the buildings he was circling. He kept moving slowly, glancing every few seconds at the console to make sure that his cell phone was still turned on.

Walter was once again approaching the red area, which served the center of the complex through the main doors of one of the anchor stores. The phone sounded.

"Turn left in red CC. You got it!"

"Yes. I'm coming up to it. Turn left."

"Yeah. And then drive toward the front doors. I want you to get as close as you can and park in the first empty space that has parked cars on both sides."

"What number?" Walter asked as he turned his car into aisle CC.

"The closest empty one. But it has to be a single space with cars on both sides of it. Understood?"

Walter's temper was close to its boiling point. It would be hard to control when he found himself face-to-face with the sick son of a bitch. Every instinct would drive him toward murder, but he was ready to put up with whatever indignities were fired at him in order to assure Emily's safety.

He saw a single spot to his left. But was it the one closest to the front door? "Should I take this one?" he yelled toward the phone before realizing that the caller had long since hung up. He hesitated, then decided to try even farther up the aisle. It seemed like a dumb move, when each of the aisles proved to be packed solid. But then, ahead on the right, only a dozen spaces from the door, a small sedan backed out. Walter stopped, let the car pull clear, and then swung into the empty space.

The phone chirped immediately. "Okay, okay. Now get out of the car and take the leather case. Leave the package inside and leave all the doors unlocked."

"When do I see my wife?"

"Take the briefcase, get out of the car, and come inside the mall."

"I'm not getting out until I see her . . ."

"Then you won't be seein' her at all. I'm not lettin' her go until I'm sure I haven't been followed and I get to count all the money."

"I have to see her . . ."

"No way, pal. Either you walk through the front door carryin' that case within one minute or the deal is off. And the money better be in the car or you're going to get the first piece of her ass in tomorrow's mail. It's your call!" The voice was firm and defiant. Walter didn't think the man was bluffing. He climbed out, taking the briefcase with him. He did a final check to make sure the doors were unlocked and then he strode off purposefully toward the bank of glass doors.

Walter never noticed Mike, who was exiting from the farthest door just as the glass panel in the center slid open automatically for him. There was no reason to. Mike was just another blank face in the constant stream of shoppers, wearing a bland sweater under a baseball cap. He stayed close to a woman pushing a baby carriage as if he were part of the family.

Once he was inside, Walter's eyes began darting about, looking for a face that would fit the voice he had come to loathe. He thought he would recognize it the instant it came into view. But all he found was confusion. There were men of every conceivable size and shape, bobbing on a sea of hurrying women. They all looked lost and confused. There was not one menacing expression. He kept moving through the store, toward its back doors, which connected to the interior of the mall. He carried the briefcase out in front of him where he thought it would be more easily seen.

Mike walked up the CC aisle, his head down, his hands thrust into his trouser pockets. He kept his eyes centered so that he would seem to be uninterested in anything that was around him. But all his attention was on his peripheral vision. He was looking at each car he passed, checking to be sure that there wasn't anymore seated inside or crouched between cars. He walked by Walter's parked car as if it weren't even there, but in reality he searched very carefully to make sure that no one was loitering anywhere near it. He stopped near the end of the aisle, waited for a cluster of shoppers, and then joined in with them in walking back toward the stores. He took the cap off and slipped it under the edge of the sweater, then stood up tall and let his hands swing freely. The simple changes gave him a very different appearance.

Once again, he ignored the car as he passed, but carefully cased the area. His spirits were rising. No one had followed Walter's car into the mall or through its parking lot. And no one was near it now. The $50,000 was only a few seconds away.

Mike went back into the store and quickly spotted Walter, who was shifting from foot to foot near the main door, seemingly offering the case to everyone who walked by. Jerk, Mike thought to himself, sneering visibly. He lifted a windbreaker from a display rack and carried it to a cashier. He had already tried it on, so that he was able to wear it as soon as she had given him his change. A final glance back confirmed that Walter was still waiting to be contacted. He had stepped through the doorway and was looking up and down the inside mall, waiting for someone to approach.

In the new identity that the windbreaker provided, Mike went out into the parking area. He stood for a moment on the edge of the curb, straining to see if there was anyone else watching the aisle of cars. Satisfied that it was safe, he started down the CC aisle.

It should be a very simple pickup. His van was already parked in the aisle, only three spaces from where Walter had finally settled. He would just step to the back door of Walter's car, pull it open, and reach down for the package of cash. Then, only a few steps later, he would be driving away in his own van.

This time he didn't try to hide his interest in the parked cars. He looked carefully out over the sea of steel roofs, searching for a face that was looking back. As he neared the parking stall he bent low so that he could look into the windows for someone waiting nearby. There was nothing. Everything seemed normal. It was just as he planned. Walter Childs had been too terrified over what might happen to his wife to even think of involving the police. He had come to market like a little lamb, hoping that the ax stroke wouldn't hurt too much.

Mike moved past Walter's car until he was right in front of his own van. Then he turned quickly and strode back, turning into the narrow space between cars. He couldn't help but smile at the unlocked rear door and when he pulled it open, he saw the paper-wrapped package, exactly as he had imagined. He reached across the seat and had his fingers looped through the string.

"Freeze!"

The word was shouted from behind him.

Mike backed out of the car, leaving the package.

"Stay right there." The words came from a solid-looking man in a business suit who was approaching from the front of the car. All around him, Mike could hear car doors slamming, footsteps running, and voices shouting. He did an instant pan of the area. Another man was approaching from a car that was parked on the other side of the aisle. And there were two others converging on him, one from the direction of the stores, and the other from the very end of the row of parked cars. They had him surrounded!

He set his feet squarely and grasped the open door firmly as he watched the closest of the men approach from the front, moving between the cars. The instant he came into range, Mike swung the door with all his strength. The quick movement caught the man off guard and the sudden impact sent him sprawling. Mike slammed the door shut and then kicked out viciously, nailing the man squarely in the groin. Then he stepped over him, ducked between the cars, and bolted out into the adjacent parking aisle.

"Stop! Stay where you are!" The screams seemed to be coming from all around him. He raced toward the stores, putting two of the men behind him. The only one who was ahead was the man who had been coming up the aisle from the mall buildings and he would have to cut through two parking rows in order to cut Mike off.

He reached into his pocket as he ran, pulling out the snub-nosed revolver. Then he waved it toward the man who was attempting to intercept him.

"He's got a gun!" the pursuer screamed, and then he flung himself to the ground in the protected space between parked cars. Mike knew he was going to be the first through the doorway.

The parade of shoppers had been slow to react. Only a few heads had turned at the first order to freeze. Several more had stopped to look around when the shouting began. But women had begun to scream when Mike broke out from among the cars, running at top speed. They began to scatter the instant he had brandished the pistol.

As he ran, the shoppers dove away from him, women clutching their children to save them from the madness. The mob parted like the Red Sea, giving him a clear path to the front doors that slid open automatically. At the same time, the fleeing shoppers created barriers to the men in pursuit. People backing away from Mike collided with those giving chase. One of Helen Restivo's detectives tripped over a baby stroller and tumbled head over heels along the pavement. Another had to pull up abruptly to keep from running over an ancient woman who was shuffling behind her aluminum walker.

"Halt! Halt or I'll shoot!"

Mike didn't even bother looking back over his shoulder. Go ahead, fucker, he laughed to himself. Shoot up a shopping mall. Kill a couple a dozen brats. He was right. No shots followed the threat.

And then he was inside, looking at the terrified faces of shoppers who had heard the commotion outside and turned just in time to see the danger rushing toward them. Again they pulled away, leaving him a zigzag path between the clothing racks and the dummy displays. He ran like a halfback, cutting back and forth, finding the best path to the inside door. Directly ahead of him, Walter was turning back into the store from the mall corridor, still carrying the leather briefcase out in front of him.

Walter never made the connection. With the store exploding in screams and a man rushing toward him, he might have assumed that the commotion was connected to the ransom money he had left in the car. But he was expecting to be approached by Emily's kidnapper who would want everything kept quiet and inconspicuous. There was no reason why the ransom payment should turn into a riot, or why his contact should be running for his life. His immediate assumption was that he had wandered into a burglary, or that he was in the path of a shoplifter. Walter did what everyone else in the store was doing and dove to safety behind a display of slacks. He didn't even notice Mike's face when the man flashed by.

Another man ran through the parking lot door in full pursuit, slowing only to glance around and assure himself that the kidnapper had continued out into the center of the mall. He darted though the same aisle that Mike had created and then out into the main corridor.

The commotion told him instantly which way the fleeing suspect had gone. Heads were turned toward the central plaza of the mall that connected the walkways into the numerous shopping areas and served the escalators that climbed up into the higher floors. Dozens of storefronts surrounded the main plaza and together with the aisles, elevator banks, and ascending stairways they created an enormous bazaar. He charged ahead, yelling at the people he passed, "Where did he go? Where is he?" Faces looked back blankly. Voices called contradictory directions. The kidnapper might be right in front of him, perhaps only twenty paces away, but he had effectively vanished.

Another of Restivo's men raced out into the central aisle and followed the screamed confusion into the plaza. Together, the two men started down aisles and poked their heads into store after store. Then one of them found the dark blue windbreaker that Mike had just purchased lying abandoned under a resting bench. Their man had already changed his looks. There was every chance that he had escaped through their fingers.

Walter saw the light when Andrew Hogan and Helen Restivo came through the parking lot door and strolled through the store toward the mall. The man running must have been the kidnapper. The men in pursuit were working for Hogan. Somehow, they had followed him and then made their move to capture his contact. He followed Hogan and the woman toward the plaza where the frantic, troubled expressions of the pursuers confirmed his mounting fear. They had blown it again! The man who had threatened to hack Emily into pieces had made his escape. Now, there was nothing to stop him from making good on his threat.

"You son of a bitch! You bumbling son of a bitch!" Hogan turned to the voice and Walter dropped the briefcase so that he could aim a punch at Hogan's mouth. Andrew ducked and then wrapped a bear hug around Walter and dragged him out of the aisle.

"Take it easy, Walter. Take it easy," he consoled.

"You bastard. How did you get here? Why did you come? You've fucked up everything. You've killed her."

"He won't get away, Walter." Andrew kept repeating. "We've got the doors covered. There's no way he can get out of here."

Walter calmed enough to get control over his urge to kill Andrew Hogan. "Who told you. Who told you about the meeting?"

"We've got your phones covered," Hogan explained, still holding on to his bear hug. "We heard his threats and we were monitoring your car phone."

"Jesus Christ." Walter twisted out of Andrew's grip just as Helen Restivo ran up. "Someone thinks they saw him run out one of the plaza doors. It leads out to the yellow lot. My guys are on it!"

Walter yelled into Helen's face. "Like they were on it in Grand Cayman, you idiot." Then he turned back to Hogan. "There are thousands of people out there. You're never going to pick him out of the crowd."

"His car is probably parked near Walter's car," Hogan said to Helen.

"We got another guy out there," Helen answered. "There's a van that fits the description of the one that Emily was dropped into."

Walter couldn't keep his rage bottled up. He screamed at Helen, "His car could be anywhere. He could be in it already, driving back to wherever he's keeping her." Then he looked fiercely at Andrew. "And you know what he's planning to do once he gets there."

. . .

"He brought the cops," Mike kept repeating to himself. "The mother brought the cops." He had peeled off his jacket as soon as he turned into the center aisle, thrown it under the bench, and then walked into the plaza. Only a few of the people who had seen him run out of the store kept following him. To others, he had suddenly become a faceless part of the crowd. He had walked out one of the plaza doors and into the yellow parking lot just as the witness had described. But he walked along the side of the building and then back in through another door only a few seconds later. Once inside, he had picked a direction opposite from the one from which his pursuers had come, walked into the aisle, and then turned almost immediately into a sporting goods store. He was calmly examining sets of barbells while confusion rippled through the corridor outside.

After several minutes he left the store and continued away from the plaza. At the next bank of elevators, he rode up to the third floor. Then he strolled back past the central plaza and stepped into a music store. He spent half an hour playing records by artists he had never heard of and then took an escalator back into the plaza. As he walked out into the blue parking area, he knew that he had escaped.

Now that he wasn't afraid of capture, he could give full vent to his rage. The lying little bastard went to the cops, he repeated over and over to himself. He didn't come to pay the ransom. He came to be a hero! He heard himself say, "I'll fix his ass so he'll never forget it."

As he walked down the aisles of cars, he looked for a discarded clothing hanger and for a specific compact car model that he knew would be easy to steal. Minutes later, he was dropping a hooked wire hanger down beside the driver's window of a Ford Escort. In another few minutes, he was out on the parkway, headed back to the woman whose husband had taken him for a fool. "You're gonna pay," he kept mumbling. "Christ, but I'm going to make you pay."

Walter sat across from Andrew in a mall coffee shop. He had calmed down enough so that he could steady the cup if he held it in both hands. But he was still unable to form the words of a complete, logical thought.

"He just . . . took a car . . . ?" Walter mumbled in an intonation that made it a statement of wonder.

"We don't know that," Andrew said patiently. "There are probably a dozen cars stolen out of these lots every day. There's no reason why this one is connected with our man." The statistic was close to true, but was irrelevant to their situation. They both knew the instant that the stolen car was reported that Emily's captor had slipped out of their trap.

Walter's eyes stared blankly over the rim of his cup. He sipped the coffee without tasting it and heard Andrew Hogan's voice without understanding it. "Just walked out . . . and took a car . . . and drove away," he allowed. He shook his head slowly.

"Maybe," Andrew said. "There's a chance he's still inside. But I think it's obvious that Emily is being held somewhere in the area. We've alerted all the local police forces with a description of the car. Something is bound to turn up."

Walter suddenly exploded, hissing his words loudly enough to turn heads all around the coffee shop. "If you just let me pay the money. I wanted to pay the money."

"It wouldn't have done any good," Hogan answered more quietly. "He wouldn't have turned Emily loose. It isn't his call to make."

"You don't know that. You're guessing. You're gambling with her life."

"Walter, for God's sake. We know this guy is only minding her. It's not his operation. He was just trying to shake you down for a little money for himself."

"It was the only chance that Emily had left. You screwed up the major deal in the Caymans. And now you trampled all over this one."

"You're right," Hogan allowed glumly. "I shouldn't have tried to handle this on my own. I should have gone right to the chairman."

Walter had no sympathy for Andrew's misgivings. "She was right," he said quietly. "It couldn't have been worse if you wanted to destroy me." He looked up from his daze and focused clearly on Hogan. "Andrew, I want you to back away from this whole affair. Just leave me alone. If I get another chance, let me do what I think best."

Hogan thought and then nodded. "I'll keep looking, Walter. But I won't interfere with you. On Monday, we'll go to Hollcroft. I'll take full responsibility for the delay."

Helen charged into the coffee shop, looked around, and then darted between the tables until she was standing next to Hogan. "That van out in the parking lot. We ran the registration. It belongs to a woman named . . ." Helen stopped to consult a slip of paper she had pushed into her jacket pocket ". . . a woman named Rita Lipton."

Hogan nodded his approval but with no particular enthusiasm. They were looking for a man, not for a woman. And the van's only crime was that it had remained parked near the spot where Walter had been ordered to park.

"Here's what's interesting," Helen went on. "The address is only about ten minutes from your house, Walter."

Hogan's head snapped up, his grim expression suddenly enlivened. "Screw due process," he said to Restivo. "Break into the van and see what you can find."

She smiled. "It won't be hard. The damn thing isn't locked."

"What's she talking about?" Walter Childs asked, slowly recovering from his stupor.

"There's a van parked near your car that sort of fits the description of the one that your wife was left in. It's been there all day. It could be the one that our guy used to get here."

Walter's eyes were suddenly alert. "Whose is it? Do we know?"

"A lady named Rita Lipton. Does the name mean anything to you?"

Walter searched his memory, then shrugged his shoulders. "I don't think so. Maybe if I knew more about her."

Andrew Hogan snatched up the check. "You will in just a few minutes." Walter followed as Hogan rushed to the cashier.

Walter was sorry he had decided to drive himself. Andrew Hogan had tried to push him into the backseat of Helen Restivo's car for the journey. But once he realized that the address they were heading toward was only a few minutes from his home, it made sense for him to take his own car. Now he was sitting ramrod erect, his hands white-knuckled on the steering wheel, trying to keep up with Restivo and Hogan as they wove through traffic at better than eighty miles and hour.

He was doing his best to close the space. When Helen darted out to the fast lane, her headlights flashing to scatter the traffic ahead, Walter followed. But then, somewhere up the line, a car refused to give ground. Restivo rocketed into the middle lane, leaving Walter hung up on the outside. Then, well up ahead, Restivo's car snapped into the slow lane. About the time Walter found an opening and began to gain in the center lane, the car he was trying to follow bolted across the center lane and back into the high speed traffic that Walter had just left. Finally, he decided to take his eyes off Helen Restivo and simply drive as quickly as he could, making whatever lane changes were available. That gave him his best speed

174

and the chances of his racing past Helen and Andrew were too small to even consider.

He understood the urgency. The stolen car had been reported half an hour ago, which meant that, even if they were headed to the right house, the madman had at least half an hour to take out his frustrations on Emily. The thought of Emily suffering even a few minutes of his rage was more than Walter could bear.

But, still, he shouldn't be driving like this. The past week had overloaded his nervous system to the point where he could feel the connections overheating and flashing into flame. His brain was dealing with pain signals from nearly every corner of his body, creating a current overload that had squeezed his throat shut and set up trembles in his hands and fingers. It took all his concentration just to hold the car in a straight line. The high-G lane changes were pushing him to the edge of his physical endurance.

If it were the right van, then they had the name of the registered owner. But it wasn't certain that the van was anything more than legal transportation for an all-day shopper. And if the van had been stolen, then they might be racing toward nothing more dramatic than a woman who would be happy to get her car back. But, despite the odds, they had to act. None of them could stand another second of sitting in a coffee shop, waiting for reports from the local police, or the results of credit card checks to confirm that someone named Lipton had actually been shopping at the mall.

Up ahead, Walter saw the car zigzag to the right and then peel off into an exit lane. He checked his own spacing and then followed onto the access road. He knew the area well, his own home being just one exit farther and then a few miles to the north. But as they turned left over the highway and headed south, he was unsure of the immediate surroundings. This was a commercial area, sprinkled with light industry, that was outside the perimeter of his country club set. He had generally driven around it rather than through it.

Helen pulled up to the curb and Walter screeched to a stop behind her. When he walked up close to the two detectives, he was aghast to find each of them checking a pistol. "You wait right here," Andrew Hogan ordered. Walter nodded. There was nothing in his makeup that yearned for a gunfight.

He watched Helen dart across the street and move briskly down the other side. Andrew waited for a few moments and then began easing along the street on his side. Helen passed the target address, an attached wood-frame house, and then cut back across the street. As she was stepping up on the rotted wooden porch, Andrew was pressed flat against the building, where he could see through the window and spot whoever came to answer the door.

There was the sound of Helen's knocking and moments later, Walter saw the door open. Helen lingered a moment, apparently in conversation with someone inside. Andrew left his post by the ground floor window and came around to the porch where he joined her. The conversation went on for another minute, with Hogan taking out a pad and writing notes. Then the two detectives came down the steps and walked quickly toward their parked cars.

"We're late," Hogan said.

"He got away?" Childs demanded.

"No, moved out two weeks ago. Rita Lipton lived her for a few months. She moved out without saying where she was going."

"Christ," Walter cursed.

"Walter, that house belongs to a social services charity, the Urban Shelter. You remember that was the same outfit that your first messenger had worked for."

Walter tried to remember. The night when he had found the man waiting in his living room seemed a century ago.

"You were on the board of that outfit," Helen Restivo joined in. "That was the only link we could find between you and the messenger."

Walter nodded slowly. "That's right," he allowed. "Emily did volunteer work for the Urban Shelter. I was more of a figurehead than a worker."

"I want you to do something for me," Andrew said to Walter. "I want you to get together with your daughter. She's been searching through Emily's papers for the names of everyone connected with that group. Correspondence, membership lists, programs she was involved in. Go over the records with Amanda. Look for anything that rings a bell. Anything!"

Andrew looked incredulous. He thought that Amanda had been going through Emily's files simply to embarrass him. He had no idea that she was working with Andrew Hogan. "But Amanda isn't . . ." he started to argue.

"Do it, Walter. This is too much of a coincidence for me to swallow. First, the guy with the ransom note worked there. Then, the two guys who took her out of the shower were defended by the shelter. And now the one who comes to pick up the ransom was living in housing paid for by the shelter. That has to be the connection.

"Okay . . . okay," Walter agreed.

"Helen and I are going down to their offices to get someone to let us in. We want to see if anyone knows Rita Lipton. Maybe her new address is on file."

"That could take hours," Walter protested. "Isn't there some faster way to find her?"

"We'll try everything we can think of," Hogan assured. "And you do everything you can to find those records."

Mike stepped off the bus just a few streets from Rita's old house, the one that the agency had provided while she was working on his release from an assault charge, but he turned in the opposite direction to begin walking to his new address. They had moved the day that the down payment for "minding the lady" had appeared in his mailbox. Rita had known that the old house wouldn't work. They had needed a place with a sealed-off section if they were going to make the lady comfortable and still be damn sure that she wasn't going to get away. He had never figured that the more remote location would be a problem. They had Rita's van, which had been her home from time to time, and there was plenty of money for gasoline.

But now the van was gone, all because that son of a bitch had brought the cops back again. And he was walking because he didn't want to ditch the stolen car anywhere near his new home. His temper flared with each step he took. Instead of picking up the $50,000 he had been counting on, he had lost the van that he and Rita needed. He had to take the bus with all the damn deadbeats and now he had to *walk* like some kind of fucking drifter. It was all that bastard's fault. He had warned him not to call the cops. He had told him exactly what was going to happen to his wife's ass if he tried any of his dumb tricks.

Mike stumbled on pavement that was heaved up six inches above the curb level. "Son of a bitch," he snapped. His shoes were scuffed and covered with dust. His teeth began to grind and his fists tightened in a spasm of rage. He'd take a belt to the bitch. And he'd make a recording so that Walter Childs would hear every lash and the screams that would follow. Maybe he'd never see his wife again, but he'd know exactly how she died. He'd spend the rest of his life wishing he'd done what he was told. This was going to be one tape that the smart-ass son of a bitch was never goin' to be able to forget.

• • •

Walter stepped wearily into the kitchen where he found Amanda and Alex waiting anxiously. He simply shook his head slowly, his defeated expression all the information they needed. Amanda put her arms around him and hugged him. "It'll be all right," she whispered in his ear.

Over her shoulder, Walter spotted the courier package resting on the end table in the family room. He broke free from his daughter. "When did this come in?"

"This morning. It was in the mailbox," Alex answered.

Walter began ripping the tab. "You should have opened it," he said.

"But it was just something from your office," Amanda responded.

He paused for an instant. She was right. The sender's address was his own office. His was the name that had authorized the delivery. He pulled the envelope open and took out a sheet of paper. His dark expression brightened as he read:

Now you know what it feels like to screw up the one chance you had to rescue your wife. Her blood, and there will be blood, is on your hands.

Her death agony starts Monday morning at 9:00 A.M. your time unless our courier leaves the Fassen Bank, in Zurich, with $100 million at 9:00 A.M. Zurich time. If the money is safe in our hands at noon, Zurich, your wife will be set free at 9:00 A.M. New York time.

We are very close to you, and will know instantly if you inform your security officer or notify the police.

The note was signed with a routing number and bank account number.

Walter smiled as he read it and passed it to Alex. Amanda stepped close so that she could read over Alex's shoulder.

"These are the people who are behind your mother's kidnapping," Walter told his children. "These are the ones who have the power to order her set free."

"What about the people you were dealing with today?" Alex asked.

Walter remembered that the man who was actually holding Emily had fled from the shopping mall without his money. He could only hope that his threats of cutting her to pieces hadn't been real and that he could still save his wife. He had been given another chance. Despite all of Andrew Hogan's screw-ups, he still might come out ahead.

"Can you do this? Can you do what they're asking?" Amanda wanted to know.

Walter knew that there was still a chance that Hogan and his lady detective might be able to rescue Emily. "If I have to, I can do it," he answered.

Emily could feel her heart begin to pound the instant that Mike slammed the upstairs door. "We've been fucked over!" he screamed to Rita and then followed his greeting with a stream of obscenities. Emily could hear Rita trying to calm him down, reminding him that he had gotten away, and that he obviously hadn't been followed. Their voices dropped to a conversational level and Emily couldn't make out the words. But suddenly Rita became agitated.

"You left the car?" she asked in disbelief. "You left it right there in the mall?"

"I had no choice. That's where the police were staked out. I couldn't go back there."

"Oh, Jesus," she said. "Oh, Jesus."

Mike snapped at her. "Will you knock it off! It's only a car. I can get us another one tonight."

"Damm it, Mike! You and I are all over that car. Our prints are on the wheel and the door handles. My registration is in the glove compartment. Your court papers are probably still under the seat. Don't you understand? If they find that car, they find us."

There was a moment of silence and then Mike asked in a chastened voice, "Okay, so what do we do now?"

"We get our asses out of here."

"What about the bitch downstairs? What are we going to do with her?"

"Leave her where she is," Rita answered. "The best thing we can do is put a couple of time zones between her and us."

"No fucking way," Mike roared. "She can identify us."

Rita's response was sarcastically logical. "Honey, if they already have our fingerprints, my registration, and your court papers, how much do you think anything she tells them is going to add. They *know* who we are."

"Yeah, but none of that stuff counts as much as an eyewitness. And besides, I owe her. Her and her double-crossing husband. I promised him a piece of her and I always keep my promises."

"Don't be such a thug! Use your head! We've got things we have to do!"

"I'm not leaving her to pick me out of a lineup."

"Okay, okay! But first we've got to pick up a car and get ourselves some plane tickets." Their voices dropped off to a conspiratorial level.

Emily shuddered. She had played it wrong from the beginning. Now she realized that she should have broken out as soon as she had her chance. She had been too careful in working the headboard. It had taken much longer than it should. She had tried to handicap the risks, deciding to wait out the day and make her move when they were both asleep. But now they wouldn't be sleeping.

If they just left her behind, she could break free at her leisure. But she knew that before they left, she would have to face one more meeting with Mike. She could picture him standing over her, his eyes dancing with delight and his mouth pulled into a mocking sneer. There would be no point in begging. That was what the sadistic son of a bitch wanted. She began to plan how she was going to struggle with her arms chained above her head.

Bill Leary turned off the court lights and sauntered down the tiled hallway to the men's locker room, wiping his face with a sweat-soaked towel. The last of the club members had left and the day's schedule of lessons was over. Now came the demeaning part of his job when he was more janitor than tennis professional, responsible for shutting down the air conditioning, locking all the doors, and turning out all the lights.

He pushed the swinging door open and stopped short when he found the room in darkness. His hand slid along the inside wall feeling for the light switch. At that instant, a fist fired out of the darkness and exploded against the side of his face. Leary pitched sideways, crashing against one of the metal lockers and setting it vibrating like a snare drum. Then he dropped to the floor.

He never lost consciousness, so he felt the stabbing pain in his cheek and the rush of blood that flooded across his face. He was blinded by the flash when the lights were turned back on and took him a second to fill in the features of the shape that was standing above him. It was a young man in his mid-twenties, about Billy's size, and probably a gym rat judging by the oversize proportions of his arms and shoulders. He was wearing tan slacks and a striped dress shirt with the collar open and the sleeves turned up.

"What the fuck?" was the best he could manage. The side of his face was swelling already.

"Emily Childs sends her regards," the young man said, and then he aimed a soccer kick between Billy's splayed-out legs, directly into his groin. The pain sent streaks of color through his already clouded vision. He wanted to scream, but there was no air in his lungs. Billy rolled onto his side like a doomed ship getting ready to sink. It was a full minute before he could manage a sound. "Who are you?"

"Alex Childs. You've been blackmailing my mother."

It would be another minute before he could speak the words that would deny the charge. Instead, he shook his head.

Alex sat down comfortably on the bench above the writhing form. "I need some answers," he said, as if he were addressing a business meeting. He planted his foot firmly on Billy's neck. "I'm going to break some bones if I don't get them." He waited patiently until the pain dimmed a bit in the tennis coach's eyes. Then he asked, "Why was my mother paying you a thousand a week?"

"A week? Nothing like that," he answered between gasps.

"My sister went through my mother's papers. There's a check to you every week. Most of them are for a thousand dollars. What was she paying you for?"

"Tennis lessons," Billy said, each word dripping with pain.

Alex's foot got heavier. "Ten thousand dollars worth of tennis lessons? She'd have won Wimbledon." His voice became more threatening. "What did you have on her?"

"I swear. We were working a couple of hours every day."

"You're lying," Alex said. He began to stand up slowly. Leary could feel his tongue being squeezed. He waved his arm in surrender and Alex eased back on the pressure.

"Christ, let me talk," he said.

"That's why I'm here," Alex answered. "Just don't talk about a thousand dollars a week for tennis lessons."

Billy got a hand under his body and slowly raised himself to a sitting position. He picked up the towel and blotted the blood on his cheek. He tried to stand.

"Stay right there," Alex threatened.

"Christ, you broke my jaw. I have to get to the hospital."

"After we talk. After you tell me where my mother is?"

"I told the police. I have no idea. I was shocked when they told me she had been kidnapped."

"You were in her bedroom when she was taken."

"No! After! After she was taken. The place was a mess. She was already gone."

"What were you doing in her bedroom?"

Billy hesitated. He didn't want to say anything to anger his attacker. "We had . . . an appointment. She had just lost a match she should have won. She . . ."

"You're not going to say 'tennis lesson,' " Alex threatened.

Leary's eyes rolled hopelessly. "She wanted to win . . . she couldn't stand losing."

He looked suspicious, but he didn't react violently, so the tennis pro went on. "I got to the house and nobody was there. So I waited at the tennis court. When she didn't show up I thought something might have happened to her. I called into the house and when I didn't get an answer, I began looking around."

"In her bedroom?"

"Just upstairs. Her bedroom door was open and I could see there had been some kind of a struggle. I thought someone might have hurt her. But I couldn't find her. There was just blood and the place was in shambles."

"Why didn't you call the police?"

"I don't know. I guess I panicked. I thought I'd better get the hell out of there."

"Why, if you were just there to give her a tennis lesson?"

"You know. I mean, how would it look? Me in her bedroom?"

Alex's fist tightened. "It would look as if you came to pick up your blackmail check and she told you she wasn't going to be paying you anymore."

Billy was frantic. "What in hell would I be blackmailing her with?"

"I think you conned her into sleeping with you. Isn't that it?"

Leary thought quickly. Emily's son had put it into words. Maybe he wasn't totally offended by the idea. And he had to say something credible. Alex's knuckles were showing like cast iron through his skin. Billy nodded. "Yeah," he admitted. "We had a . . . relationship."

"And you were charging her a thousand a week to keep it quiet," Alex added instantly. "She knew if she didn't pay, you'd tell my father."

Billy shook his head. "Jesus, no. Nothing like that . . ."

"What did you have? Pictures? A recording?" Alex went on with his accusation as if Leary had never denied it. "She wanted them back and you had a fight?"

"She wasn't hiding it from your father," Billy suddenly shouted. "She was doing it to get even with your father." He cowered from the new round of blows that he had every right to expect. But it was Alex who seemed to have been suddenly punched in the gut. He took a step backward and settled slowly onto the bench like a balloon that was leaking air.

The tennis bum was telling the truth. Amanda had already shown him the proof that their father was cheating. He had read the detective's report and his father had not denied the evidence when they had confronted him. His eyes settled slowly on Leary. "And she was paying you . . ." There was loathing in his voice.

"It's not the way it sounds," Billy protested. "I *was* spending a lot of time on her tennis game. The other thing was something she just . . . wanted to happen." He could see that Alex was skeptical. "I guess she was paying me for more than just . . . tennis. I suppose I was good for her ego. She was being thrown over by her husband. She felt awful. Maybe she wanted to hear that she was still young and still beautiful." And then, as an afterthought, "She was young and beautiful. And spirited. I really liked her. I think I was good for her."

Alex was only half hearing. His father had another woman. But his mother wasn't going to step aside quietly. Christ, she was sleeping with a tennis player. She was going to get really ugly and make him look like a fool and he knew that was one thing that his father would never be able to tolerate. He would part with his money, but not with his self-image of being fully in control. He would never allow himself to be mocked. The only question was how far would he go to preserve his demanding self-respect. As far as getting rid of his own wife?

Walter sat at the home computer, checking through Emily's files and printing out all references and correspondence that had anything to do with the Urban Shelter. He read, with growing amazement, how deeply she was involved with the shelter's work for the indigent. She managed the legal defense fund that paid for investigators and lawyers to help poor people defend their legal rights. She was involved in soliciting contributions from supermarket chains for half a dozen soup kitchens and from building contractors for a habitat program that rehabilitated old homes. She ran a real estate service that found low-cost and subsidized housing for homeless families. He had assumed that the shelter was a conscience-soothing diversion for the wealthy ladies of the riding and golfing set. He had never realized that Emily didn't mind getting her hands dirty.

Amanda was going through printed records and files, sifting for the same type of evidence. But she was lingering over the investigative services that her mother had employed, remembering that one of them had taken on the private assignment of following her father. Walter brought her some new files that he had printed out and was annoyed to see her pouring over the evidence of his infidelity. He pulled the file out of her hand. "I don't think we have time for that right now!"

"How could you," Amanda snapped.

Walter made a show of summoning up all his patience. "When your mother gets home, she and I will have a long talk. And then, if it seems pertinent, one of us will try to explain to you how these things happen."

He was back to the computer when she answered, "These *things*? Is that what you call betraying her?"

He wheeled. "Damn you! I don't owe you any explanations. You lost your right to give morals lectures a long time ago."

"So did you," Amanda fired back. "But that didn't stop you from lecturing me. How in hell could you look down your nose at my lifestyle when you were humping some slut in the secretarial pool."

His hand flashed across her face. "Don't you say that. Don't you dare say that."

Her eyes flared angrily. Her fingertips went up and touched the red print on her cheek. "You pig!" she cursed.

His hand closed in a fist, but he was able to stop it in midair. He stood helplessly in front of her, his body trembling in rage. "I didn't care what you were doing," he said. "What I couldn't stand was the one you were doing it with."

"You didn't bother to know him. You just decided for yourself that he was no good."

Walter's hand fell to his side, but his fingers were still squeezed together. "What is he? A lowlife photographer?"

"He's an artist, and a damn fine one."

He relaxed into mocking laughter. "Oh, Jesus, an artist? Is that what they call shiftless womanizers these days? Maybe you mean a con artist. He's unemployed and living off you."

"You never came to his shows. You never once even looked at his work."

"I know all about his work, or I should say his lack of work."

The doorbell chimed. Amanda's response stayed on her lips. Walter was suddenly terribly embarrassed by his tirade. They looked at each other with apologies forming in their eyes. The bell chimed again. Walter walked silently around his daughter and went to the door, opening it in front of Andrew Hogan.

He carried a carton of records that he and Helen had taken out of the offices of the Urban Shelter, and began laying them out on the dining room table. "These are the pieces," he announced, "and they all fit together." He nodded to Amanda as she entered from the den, but kept arranging the files.

"Here's Thomas Beaty, who brought you the ransom note. He worked in the office a few days a week so he probably knew Emily by sight. Chances are he thought of her as just one of the volunteers and she probably didn't pay any particular attention to him. But someone knew both of them."

"Who?" Amanda interrupted.

Hogan opened some other files on the table. "Probably someone who also knew these two characters. They're the ones who carried your mother out of the house. What's significant is that Beaty filed a motion for these two creeps when they were arrested for a burglary not half a mile from here. So it looks as if someone knew all these people as well as Emily."

Walter and Amanda stared at the mug shots of the two minor felons. Walter shook his head. "I don't think I've ever seen either of them," Amanda said.

"How about these two?" Hogan asked. He dropped two grainy black-and-white photo prints on the table, one of a woman with straight black hair, the other of a man with closely cut black hair and a nicely trimmed moustache. "The lady is a small-time confidence hustler. One of her names, Rita Lipton, was on the van registration. She used the registration as her identification when she rented a subsidized house through the Urban Shelter. She needed an interview and a caseworker report. Mrs. Childs was the interviewer. The caseworker is a professional social worker who lives in Newark. We've got people looking for her right now."

Walter was concentrating on the image. "I've seen her. Where in hell have I seen her?"

"The bank?" Hogan asked.

Walter shook his head. "No, not the bank. But recently. Maybe not this woman but someone very much like her."

"Who's the man?" Amanda asked.

"A guy named Micklcievski. He skipped bail on an assault charge. The lady, here, guaranteed his bail. The bondsman is looking for both of them."

"The bar," Walter suddenly remembered. He jabbed his finger at Rita's picture. "She was the woman who was talking to your two men. I thought she might be working for you and that the two guys were my ransom contacts. The van belonged to her?"

Hogan nodded. "Yeah. And she was living in the house we went to. It looks like these are the two who are holding her. Obviously, they tried to make a little money on the side for themselves."

"Where are they?" Amanda demanded.

"Probably not too far from the house she was renting. The car that was stolen from the mall turned up only a mile from there. Helen Restivo is making photoprints of the two of them. Her guys will be on the street, looking for these two all over the neighborhood."

"And when we find them, we find my mother," Amanda realized in an optimistic voice.

"Right," Hogan answered. He exchanged a knowing glance with Walter Childs. Both of them knew that the longer it took, the less the chance of them finding Emily alive and in one piece.

Mike watched the Nissan SUV swing into the suburban parking lot and pick a space close to the platform entrance. The lot had been thinning out with the arrivals of trainloads of commuters and now the reverse flow of people headed for an evening in the city was in progress. Several cars had pulled in and been abandoned by couples who were now at the edge of the platform, leaning out in hope of finding the approaching train. A young couple jumped out of the sports utility vehicle, aimed their keys at the car, heard the reassuring chirp as the locks clicked, and then ran to the train platform. They were just in time to catch the last car of the city-bound express.

That was the car he wanted, but he waited to be sure that no latecomers came racing into the lot. Then he stepped casually out of the waiting room and walked to the van. He took an electronic device from his pocket, keyed it, and then let it swing in his hand. The device scrolled through the six-digit combinations available to keyless entry devices, broadcasting the signal for each numerical combination. In less than a minute, the SUV signaled, blinked its lights, and snapped up its door locks. Mike took a last glance around and opened the door.

The same number combination had simultaneously connected the car's engine control computer. All Mike had to do was release the hood latch, find the ignition wires, and make the same kind of connection that would have started any car before the advent of antitheft systems. He was driving the car out of the lot less than ten minutes after the train had pulled away from the station.

He allowed himself a single sigh of satisfaction, but it was instantly choked by the anger that was still gagging in his throat. The bastards had gotten the better of him. He had been way ahead when he set up the roadhouse for the meeting. It had been a dumb place for a payoff because it was easily watched and there was no convenient escape. But it had been a perfect place to find out if his mark had brought in the cops. His recording, he figured, had scared the lady's husband shitless. He would have bet anything that he would have come to the second rendezvous alone and ready to pay.

Even then he had everything figured out. He was going to make the exchange without ever being seen. And he had a hundred escape routes if anything went wrong. It was all perfect, except for the car. There had been an army of them and there had been no way to turn back. So now, instead of pocketing fifty thousand, he was involved in another brainless car heist. Instead of being on the top of the world, he and Rita were on the run.

He seethed when he thought of the self-satisfied son of a bitch who had cared more about his money than about his wife. Maybe he didn't believe the threats. Or maybe he had figured that he was smarter than anyone involved in a kidnapping and that he could get the bitch back, catch the kidnapper, and save himself fifty big ones in the process.

Well the smart-ass bastard had gambled and lost. He put up his lady as a bet that he was smarter than Mike. He had his moment when Mike was running for his life through mobs of screaming shoppers. But now it was his turn to pick up the chips. The lady was his and when he was through with her, the double-crossing little prick was going to know that he had lost big-time.

He turned onto the industrial street that their rented house shared with a row of light assembly factories, warehouses, and a few other run-down wood-frame boxes that were the last remnants of a residential neighborhood. He pulled past his overgrown driveway so that he could back the SUV up to the garage door. Then he lifted the door, backed the car under cover, and went around the house and in the front door.

"Got it," he told Rita. "A big four-wheeler."

"Gas?" she answered.

"Yeah, gas! What do you think?"

She was seated at the kitchen table, dressed in a smart, tailored suit, with straight dark hair hanging to her shoulders. There were a dozen credit cards spread out in front of her and a stack of driver's license forms. Mike stood behind her, glanced over her shoulder, and studied her work.

"What do you think?" Rita asked.

He whistled. "Great stuff. The guys I used to work for would want to keep you full-time. I don't know why you do anythin' else."

"Because I don't want to do anything full-time," she said without looking up from her work.

"Where are we goin'?" He asked.

"I thought maybe the West Coast. I'll go out to the airport as soon as I'm finished and book whatever I can get seats on. Whatever takes us the farthest away from here."

Mike couldn't hide his smile. He was going to be alone with the lady downstairs for a couple of hours. At least he'd get something for his trouble. And he'd make a recording that would tell her husband exactly how she had paid off his gambling debt.

"Get all our stuff together so we can pack the car as soon as I get back," Rita said.

"We leavin' tonight?" He was disappointed that he might not have time for his revenge.

"No, I won't be able to get us on anything until sometime tomorrow. Probably in the afternoon. But we want to be ready to pull out of here on a minute's notice. There's no way of knowing how close to us they're getting."

"Sure," he answered.

Rita picked up one of the credit cards and the matching driver's license she had just forged. "And for God's sake, Mike, forget about the lady downstairs. It's not her fault that we didn't get the money."

"We're not even goin' to get the second payment for holdin' her," he reminded Rita. "We'll be gone before we have a chance to collect."

She was walking toward the front door when she told him, "That's not her fault, either. The way you stay ahead in this game is by knowing when to cut your losses. Believe me, this is the time to cut. Nothing that happens to her is going to make us any richer."

Andrew Hogan's name carried weight with the State Troopers, but not enough to hold down Lieutenant Borelli's temper. "You're saying that a lady around here was kidnapped a week ago," the lieutenant said, "and you're just getting around to telling us about it."

"We had no choice," Helen Restivo explained. "We could have gotten her killed and maybe caused serious problems for a very important bank."

"So the former police commissioner of New York turns to you and your half-assed amateurs instead of the police. And then you guys run an investigation in my area without bothering to let me know."

"Don't you see. If this had gotten out . . ."

"Oh, that's it," the lieutenant interrupted. "Hogan figured a bunch of idiots breaking into office buildings, grabbing files without a court order, and interrogating innocent citizens would be more secure than a professional police force."

"I didn't mean that!" Helen snapped.

"I don't give a damn what you meant," Borelli screamed, "because you have to be too stupid to worry about. It's Andrew Hogan that pisses me off. He's a pro and he ought to know better. All I'm going to do with you is toss you in the lockup and then wait for Hogan to come and claim you."

"Dammit, do whatever you want with me." Helen was on her feet leaning across the desk. "But get your people out on the street. This lady is only a couple of blocks from here and she's going to get killed unless we find her."

Borelli's eyes blazed into hers and then dropped slowly to Helen's hands, which were resting on his desk. He noticed the space where two of her fingers used to be. Helen followed the state trooper's focus and instinctively pulled back the wounded hand. "I lost them making an arrest," she said as she settled back into her chair. "I used to be a cop."

His expression changed from anger to a curious respect. "Tell me again about this lady," he said.

Helen had been making slow, workmanlike progress. She had gotten the photographs—license-type mug shots—from friends in the New York City Police Department who had processed the fingerprints from the van. She had made photocopies, which were even less detailed that the originals, and had her people show them around the neighborhood of the house they had visited. She had gone to the local police to enlist their help.

Her problems had begun when the local police, who were ill equipped to investigate anything more than a lost dog, contacted the troopers for help. Borelli didn't like learning about felonies a week after they had been committed. Next, the business manager of the Urban Shelter had called the police to ask who authorized the search of his records. No one that Borelli could tell him about! Then, minutes later, one of her people had buttonholed a derelict in a doorway and shown him the photo of Rita. The derelict turned out to be a trooper who was on a surveillance assignment. Now Helen was about to be jailed in the local state police barracks and troopers were combing the neighborhood looking for the rest of her operatives.

"You should have come to me right from the start. Day one! The first time you heard about a kidnapping. Then we could have given you a hand. Now what am I supposed to do? Give you a hand breaking into some other offices? You want my help in hassling a few more private citizens?"

"There were very important reasons why we couldn't involve police . . ."

"More important than doing things legally," Borelli interrupted.

Helen slumped down in defeat. Lieutenant Borelli had all the questions and she didn't have any decent answers. Of course they should have gone to the police. Certainly they should have gotten search warrants. There was no acceptable explanation for apprehending citizens and trampling all over their rights.

"Lieutenant," she said softly, "take all the time you want to kick my ass around here. But we probably have only a few hours to save this lady . . . if she's not dead already."

For the first time since she had been brought into his office, the trooper seemed sympathetic.

"Those two photos," Helen continued, pointing to the copies that the troopers had taken from her, "are the people who are holding her. The lady owns the van that the victim was dumped into. The man is the one who drove it to the mall to pick up the ransom. They used to live three streets from here. We figure they're still in the neighborhood."

Borelli lifted the pictures from his desk. "These aren't very good."

"They're not even accurate," she told him. "The guy we chased through the parking lot didn't have a moustache. And the lady is a con artist. She probably has as many looks as she has names." Then she added, "The problem is that they're all we have."

Borelli picked up his phone and dialed an extension. "Get in touch with the photo lab," he ordered. "We're going to need a rush job. Super rush."

"My people?" Helen mouthed softly.

He nodded and then said into the phone, "And tell our cars to leave the freelancers alone for the time being. We can use all the help we can get."

He disconnected and then dialed another number. "Where's my call to Andrew Hogan?" he barked. Then his lips curled in disgust. "Of course he's not in his office. It's Saturday. Maybe you ought to try his house." There was another pause and then Borelli's eyes rolled to the ceiling. "Well now, you ought to be able to find his address. You're a detective, aren't you." He slammed the phone down, embarrassed that a fellow officer had witnessed the exchange.

Helen stood up long enough to write Andrew's cell phone number on Borelli's desk pad. "You can get him here," she said, and then added, "thanks for giving me another chance."

"Yeah," he said gruffly. "But it's the lady's chances that I'm worried about."

"Payback time!" Mike announced from the top of the stairs. He closed the door behind him and came down the basement steps slowly. "Your old man decided to keep his money and give you away instead. So, I guess you owe me fifty thousand big ones. How are you figurin' on working it off?" He was chuckling in anticipation of the terrified eyes that would greet him.

"No problem," Emily's voice fired back. "It'll only take a few seconds to give you all you can handle."

He stopped in midstride. The sneer disappeared from his curled lips. He bent down so that he could see into the room and make certain that she was still shackled to the bed. "Saucy little bitch," he said, striving to re-capture his usual bravado. "I'm goin' to take my time with you."

Emily laughed. "Take your time? Little boys like you don't know how to take their time. You better hurry before you lose it all down your leg."

His contemptuous cool melted in a blaze of anger. "Keep up the lip, lady. You're gonna get it good!"

"You're all talk, sonny. You haven't got anything!"

His face went red, his eyes narrowing to slits. "You shut your fuckin' mouth."

"Oh, I'm sorry. Is it over already? I hope it was good for you."

Mike screamed like a soldier leaping out of a trench. He flung himself on Emily, one hand on her throat, the other ripping at the top of her nightgown. His teeth flashed like sabers as they went for her breast.

Emily pulled a wooden rung out of the sprung headboard and whipped it like a forehand smash across the back of his head.

"Ahhh!" Mike's face came up from her body just in time to see Emily's two-handed backhand. It hit him squarely under the right eye. He tumbled backward from on top of her and had to grab the corner of the mattress to keep from rolling onto the floor.

Emily pulled her knees up and fired a kick into his throat, launching him over the back of the bed. She jumped up, part of the headboard still chained between her hands. Mike was still rolling on the floor, trying to get his balance while at the same instant trying to stem the flow of blood from his face. She raised her arms and shattered the headboard remnants across his back. Her swing had been awkward and she had not struck solidly. But it was enough to knock him flat on the floor. Emily ran around him and bolted for the stairs.

"You're dead meat," his agonized voice screamed behind her. She stole a glance back as she reached the steps. Mike had recovered to all fours and had already begun stumbling after her. When she was at the middle of the stairs, she heard him reach the first step. He was gaining, but that didn't matter. All she had to do was reach the door and close it in his face. Then she would have all the head start she needed.

Her hand was on the knob, twisting and pushing. But the door was heavy; a metal-covered fire door mandated by an obsolete building code. It moved slowly. Emily threw her weight against it and began squeezing through the opening as it widened. She was halfway through when Mike's hand caught the hem of her gown.

For an instant, they hung in balance. One more step and she would be able to throw her weight against the back of the door. Then, if she could just close the bolt, she could leave him holding the gown from the other side. But Emily couldn't plant the one more step that she needed. She was still in the space between the door and the jamb, and a fraction of an inch at a time she was being pulled backward.

She turned abruptly and punched with her fist, smashing her fingers against the top of his head. She slashed with the chain that hung from her wrist. She tried to kick, but the twisted gown bound her legs. And then Mike's other hand got a grip on her hair. Her fingers slipped off the doorknob.

She spun around and saw the rage in Mike's bloody face. And then she was flying. She was lifted off her feet and tossed like a rag doll down the well of the stairs. She hit two steps from the bottom and then she flipped forward, crashing against the painted cement floor.

"I'll kill you," Mike screamed as he charged down the stairs toward her. He twisted his fingers through her hair and dragged her to her feet. Emily slashed her fingernails across his face. He howled and then cracked a short, tight punch to the point of her chin. She felt her body go limp and tasted the nausea that she vaguely remembered from the drug. Then her world went black and vanished.

She had no sense of lost time. There was just his voice, which seemed to be echoing from the distance, screaming obscenities. But he couldn't be at a distance. She could feel his body pressing down on hers. His fingers were locked around her jaw, shaking her face from side to side. Light began to come back into her eyes and there was his face, soft and out of focus, yet distorted and grotesque.

She tried to push him off, but her arms wouldn't respond. She knew he was on top of her, his weight pinning her down. But that wasn't what suddenly terrified her. It was that her arms and shoulders had no feeling. They seemed disconnected from her brain. She thought she was paralyzed. "Oh God," she managed to gasp.

"You like it, don't ya! Tell me how much you like it, bitch."

Feeling was coming back into her body. She could feel a tingling in her fingertips.

He shook her face violently. "Tell me you like it!"

Then she realized what was happening. She was in the bed, her legs splayed apart, and he was pressing down between them. The nightgown was bunched up under her chin. She was being raped. "You love it, don't ya, bitch. It's what you've been wanting since you laid eyes on me."

Emily began to laugh.

He was ridiculous, trying to look suave when his eye was black and the side of his face was a smear of clown's rouge. His bouncing made him look more like some sort of dashboard ornament than like a lover writhing in passion.

He stopped moving when he heard laughter. "Tell me you like it!" he screamed into her face.

"I can do better by myself," Emily taunted.

His eyes went insane. "Oh yeah!" He bounded off her and nearly tripped over the trousers that were down across his knees. She was still laughing at the comedy he was creating as he pulled up his pants. "I'll take that fuckin' smile off your face."

When he turned back to her, Emily saw the flash of the blade that sprung out of his hand. Then he was behind her, twisting her face to one side. He pressed down on her temple with the heel of his hand, driving her head into the mattress. There was an instant when the blade felt ice cold. And then, miraculously, it turned white hot. A warm ooze flooded across her cheek and into the corner of her mouth. She tasted her own blood.

"Let's see you do that by yourself," he hissed. "Let's see what your old man thinks when he gets this in the mail."

Her hand moved. She reached up to touch her face and realized she couldn't find the top of her ear. The overpowering sickness came back and she drifted back into the peaceful blackness.

Angela bent over the wash basin, combing the brunette coloring through her blonde hair. Then she stood up straight and laughed out loud at the image peering through the steamed-up mirror. Even she couldn't be sure who she was.

As soon as Walter had left, she had gone into action. She spent a good part of the afternoon erasing all her computer records, reformatting her disks over the files, and then erasing every record from her hard drive. Next she cleaned her file drawers, feeding the pages into a portable shredder and then dumping the shreds into a garbage bag.

She packed carefully, selecting only essential clothes that would fit into one small overnight travel bag along with her jewelry box. The designer knockoffs and fashionable casuals that hung in her closet got only a brief, nostalgic glance. She could replace them with designer originals if she wanted.

Next, she had taken the scissors to her hair, raising the length up from her shoulders to her ears and thinning out the top. And then she had applied the hair coloring, working it down to the roots and rinsing it until the water in the wash basin ran clear. The results were hysterical. Her perfect face seemed suddenly too wide and the color of her eyes no longer seemed appropriate. Nothing worked with the wild hair that stood out from her scalp like fire-scorched grass.

Angela attacked with a curling brush and her hair dryer until she had a neat, if casually offbeat coiffeur. The new color, combined with an entirely different makeup palette, gave her a vastly different appearance. Walter could pass her in the bank lobby and would probably walk on for a few more steps before he made the connection. Andrew Hogan's Keystone Kops, who had met her only briefly, wouldn't recognize her at all.

The next step was the picture. She put her Polaroid camera on the edge of the kitchen counter, set the timer for ten seconds, and then ran around to look into the lens. By trial and error she finally got a photo of herself where her head was about the size of a postage stamp. She held the photo against the window, ruled the back, and then cut out a passport-size photo of the young brunette with short hair. This fit perfectly onto the first page of a Canadian passport just above the name Susan Schwartz. Angela slipped the passport into the outside pocket of her travel bag.

She gathered up her trash—the stained cloths, the empty hair coloring bottle and package, the paper towels that had wiped the basin, the film boxes and wrappers—and stuffed them into a paper bag. She added this to the sack of shredded files and carried them out to the incinerator drop chute.

The apartment had to have a lived-in look. Certainly, the full wardrobe of clothes, the cosmetics and toiletries still in the medicine cabinet, and the clothes in the hamper combined to give the impression that she was still living there, and would be back shortly. Now Angela added other touches. She filled two pots with soapy water and left them in the sink. In the refrigerator, she uncapped the milk jug and left a half stick of butter on a desert plate. She spread the *Times*, with the pages opened to the crossword puzzle, across her unmade bed. When she looked around for her final survey, she could hardly believe herself that this was the last time she would ever see the apartment.

Finally, she slipped on a denim jacket, added a colorful scarf at the neck, and threw the strap of her travel bag over her shoulder. She locked the door behind her and took the elevator down to the first floor. There, she shifted over to the fire stairs and let herself out the back door.

Angela went around the building, crossed the street, and walked past the front of her apartment building on the opposite side of the street. Helen Restivo's man was behind the wheel of a parked car directly across from her doorway. In the light of a streetlamp, she noticed him raise his glance as she approached, and run his eyes appreciatively over her full length. Then, as she reached the car, he turned away, resuming his vigil of the front door. The woman he was waiting for would never appear.

She walked to Park Avenue, crossed to the downtown side, and signaled to a passing taxi. "Kennedy Airport. International departures," she told the driver. He dropped the flag on his meter.

Walter's living room was like a funeral parlor, with the deceased there in spirit if not in person. He sat hunched on the edge of a soft chair, his head sunk down between his shoulders and his eyes fixed on the pattern in the oriental carpet. Amanda sat back into the cushions of the sofa, her attention focused on the blank surface of the ceiling. Alex had turned a straight-back chair around so that he could straddle the chair back and lean his folded arms across the top. His attention was fixed on the telephone, willing it to ring.

Their conversation consisted of random phrases, unrelated to one another, but all concerned with their wife and mother. "They've got their pictures," Walter had announced. "Somebody must be able to recognize them." Then, after a ten-minute silence, Amanda had contributed, "Mother is a very strong person. She'll come through this all right." Five more minutes had passed and then Alex had commented, "There must be some way they could keep us posted on their progress."

But while the conversation was sparse, the atmosphere was burdened with guilt. Walter could feel his son's moral indignation that his mother had been treated so shabbily by his father. Alex, who had been the reasonable arbitrator between Walter and Amanda, had returned from the tennis club firmly on Amanda's side. He hadn't questioned his mother's affair with the tennis pro. Rather, he had demanded of his father, "How could you have driven her into the arms of that creep?" His voice had been filled with censure and his eyes heavy with disgust.

Amanda could hardly bear the sight of him. She was immersed in the hypocrisy of her upbringing. Bad enough that her entire adult life had been condemned as shabby, purposeless, and immoral. Now she knew that the stinging, hurtful words had come from a figure of righteousness whose sins were far blacker than her own. Her father didn't disapprove of her sleeping around, he just wanted her to sleep with someone of his own class. To him, Wayne was a greater disgrace than either fornication or adultery. Her judgment was more offensive than her morals.

Walter was trying to keep his problems separated. He clung to Angela's words that their affair wasn't the cause of Emily's kidnapping. Even if that weren't true, his marital infidelity certainly couldn't be blamed for the gross threats of the madman who was holding her. When he had decided to go along with Hogan's plans for catching the kidnappers, he had assumed that Emily would be kept safe. How could he have known that a deranged felon would be willing to mutilate her for what he regarded as pocket change? Walter could almost believe that he wasn't responsible for his wife's predicament.

The exposure of his moral failings was another problem. He would have preferred to explain the changes in his life to his children positively and in good time. He knew how devastating it must be for them to have their father's philandering thrown into their faces, particularly at a time when their mother was in grave danger. But eventually he would have told them, and he had already taken their disappointment into account.

His status at the bank was still a different concern and one that had slipped beyond his control. If Hogan and his lady detective were able to find Emily within the next few hours, then his adherence to bank policy and his refusal to pay the ransom would be seen as extreme devotion to duty. He could order the brass plate with his name for the door of the chairman's suite. If Hogan didn't find her, then he would pay the bank's funds as ransom and leave with Angela for the life of a well-heeled exile from the banking industry.

But as he sat brooding under the watchful eyes of his children, it was difficult for him to keep the problems separate. It seemed that his whole world had come crashing down on his head; his wife brutalized, his children traumatized, and his self-worth minimized. His adulterous affair was the root cause of all his problems. He couldn't help wondering if Angela was suffering as much for their love as he was.

In all his self-loathing and self-pity he had completely forgotten that they were gathered for Emily's wake rather than his own. And then the telephone rang.

Alex was the first to the receiver, where he exchanged little more than a grunt with Andrew Hogan and handed the phone to his father. Walter nodded gravely as he listened, nodding encouragement to Amanda and

Alex who were hanging on his half of the conversation. "I see . . . I understand . . . let's hope so . . ." Then he asked Hogan to hang on for a second while he told them, "A convenience store clerk recognized them. He thinks he knows the area where they live. And a car was reported stolen from the train station. The owner thinks the man was waiting at the station. Andrew says they could find them at any moment."

"Sure," Amanda said sarcastically, turning away from her father. "Andrew couldn't find them when they were sitting in a bar that he had under surveillance." Alex went back to his straight-back chair.

"Andrew," Walter said. "I need you to pull your people off me." He listened for a few moments, his expression showing his displeasure. "I know what your responsibilities are. I also know that they don't include snooping into the affairs of senior bank officers." He listened for a full minute. Then he said, "No, it can't wait until Monday. On Monday, you can do whatever you want. I need your investigators out of my life now."

His angry voice had gotten Amanda and Alex's attention. They suddenly understood that their father was a suspect in their mother's kidnapping. They exchanged wide-eyed glances.

Walter's next remark was as much for their benefit as to persuade the bank's security officer. "Andrew, you have no idea what it's like to make a mistake with a woman you love and know you're going to live to regret it. If you can muster up an ounce of human feeling, I want a free hand for the next twenty-four hours."

He listened, nodded, and then said, "Thank you." When he turned back to his children he thought he saw a faint flickering of respect.

Sunday

EMILY'S FACE WAS GLUED to her pillow by a paste of dried blood. She lifted her head slowly, wondering why the pillowcase was pulling at her skin. Then she remembered the hot slash of the knife. She was about to scream at the image of horror she recalled, but she stopped the sound in her throat and instead prayed, Oh Jesus, oh sweet Jesus, what have I done?

She remembered that she had freed the crossbar of the headboard and had been able to slide the locked handcuffs off. She could have bolted into the ceiling and began her crawl to freedom. But they were still walking back and forth right over her head. They would certainly hear her pulling down the ceiling tiles. She had decided to wait until they went to bed.

Then she had heard Mike leave, banging the door angrily behind him. Maybe this was her chance. Maybe she should slam down one of the ceiling tiles and make a racket by knocking over the table and chair. That would bring Rita charging into the room. Emily was just as big as the other woman and probably a lot stronger. She would have the element of surprise working in her favor. She could overpower her jailer and then simply escape out the front door. But suppose Rita had a gun? Then there would be no struggle. All she would be able to do was watch helplessly while she was reshackled to something more durable than the bed frame. Maybe the water pipes under the bathroom sink. Then there would be no possibility of escape. Once again, she had made a terrible mistake in judgment. She had decided to wait.

Emily had realized the enormity of her mistake when Mike returned and Rita left the house. Now she was alone with the man who had promised to ravage and mutilate her. She had no doubt that he soon would be coming down the steps to deliver on at least part of his threats. That was when she had formulated her plan. Lie still. Pretend she was still tied to the bed. Do something to distract him so that he wouldn't notice that the chains were hanging freely. Then, when he got close, crack his skull with the bedpost and lock him in the basement.

It had been a good plan. It had come within one footstep of succeeding. But in the end, it had failed awfully. She had paid a terrible price.

Emily sat up slowly. Her jaw ached. Her ear was throbbing. Her knees and elbows were skinned from her fall down the stairs. She lifted each arm and kicked each leg to make sure that the muscles were still working. Lastly, she felt for her ear, and recoiled at the touch. It ended abruptly in a ridge of dried blood that was attached to her hair. There was a small mirror in the bathroom, but she was afraid to see how badly she was damaged. She had to keep focused on her escape.

She listened carefully. The house was completely quiet. There were no footsteps nor rumbles of water running through the pipes. Her keepers were asleep, probably two floors above her head.

She tied the torn corners of the nightgown into a knot, keeping the ripped neckline from falling down around her arms. The gown almost fit, giving her freedom to move. She folded the legs of the table, carried it into the bathroom, and set it up directly under the ceiling tile that she had been able to pop out so easily. Then she went back for the folding chair and used it like a step stool so that she could climb silently up onto the table.

When she raised her hands, the free ends of the shackles swung together, rattling like the rumble of an anchor chain. She paused with her hands over her head, listening for any response from upstairs, and then breathed in relief when there was none. You're panicking, she chastised herself. The sound had been hardly audible, amplified by her own fear. She looped the chains around her arms and then pulled the sleeves of the nightgown over them to keep them silent. The ceiling tile moved away easily.

She was staring into heavy darkness. Far ahead there was a faint trace of ambient light; probably a distant streetlight shining through the window that had illuminated her goal during the day. Emily waited a few seconds until her eyes adjusted enough for her to make out the edges of the rafters. She reached as far forward as she could and dragged herself up into the narrow channel. When her waist reached the edge of the ceiling opening, she let her weight settle on the top of the tiles. The suspended ceiling groaned under her, but she didn't sense that it was sagging. It was going to hold up.

She started forward, but the neck of the nightgown pulled her to an abrupt halt. When she pushed backward with her knees, she was pulling the gown back instead of forcing herself ahead. Emily lifted up and pulled the hem up to her thighs. The tiles were like sandpaper against the welts left by her fall.

In a matter of seconds, she was breathless. The space was much too small for her to get to her hands and knees. Instead, she had to twist her body completely just to edge her knee or elbow ahead a faction of an inch. The effort was exhausting, particularly in the hot, dead air that was trapped under the floor. She was able to twist her head back and catch a glimpse of the space that she had climbed through. It was only a few inches beyond her toes. It had taken all her effort to move just the length of her body.

She gulped down air and then pushed ahead. She tried to find a productive body rhythm. Press herself hard against the right rafter, advance her left knee and elbow until they were grinding against the splintery wood, and then roll to her left as she pushed forward with the knee and elbow. But there was no way she could find a pace. Her knees had to be fitted carefully over each of the ceiling frames. Otherwise, she would be cutting herself to shreds. The rafters were rough-hewn. Splinters gripped the fabric of the gown and stuck into her bare skin. Every movement had to be executed slowly and precisely. There was no way she could hurry, nor any alternative to the exhausting effort.

The light ahead seemed a bit brighter, perhaps because she was getting closer, but probably because her vision was acclimating to the environment. She could see the open rafters where the ceiling ended, giving her plenty of space to drop down into the other room. Just that flicker of encouragement was enough to keep her struggling forward.

There was a sudden roar, starting far off and tumbling toward her like an approaching train. Water was running in the drainpipes. One of them was awake and Emily tried to listen through the cascade for the sound of footsteps. There was an instant when all was quiet again. Then the floorboards directly above her head groaned.

She lay perfectly still, holding her breath as if even the slightest movement of air would give her away. Footsteps shuffled above her. The refrigerator door creaked as it swung open and then seemed to explode as it was slammed shut. There were more footsteps; his, she thought. In her mind, she plotted his route back and forth across the kitchen, tensing when he seemed to be moving in the direction of the basement door. If he came down the stairs, there would be no escape for her. He could beat her to either end of the tunnel in which she was now trapped and be waiting in rage when she finally lowered herself out of the ceiling.

The refrigerator creaked open again and once more there was the loud slam when it was closed. Footsteps sounded directly over her head and then diminished as he climbed back up the stairs. Emily let herself breathe normally for a few seconds. She blinked the perspiration out of her eyes. Then she wiggled ahead, gaining an inch at a time toward the faint light ahead. Her shoulders ached. The muscles in her legs were verging on spasm. She could feel fire where her skinned knees had been rubbed raw.

Slowly, painfully, she was approaching her goal and now she could begin to weigh the problems she would face when she reached the other room and the ceiling that was supporting her came to an end. She would enter the open space head first, with no room to turn herself around. That would mean dropping from the ceiling height to the floor with nothing to break her fall but her outstretched arms.

She thought of alternatives. Perhaps, when she reached the end, she could lift out the last ceiling tile. Then, if she could manage to cross the open space with just the framing for support, she would leave herself room to lower her feet and get herself turned around. Or maybe the top of the wall that framed out the space she was escaping would give her a handhold. Then she would have something to hang from while she dragged her feet out from the narrow space over the ceiling. She couldn't be sure what she would find, but just thinking of the possibilities was a distraction from her agonizingly slow passage. Emily figured that she had been in the ceiling for about half an hour and was still only halfway to her destination.

Again and again she paused, stretching the pain out of her limbs and gasping down swallows of the still, dusty air. At one point, she exploded with a sneezing fit and then lay absolutely motionless while she listened to hear if her keepers had been aroused. At last, her outstretched fingers locked over the framing that held the last tile in place. She was able to drag her head out into the open.

She was peering down into a small room, bounded on one side by the studs of her framed-out prison and on two other sides by concrete walls that she took to be the foundation walls. The fourth side was a metal fire door.

Directly below her was a small heating unit. Hot water pipes rose from its boiler and disappeared through the flooring above. Directly across from her was the source of the sunlight she had seen during the day and now the hazy moonlight that had been her goal for the past hour. A small window, high on the wall, opened out to a window well. It looked to be about two foot wide, and maybe eighteen inches deep; plenty of room for her to wiggle through if it could be opened and if she could find something to stand on so that she could raise herself up to the sill.

She stretched out to the heating pipe and found it warm but not too hot to touch. Clutching it in both hands, she dragged her body across the last ceiling frame. She dropped one leg and then let the other slip off the edge. Her body cartwheeled, tearing her hands from the pipe and sending her crashing down to the floor. He legs buckled and she sprawled out onto her back. She lay still for a moment, taking inventory of her pain. Then she smiled. A nasty fall, but not much worse than many of the dives she had taken on the tennis court. Nothing was broken and she had escaped from her cell.

Emily eased to her feet. She listened to make sure that the sound of her fall had gone unnoticed. Then she went to the door and gently grasped the knob. But it wouldn't turn. The door was locked from the other side.

She bent low and looked for the locking mechanism in the minute crack between the door and the frame. Then she dropped down to her raw knees to look under the door. But there was nothing to see. There was no trace of light from the other side. The lock seemed heavy. She wouldn't be able to wiggle the door open.

She felt herself beginning to tremble and had to struggle to get hold of her nerves. Then she waved her arms through the darkness until she made contact with a pull cord that was hanging from an overhead bulb. The light would certainly shine through the window and, even with the well, would be visible from outside. But her jailers were probably still asleep. And even if one of them were awake, the odds were that their bedroom would be on a different side of the house. Emily had to know exactly where she was and what she had to work with. She pulled the string and light flooded the room.

It was a furnace room, accessed from outside by the locked door that probably led to the garage. There was the small, squatting furnace and a tall, thin water heater, surrounded by a maze of cross-connected copper pipes. An oil line came out of the concrete floor and bent into the face of the burner. A round, sheet metal flue disappeared through the wall a few feet over the door. Other than that, the room was empty. There was nothing she could use to pry at the door jam. No tools that she might use to knock the bolts out of the door hinges. Worse, there was nothing that she could climb on. No workbench, nor cartons, and certainly not a ladder. When she went to the window, she could just manage to curl her fingertips over the sill. With such a weak handhold, Emily couldn't even lift her toes from the floor.

She spent the next fifteen minutes in a frantic search for things that she might put to use. She tugged on the pipes to see if a section could be pulled free. She tried to lift the small firebox door from the boiler. She even tried to tip the hot water heater so that she could free one of the bricks on which it rested. But everything was secure.

Emily stood in the middle of the barren room, battered, barefoot and clad only in the ripped nightgown. She had been clawing her way forward for more than half an hour and yet she was less than twenty feet from the spot where her broken bed stood. She had escaped her prison cell only to lock herself in an another cell. She had freed herself from her tormentor, but all she had really done was given him a new reason for his terrifying anger. She felt herself choking on her own frustration.

One of the handcuffs dropped down from under the sleeve of her gown. Emily stared dumbly at the eighteen-inch length of chain with the closed manacle hanging from its end. She tugged at the other sleeve, freeing the second chain. Her eyes scanned the heavy metal extensions of her arm and she grasped the chains just below the cuffs that fastened them to her wrists. A weary smile crossed her lips and then she pulled the string to douse the light that was shining out into the window well. She wasn't beaten yet.

Andrew Hogan caught up with Helen Restivo at an all-night diner, where she was having the standard field breakfast of a doughnut and a cup of coffee.

"Just the coffee," he told the waitress as he slid into the booth.

"Smart call," Helen told him as she pushed her partly eaten doughnut away. "They get worse with the years."

She filled him in on the street activity. The State Troopers were doing the most efficient thing by talking with all the street toughs and lowlifes who worked the neighborhood. It made sense that any newcomers would be thoroughly cased as potential burglary victims or as targets for pension check and social security rip-offs. Someone must have noticed them.

Her hirelings were doing the gumshoe work, showing photographs to taxi drivers, gas station attendants, and convenience store managers. The police photo lab had printed up shots of the two that had been arbitrarily retouched. Rita appeared with hair of varying lengths and shades while Mike was in both clean-shaven and bearded versions. It was the clean-shaven Mike, without the moustache, that the owner of the stolen car had recognized. Two people had identified shorthaired versions of Rita.

"We're going door to door selling magazine subscriptions," Helen reported. "I feel as if we're standing right on top of them. It's amazing that we haven't had a hit by now."

"What about the troopers?" Andrew asked as a cup was set in front of him.

"Nothing at all," she answered. "Apparently our couple are experienced enough not to make waves in a community. As far as the local scum knows, they don't even exist."

He glanced at his watch. "Almost six," he mumbled absently. Then he turned to Helen. "So what do you think?"

"I don't want to be grim."

Andrew nodded. "That's what I think, too. She has to be dead by now. And to tell you the truth, I feel more than a little guilty."

Helen seemed surprised. Andrew Hogan wasn't the kind of policeman who let himself get emotionally involved with anyone. In his world, both the victims and the criminals were simply data. With all the suffering he dealt with, indifference was the only way to survive.

He noticed her interest. "I've been thinking that if I had left Walter Childs alone, he might well have saved her. He had two chances to pay the ransom. Either one might have brought her. I screwed up both of them."

"We can't always succeed, but we have to always try," she quoted from one of the inspirational speeches he used to give to the troops.

"Mindless idealism," he answered.

"Besides, if we're going to start blaming ourselves, then I have to come in for a share," Helen told him. "It was my team that missed whoever was waiting in the airport at Grand Cayman. And it was my people who lost the guy in the shopping mall. I'd say that I was more to blame than you."

"Okay," Andrew agreed.

"Backstabbing son of a bitch," Helen accused. They both laughed. The waitress poured seconds on the coffee and picked up the remnants of Helen's doughnut.

"It's not that I screwed up," Hogan went on. "It's that maybe I didn't care enough about the consequences."

" 'You can't let yourself care.' You must have said that a thousand times."

"So maybe I was wrong a thousand times."

Helen's expression was puzzled. "What's with you?"

He shook his head. "Nothing important. But I want you to pull your people off Walter Childs."

"What? You know what he might try to do."

"Maybe he will. It's his wife."

"Probably he will, and it's the bank's money. You have to be kidding."

His expression showed that he wasn't. "Right away. Get in touch with whoever you have watching the Childs house and tell him to take the rest of the day off."

She pushed her cup away and took the cell phone out of her purse. "Andrew, why are you doing this?"

He turned his hands up in a gesture of ignorance. "Walter said that I never made a mistake with a woman I loved and had to live my life regretting it. I guess I'm beginning to understand that something like that would be awful."

Helen shook her head slowly. "Why would you listen to the philosophy of Walter Childs? He's a heartless bastard. Even if he gets his wife back, he's going to dump her for this year's model. For all we know, he's going to pay the hundred million to himself."

"Indulge me," he said, pointing to her telephone. "Make the call."

She was angry as she dialed. "Maybe you're letting him send the bank's money to that tennis stud. He'll never get his wife back."

Andrew gestured again toward the phone.

"Or to Mitchell whatever-his-name-is. He gets a hundred million he doesn't need. And you get canned in disgrace." Helen heard the voice of the man she was calling. She put her hand over the phone. "Please, Andrew. Don't do this. You're putting your own neck in a noose to ease Walter Childs's conscience. For God's sake, he doesn't deserve it. He's been screwing young ladies who can't afford to say no."

Hogan pointed impatiently toward the phone. "I'm not worried about his conscience. I'm thinking about my own."

Helen shook her head in despair and gave the order. She had to repeat it before her man really believed what she was asking.

He paid the bill and then walked her to her car. She was going back to ringing doorbells. He was headed to the State Trooper barracks, hoping that the professional police had turned up something. He held her door open and then bent through the window.

"Helen, you knew what I meant, didn't you?"

She didn't answer.

"When I said I had never made a mistake with a woman and lived to regret it? Because it's not true. I did make a mistake with you."

Helen made a point of looking directly into his eyes. "The answer is still no, Andrew. There's no way I'm ever going to get tied up with someone who feels responsible for me."

The automatic window closed in his face and the car pulled away.

Walter was in a daze, numbed by the horrors of the past week. It was not that he had forgotten the miscalculations and blunders that he had made in his dealings with Emily's jailer, nor that he could block out the thought of the pain he had probably caused her. It was simply a case of overload. There were too many tragedies for him to deal with rationally. So many of the structures that supported his version of reality had been undermined that he felt like the pathetic victim in a bad dream. He had lost control of his fate. All he could do was hope that he survived until the sunlight woke him in the morning. And then he would go on from there.

His family was finished. He had killed his wife and even if she managed to survive her ordeal, she would never forgive him. His children despised him. Somehow, he had nourished the hope that he could maintain a civil relationship with his old life even as he started a new one. But now he understood that could never be.

But even his new life was in jeopardy. He had broken faith with Angela, doubting her explanation of the events in Grand Cayman. And, if she were lying, then it was certain that she had broken faith with him. He loved her as much as ever, but he was no longer certain that she really loved him.

His career was in ruins. The chairman would already have good reason to doubt his judgment. And once he reached his office, there would be ample evidence to doubt his honesty. He was going to have to learn to live without the big office that he had coveted.

Walter drove out of the tunnel onto the West Side streets, headed uptown, and then cut across Central Park. The park road was strangely empty and the footpaths inviting to the Sunday morning joggers. The air was still, the grass tinted to a fresh spring green, and there were buds on the flowering trees. For a few minutes, there was beauty in Walter's dismal world and he couldn't help thinking how hopeful his life had seemed only a few days before. All he could do was salvage what was left. In a few minutes, he would collect the ransom from InterBank and pay it into the private account in Zurich. Maybe this would save Emily. Maybe it would save him. He was determined that this time there would be no tricks. This time he would be calling the shots, not Andrew Hogan.

He had thought over and over again of Angela's comment that Hogan couldn't possibly be causing more problems if he were trying. "Is there any reason why he'd want to destroy you?" she had asked. Any number of reasons, Walter had decided. He could count a dozen slights that he had inflicted on the former police commissioner without stretching his memory. Petty things, certainly. Correspondence ignored. Changes to procedure made without consulting Andrew's department. Greetings in the elevator that were condescending rather than sincere. Hogan was a proud man who had reached the pinnacle of his career. Even the most accidental slights from the princes of banking could seem like expressions of disdain for his humble beginnings.

But none of this would justify his placing an innocent woman in danger. And that was what Angela had implied. She thought that Hogan was impeding Emily's rescue just to keep Walter swinging in the wind. Unless they could find some other way to free Emily, there was no question that Walter would have to pay the ransom. And that, Hogan knew as well as anyone, would be the end of the Walter's banking career.

He parked his car, walked to the bank's main doors, and signed in with the security guards. The overhead lights were on throughout the executive floor, acknowledging that global banking had become a seven-day affair. Walter walked past Karl Elder's suite of offices where two of the secretaries were at their desks, jumping at each command that boomed through his open inner door. Walter walked quietly by, trying to pass unnoticed. Karl always had time for long stories about his global affairs, boring at best and infuriating when there was work to be done. There was no time for stories now.

He was relieved that none of his staff had come in. Certainly, once he closed his door no one would bother him. But he was about to violate the trust of all his associates and he knew it would be easier if they were nowhere in sight. He slipped his jacket off and threw it at the sofa. Then he pulled down his tie, opened his shirt collar, and rolled his chair up to his computer terminal. At the touch of a key, his monitor lit up and after a few dialogue exchanges with the security menu, he typed in his personal authorization code. There were only eight code numbers that opened every door in the InterBank local area network, giving complete access to every file in the bank's information vaults. Walter's was one of them.

In rapid sequence, he opened the accounts in which he had parked the bank's funds, transferring their balances into a single account. With each transaction, the amount in the designated account rose, until it finally flashed $100,000,000.00. In effect, he had packed the entire ransom into a single bag.

The "bag" was set down in a corner of the screen while a new series of communications began. Walter logged onto a high-speed data link that the bank owned, actually a fiber path to an earth station in Atlanta, and an uplink to an equatorial satellite that was in a parking orbit off the coast of Brazil. The satellite's footprint covered the eastern two thirds of the United States, the northern half of Latin America, the North Atlantic, and Western Europe. One of Fassen Bank's rooftop antennas was aimed directly at it.

Walter typed in the routing code that would link his account with the target account in Fassen Bank. Once again, the system demanded a code number, this one a special authorization required before any funds beyond a threshold amount could leave InterBank. Walter responded with a new number, generated by his secret cipher, which appeared as asterisks on the computer screens. He raised the ransom "bag" into the space reserved for the transaction source and then ordered the system to send.

Walter sat for a full minute, staring at the face of the screen. With a few keystrokes he had just changed his life forever and the enormity of the event was weighing on him. Technically, he was a thief. He had just robbed a bank. Not embezzled, or defrauded, or misappropriated, nor any of the gentle words used to describe white-collar crime. But *robbed*, just as if he had gone up to the teller's window with a note and pointed the barrel of a shotgun through the glass. He had gone to the vaults, tossed the money into a sack, and carried it out of the bank building.

There was no doubt that he would be caught and probably no later than noon the following day. Karl Elder would notice the large transfer and come to ask for the details. If InterBank had just enriched Fassen Bank, he would want to take full credit for his generosity. Mitchell Price would find the transaction printed out as an *exception* to one of his computer security procedures. He would want a full explanation. Sometime before noon, there would be a call from the president's office. "Mr. Hollcroft wonders if you could spare him a moment?" the executive secretary's voice would ask politely. And then, after the usual small talk about their weekends, Jack Hollcroft would say, "Walter, you sent money to Fassen yesterday and I'll be damned if I can remember what's involved."

There would be inescapable guilt, but there would also be a measure of understanding. "It must have been a terrible ordeal, Walter. And how is Emily? Home? Feeling well? Nothing is more important than her welfare."

But, of course, there was policy. An institution like InterBank had to follow procedures. That was the final defense for any mistake or transgression. Not following procedure eliminated any ambiguity that surrounded a misdeed. It was proof of guilt.

There would be nothing personal. No hard feelings and certainly no cries of anguish. After all, the damn money was insured by policies that were spread across the entire global reinsurance industry. But there would be no doubt that Walter had violated policy, which was the ultimate example of poor judgment. His was certainly not the hand that the directors would want on the tiller.

Walter started to button his shirt collar and then realized that proper bank attire was no longer important. He left it open and instead of pulling up the knot in his tie, he dragged it down and slipped it over his head. The lobby security guards couldn't believe their eyes when he stepped out of the elevator in what appeared to be a sports shirt, his jacket folded casually over his arm.

He crossed the street, reclaimed his car from the parking garage, and drove uptown toward Angela's apartment.

Emily sat on her haunches, looking at the print of the window formed by the stream of sunlight on the opposite wall. She was exhausted, from her climb through the space over the ceiling and then from spending the night pacing her tiny prison cell. But she couldn't let herself sleep. Not when one of them would be coming down at any moment.

She had expected them long ago, when the daylight had first crept through the window. She had heard someone—Rita, she thought—moving around in the kitchen. It was hard to tell what was happening. In her new room she was no longer directly under the kitchen and the sounds were much harder to interpret. But she had guessed that it was Rita fixing breakfast and had braced herself for the onslaught she could expect once she came down the stairs and found her missing.

But then there had been voices. She heard continuous murmurs, interrupted by staccatos of shouting. And then the shouting had become continuous. At one point, she had been able to make out Mike saying, "Nobody's goin' to call! If they didn't call on Friday, they're not goin' to call now." The haggling grew more heated until Rita's voice cut through with, "Maybe they didn't find the van. Maybe no one is looking for us." Seconds later, Mike had shouted, "You said yourself it was time to cut. Let's just leave her and get out of here."

There was a long period of quiet movement in the rooms above. The little bit of conversation was too soft for Emily to hear. She wondered about Mike's insistence that "they just leave her." More than likely, he didn't want Rita to know what he had done to her. She prayed that Rita would agree, because if they left without checking on her, then she could use the swing of her chains to break the small cellar window. Then she could scream until someone came to her rescue.

"I'm bringing her some breakfast," Rita's voice shouted from above.

"No!" Mike yelled immediately from another part of the house. "Leave her. We've got to get out of here."

She heard the door open and then Rita's footsteps on the stairs in the other room.

"Don't go down there!" Mike's voice yelled. There was the pounding of his running footsteps.

"Jesus!" It was Rita screaming from the other room. "Jesus, what did you do to her?"

"Don't go down," Mike repeated. His footsteps pounded through the kitchen.

Rita's voice yelled, "Her bed is all bloody. What did you do with her?"

Then Mike's voice, "Where the fuck is she?"

"What did you do, cut her up?"

"She was here, in the bed. I left her here."

"Drowning in her own blood, you goddamn thug?"

"The ceilin'. She went out through the bathroom ceilin' . . ."

"It looks more like you stuffed her down a drain. What the fuck is the matter with you?"

"Will you shut up and help me find her?"

"She couldn't have gone anywhere. That ceiling just leads to the furnace room. What in hell did you do to her?"

"She's in the furnace room," Mike yelled and she heard his footsteps racing up the stairs.

Emily moved quickly and took up her position, pressed to the wall behind the locked door. It was only seconds until she heard hurried footsteps outside and then the sound of the garage door opening. She set her weight as if she were positioning to hit a hard, cross-court backhand. Her body was coiled and her fingers were wrapped around the shackle chains that hung from her wrists.

A dead bolt slid on the outside of the door. The knob turned and the heavy door swung open. Mike stepped into the room, leading with the pistol that he held in his hand.

She started her backhand, beginning low near the floor and whipping her arm around and upward in a topspin motion. The chain followed like a whip the handcuff at its end picking up momentum. It was nearly whistling when it struck Mike on the side of the head with a sharp, metallic crack. His head snapped sideways and the gun clattered to the cement floor. Then he sagged against the hot water tank and slid down the face of the tank onto his knees. His vacant eyes circled toward Emily and tried to focus.

This time both chains came from directly overhead. She had jumped out next to him and was bringing both hands down as if she were aiming a sledge at a log splitter. The cuffs hit the tall wave across the crown of his head. Mike didn't make a sound. He simply fell forward and landed on his face.

Emily bent down and picked up the gun. She was holding it in both hands when she stepped through the door and out into the garage and came face-to-face with Rita. The two women stared at each other.

"Turn around," Emily ordered.

Rita was shocked by Emily's battered condition. She reached out to help, but stopped suddenly when she saw the gun, its muzzle bouncing around in Emily's trembling hands.

"Be careful with that. You don't want to hurt anyone."

Emily laughed at the irony. She had been hurt terribly. "Turn around and walk slowly back up into the house. I'll be right behind you."

Rita hesitated. "You won't shoot me."

"I don't want to," Emily said in precisely clipped words. "But if I have to leave you behind me, I'm going to make sure that you can't come after me." She steadied the gun and then lowered it until it was aimed at Rita's knees.

"No," Rita said instantly. "I'll go." She turned slowly out of the garage and went to the steps that led down from the side of the house. Emily followed a few paces behind.

The house was an old, wooden-frame structure, facing the blank back wall of an industrial building that was directly across the street. Farther down the road, there were a few other houses, all tired and in need of repair. Mike and Rita could have shouted at each other forever and Emily might have screamed her head off. There was no one close enough to care.

The layout was pretty much as she had pictured it. The basement room where she was held had once opened out into the garage. But that opening, along with the heating plant, had been walled off, creating a separate furnace room that accessed the garage. When she had crawled over the drop ceiling, she had found her way into the other part of the basement.

Rita went into the house, holding the storm door just long enough for Emily to catch it. They crossed a hallway with a linoleum floor and then walked into a sparsely furnished living room.

"Where's the telephone?" Emily demanded.

"In there!" Rita nodded toward the kitchen and Emily waved her ahead with the barrel of the gun. She went in slowly and hesitated near the door.

"All the way in. Get over there. By the stove."

She did as she was told, clearing the center of the room.

Emily glanced around and spotted the door that opened to the basement steps. She circled around close to the walls, keeping as much distance as possible between herself and the other woman. She slipped the bolt, eased the door open, and then moved back into the center of the kitchen.

"Go downstairs into the basement," Emily said. "And close the door behind you."

Rita moved carefully, never taking her eyes off the gun. "Listen, I'm not the one who hurt you. I was just watching you." Her voice oozed sympathy. Rita was a con artist for any occasion.

"I'm not going to hurt you. I'm going to lock that door, call the police, and give them this address. Then I'm going to sit down and wait. But if either of you come up into the room, I'm going to do my best to shoot you."

Rita was in the doorway. "What about Mike?" she asked. "Is he going to be all right?"

"You know what, Rita? I don't give a damn. And neither should you." Emily reached across her and slammed the door shut. She reached for the bolt.

Suddenly she was slammed back against the wall, the pistol driven into her stomach so that it knocked her breath away. The door had snapped back, into her face, and right behind it came Rita, moving like an athlete. She grabbed the gun and tore it out of Emily's hands, sending it skidding across the kitchen floor. Then she took Emily around the neck and began banging her head against the wall.

It took Emily a long second to react. As soon as she had closed the door, Rita had hurled it open from the other side. Before she knew what had hit her, she was being pounded. Her rage flashed and she swung her hands up inside Rita's arms, grabbed her face, and then pushed her thumbs into her eyes. Rita pulled away, screaming in pain, giving Emily the room she needed to hurl a roundhouse right squarely into Rita's jaw. Then she pushed with both hands, driving the shrieking woman back through the open door. But before she could slam it shut, Rita came charging back, this time with her head down. She flung Emily backward, away from the door and out into the kitchen. For an instant, they stood on opposite sides of the room, staring furiously at each other. Simultaneously, they saw the discarded pistol that lay between them.

Emily moved first and dove toward the gun. Her hand was reaching out for the weapon when her fingers suddenly pulled up short. Rita had leaped down beside her and caught the shackle chain that was dangling from her wrist. Emily tried to get to her feet, but Rita held the chain and pulled her back down to her knees. She twisted Emily over onto her back, took the length of chain in both hands, and began forcing the links down onto Emily's throat.

It was a struggle of strength for which Emily was poorly matched. Rita was up on her knees so that she could lean her weight across the chain. Emily was on her back, able to generate little resistance. The links were pressing into her flesh and against the hard edge of her windpipe. She gagged as she tried to scream. All the strength she could muster wasn't enough to back the chain off her neck.

Emily let go with her free hand, taking all of Rita's choking pressure. Instead of continuing the losing struggle, she swung the free chain and handcuff into the murderous face that was high above her. Rita struggled through the first blow, resuming her chokehold after it released for a split second. But the second blow hit into her eye and she let out a scream. One hand flew up to her face, giving Emily freedom to swing another blow. This time the iron cuff tore across Rita's nose. Both hands went to her face, letting Emily grab the chain that had been pressing on her throat and quickly force it under Rita's chin. Their roles changed as Rita lost her balance and fell heavily from her knees onto her side. Emily spun around on the floor to open some distance between them. She kicked out viciously, leaving her opponent in a helpless ball. Then she scrambled to the gun, snatched it up, and struggled to her feet. She stood wobbling for an instant and then fell back against the wall.

"Don't move," she managed when Rita tried to lift herself to her feet. "Stay right there or I'll start firing. I swear to God, I will." Rita settled back and sat on the floor. Emily stood watching her, the gun wavering as she panted for breath. From the corner of her eye, she spotted the telephone, mounted on the wall on the other side of the doorway. She began to slide toward it, keeping the gun oriented in Rita's general direction. Emily knew that she couldn't aim precisely, but she was sure she could hit her target at the close range between them. There was no doubt in her mind that she had the courage to fire and to keep firing until Rita was no longer moving. She eased past the open doorway.

There was a fraction of an instant when she thought she was aware of Mike, a sense of his presence or possibly the sound of his breath. But long before she could react, an arm swung around her neck. A hand reached across her and grabbed for the pistol. She tried to swing the gun at her attacker. A shot exploded in her face. There was a thud over her head as the bullet tore into the ceiling, sending down a shower of plaster. Then the gun was ripped out of her hand.

She flew forward, crashing into the kitchen sink. When she turned, Mike was a distance away, still in the doorway and leaning against the jam. His face was contorted in rage. A web of bloodstains trickled out of his hair and across his face. The handle of the gun dangled from his grip.

"Shoot the bitch," Rita groaned from her seat on the floor.

"Yeah ... yeah ..." Mike promised between gasps for air. "But not here ... down in the washroom ... where the blood won't matter ..."

He didn't bother to turn the gun in his hand so that he could hold the grip and put his finger across the trigger. Instead he stood away from the door jamb, wobbled for a moment while he found his balance, then stepped across to Emily and twisted her hair between his fingers. Without a word, he began dragging her to the open basement door.

She knew she should flail out with her hands or turn herself around so that she could aim a kick. Anything that would keep him from dragging her to her execution. But there was no struggle left in her. She had used up every bit of her strength and all her will to fight. She moved along meekly to the top of the stairs.

The telephone rang.

Mike froze. His grip on her hair relaxed and his labored breathing seemed to stop. Rita, who had been trying to pick herself up, hesitated with one knee still on the floor. Emily looked at the phone as if she expected it to begin talking.

It rang again. Mike looked from Rita over to the phone and then back to her again. He listened and with a quick jerk of his head ordered her to answer it. She moved quickly and lifted the handset during the third ring.

"Yes?" There was fear in her voice. She listened for several seconds. "Yes," she said again and then listened in silence for half a minute. "No. No need to repeat anything. I understand." She put the phone back on the hook and then stood and stared at it as if she expected it to ring again.

"What?" Mike demanded.

"We have to let her go. Then we pick up the rest of our money." She and Mike stared at each other.

"Fuck it," Mike finally managed. "We owe this bitch."

"We let her go tonight and we pick up five thousand tomorrow," Rita corrected.

"No. We finish her so there's no witness. And then we get our asses out of here. I'm not leavin' her to have the last laugh on me."

"She'll be laughing at both of us if we've been through all this and don't have anything to show for it. And her remembering us won't mean a thing. Sooner or later they're going to open that van and figure out who we are."

He turned the gun in his hand and then pushed the muzzle against Emily's cheek. "I don't want to leave her behind. It's too dangerous."

"And I don't want to walk away from five grand. That's just too stupid. Look, we drop her off tonight and as soon as they see she's okay, they tell us where to pick up the money."

"There won't be any more money!" He shouted at her.

"Not if they don't get her back. That was the deal and that's the way they're playing it. You said there were probably some heavy hitters behind this. I don't think it would be safe to cross them."

Mike shook with frustration. Then he took a deep breath and screamed. "Ahhhh!" He shook his grip on Emily's hair as if he hoped to tear her head off. Then, when his venting was over, he flung her through the open cellar door. She grabbed the banister and spun with the momentum of her own weight, but managed to keep her footing. When she heard the door slam above her, she slumped in defeat on the bottom step, back in the room she had escaped.

Monday

MIKE WAS SUDDENLY SUSPICIOUS. "Rita," he said in a stage whisper. She came out of the kitchen wiping her hands in a towel. "Ya ever see that guy before?" He was standing close to the front window and the jerk of his head indicated that she should look outside.

She reached for the curtain, but Mike grabbed her hand. "Just look! Don't let him see ya!"

She squinted through the dusty lace curtains. "The guy with the cap?" She shook her head. "I don't think so. Probably someone from the factory."

"Now? It's past midnight. No one is going to the factory."

She looked again and watched as the figure continued around the corner. "Let's not get jumpy. We'll be out of here in an hour." She went back to the kitchen and ran some water into a pan. Then she called, "I'm taking a washcloth downstairs so she can clean herself up a bit. And I'm bringing her down some old clothes."

"As far as I'm concerned," he called back, "we can dump her just the way she is now. You think anybody is goin' to give a damn?"

"Just watch the top of the stairs," Rita told him. "I want you nearby in case she has some other tricks she wants to try."

Mike shuffled into the kitchen. He hated the thought of Emily going free. They were already set up for kidnapping charges and he had added rape and assault. There was no longer sentence waiting for them if they just buried her behind the house. He wasn't sneering at the extra money. He just didn't think it was worth giving her the chance to point him out from the witness stand.

But Rita had made one point that had registered with him. Some crime boss might be behind the kidnapping. He had stuck his neck out for a shot at an extra fifty thousand. But he didn't want to cross anybody big just for the satisfaction of putting the crazy bitch away.

Rita came up from the basement. "No more trouble from her. She's sitting down there sucking her thumb. Never even moved while I washed her off."

"Did you have to dress her, too?" he asked sarcastically.

"No, she's doing that herself. In slow motion."

He walked back into the living room. He and Rita had been pacing around the house since they had packed their things into the stolen car. They had spent the whole evening waiting for 1:00 A.M., when they were supposed to take Emily out to a public school parking lot and leave her bound and blindfolded on a bench. Mike moved to the edge of the window and for the hundredth time, glanced out through the curtain. There was another man crossing under the streetlight.

He pulled back, afraid that he might be seen. He waited an instant and then leaned out again. The man was still there and he didn't seem to be going anywhere. He had walked out of the light and down to the corner of the brick factory building. But he was still standing in the shadows right where the other one had disappeared.

Mike eased over to the side window and looked across the empty lot to the cross street. It seemed as gloomy as always—another industrial building with trash piled on the street outside. This one had windows across the second story. The lights were out and there was no sign of activity. He went back to the front window and found that the second man he had seen had also disappeared. "Take it easy," he told himself. He went back into the kitchen for another glance at the clock. 12:20. They didn't have to wait any longer. What difference would it make if they dropped her off a half hour early.

It was just by chance that he saw another figure crossing to the back of one of the houses down the street. Auto headlights from a car turning at the farthest intersection panned across the open lots. They silhouetted the from of a man running from the street.

"Rita!"

She turned instantly and came up next to him at the kitchen window.

"There's somebody out there," he said, again whispering as if to keep a secret. "I saw him movin'."

"Probably lives in one of those houses," she answered. "I saw people down there before."

He hurried back to the living room. Through the front curtains, he could now see both of the earlier men at the corner of the factory building and a third man walking toward them. He went to the side windows. A car was parked on the street in front of the darkened industrial building. He caught sight of a person moving from the car to the building and then of a steel door swinging open. In the dim light behind the door, he could see other people inside.

"Christ!" he called out as he pulled away and ran back into the kitchen. "There's cops all over the place."

Rita looked at him, her eyes a wide open question. "You sure?"

"Look for yourself," he told her. "You have any more bright ideas?"

She thought for an instant. "Yeah, I do. I think if they have us surrounded we'll have a much better chance in court."

"We're not giving up," he snapped.

"You'd rather shoot it out with the entire New Jersey state police? For Christ's sake, Mike, the judge won't blow you away with an assault weapon."

"Get the bitch up here, quick."

"I'd rather give up before someone sees what you did to her."

"Get her up here. She's going to be our ticket through all that heat."

"Mike, please! They have sharpshooters. Don't think like a gangster. Give it up and take your chances."

"Get her, dammit. If I die then she dies, too."

"Okay," Rita said. "But I'd rather not be included. Let me go out waving a bedsheet."

"No, fuckin' way. We're goin' to need someone holdin' her and someone drivin'. We're doin' this together."

She moved slowly to the basement door, but hesitated.

"Hurry up," he called after her. "The fuckers are closing in!"

Emily was sitting on the corner of the bed, dressed in the plain house-dress that Rita had brought down and resting her head in her hands. Rita wondered if she had enough strength to make it up the stairs. She lifted Emily's face and the dead eyes confirmed what she had already guessed. They would have no more trouble with their prisoner.

"C'mon. We gotta get you outta here." Emily rose slowly as Rita prodded her shoulder and shuffled toward the steps.

Mike had doused the light on the back of the house and crept into the darkened bedroom where he could look outside without being seen. Another car had pulled up at the factory building. There was someone moving along the fence at the back of the property. Then he noticed another man, crouched low, already in position.

Two out front and two in the back, he counted mentally. There's a whole bunch of them in the factory, probably up in the darkened windows. And maybe there are a couple of backups still in the cars. Then he remembered the one he had seen across from the street to the back of the neighboring houses. They probably had guys hidden in the shadows over there, too. Eight, maybe ten of them all together, covering the house from every side, getting into position to rush the place. Or maybe just planning to wait, knowing that he had to come out eventually.

He heard footsteps in the kitchen and went back to find Emily standing in the middle of the room with Rita practically holding her up. He moved directly into Emily's face.

"Pay attention, because if you don't, you could get yourself killed."

Her eyes struggled back into focus.

"There are cops out there with guns. They have this place surrounded."

Rita's face jerked around. "What guns?"

"They're cops! They're not doin' parkin' tickets!"

She started for the window.

"Stay away from there," Mike snapped. He reached to the wall and switched off the light. "You could get your head blown off."

"Mike, this is crazy. We never bargained for a gun fight."

"They won't fire if they see this bitch in front of us."

Emily was taking in the situation. Color was returning to her face. Mike pushed her back into a darkened corner. "Now listen," he hissed. "We're going to walk out the side door, open the garage, and get into our car. And then we'll drive right out of here. All of us, includin' you. Nobody is going to stop us, and there won't be any shootin', because they won't risk you gettin' blown away. So just stay right with me, keep your head up, and walk nice and tall, you understand?"

Emily showed a trace of a smile. "Fuck you," she said to Mike.

His hand shot to her throat. He pulled the gun out of his pocket and touched it to the bridge of her nose. "I could kill you right now."

"Go ahead," she answered. "Just as long as I know that you're going to get yours."

He pulled her away from the wall and pushed her into the darkened living room. "You're goin' out first and you're goin' to tell them, 'Don't shoot. Hold your fire.' Loud and clear, so that everyone understands it. Then you yell, 'I'm Emily Childs.' You read me?"

Emily laughed. "I'm going to tell them they're a bunch of wimps. I'll dare them to fire."

Mike reached for the door handle. "Say whatever ya want. They'll see you." He looked back at Rita. "Ready?"

Her face was ashen. "As ready as I'll ever be . . ."

"Stay close to me," he said. "Right behind me." Then he told Emily. "You move nice and slow. If you try to take off, you're dead!"

The front doorbell rang!

Mike and Rita froze. Emily laughed. "Give it up, Rita. You're in enough trouble without murder."

"Shut up!" Mike wrapped an arm around her neck, putting her in a chokehold.

"She's right!" Rita pleaded.

Mike's eyes darted from the side door to the front door. He couldn't walk out the front door, right into their arms. And there were probably more of them at the side door, as well.

"I'll tell them you never hurt me," Emily coached Rita until Mike's arm cut off her breath.

The bell rang again.

"Let's give it up," Rita said.

"We're not givin' anythin' up. Not while we have her."

"Well, what's your next big idea?" The sarcasm in Rita's voice masked her fear.

Mike tightened his chokehold. He backed Emily into the darkened kitchen.

A fist pounded on the outside of the front door. "Open the door, Rita," a voice boomed. "This is the police. We need to talk to you."

Rita turned to look at Mike, then back to the door and finally back to Mike. "What should I do?"

"Tell them to come on in. Tell them door is open."

She was shocked, unable to move.

Mike's voice hissed out of the darkness. "Do it!"

She turned back to the front door. "C'mon in. It's open."

A silent pause and then a voice said, "Come to the front door and open it, Rita."

"Don't," Mike called. "Sit down on the couch. Quick." She moved over to the sofa and lowered herself easily.

"Come to the front door, Rita, and open it slowly."

"Tell them you can't walk. Tell them to come on in."

Rita didn't understand the strategy. But she yelled through the door, "I can't. I can't walk. You'll have to let yourself in!"

There was no response. The only sound was the hiss of Rita's breathing as she wondered if they might have gone away. Then the door exploded open, swinging freely until it slammed against the wall. But there was no one there. The open doorway was filled with blackness.

"Where are you?" Rita screamed.

The response was a dark-clad figure that sprung through the opening and tumbled into the room. He rolled into the shadows and came up on one knee with a stubby assault rifle aimed directly at Rita. Her scream pierced the air. Another form turned around the edge of the door and pointed a blinding light into her eyes. "Don't move," he warned, and then he stepped carefully into the room, aiming a pistol with his free hand.

Rita's hand started up to block the light from her eyes.

"Don't move!" the voice screamed. She froze like a statue. Then her wide eyes panned from one man to the other. They were dressed in black, with their pants tucked into boots. Each wore a helmet and a thick black vest.

"Where is he?"

Rita stuttered.

"Where's Mike? Where is he?"

"Right here!" Mike pushed Emily into the kitchen doorway. Then he rose up behind her. The flashlight illuminated both their faces and then glistened off the pistol that was pressed into Emily's ear.

"Get that fuckin' light out of my face," he ordered. The officer saw Emily's fear and lowered the light. "You can see I got the lady," Mike said. "Who's goin' to kill her? You guys? Or me?"

A third assault trooper bounded into the doorway.

"Come on in," Mike said. "Join the party."

The new arrival saw the situation and glanced at the two officers who were already in the room. Their weapons were poised, but their faces were raised from their sights. They had already decided not to fire.

"Close the door," Mike ordered. The new officer looked to the other two for directions. "Close it!" he screamed insanely, and the man reached behind him, found the doorknob, and swung the door closed.

"Good." Mike was beginning to feel the thrill of power. "Real good.

Now, I want all of you to lay the guns on the floor and then push them away, under the coffee table."

"No way," answered the one with the flashlight.

"Then you better start usin' them. Because at three, I'm goin' to use this one." He pushed the muzzle of his revolver harder against Emily's face.

"One . . ."

"Okay!" The trooper with the flashlight bent over and carefully placed his pistol on the floor. His partner, still on one knee, slowly set down the rifle and then the third officer let his automatic pistol drop from his hand.

"Under the table," Mike ordered. Rita watched openmouthed as the black-clad figures obediently pushed the cache of weapons up against her toes.

"You two," Mike said, nodding at the two original invaders, "get flat out on the floor. Down on your faces." They moved slowly to all fours and then stretched out on their bellies. "Spread eagle. Hands and feet out!" The two followed his instructions.

"You get out of here," Mike said to the third policeman. "Go back to your boss and tell him exactly what's goin' down in here. Anybody comes near this place, and your buddies' brains get spread all over the rug. Then tell someone to call me. Someone high up, because there are things he'll have to do for me if he wants these guys to stay alive."

"You'll get yourselves killed," the officer warned. His glance lingered on Rita.

"That's for sure," Mike said, "because you're not takin' either of us alive. So you understand your choices. You either let us go, or all of us die together. Including your friends and this lady here."

The officer eased open the door, keeping his eyes on Mike, and then backed through the opening. Only when he was on the outside step did he turn and dash off into the blackness.

"Get the guns," Mike told Rita. He stuffed his own pistol into his belt, exchanging it for one of the assault rifles. He took one of the police automatics and slipped it into his pocket. Then he released his grip on Emily's throat and pushed her down onto the sofa, keeping the assault rifle trained on her head.

"Check out these two." He nodded at the two men stretched out on the floor. "Careful. Go around behind them. Lift the vests and check their belts." Rita removed a handcuff set from each of them and took the pistol that one of them was wearing at his back.

The telephone rang. Rita looked expectantly at Mike.

"Let it ring! We're not ready to talk to them yet." He raised his voice above the telephone's interruption. "Both you guys put your hands behind your backs."

"Look, Mac . . ." one of the assault troops began.

"Shut up! Behind your back! Now!"

Their hands moved until Rita could pull them together and snap the handcuffs into position. "You'll never make it," the other officer warned.

"Then neither will you guys" Mike smirked.

The telephone stopped ringing. Rita looked even more frightened. "They hung up," she said. "We should have answered."

"Fuck 'em! I might not answer the next time, either. Let them sweat a bit."

It was almost 2:00 A.M. when Andrew and Helen arrived on the scene. The negotiations had already begun, and Lieutenant Borelli pulled the two of them into the industrial building on the next street that he was using as his command post. Together, they peered out of the darkened second-floor windows at the blank shape of the house.

"I have two men trapped in there," Borelli said, his tone suggesting that Hogan and Restivo might be responsible for their situation.

"I'm sorry," Hogan answered. "I know I've got a lot of explaining to do."

The lieutenant put aside some of his hostility and took on the tone of a professional. "We've been talking with him on the phone. There's a negotiator on the line with him right now. But we're running out of time."

Hogan's expression changed to a question.

Borelli went on. "He wants safe passage out of the neighborhood and a one-car escort to the airport. From there he wants a plane."

"What for?" Hogan asked. "He's got to know that someone will be waiting for him wherever he lands."

"That's what the negotiator is trying to sell him. But this guy isn't making a lot of sense. He's enjoying the attention. We've got one hour to agree and to tell him that his plane is waiting."

"Or what?" Hogan asked.

"He shoots one of my men and has the other roll the body down the front steps. Then we get another hour until he shoots the other officer and tries to fight his way out. He'll be using your lady as a shield."

Andrew nodded. It was a situation he had been in many times himself. Rita and Mike were finished and they probably knew it. But they also knew that they would be facing life in prison and they weren't going to let that happen.

Just as certainly, there was no way the State Troopers were going to give them an escort to anywhere. The whole purpose of the standoff was to keep them from hurting anyone else.

"What's the plan?" Helen asked, hoping that the cooling of Borelli's earlier rage applied to her, as well.

"We're going to agree, provided they leave both of our men in the house. We'll tell them that if either one is hurt, there will be no plane. Then we'll take him when he comes out in his car."

"What about Emily Childs?" Hogan asked.

"We won't shoot first, except to take out his tires. Maybe when it's obvious that he's not going anywhere, he'll decide that there's no point in getting him and his girlfriend killed. Because we'll make it clear, if he shoots the lady anywhere along the way, then we start shooting."

It was the same decision that Hogan would have made himself. Assure the safety of his officers first, and then try to save the hostage. He also agreed with stopping the car as soon as it cleared the house. There was no point in trailing them out to the airport. Then the showdown would have to happen when they tried to board the plane. And there was absolutely no sense in letting them get on the plane. All that did was move the showdown to another city. The fact was that at some point, Rita and Mike would have to decide if they really would rather die. If they did, nothing could save Emily.

"Can I help?" Hogan asked.

"Not now," Borelli answered. "You and your friend have helped enough."

Mike stood in the kitchen doorway, tugging the telephone cord to its full length. He had the assault rifle at his hip, panning in the general direction of the two officers lying on the living room floor. Rita was sitting across from Emily, half aiming a pistol in her general direction.

"One car," Mike was saying, "with just one cop inside. I don't want to see another cop car around here. In fact, you better make damn sure there aren't police cars anywhere along our route." He listened for a few moments. Then he snapped, "I don't give a fuck about other towns and other jurisdictions. You get ahold the other jurisdictions and tell them no cars along the route. If you can't do that, then put someone on the line who can."

His voice was spirited, almost cheerful. Mike was enjoying the power. He had the whole state of New Jersey out there begging him to come to terms.

They had started with assurances that he wasn't actually a kidnapper. Someone else had taken the woman by force. Sure, he was in trouble, but it was the kind of trouble he might be able to get out of, *if* he didn't make things worse. Give up the two officers right away. Everyone understood that he had taken them in a moment of panic. And then negotiate the release of the lady. Of course, they would have to take him and Rita in. But they would have an attorney appointed within the hour.

Mike mocked those offers. The guys in the black suits who had charged into the house with assault weapons didn't look like lawyers. He wanted a car to the airport and then he wanted a plane.

Each negotiator claimed not to have the authority to give in to his demands and Mike kept asking for someone who did. They kept going to higher and higher officials and, one by one, he kept telling them to fuck off. Maybe he should demand to speak to the governor.

"He's going to get us all killed," Emily repeated to Rita. She had been explaining the scenario ever since Mike had answered the phone. The three of them would walk outside with her in the front as a human shield. Once they were away from the front steps, she was going to turn on Mike, kicking at him until she broke free. Then she would run to the police. Whether she got free or not, Mike would have to kill her because there was no way she was going to get into his car. And once he did, then Rita and Mike would be standing in the middle of an army of troopers, all of them armed and mad enough to fire. "You don't have to get shot to pieces," Emily whispered. "All he has to do is tell them you're coming out without your guns. Then they can't fire at you. They have to arrest you. And I'll tell them, I swear to you, I'll tell them how you tried to help me."

Rita stood up and looked at Mike, who was smiling as he listened to the pleading over the telephone. "This isn't going to work," she suddenly announced.

He snarled at her. Then he yelled into the phone, "No! No! No more time. I told you what I want and when I want it. You have five more minutes. Then I kill one of these guys. Maybe that's what it's goin' to take to get through to you." He backed into the kitchen for the length of time it took him to hang up the phone. Then he returned to the living room and walked around behind the two prone police officers. "Doesn't sound like your buddies out there are takin' me seriously. So who's it goin' to be? Which one of you guys wants to be first?"

Angela's plane had left Heathrow just before midnight, in time to get London's bankers to Zurich before the Swiss banks opened. Despite the hour the plane was crowded. Apparently the English were very appreciative of the Swiss financiers' legendary discretion.

She had landed in London early in the morning, checked into a business suite, and connected to her office computer over one of the bank's leased circuits. In the early afternoon—early morning in New York—she had watched Walter's transaction, transferring funds to Fassen Bank. Instantly, she had sent the recorded phone message that would free Emily. Then she had freshened up, and gone back to the terminal for her Zurich flight. She had slept comfortably in her First Class seat until the wheels went down on final approach.

As soon as she came through the door she saw the lights of Zurich, still glowing even though the sky was beginning to fill with morning light. Close by, there were the garish logos of global companies, flashing in neon at the tops of the buildings. Farther off, she could see the streetlights of the old city, with the occasional flicker of automobile traffic. It was less than spectacular. Zurich insisted on being unobtrusive. There was nothing dramatic about the city until daylight brought the background of jagged mountains into view.

A taxi was waiting at the head of the queue with the passenger door open. Angela slid in, pulling her bag into the seat after her. She gave the name of a modest hotel in the banking district that was even more discreet than the banks. She knew that she would attract very little attention. Businessmen using the hotel frequently arranged for companions to join them in their rooms. She had stayed there once herself and had been approached in the bar by an Englishman who thought she had been sent over by the service.

At the desk, she signed in as Susan Schwartz and smiled at the clerk when he tried to compare her with the passport photo. Then she refused the services of the bellman and saw herself to her room.

The morning sun was pouring in through the starched curtains. Angela tossed her bag on the bed and went to the window. Traffic was building in the streets and there was a crowd pouring out through the doors of the streetcar at the corner. There wouldn't be any time for her to catch up on her sleep. Hardly enough time to take a shower. The banks would be opening soon and she wanted to be in and out of Fassen Bank as quickly as she could. She checked her watch and calculated that it was two in the morning back in New York. By now, Emily Childs had been dropped off in a school parking lot. Within a few hours, her safety would be assured. Angela knew that once Emily was safe, someone would have to think about sending a message to stop the transfer of funds that Walter had initiated. She wanted to have the money out the door and into another bank before that message came.

A minute before his deadline, Mike heard the telephone ring. He broke into a smile. "I hope it's for you," he said toward the two officers. "Otherwise, your time is up!"

He backed into the kitchen and returned with the handset. "Yeah," he said. Rita watched his face darken and felt certain that the police outside were calling his bluff. But then one corner of his mouth curled up into a sneer. "Yeah," he said again. "Only not in fifteen minutes. Now! I want everyone out of that buildin', and I want all the police cars out of here. Just one car, out in the street, clear of the driveway. And one driver. I'm going to take a long look around and if those two jerks are still standing across the street, or if one of those mothers is still in the backyard, then the whole thing is off. Each of your guys gets it in the back of the head. And then me and the lady here take our chances."

He listened for a few seconds and enjoyed what he was hearing. "Okay," he finally said. "You have five minutes to clear everyone. Make sure you get 'em all. You don't want to make any mistakes."

Mike let the phone fall to the floor. "Well, what do you know," he announced proudly to everyone. "We're getting a police escort to the airport."

They waited quietly, listening to the sounds outside the house. Voices called to one another. Auto engines burst into life, followed by transmission sounds and the squeal of turning tires. Then there was silence, broken only by the sounds of their breathing. The captured officers listened with trained ears, trying to identify what was taking place outside. Rita looked about carefully, as if the enemy might already be in the house. Mike checked and rechecked the position of the pistols in his belt and pocket and then wiped the sweat from his palms down the legs of his trousers. Emily sat at the edge of the sofa, tense as if waiting to spring. She didn't care about the police outside. All her energies were focused on the man who had delighted in torturing her. No matter what anyone else did, she would make certain that he didn't get out alive.

Headlights flared in the front window curtains and Rita crossed the room to look out. "It's the police car," she said, her voice fearful of the ordeal that it represented. The moment had come. She would be stepping out into a no-man's-land.

"Pull the curtain," Mike told her. "Look around. Tell me if you see anybody."

She looked carefully, touching her forehead to the glass so that she could widen her field of vision. "Nothing out there," she said. She kept looking. "Just the police car. Nothing else."

"How about the factory?"

She went to the side window. "The cars are gone. The lights are out. But I can't tell if anyone's there. It's too dark."

He thought. There were probably people still in the second floor windows. Maybe a sharpshooter. Sure. If they caught him out in the open, it would make sense to take him out. But he could handle that. He had a bulletproof shield. As long as he kept close to the lady, no one would dare fire.

"Okay, now check out back. There were two of them back against the fence. Take that flashlight and look out the window. All along the bottom of the fence."

Rita went close to the prone policeman and lifted the lamp from the floor. She stepped over their bodies on her way to the back of the house. When she snapped on the light, she was startled by its brilliance. Aimed through a back window, it illuminated half the yard and let her see even the spaces between the fence planking. She panned slowly. There was no one there. Then she went to the kitchen window and moved the light back and forth across the litter-strewn lot between the house and the next cluster of buildings.

"They're gone," she called from the kitchen.

Mike's mouth drew into a narrow smile. "They're not gone. They're just hiding, waitin' to pop up the minute we show our asses. But the only thing they'll see is the bitch's face."

He slung the assault weapon over his shoulder and pulled the police automatic from his pocket. In one step, he was hovering over Emily. "On your feet!" She stood immediately.

"Fasten the cuffs," he ordered. Rita looked at the manacles dangling from Emily's hands and then took the key from her pocket. She unlocked the cuffs that had been fastened to the bed and then connected each of them across to Emily's other arm.

"Okay," she said. Mike prodded Emily toward the door and then reached around her for the knob. The door swung back from its shattered frame.

Instantly, his arm was around her throat and the muzzle of the pistol against her ear.

"We go real slow," he told Emily. They moved through the doorway, with Rita pressed close behind.

"One step, then stop." His chokehold lifted Emily off her feet and deposited her on the next step, where he joined her immediately. Again and again he moved her down until they were on the path leading to the driveway. Emily had imagined that she would be able to throw an elbow or get her fingers close to his eyes. But the handcuffs kept her hands in front of her and his hold was like a vise. She was choking each time he lifted her feet off the pavement.

He moved her slowly to the driveway, always keeping her on the street side, with his back to the house. Rita moved with them, hiding behind the shield that they afforded. Then they backed up to the garage door, which Rita raised.

"Turn on the light and look around."

She did, and opened the car door to look inside. "All clear," she whispered.

"Kill the light and get into the backseat."

She switched off the light, stepped around the car, and climbed into the back behind the passenger seat.

Mike took one last look up and down the street. There really was no one beside the uniformed policeman sitting behind the wheel of the waiting cruiser. He pulled Emily back into the garage, along the driver's side of the automobile.

He opened the back door, ducked down behind it, and pushed Emily into the seat next to Rita. "Put your gun right up against her head. Up high, so they can see it." Emily felt a new weapon against her temple, but Rita wasn't pressing it into her skin.

Mike reached over the driver's seat and pushed the front door open. He used this as his shield while he closed Emily's door and slid in behind the wheel. He started the car, turned on the high-beam headlights, and rolled slowly out of the garage, his face below the height of the steering wheel. If they were going to turn a marksman loose, this would be their moment. But there was no hint of an attack as they rolled slowly down the driveway and bounced onto the street. Mike straightened up in time to see the cruiser pulling slowly away, its red and blue lights spinning furiously. He fell into line behind it and followed it toward the corner, which was masked by the wall of the factory across from the house. "Make sure they can see the gun," he snarled at Rita. "Keep it up high." The cruiser turned the corner. Mike leaned forward to see if anyone was waiting on the other side of the building. It looked clear and he made his turn keeping close on the taillights of his escort.

The shots went off together, sounding like a single explosion instead of series of small pops. The sports utility truck lurched as two of its tires were shot out. Something struck the back of the car like a fist, setting the frame resonating like a kettledrum.

"Shoot her!" Mike screamed. He fought the wheel to keep the car on line and stepped down on the gas pedal. "Blow her fuckin' head off! Shoot her!

But Rita was already falling forward, an expression of total amazement distorting her features. The gun she was holding dropped with her hand into her lap. She pitched ahead until the top of her head hit the back of the front seat. Then she crumpled into a kneeling position and fell against the door. There was a spreading bloodstain in the middle of her back, matched perfectly to the round hole that had been punched through the back of the seat and was leaking upholstery.

Emily couldn't reach the pistol that was falling away with Rita. She was being tossed first to her left and then to her right by the abruptness of the car's maneuvers and then slammed forward by the sudden crash. As the gunshots had sounded, the police cruiser had accelerated ahead and then swerved sideways to block the road. A figure had bounced up in the back-seat and begun aiming an automatic weapon. Mike had kept the pedal to the floor as he veered right to circle behind the police car. When he had seen the rifleman in the backseat, he had cut to the left, aiming straight at the gunman. His truck deflected off the rear quarter of the cruiser, slamming both policemen against the inside of their own car. The weapon fell harmlessly out the window.

Mike swung the wheel to the right, tearing the bumper and half the trunk from the cruiser and scattering it across the road behind him. He hadn't planned it, but he had turned the escorting patrol car into a barricade of debris that blocked the two police cars coming in pursuit.

Shots rang out from every side. The windshield starred and the passenger window shattered. There were more thumps against the sides of the car, one striking Rita's body and pushing it over against Emily. But even with the blown tires, the truck was gaining speed, leaving the rattle of gunfire behind. And there were no cars with wailing sirens gaining on them. Just a few more seconds were all that he needed to put enough space between him and the police so that he would have a chance to make a getaway.

He caught only a quick glimpse of Emily rising up behind him, not enough time for him to get his hand back from the wheel to protect himself. Certainly not enough to reach for the automatic that was in the seat next to him. Emily threw her hands up over his head. The chains that he had fastened to her wrists fell heavily across his chest. Then she heaved back, pulling the links across his throat.

Mike wasted an instant trying to steer the car and then lost another precious moment when he fumbled for the weapon. By the time he got his hands up to the chain it was already biting into his flesh.

Emily raised her knees against the back of Mike's seat, letting her use every muscle in her body for leverage. Then she pulled back, ripping his head back and lifting him right out of his seat.

His arms flailed wildly. His hands reached around behind his head so that he could get a grip on the chain. But in that position, his strength was no match for the force Emily was generating. He felt his windpipe snap and could taste his own blood in his mouth. And then there was no air. Mike's feet were off the pedals, kicking frantically in search of any kind of leverage. His heel flew forward and smashed the center out of the dashboard.

The truck kept rolling ahead, angling gradually toward the sidewalk. It was still traveling at a good rate of speed when it jumped up on the curb, sheered off the top of a fire hydrant, and ricocheted off the wall of a brick building. From there, it angled back into the road, crossed the street, and slammed into an industrial trash Dumpster on the other side. All the while Mike was struggling, his efforts getting weaker. All the while Emily kept her knees braced and her body taut as she pulled back with all her strength.

When the car came to rest, Mike made no movement to escape. His finger never even twitched in the direction of the pistol or the assault weapon.

Emily thought that he was dead. But she kept her weight hanging from the chain that was looped around his neck. She was crying hysterically when the police pried open her door and lifted her out.

Walter had been up all night, drinking black coffee and pacing in circles around Amanda, who was dozing on the family room sofa, and Alex who had finally nodded off in a soft chair. His fear and anxiety were driving him like rocket motors.

He should have heard by now. There was already sunlight in the windows, which meant that it was late morning in Zurich. The money should already be gone from Fassen Bank. The order to free Emily, it should have been given hours ago.

She was supposed to have been left off safely, in a spot where she would be easily found. But that hadn't happened. Maybe she had never been set free. Or maybe her jailers had dropped her deep in the woods or in some deserted building where she would never be found. Walter didn't know. All he could do was agonize over the dreadful possibilities.

It had to be the sadistic pervert who had been holding her. The fiend had taken such pleasure in describing how he planned to violate her and mutilate her if he wasn't paid. Walter had believed he really meant it and wanted to meet his demands; $50,000 was a pitifully small amount compared to what was at stake. But Andrew Hogan had never taken him seriously. Hogan had insisted that the bastard was only a hireling, useful only in as much as he might lead them to Emily. Now it seemed obvious that Hogan had guessed wrong. Emily had not been released on schedule.

The one thing Walter couldn't let himself think about was what her keeper might have done to her. Twice, he had given assurances to the man, and both times he had broken his word. Once, it was because he had cooperated with Andrew Hogan, the second time because Hogan had barged in with a blundered attempt of his own doing. The deceptions could have driven the psychopath beyond his point of control. Emily might have paid the full price of his madness.

"Nothing? No word at all?" Amanda's sleepy voice asked as she snapped out of her slumber and read her father's anxiety as he paced with his coffee gripped tightly in his hand. She lifted up from the sofa and glanced over at her brother. "I guess we haven't been much company for you." Then she moved slowly by him and into the kitchen, where she poured the dregs of the pot into a cup.

"She should have been found by now. I sent the money. They were supposed to let her go." He shook his head in self-recrimination. Then he sank into the sofa that Amanda had just left. She leaned on the kitchen counter. "We'll just have to wait . . . and hope."

"I tried. I did everything I could," Walter said, shaking his head in despair. He raised his eyes to his daughter, expecting a consoling word or expression. But she remained dark and silent. He knew she would never completely forgive him.

The telephone rang and Amanda sprang to answer. Alex bolted out of his chair and rushed to her side. Walter stood, looking after them, too frightened to follow. He watched her lift the receiver, but didn't hear her say a word. For what seemed an eternity, she listened gravely.

"What is it?" he finally managed.

She held up a hand, telling him not to interrupt.

"Jesus, is she all right?"

Amanda was nodding, but he couldn't tell whether she was answering him or agreeing with something that was being said over the phone. "Okay," she said. And then, "Yes, I know how to get there . . . of course . . . he's right here . . . certainly he'll come . . . we'll all be leaving right away . . ."

"For Christ's sake, tell me. Is she all right?"

Amanda smiled and nodded enthusiastically, but then her expression narrowed as she went on listening. With her change of mood, Walter's sudden joy was dashed.

"What happened? What's wrong?" he begged.

She waved the questions away and went on listening. "But that's not serious," she interjected. She nodded at what she was hearing, thanked the caller several times, and finally hung up the phone.

"They've found her. She's okay. She's going to be just fine." She hugged her brother and they locked together in a swinging, dancing embrace.

"What was the problem?" Walter demanded again.

Amanda hesitated for an instant and then explained that there were superficial wounds in the course of the rescue. "They're going to keep her in the hospital for a day or two. Just to make sure everything is all right. It's routine. Just a routine precaution."

・・・

He bought an armful of flowers from the florist in the hospital lobby and smiled at everyone on his way up to her room. As he neared her doorway, he stopped for an instant to check his tie and smooth down his hair. He started into her room but was stopped in his tracks by her battered appearance.

Her face was swollen around a red welt that she had gotten during the car crash. An enormous white dressing circled her head. Both her hands were bandaged to protect cuts she had gotten from her shackles. There was a terrible fatigue in her expression, undoubtedly the result of her ordeal, and a simpleminded look in her eyes that probably came from the solution that was being dripped into her arm. He ran to her, dropped the flowers at her feet, and lifted her into his arms. "I'm so sorry," he said, and then he repeated it over and over again.

He left Emily asleep, with Amanda by her bedside, and went down to the hospital cafeteria to join Andrew Hogan. Andrew took him step-by-step through the last hours of her captivity, the attempted escape, and the car crash that had killed her captors.

"She told me she had killed someone," Walter said, as soon as Andrew had stopped speaking. "I was holding her, trying to console her. She wasn't fully conscious. But she mumbled, 'I killed him, Walt. I killed him.' Who? What did she mean?"

"Emily is heavily sedated," Andrew said.

Walter nodded. "I know, I know. She's in a daze. But she seemed positive that she killed someone."

Andrew went into more detail than he intended about the last minutes of Emily's captivity. "At some point, probably after the woman was shot, Emily got the handcuff chain around the guy's neck. She pulled back hard, obviously trying to make him stop the car."

"And that's what killed him? She garroted the bastard?"

Hogan shook his head. "No, I don't think so. The man died in the car crash. The impact broke his neck. That's what the police officer on the scene is going to write in his report. He assured me there would be no problems for Emily."

"But, she thinks . . ." Walter persisted.

"She'd been through hell," Andrew said. "She has every reason to hate the prick who caused it. And yet killing someone is hard for her to accept."

Walter felt indicted. "I never intended for her to suffer. I never wanted to see her hurt."

237

"Oh?" Hogan asked. "What did you intend?"

Walter looked flabbergasted. "Intend?"

"Yeah. When you and your young lady planned this whole thing, what was it you intended?"

"You think . . . that I . . . ?"

Hogan walked toward the exit. Walter kept pleading his innocence until he realized that no one was listening.

He finally fell off to sleep in the backseat of the car while Alex drove them back home. "Her ear," Amanda kept repeating. "It's gruesome! It must have been awful for her."

"There's plastic surgery," Alex finally offered. "They do wonders."

"But the shock! Do you think she'll ever get over it?"

"Mom's a strong lady. I think she'll do just fine. I really do."

Walter was scarcely awake when he noticed the blinking light on his telephone answering machine and played back his secretary's message. "Mr. Hollcroft called," Joanne said, her tone conveying due reverence for the president and chief executive officer. "He heard about Emily and he wants you to know how shocked he is. He insisted that I tell you that he and the bank are completely behind you. He wants to know if there is anything he can do for Emily, or for you."

"That's most considerate," Walter said, hoping that his secretary might carry the remark to Jack Hollcroft's secretary. "I'll call him right away."

"Oh, you can't do that," Joanne cautioned. "He's going into a meeting with a few of the directors. It's expected to run late. But his secretary did say that he hoped to talk with you at your earliest convenience. He didn't mention anything specific, but she said she thought it concerned some international transactions that he didn't completely understand."

Walter breathed deeply. There was very little that the chairman didn't completely understand.

Tuesday

JACK HOLLCROFT, ACCORDING TO *Fortune* magazine, was the most conservative man in global business. "Among the sixty suits in his closet," the editors jibed in a feature article, "there isn't one lighter than charcoal gray. He regards colored shirts as the gaudy uniform of advertising hucksters and once told a colleague who appeared before him in suspenders that he looked like a sideshow barker." It was an accurate description of the world's most respected banker. Everything about Jack Hollcroft assured depositors that he would never gamble with their money.

He was an unimpressive-looking man of average weight and average height, with thinning gray hair, gray eyes, and a complexion that was slightly tanned all year round. His most remarkable feature was an easy smile that made him look a bit like a southerner even though he had been raised in the suburbs of Boston. His voice was perfectly modulated and never elevated in volume. He was known to be a generous patron of causes that involved small children and helpless animals. Yet successful men, with personnel entourages much larger than his, were known to stop in the men's room and throw up their lunches before entering his office. You had to be well prepared for Hollcroft because, while he would allow a puppy to pee on his shoe, he couldn't stomach fools.

He stood to meet Walter Childs halfway between his office door and his desk and then walked him over to a setting of antique furniture that was one of three informal groupings in his office. "What a terrible ordeal you've been through," he sympathized. "Your wife kidnapped. I can't imagine anything worse. You really shouldn't have come in so quickly. What was it? Just yesterday that she was released. Really Walter, there's nothing here that's at all important compared with her recovery."

He helped Walter into a corner of a sofa as if he were an infirm patient. "How is she?" he asked with genuine concern. "And how are you? It must have been horrible for you."

Walter explained her harrowing escape from the clutches of a madman, elaborating on the police assault, the hostage situation, and the high-speed chase through a field of automatic weapons fire. "It's the stuff of movies," he told the president. "Horror films, I suppose."

Hollcroft's eyes were filling. "Awful. Just god-awful." But after a discreet pause he added, "Andrew Hogan told me just yesterday about the kidnapping. And, of course, about her escape. But I had no idea of the degree of danger she was in. I really have none of the details."

It was his invitation for Walter to fill in the details. He cleared his throat. "I imagine Andrew told you that the bank was the real target. I was nothing more than the key to the vault. It was the bank's money they were after."

The chairman nodded, but continued to give Walter his full attention. He wasn't going to help him skip through the details of his disregard for the bank's money. It was up to Walter to choose the right words.

"I was in a terrible dilemma, Jack. As you'll see when Andrew gives you a copy of the ransom instructions, it was obvious that this person . . . or persons . . . was completely familiar with our operations. I thought, and Andrew agreed, that it could very well be someone inside the bank. The note said explicitly that they would know instantly if I contacted any of the bank authorities or, God help us, brought in the FBI or the police. If I did, I'd never hear from them, or from Emily, again."

Another nod from Hollcroft. This time he adjusted the crease of his trousers, crossed his legs, and looked up expectantly.

Walter went on, dramatizing the agony as he had carefully, and responsibly, weighed his choices. "The only answer seemed to be to pretend to go along with them, and use the promise of . . . cooperation . . . as a way to trap them and ultimately reach Emily. That's the way that Andrew and I tried to play it." He kept bringing up the name of the security officer. He hoped that Hollcroft might be concluding that he hadn't really violated bank policy. He had gone straight to the security officer the very next day.

His tale wove on to the events of Sunday morning, when he had finally realized that there was no other way to save Emily's life. He detailed how he had wired the money to the numbered account in Fassen Bank. "We have to put a trace on that money," he concluded bravely. "That's why I wanted to come in as soon as I was sure of Emily's health. I want to get working with Andrew to see if we can find where the money was delivered."

The chairman's hands rose defensively, indicating that he was over-whelmed by Walter's thoughtfulness. "I wouldn't hear of it, Walter. We have people here who will know exactly how to handle this. You belong with Emily."

He stood up and Walter stood with him. "Jack, I'd really like to see this whole thing through to the end."

Hollcroft was shaking his head. "Walter, there really isn't much you can do. I'd be disappointed in Fassen Bank if they even admitted to paying out the funds, much less help us identify the person who received them. Herr Vogler has been running operations over there since he was a boy and I've never heard him admit that he had even a single depositor."

They shook hands and then Walter took one last glance around the office that he had hoped would one day be his. He doubted that he would ever see the office, or Jack Hollcroft, again.

Helen Restivo was surprised to find Andrew Hogan in her office. She had gone from the carnage of Emily's rescue to her home for a hot bath and a much-needed nap. She had assumed that Andrew would be sleeping for the next three days.

"You look like hell," she said by way of greeting.

"Thank you," he said, rubbing his hand over the stubble of his beard and confirming that she was undoubtedly right. "I have a few more things to do before I have the luxury of rest."

Helen nodded knowingly. They had managed to rescue Mrs. Childs, but the rest of their investigation had been a disaster. Andrew would have to explain the botched traps that they had set for the kidnappers and worse, the loss of a great deal of his employer's money. It was very probable that Andrew would join Walter Childs on the unemployment rolls. "I don't envy you," she said sincerely. "InterBank won't be a fun place today."

"Screw InterBank," Hogan answered. "They were hit and they lost some money. They don't need my report to tell them that. All those MBAs ought to be able to figure it out by themselves."

Helen was stunned. She had assumed that Andrew's defense would be a detailed indictment of Walter Childs. He had a senior vice president's word that no funds would be transferred. He had no authority to direct a senior officer's actions. "You're not going to tell them what happened."

"The money is gone and so is Walter Childs. That's what happened."

Helen smiled in disbelief. "What about his affair with the lovely Miss Hilliard?"

"Like you said, it's his affair. And by the way, it appears that Miss Hilliard has decided to leave the employ of the bank."

"What?"

Andrew nodded. "She's cleaned out all her files, cut her ID card in half, and left no forwarding address."

"But you must know where she is," Helen said, tipping her head suspiciously.

"If I had to guess, I'd guess Switzerland. Isn't that what we always say? 'Follow the money.' "

"Then it was Angela who set this whole thing up."

He shrugged. "Could be, although she would have to have been working with someone else. I noticed that there was a tennis racquet on the shelf of her closet. You don't suppose she's taking lessons from Billy Leary?"

"No damn way," Helen said. "They come from two different planets. He's from Pluto, or wherever idiots originate."

"Or maybe Walter Childs wasn't the only senior executive she was favoring," Andrew suggested. "Did you ever pick up any dirt on Mitchell Price?"

She was bewildered by his attitude. Andrew Hogan didn't generally make light of crime. And she had never known him to drop an investigation until he had most of the answers. "Do you know who did this?" she demanded. "Because I've taken my lumps on this case. I'm entitled to know."

"Could be a lot of people," he said. "Walter Childs is still my prime candidate. I wouldn't be surprised to hear that he's left for Zurich himself."

"And you don't care?" Helen snapped.

"Not really," Hogan said. "I've decided to leave the bank. If the MBAs want to run down the bank robbers, let them do it on their own."

Helen sat staring at him. She was dumbfounded. "Then what is it you have to do that's so important?"

He smiled and glanced shyly down at his hands. "I had to talk with you."

"About the investigation?"

He shook his head. "No, about us. You and me."

Her blank expression suddenly registered. "About us? Didn't we have this conversation a couple of days ago?"

"Yeah, but I've been thinking about what I said. I want to make it perfectly clear that I don't feel responsible for your wounds, nor the least bit guilty about your lost career. That's not why you're my responsibility. I'm responsible for you because I'm very much in love with you. I have been for a very long time."

Her expression went back to bewilderment.

"So what I had to do was ask you to marry me."

"Again?" Helen asked.

"Yeah, but this time I have a better reason. I need you, and even though I've wasted the best part of my life, I need to spend the rest of it with you. If I don't, then I'll have wasted the whole thing."

He kept staring at his hands, hoping for some hint of her reaction. There was every chance she would simply repeat her no. Even worse, she might just break out laughing. But there was no response. He had to take his chances and look her in the eye.

He found her smiling.

"You think I'm an idiot," he said.

"I think you need to get some sleep."

His lips pursed. "I guess that means no."

"No," Helen said. "It means yes if you still want to marry me after you've gotten a good night's sleep."

Hogan smiled broadly as he stood. "I'll call you tonight."

"Andrew." He stopped and turned back to her. "Are you the one who hit the bank?"

"How'd you guess?"

"Because you're quitting your job, getting married, and going into retirement. When did you become filthy rich?"

It took him a while to answer. "About ten seconds ago," he told her.

Walter let himself into the back door of Angela's building and then through the steel door to the fire stairs. He had raced all the way to her floor before he realized that his heart was pounding and that he was gulping for every breath.

The key didn't fit into the lock and he kept changing its position and trying to force it. Then he got hold of himself, paused to take a few breaths, and found that the key worked easily. He stepped inside, closed the door behind him, and stood leaning on it while he looked around. Everything seemed normal. Absolutely normal. What the hell had Andrew Hogan been talking about?

He glanced at the computer as he crossed the living room. The power light on the scanner was glowing green. Christ, her computer was still connected. In the bedroom, he threw open the closet door and ran his hand across the clothes. Some of the outfits he recognized as her favorites. What did Hogan think? That she would just walk away from several thousand dollars worth of clothes? He dashed into the bathroom and slid open the medicine cabinet. Nothing had changed. Her prescription medicines were sitting there in their brown bottles. Then he walked through the kitchen. She had to be coming back.

He was halfway out the door when he remembered her jewelry. It was a small collection, but they were all exquisite pieces. Angela would never leave them behind. He raced back to the bedroom, crawled into the closet, and pulled free the six-inch molding. Her jewelry case was gone.

Walter's return to the bank was disastrous. Word of his situation had apparently reached the secretaries and been carried instantly down to the elevator starters. The security guard didn't even look at him as he signed back in, and in the elevator he had the feeling that two complete strangers had pulled back from him as if his cancer were showing. His office staff became instantly busy as soon as he opened the outer door, with not a single face looking up from the desk. Even Joanne turned away to hunt in a file drawer, acting as if she wasn't aware that he had passed within a foot of her.

There were no messages on his desk, which meant that if anyone had called Walter wasn't expected to call back. And when he settled into his chair, the phone that was always ringing remained terribly silent. He was gone already. His office was empty. How long he chose to leave his body at the desk was entirely up to him.

He tried Angela again on his private line and then tried her apartment. The recorded voices seemed mocking, as if she were listening to monitor the calls, knew it was he, and couldn't help smirking. He sat through a silent hour, then called for a limousine and headed back out to Short Hills.

Emily was up and fully dressed, moving about the house with her usual energy. Walter commented on how well she looked. "Makeup does wonders," she answered. Unconsciously, her hand went up to the side of her face, toward the place under her hair where the top of her ear had been severed. But she stopped her fingers short. That's a habit I don't want to get into, she reminded herself. The disfigurement was minimal and she had to train herself to stop calling attention to it.

All her physical injuries had proven minimal, which was why she was back home after only a day of hospital rest. A plastic surgeon had tended her ear and assured her that it could be totally reconstructed. Emily had looked in the hand-held mirror and decided not to bother. Her hairdo concealed the damage adequately. X rays revealed that her jaw and cheekbones were intact, and although the discoloration was increasing, the swelling was already subsiding. The other wounds, to her hands and knees, were superficial.

Less certain was the severity of the wounds to her mind. Her terror had been prolonged. Her jailer's horrendous threats had been convincing. Her preference for dying had been real. "She's been through more horror in just a few hours," the hospital psychiatrist had explained to her family, "than most of us face in a lifetime." Her bravado, he warned, was just that—a public glossing over a severe private pain.

Walter knew that the pain went even deeper than the doctors suspected. For several months, Emily had been glossing over the pain of being abandoned. She had known of his affair and suspected his intentions for her and yet had pretended that their family life was going on happily.

Amanda, with her usual lack of delicacy, had stated the situation clearly. "Everything was a lie, wasn't it? You were pretending to love her while you were getting ready to dump her. That must have hurt her terribly."

"I wasn't pretending anything," Walter had argued. "I have always loved your mother and wanted the best for her."

"Well, are you still going to dump her? You have to decide, Dad. And you have to tell the truth. The lying has to stop if Mom is ever going to get better."

He hadn't been able to give his children an honest answer. There was no corner of his life that wasn't in turmoil. All he could tell them was that he and their mother would have a great deal to talk about and important decisions to make. But he did promise that the lying would stop.

Alex and Amanda had planned to stay for a few days until Emily was back on her feet. But she had sent them back to their own lives, assuring them that she was completely capable of taking care of herself. Then she and Walter had shared a quiet dinner ordered in from an Italian restaurant and transferred from the tinfoil pans directly onto their everyday china. Walter had offered to brighten the event with a bottle of Brunello from his modest wine rack. Emily had put the meal in perspective by settling for ice water. Then Emily went back to repairing the damage the house had suffered while in the care of her husband and children, while Walter followed her about. They commented cordially about the things that had been misplaced and disorganized. But they never talked.

Walter was staring blankly at late-night television news when Emily touched him on the shoulder and announced that she was going to bed. She mentioned that she had made up another room, which was a polite way of telling him that he wasn't invited to join her.

He followed her to the foot of the stairs. "Emily?"

She broke her stride and turned back to him.

"We should talk . . . about . . . things . . . us. . . ."

She nodded. "You're right, Walter. I'll let you know when I want to talk."

Then she continued on up to their bedroom and closed the door behind her. He heard the lock click.

Walter went to his car and used his cell phone to call Angela. It wasn't a legal precaution, because he knew his wireless calls could be traced and reported just as easily as the ones he made from a house phone. But, now, it didn't seem fair to be calling Angela from Emily's kitchen. He dialed, listened to the ringing, and then to Angela's recorded voice directing him to leave a message and promising to "get right back." It was the same promise that he had been hearing all day.

Wednesday

WALTER DREADED HIS ARRIVAL at the bank and the agonizing minutes that would fall like a hammer on an anvil as he waited for the board's decision. The usually chatty Omar sat stone-faced behind the wheel, not even glancing into the mirror. Did Omar already know that he was driving a hearse? Once again, the security guard made a point of being busy with critical paperwork while Walter signed in. In the elevator, everyone was too busy watching the floor lights flash to look him in the face. His outer office could have been a prison camp. When he passed Joanne's desk, he asked her to bring in his coffee.

"Sit down," he told her when she set the cup on his desk. She did, still managing to avoid any real eye contact. "Would you look at me, please?" he said. It was a request rather than a directive. "What do you see?"

She blinked several times. "I don't know what you mean."

"Is there a big letter L as in loser carved into my face? I only ask because I seem to have become so horrible that no one can bear to look at me."

"I'm sorry, Mr. Childs. I'm so terribly sorry." He knew she meant it, and not just because no one was speaking to him. She meant she knew that he was about to be axed for reasons that seemed totally incredible and she was genuinely sympathetic to his plight.

"Thank you," Walter acknowledged.

Joanne got up and was nearly to the door when he called her. "You've probably heard a lot of nasty rumors. You're going to hear more. There's no need to defend me because some of them are undoubtedly correct. But there's one you might try to put a stop to."

Her expression answered that she would gladly be helpful.

"I did not arrange to have my wife kidnapped. I did nothing to harm her and did everything I could, including robbing this bank, to save her. I may be a cad. I'm not a monster."

The chairman's message, delivered by one of the outside directors, was

247

more merciful than it need have been. An ex-navy admiral, who had been added to the board as the kind of patriotic signal that couldn't hurt in the bidding for government bonds, came to his office, asked after his wife, and then told him the verdict.

"As you'll appreciate, Walter, these events make it difficult for us here at the bank to continue placing our unquestioned confidence in you. And no victory can be won without confidence."

Walter's eyes dropped down humbly.

"Understand, there is absolutely no animosity. We are all terribly sympathetic."

"Thank you," Walter managed to mumble.

"And it goes without saying that there is no thought of prosecution over the misappropriated funds. Insurance will make up any losses and we'd rather not announce to the banking world that our security isn't water-tight."

That was a relief, although Walter wasn't surprised to learn that Jack Hollcroft would find loss of face much more painful than loss of funds. Discretion was an essential for survival in the banking world, and no bank could afford to admit that there were crooks in its boardroom.

"It's just that we have a bank policy to deal with exactly this kind of situation," the admiral went on. "It's a policy that's designed to protect us all from intimidation. And in breaking that policy, you really broke a trust."

He nodded in contrite agreement.

"We thought it might be best if you tendered your resignation. Under the circumstances, you could certainly cite personal reasons. We'll accept with regret and insist that you take your full benefits with you. Hopefully, that sort of arrangement won't limit your opportunities should you decide to get back into banking at some future date."

Walter was truly surprised. "That's very generous of you," he said.

Walter began drafting the resignation as soon as the admiral left. He felt relieved that it was all over and that his sentence had been so light. They could have jailed him. Instead, they were content to simply cast him out into the darkness where there was weeping and gnashing of teeth.

During his last limo ride home, Walter tried his best to fight back the morose thoughts. He didn't want to believe that Angela had deserted him, despite the mounting evidence that she had vanished. Hogan's investigators had opened her desk files and found them completely cleaned out of all records and correspondence. Her e-mail, which could be read from anyplace that offered telephone service, had gone unopened. Her telephone numbers continued to play her recorded voice.

Worst of all, he didn't want to believe that she had taken his money. Hogan said that there was evidence that she had gone to Zurich, but that had to be simply the most obvious suspicion of a frustrated cop. Because if that were true, then it was also quite likely that she had been after the money all along and had been playing him for a fool. He couldn't bear to think that she had never loved him. Worse was the possibility that her moments of ecstasy while locked in his embrace had been faked. He had never deluded himself that her desire for wealth and power had not been part of his appeal to her. But he had never suspected that had been his only appeal.

He fell into a black hole whenever his thoughts focused on Emily. During her terrible ordeal, when it had seemed that he might never see her again, he had longed for her. The moment he had seen her in the hospital, he knew that he certainly cared for her. But what did she feel for him? Love? Pity? Loathing? Any of the choices might be right. All of them could be wrong. Her mind was completely shut to him. They had to talk.

Even though they were driving through beautiful country on a perfect day, not a single ray of sunshine penetrated Walter's thoughts. Would he ever be able to get back into the banking fraternity or would a raised eyebrow from Jack Hollcroft condemn him forever? Could he keep the house? Walter was nicely funded and even the fractional vesting of his pension would give him a decent income. But his lifestyle was based on expectations that had vanished from the horizon like a sinking ship when Angela had vanished with the money. A cutback—a very severe cutback—was inevitable.

When they reached his house, Omar raced around the car and opened the door. Walter started past him with his usual nod, but then realized that a personal driver was one of the perks he had forfeited. He turned back. "You may have heard, Omar . . ."

"I did, Mr. Childs," the driver answered, still standing at attention with the door in his hand. "And may I say how sorry I am." The musical accent made the words even more of a dirge. "I will certainly miss our conversations and I only hope that we will meet again."

Walter put a grateful hand on the man's shoulders. But he didn't speak.

His only thought was that if there were a next time, there was an even chance that he would be driving Omar.

He opened the front door and nearly tripped over Emily's luggage in the front hall. There were two matching suitcases, each bulging and obviously heavy to lift, and a smaller travel bag. He looked up from the luggage in time to see his wife coming down the stairs in a knee-length skirt and a dressy blouse, not her usual daytime attire.

"Hello, Walter. You're home early." She stepped past the bags without seeming to notice them and went into the kitchen where a glass of wine was waiting for her. Walter followed silently. "Fix yourself a drink," Emily suggested. "I'm ready to talk now, but we're a bit short of time. My car is due in twenty minutes."

Her high heels clicked on the tiles as she crossed the family room. Walter stood paralyzed as Emily settled into a single chair on the far side of the coffee table and adjusted her skirt below her knee. Then she looked up and gave Walter her full attention. He didn't have any idea how he should begin.

"What was it you wanted to say," she prodded.

"The luggage . . . are you . . . going away?"

"Yes. I'll send for the rest of my things once I'm settled. Hopefully, that won't take too long."

"Where? Where are you going?"

"Right now, I'm going to stay with a friend in Savannah. Then I thought I might take a trip for a few months. I'm really not sure where I'm going to end up."

He went to the wet bar, fixed a drink of his own, and carried it to the sofa. He sat, fidgeted with the ice cubes for a moment, and then raised his eyes to find her looking at him expectantly.

"Emily . . . I love you. I know I've been a fool, but I know that I love you. I'm begging your forgiveness . . . even though I know I don't deserve it."

Her expression didn't change, but her voice softened a bit. "Thank you, Walter. And I do forgive you, even though I agree that you don't deserve it. Fundamentally, you're a decent man and I never want to have bad thoughts about you. I really do wish you the best."

"Do you have to leave? If you could stay for a while. A few weeks, maybe. I'm sure we could work everything out."

Emily shook her head slowly. "No, I don't think so. We both still have long lives ahead of us. I don't think we should spend them mourning over a dead marriage or trying to breathe some heat back into cold ashes."

He was shocked. "A dead marriage? Dead?"

"I think that's the right word," Emily said softly. There was no anger to her tone. If anything, her voice carried a note of sadness.

"But if you can forgive me . . ."

"I do forgive you, Walter. You have to believe that. But that doesn't change the fact that out marriage is over. I don't see any reason why we should go on living together like old friends sharing an apartment. I want what you want. To be married to someone."

"But damm it, I said I was sorry, and I am."

"I know you are and I hope you can get over it. You're not the only one who's at fault. I'm sure I did as much to wound our relationship as you did. But you're the one who . . ." She raised her hand with a finger and thumb extended to simulate a pistol and then she squeezed off a shot ". . . shot it dead."

His face registered his confusion. "I know I cheated on you. I was . . . unfaithful . . ."

"Is that what you think? That I'm leaving because you were . . . unfaithful?" She shook her head sadly. "God, but you must think I'm some kind of prig."

Walter's voice climbed in frustration. "No! I don't think anything like that. You have every right—"

She raised a hand to silence him. "Please, just listen, Walter, because I want to make sure you understand this. I want you to know exactly why I'm leaving."

He jumped to his feet and began pacing. "I know why you're leaving," he told her. "You want to get back at me. To punish me. And I don't blame you. It was terrible of me . . ."

"Will you please sit down," Emily ordered. "Just sit down and listen!" She waited patiently until he had lowered back into his chair. "You think I'm leaving because you're having an affair with a woman at your office."

"That's over," he interrupted. "I've been trying to reach her for the past few days to tell her that it's over."

"I don't care whether it's over."

His jaw slackened "You don't care . . ."

"Not any longer. I did care when I first learned about it. But I loved you, Walter. Oh, of course I was hurt, but I wasn't shocked. You're a good-looking man on the way to the top. I'd have been a fool not to realize that young, attractive, and very bright women would be attracted to you. Some of them would be just on the make. But some of them would honestly see you as the answer to their prayers. Someone that a fairy godmother had arranged for them to meet."

He nodded his understanding. "Of course, but I shouldn't have . . ."

"Of course you shouldn't have let yourself be seduced. And believe me, the image of you getting it on with another woman was a bitch for me to face. I imagined that she was startlingly beautiful and when I looked at myself in the mirror I began to think that I was an old hag. And then I saw her, Walter, and she was more beautiful than anyone could have imagined. Jesus, I couldn't even bare to look in the mirror."

"I *am* sorry. Truly, sorry." His voice was choking with remorse.

"But that didn't kill our marriage," Emily went on. "I mean, it was damn tough to take, but it wasn't something directed at me. I figured that you had been offered a smashing piece of ass to play with and that it was too much to pass up. You were tempted and you gave in. You were weak, not evil. You weren't perfect, but I've never demanded perfection from myself and I certainly wasn't going to demand it from you. I thought you'd have your fling, be crushed with guilt, and try to sneak back into the house. And I wasn't going to make it tough for you. Just let you know that I knew so that we both wouldn't be living a lie. Accept your apology, just as I have now, and then try to get on with our lives."

"But, then . . . what?" Walter wasn't sure whether she was leaving him or coming back.

"Our marriage didn't die because you were screwing Angela," Emily said, using her name for the first time. "It ended because you were screwing me."

He was bewildered. His hands came up in an imploring gesture. "I don't think I understand . . ."

"You decided that I wasn't good enough for you. You wanted to trade me in and start all over again with a new model. You decided I wasn't flashy enough to capture the attention *you* deserved. I wasn't smart enough to mix it up with the circle of friends *you* belonged in. I didn't speak all the languages of *your* global empire. I wasn't hot enough to make everyone envious of *you*. I wasn't good enough in the sack to satisfy *your* needs. You wanted a goddamned trophy to stand in your house as a tribute to what a great man *you* had become and I just wasn't big enough, or shiny enough to fit on the pedestal *you* had built."

Emily was losing her calm veneer as she recited the litany of abuse. She heard a shrill, nagging tone in her voice that she couldn't stand. She stopped, took a breath, and then drank from her wineglass. When she felt composed, she continued.

"You stopped thinking about *us*, Walter, which is what a marriage is supposed to be about. You discarded me and started to think only about *you*. And that's not a marriage, that's an arrangement. I don't think either of us should settle for an arrangement."

"I never stopped thinking about you," Walter protested.

"Oh, I'm sure I was on your mind," Emily agreed. "You must have been sick wondering what I would say, how much I would demand, whether I'd go away quietly or whether I'd kick up a fuss. But face the truth. All those thoughts were really thoughts about how I would affect *your* happiness. You see what I mean. Planking Angela wasn't nice. But throwing me on the garbage heap was the real killer. It wasn't sex that killed our marriage. It was selfishness. When I understood that, then I understood that I was all alone and that I better start taking care of myself."

An automobile horn beeped discreetly outside the front door. Emily took a final sip from her glass, set it down, and stood. "That's my car, Walter. I'd appreciate it if you gave me a hand with the bags."

He followed her through the kitchen toward the front door. "I never traded you in like an old car. How can you say I threw you on the garbage heap?"

She stopped when she reached the luggage. "Probably not in so many words. But what did you intend for me after you rode off into the sunset with your new bride? Was I supposed to be thrilled with alimony checks? Was I supposed to devote my life to tennis? Become the queen of the singles bars? We had a life together and then you went off and found another life for yourself. Now I have to find one or else I'll be as good as dead."

"But I want our life together," he said. "Angela is gone. There is no one else."

"She's gone?" Emily questioned. Walter's glum silence confirmed what she already knew. "I'm sorry to hear that, Walter. I can only hope she was wonderful in bed and that she did wonderful things for your ego. Because, God knows, you certainly have paid top dollar."

She stepped out the door, leaving Walter to struggle with the luggage. Emily waited by the car door until the driver had lifted the bags into the trunk and slammed the lid. When he was getting back behind the wheel, she turned to the confused, slumped, totally defeated man beside her.

"Good-bye, dear." She kissed him on the cheek.

"Emily, please don't go. I've lost everything. I have nothing left to fall back on. What's going to happen to me?"

She settled into the rear seat. "Don't give me set-up lines like that, Walter. Because I really do give a damn."

She pulled the door closed. The car rolled down the Belgian block driveway, leaving him standing alone by the open front door.

Sometime Later

ANGELA STRETCHED OUT ON the hot tiles along the edge of the pool and peered over the top of her sunglasses to get the attention of the waiter. He circled behind the chaise lounges so as not to cast a shadow on any of the guests and then dropped to one knee beside her.

"Ahh, Signorina. Be careful. The sun is very high. Your skin . . ."

She smiled. "I don't suppose I could get you to rub some oil on me."

The young man tried to look serious. "I think you may need it. You're already getting a little pink."

"Where you're looking, I've always been pink," she said, making a point of following his glance down under her bikini top. "And on your way back, could you bring a bottle of mineral water. Ice cold."

"Of course, and some extra ice." He looked as if he might walk on the water in his haste to fetch the suntan lotion.

The hotel was built into a cliff on the Amalfi Coast, with rooms above each other so that every guest would have an unobstructed view of the Mediterranean. The swimming pool actually projected beyond the cliff line and had no visible edge to contain the water. Instead, the water flowed over the top on the seaward side, dropping into a catch trough that was there to keep sun worshipers from falling off the cliff. From inside the pool, it seemed as if the water were flowing gently into the sea, which was actually five hundred feet below.

She glanced through the door that opened out from the small, intimate lobby. It was empty, as it had been for the past hour. There was just the desk clerk, leaning his elbows on the counter, trying to appear alert while actually sleeping. Angela tasted the first hint of apprehension backing up into her throat.

Today was supposed to be the day. This pool, at this hotel, at exactly twelve noon. An exclusive hotel, with a reputation for assuring the total privacy of its guests. An international clientele, with no particular loyalty to the laws of any country. A view that looked down on the world's finest watering holes and on a sea that led everywhere. It was the perfect place for two multimillionaires to begin their lives of luxury. But so far, Angela was the only one who had arrived.

She checked her watch and found that it was after two. Had something gone wrong? She was about to run through the list of all the possible legal and physical disasters, but then the smiling waiter appeared, the oil and water in his hands, the towel draped over his arm. He was trying to disguise his anticipation with the bored professionalism of a physician.

He unhooked the clasp of her bra and pushed the straps off her shoulders. When he had oiled her the day before, he had managed to stretch two minutes of work into nearly half an hour. Angela had found the massage exciting and his suggestions of why he should visit her room amusing. Heck, maybe she should invite him to Sardinia.

His hands and his voice began having their effect. She felt herself relaxing into a dark, hypnotic abyss, soothed by the heat of the sun and the touch of a man's hands moving under her arms. Without meaning to, she let herself drift off to sleep.

She was awakened not by a sound, but by the silence. His melodious voice had gone still, making her aware of the water tumbling over the pool's edge. And his touch was different, more medicinal and less arousing. Angela blinked her eyes opened and was reassured by the shadow that was still hovering over her and spilling out across the tiles. But then she was suddenly aware that the shape of the shadow was different. She rolled over abruptly, clutching the untied bra against her breasts.

"Ah ha! It's you. Thank god, I was beginning to worry."

Emily sat back on her heels. "You didn't look terribly worried to me."

Angela sat up, reaching back to reclasp the top. Emily stood and walked to a table, set out in the shade of a tall pine. She took off her wide-brimmed straw hat and tossed it on the table, smoothed the colorful skirt she wore under a white, sleeveless blouse, and sat. Angela wandered up next to her, pulling on a beach robe.

"Want some bottled water?" she asked.

"Seems weak for a celebration," Emily said. "Maybe a bottle of champagne."

Angela smiled. "Why not? We can afford it." She signaled to the waiter and sent him to find the best bottle in the house. Then she settled next to Emily.

"You were absolutely right," Emily said, after panning the horizons of the view. "Totally spectacular." Then she asked, "Had you been here before?"

"Just by way of the Internet," Angela said. "It looked great when I suggested it, but it was really incredible when I first stepped out of the lobby. As soon as I saw it, I knew we had picked the perfect place to meet."

"Absolutely perfect," Emily agreed.

The waiter raced toward them, carrying a dark bottle with shiny tinfoil surrounding the cork and dragging a chrome-plated ice bucket. He set two glasses in front of them, and began twisting the wire off the cork.

"Does he have time to wait on anyone else?" Emily asked.

"I try to keep him busy. In fact, I thought I might bring him with me for a few months. I could use someone who speaks the language."

"Get a phrase book. You won't get attached to it, so it will be easy to throw away when you move on to France." Emily raised her glass and held it to the sun so that it came alive with color. "Where do the bubbles go?" she asked.

"Wherever they want," Angela said. Then she gestured a toast. "Congratulations. You really pulled it off."

"It had its moments," Emily admitted.

Angela reached for the bucket to pour refills, but the waiter appeared almost magically and did the honors. "You know," Angela said as soon as he had backed away from the table, "you might want one of your own. I could ask if he has a friend."

Emily laughed. "I have underwear that's older than he is. You'd have to ask if he has an uncle."

They drank again and then Emily settled back with her face in the sun. "It had its moments," she repeated softly. "It seemed so simple, but I doubt if I could ever do it again."

"I'm amazed you could do it all," Angela added in genuine admiration. "When you first came to me, I thought you were up to some sort of trick. Something to break up Walter and me and get your husband back. And then, when I realized you were serious, I thought you were crazy. I mean, to have yourself kidnapped . . ."

"It had to be that way. It had to be set up so that even if everything went wrong, I would be in the clear."

Angela remembered their first meeting when Emily had suddenly appeared at her apartment. She had expected hysteria and then threats. Instead, she had listened to a very orderly presentation of how she could have everything she wanted, without having to put up with unwanted affections and submit to the tyranny of sexual harassment. By working together, they could force Walter to rob his own bank and then turn the money over to them.

Angela had picked holes in the plot, only to learn that Emily had already stitched them closed. How could they hire kidnappers? They wouldn't know where to find those kinds of people. Emily had the answer. Her charitable work involved her with many desperate people. She had already identified a team of petty crooks who would do the actual kidnapping and she had just reviewed the file on a woman con artist who could be persuaded to mind the victim and keep her comfortable and safe. "We had never met," Emily explained. "But her record showed an absolute genius for making money without ever doing anything violent that might attract attention. Most of the judges she appeared before had decided she was harmless and dismissed the charges."

Angela had looked at it from every angle. Emily was the one who would be in danger, while she would have very little to lose. And yet she would be getting half the reward. It was too good to be true. And things that seemed too good to be true had a way of turning out that way.

"You remember that at first I didn't like the idea," Angela said.

Emily nodded. "I remember. I thought that maybe you really were in love with Walter. I was suddenly worried that I might be cutting my own throat."

"*You* were worried." Angela laughed. "All I could think of was that you were the scorned woman, and that *hell hath no fury*. I kept trying to figure out exactly what fury you were planning for me."

"What convinced you?" Emily wondered.

Angela thought. "Walter, I suppose. He kept telling me what a wonderful person you were. Gradually, I found that I like you. Besides, I really didn't have much in the way of choices."

Emily was surprised. "No choices? I thought you were the rising star of the banking world."

Angela laughed sarcastically. "I was, as long as I went along with Walter. But if I had told him the truth and turned him down, he would have been too embarrassed to keep me around. He wouldn't have wanted to see me every day, knowing that I didn't worship at his shrine. Sooner or later, he would have found some way to get rid of me. Something nice, like the Paris branch, or an office in Hawaii. But something distant and dead-end."

"There are other banks," Emily reminded her.

"Not when you have left someone else's fast track without an explanation. It's like a big, private club. When you tell one of them to fuck off, you tell them all."

"So even though Walter thought he was the best thing that could possibly happen to you . . . ?"

"He was the worst. And there was nothing I could do about it. There was no way I could be his trophy and still have a life of my own. That's why I loved your little scheme. It got me what I wanted and Walter what he deserved. It was absolutely perfect."

The waiter reappeared to empty the rest of the bottle into their champagne flutes. Then he stood like an expectant puppy with an empty dinner dish.

"Send him for something . . . *anything*," Emily suggested.

"Another bottle," Angela told the young man and he raced off again to do her bidding.

Then it was Angela's turn to satisfy her curiosity. "What I never was sure of was how you could be so certain of me. I mean, suppose I had been truly in love with your husband. I could have just left you with the kidnappers. There was no reason why I *had* to call them and tell them to set you free. I could have been rid of you without the bother of an ex-wife. No messy divorce. No property settlement. I could have had Walter, everything that belongs to Walter, and the whole hundred million for myself. You were taking quite a chance putting your life in the hands of the other woman."

Emily laughed. "May I say how proud of you I am that you didn't give into your natural greed. But actually, I never saw myself in danger. The lady con artist I picked would do anything for money, but she wouldn't hurt a fly. Once she figured out the call wasn't coming, she would have let me go. Certainly, for a price. And then I could have mentioned that I had heard my kidnappers talking to you and that you were the mastermind behind the whole affair.

"But I never thought that would be necessary. I figured you were as badly abused by Walter as I was. I never thought for a second that, as they like to say in court, his advances 'were welcome.' "

The waiter came back with a fresh bottle of champagne and a bowl of salted nuts. As he involved himself with the cork, Emily reconsidered her earlier advice. "Maybe he would be better than a phrase book. There are so many things he can do without you even bothering to ask."

Angela was still concerned. "But you were wrong about the woman. She damn near got you killed. All the while I thought you were relaxing comfortably, enjoying our revenge, and you were actually hanging by your thumbs."

Emily thought. "I guess I was wrong about her. I gave her more credit than to be playing house with a violence-crazed gangster. But she turned out to have the same failing that we all seem to share. We do make some very dumb decisions when it comes to the men we hand our lives over to."

"This guy was really bad," Angela said sympathetically.

"Worse than anything I could ever have imagined. Once he came on the scene, I gladly would have called the whole thing off just to get away from him. When Friday came and went I thought that Walter must have decided not to pay. I realized that if you had double-crossed me, you were going to get away with it. I wasn't going to be able to talk my way around that pervert. And Walter's blundering had eliminated any chance that I would be able to offer them money. By Sunday night, I was sure the whole thing had backfired on me. I was sure I was going to die."

"We almost didn't make it to Sunday," Angela added. "It almost ended on Friday. Friday was a disaster. They had set a trap for the kidnapper and I walked right into it. That's why I couldn't call them to have you set free until Monday."

"Well, you didn't call a moment too soon. Do you know what was happening when the telephone rang?"

"No. What . . . ?"

"I was being led downstairs to the basement where he was going to blow my brains out. I was hoping that he would just shoot me. My biggest fear was that my last memory of earth was going to be getting laid by that sick bastard."

"It was that close," Angela said in amazement.

"That close. But it still wasn't over. I guess you heard about his using me as a shield while he tried to shoot it out with the police."

"No!" Angela's eyes were wide with amazement. "I had no idea."

"It had its moments. We certainly earned our money."

"Indeed we did," Angela joined in. "But now comes the real challenge. How are we going to spend it?"

Emily glanced around. "Obviously, you've had a head start." She focused on the waiter. "It looks like you've already found someone to help you spend it."

"Oh, no," Angela said. "That would make me just like Walter. Paying for a great-looking companion to massage my ego."

"We don't need trophies," Emily agreed.

The young waiter filled their glasses from the new bottle and then moved off to a discreet distance, awaiting their next command. They sat in silence, taking in the incredible seascape that lay at their feet, already beginning to pick up the dazzling tint of the setting sun. Emily lifted her champagne and let it sparkle in the full prism of color. "One final toast," she proclaimed. "What should we drink to?"

"That's easy," Angela answered. "To the man who made all this possible."

"To Walter," they said together.

They sent the empty glasses tumbling like snowflakes down into sea below.